Playing with Fire

L.J. SHEN

Playing with Fire

A broken boy on the path to destruction.
A scarred girl without direction.
A love story carved in secrets, inked with pain and sealed with a lie.

Grace Shaw and West St. Claire are arctic opposites.

She is the strange girl from the food truck.

He is the mysterious underground fighter who stormed into her sleepy Texan college town on his motorcycle one day, and has been wreaking havoc since.

She is invisible to the world.

He is the town's beloved bad boy.

She is a reject.

He is trouble.

When West thrusts himself into Grace's quiet life, she scrambles to figure out if he is her happily-ever-after or tragic ending.

But the harder she pushes him away, the more he pulls her out of her shell.

Grace doesn't know much about anything beyond her town's limits, but she does know this:

She is falling in love with the hottest guy in Sheridan U.

And when you play with fire—you ought to get burned.

To Chele and Lulu.

"It is never too late to be what you might have been"—George Eliot

Playlist

My Chemical Romance—"Helena"

Bikini Kill—"Rebel Girl"

Blondie—"Atomic"

Sufjan Stevens—"Mystery of Love"

Rag'n'Bone Man—"Human"

Healy—"Reckless"

Powfu—"Death Bed"

Playing with Fire

Prologue

Grace

THE ONLY THING TO REMAIN COMPLETELY UNTARNISHED AFTER the fire was my late momma's flame ring.

It was a cheap-looking ring. The type you get in a plastic egg when you shove a dollar into a machine at the mall. Grandma Savvy said Momma always wanted me to have it.

Fire symbolized beauty, fury, and rebirth, she explained. Too bad in my case, it symbolized nothing but my demise.

Grams told me bedtime stories about phoenixes rising from their own ashes. She said that was what Momma wanted for herself—to rise above her circumstances and prevail.

My momma wanted to die and start over.

She only got one out of the two.

But me? I got both.

November 17th, 2015
Sixteen years old.

The first time I woke up in a hospital bed, I'd asked the nurse to help me put the ring back on my finger. I brought the ring to my lips and mouthed a wish, like Grandmomma had taught me.

I didn't wish for the insurance money to kick in quickly, or to end world poverty.

I asked for my beauty back.

I passed out shortly after, exhausted by my sheer existence. Asleep, I caught specks of conversations as visitors flooded my room.

"...prettiest girl in Sheridan. Elegant little nose. Pert lips. Blonde, blue-eyed. Crying shame, Heather."

"Might as well been a model."

"Poor thing doesn't know what she's wakin' up to."

"She ain't in Kansas no more."

I treaded out of the induced coma slowly, not sure what was waiting for me on the other side. It felt like swimming against crushed glass. Even the slightest movement ached. Visitors—classmates, my best friend Karlie, and boyfriend Tucker—came and went, patting, cooing, and gasping while my eyes were closed.

Oblivious to my consciousness, I heard them crying, shrieking, stuttering.

My old life—school plays, cheer practice, and stealing hasty kisses with Tucker under the bleachers—felt untouchable, unreal. A sweetly cruel spell I'd been under that evaporated.

I didn't want to face reality, so I didn't open my eyes, even when I could.

Until the very last minute.

Until Tucker walked into my hospital room and slipped a letter between my limp fingers resting on the sheet.

"Sorry," he croaked. It was the first time I'd heard him frazzled, insecure. "I can't do this anymore, and I don't know when you'll wake up. It's not fair to me. I'm too young for ..." He trailed off, and his chair scraped the floor as he shot up to his feet. "I'm just sorry, okay?"

I wanted to tell him to stop.

To confess I was awake.

Alive.

Well.

Sort of.

That I was buying time, because I didn't want to deal with the new me.

In the end I kept my eyes closed and heard him leave.

Minutes after the door clicked shut, I opened my eyes and let myself cry.

The day after Tucker broke up with me in a letter, I decided to face the music.

A nurse skulked into my room like a mouse, her movements hurried and efficient. She eyed me with a mixture of wariness and curiosity, like I was a monster shackled to the bedrails. By the promptness in which she appeared, I gathered they'd been waiting for me to open my eyes.

"Good mornin', Grace. We've been waitin' for you. Sleep well?"

I tried to nod, regretting the ambitious movement immediately. My head swam. It felt swollen and feverish. My face was fully wrapped and bandaged, something I'd noticed the first time I came to. There were tiny gaps in the bandages for my nostrils, eyes, and mouth. I probably looked like a mummy.

"Why, I'll take that little nod as a yes! Are you hungry by any chance? We'd love to take the tube out and feed you. I can send someone over to get you some real food. I believe we're servin' beef patties with rice and banana cake. Would you like that, hon?"

Determined to rise from my own ashes, I mustered all the physical and mental strength I possessed to answer, "That'd be real nice, ma'am."

"It'll be here right quick. And I've got more good news for ya. Today is *the* day. Doctor Sheffield is finally gonna take them bandages off!" She tried to inject false enthusiasm into her words.

I flipped the ring on my thumb absentmindedly. I wasn't anywhere near ready to see the new me. Nonetheless, it was time. I was conscious, lucid, and had to face the music.

The nurse filled out her chart and dashed out. An hour later, Dr. Sheffield and Grams came in. Grams looked like hell. Gaunt, wrinkled, and sleep-deprived, even in her Sunday dress. I knew she'd been living in a hotel since the fire and was in a full-blown war with our insurance company. I hated that she'd been going through this alone. Normally, I was the one doing the talking whenever we needed to get things done.

Grams took my hand in hers and pressed it to her chest. Her heart was beating wildly against her ribcage.

"Whatever happens"—she wiped her tears with leathery, shaky fingers—"I'm here for you. You hear that, Gracie-Mae?"

Her fingers froze on my ring.

"You put it back." Her mouth fell open.

I nodded. I was afraid if I opened my mouth, I'd start crying.

"Why?"

"Rebirth," I answered simply. I hadn't died like Momma, but I *did* need to rise from my own ashes.

Dr. Sheffield cleared his throat, standing between us.

"Ready?" He flashed me an apologetic smile.

I gave him a thumbs-up.

Here's to the beginning of the rest of my life …

He removed the bandages slowly. Methodically. His breath fanned across my face, smelling of coffee and bacon and mint and that clinical, hospital scent of plastic gloves and sanitizers. His expression did not betray his feelings, though I doubted he had any. To him, I was just another patient.

He didn't offer me any words of encouragement as I watched the long, cream ribbon twirling before my eyes, becoming longer. Dr. Sheffield removed my hopes and dreams along with the fabric. I felt my breath fading with each twist of his hand.

I tried to swallow down the lump of tears in my throat, my eyes drifting to Grandmomma, searching for comfort. She was by my side, holding my hand with her back ramrod straight, her chin up.

I searched for clues in her expression.

As the bandages curled into a pile on the floor, her face warped in horror, pain, and pity. By the time parts of my face were exposed, she looked like she wanted to shrivel into herself and vanish. I wanted to do the same. Tears prickled my eyes. I fought them out of instinct, telling myself it didn't matter. Beauty was a seasonal friend; it always walked away from you eventually—and never returned when you truly needed it.

"Say somethin.'" My voice was thick, low, unbearably raw. "Please, Grandmomma. Tell me."

I'd enjoyed the perks of my looks since I was born. Sheridan High was all about Grace Shaw. Modeling scouts stopped Grams and me when we visited Austin. I was the most prominent actress in school plays and a member of the cheer team. It had been obvious, if not expected, that the splendor of my looks would pave a path for me. With hair rich and gold as the Tuscan sun, a pert nose, and luscious lips, I knew my looks were my one-way ticket out of this town.

"Her mother wasn't worth spit, but luckily Grace inherited her beauty," I once heard Mrs. Phillips telling Mrs. Contreras at the grocery store. *"Let's just hope she fares better than the little hussy."*

Grams looked away. Was it really that bad? The bandages were completely gone now. Dr. Sheffield tilted his head back, inspecting my face.

"I would like to preface this by saying you are a very lucky girl, Miss Shaw. What you went through two weeks ago … many people would have died. In fact, I am amazed you are still with us."

Two weeks? I'd been in this bed for fourteen days?

I stared at him blankly, not knowing what he was looking at.

"The infected areas are still raw. Keep in mind that as your skin heals, it will become less agitated, and there's an array of possibilities we can explore down the line in terms of plastic surgery, so please do not be disheartened. Now, would you like to look at your face?"

I gave him half a nod. I needed to get it over with. See what I was dealing with.

He stood up and walked over to the other side of the room, plucking a small mirror from a cabinet, while my grandmomma collapsed on top of my chest, her shoulders quaking with a sob that ripped through her scrawny body. Her clammy hand gripped mine like a vise.

"What am I to do, Gracie-Mae? Oh my lord."

For the first time since I was born, a rush of anger flooded me. It was my tragedy, my life. My *face. I* needed to be consoled. Not her.

With each step Dr. Sheffield took, my heart sank a little lower. By the time he reached my bed, it was somewhere at my feet, pounding dully.

He handed me the mirror.

I put it up to my face, closed my eyes, counted to three, then let my eyelids flutter open.

I didn't gasp.

I didn't cry.

In fact, I didn't make a sound.

I simply stared back at the person in front of me—a stranger I didn't know and, frankly, would probably never befriend—watching as fate laughed in my face.

Here was the ugly, uncomfortable truth: my mother died of an overdose when I was three.

She didn't have the rebirth she'd longed for. She never did rise from her own ashes.

And, looking at my new face, I knew with certainty that neither would I.

West

November 17th, 2015.
Seventeen years old.

The best opportunity to kill myself presented itself on that dark road.

It was pitch-black. A thin layer of ice coated the road. I was driving back from my Aunt Carrie's, sucking on a green candy cane. Aunt Carrie sent my parents food, groceries, and prayers on a weekly basis. It felt crap to admit it, but both my folks couldn't drag themselves out of bed—with or without her religious praying.

Pine trees lined the winding road to our farm, rolling over a steep hill that made the engine groan with effort.

I knew it would look like the perfect accident.

No one would assume any differently.

Just a terrible coincidence, so close to the other tragedy that had struck the St. Claire household.

I could practically envision the headline tomorrow morning in the local newspaper.

Boy, 17, hits deer on Willow Pass Road. Dies immediately.

The deer was standing right there, in the middle of the road, idly staring at my vehicle as I approached at an escalating speed.

I didn't flash my headlights. I didn't pump the brakes.

The deer continued staring as I floored it, my knuckles white as I choked the steering wheel.

The car zipped through the ice so fast it shook from the speed, skidding forward. I could no longer control it. The wheel was not in sync with the tires.

Come on, come on, come on.

I squeezed my eyes shut and let it happen, my teeth slamming together.

The car began to cough, slowing down, even as I pressed my foot harder onto the gas pedal. I popped my eyes open.

No.

The car was decelerating, each inch it ate slower than the previous one.

No, no, no, no, no.

The pickup died three feet away from the deer, coming to a full stop.

The dumb animal finally decided to blink and amble away from the road, its hooves snapping against the ice with gentle *clicks*.

Stupid fucking deer.

Stupid fucking car.

Stupid fucking me, for not hurling myself out of the goddamn pickup when I still had the chance, right off the cliff.

It was quiet for a few minutes. Just me and the deceased pickup and my beating heart, before a scream tore from my throat.

"Fuckkkkkk!"

I punched the steering wheel. Once, twice … three times before my knuckles started bleeding. I braced my foot over the console and ripped the steering wheel out of the pickup, dumping it on the passenger seat and raking my fingers down my face.

My lungs burned and my blood dripped all over the seats as I tore everything inside the pickup. I ripped the radio from its hub, throwing it out the window. I smashed the windshield with my foot. Broke the glove compartment. I wrecked the pickup like the deer couldn't.

And yet, I was still alive.

My heart was still beating.

My phone rang, its cheerful tune taunting me.

It rang again and again and fucking again.

I tore it from my pocket and checked who it was. A miracle? A heavenly intervention? An unlikely savior who actually gave a fuck? Who could it be?

Scam Likely

Of course.

No one gave half a fuck, even when they said they did. I boomeranged my cell into the woods then got out of the vehicle and started my ten-mile walk back to my parents' farm.

Truly fucking hoping I'd bump into a bear and let it finish the goddamn job.

Chapter One

Present.

Grace

"BEST NINETIES INVENTION: CURTAIN BANGS VERSUS SLAP-bracelets. You have five seconds to decide. *Five.*"

Karlie sucked on her margarita slushie, eyeballing her phone. Damp clouds of heat sailed over the food truck's ceiling. Sweat soaked through my pink hoodie. We were in the midst of a Texan heatwave, even though we were a few months shy of summer.

My heavy coat of makeup was dripping down my FILA shoes in orange spurts. Good thing we closed five minutes ago. I hated hanging outside the house with less than two thick layers of foundation caked on my face.

I was planning on a cold shower, hot food, and setting the air-con on blast.

"*Four,*" Karlie counted in the background as I scribbled a want ad. My body was angled to the window, in case late-night customers trickled in.

Karlie was officially cutting back on her shifts, something her mom and owner of the food truck, Mrs. Contreras, wasn't thrilled about. Obviously, I was sad I wouldn't be working with her as often anymore. Karlie had been my best friend since we'd both wobbled about in diapers in each other's backyards. There was even a picture of us somewhere—probably Mrs. Contreras' living room—sitting on matching purple pots, butt naked, grinning at the camera like we'd just unfurled the great secrets of the universe.

I was worried whoever was going to replace Karlie—Karl to me—wasn't going to appreciate my sarcastic nature and surly approach to life. But I also completely understood why she had to cut back. Karl's class load was insane. And that was without all the extra internships she'd picked up to decorate her CV with work experience in journalism.

"*Three.* There's only *one* correct answer, and our friendship is in jeopardy, Shaw."

I capped the Sharpie with my teeth and leaned out the window, sticking the sign on the side of the open window.

That Taco Truck is HIRING!
Help Needed.
Four times a week.
Weekends included.
$16 per hour plus tips.
If interested please speak to manager.

I opened my mouth to answer Karlie at the same time I lifted my gaze. My body froze, every inch of it seized with a mix of dread and alertness.

Crap.

A herd of Sheridan University VIPs ambled toward the truck. Eight in total. It wasn't the fact that they went to my college that sucked. No, I was used to serving my peers.

It was *who* they were in Sheridan University that made me break out in hives.

These guys were high commodity seniors. The cream of the popularity crop.

There was Easton Braun, Sheridan University's hotter-than-Hades quarterback, dragging his fingers through his wheat-hued hair in slow-mo, like in an anti-dandruff shampoo commercial. He looked sickeningly perfect. Like those chiseled guys who lived in Pinterest Land and have arm veins as thick as hot dogs.

Reign De La Salle, the linebacker with soft, tar curls and pouty lips. A Sig Ep member, who reportedly slept with anyone with a pulse (and even that wasn't mandatory, provided he was hammered enough).

Then there was West St. Claire, a completely different species from Braun and De La Salle. A myth at Sher U. He was in a league of his own.

He wasn't an athlete, but he was by far the most infamous out of the three. Best known for being a hotheaded bully who dominated the local underground fight ring unchallenged. Rude, crass, and flat-out unresponsive to people who weren't in his tight circle.

Even I, who wasn't particularly privy to town gossip anymore, knew *nobody* messed with St. Claire.

Not his peers.

Not the townsfolk.

Not his professors, nor his friends.

It didn't help that West St. Claire had ticked every sex god cliché box on the list.

His dark hair was always messy, and his emerald eyes had that dangerous glint that promised you your life would never be the same after a ride on his motorcycle. Six feet, four inches of golden skin and corded muscles. Broad, athletic, and unfairly gorgeous with thick, dramatic eyebrows, eyelashes most starlets would kill for, and narrow lips pressed into a hard, formidable line. He wore dirty Diesel jeans, faded shirts worn inside out, dusty Blundstone boots, and always had a green apple candy stick wedged in the corner of his mouth, like a cigarette.

He was widely known as Sher U's biggest catch, only no one had ever caught him—and not for lack of trying.

The girls with them were familiar, too. One of them was even a semi-friend of mine—Tess, a raven-haired beauty with more curves than a barrel of snakes. She majored in theater and arts, like me.

"*Two*! I would like an answer now, Shaw." Karlie waved an imaginary microphone in my face, but I couldn't find my voice, stuck in a weird trance.

"*One*. The correct answer was curtain bangs, Grace. *Curtain. Bangs.* I mean, hi, Kate Moss circa 1998. Fashion icon."

They were all heading toward the food truck from Sheridan Plaza, a deserted mall across the street. The so-called mall was a naked cement frame a bunch of bigwigs started building five years ago before realizing they weren't going to make any money. Everybody shopped online, especially students. The two refineries that were supposed to open nearby had decided to relocate to Asia, so the mass migration into Sheridan they were counting on hadn't happened.

Now we had a monstrous structure in the middle of town, sitting empty.

Only it wasn't technically empty. The college students used it for raves, an underground fighting arena, and hookup spots, rent-free.

These folks were probably getting back from a fight.

Tess laughed, tossing her hair to one shoulder and jumping on Reign's back, looping her arms around his shoulders.

"Gummy bears? In a slushie? That's, like, bananas."

"That's, like, *orgasmic*," Easton volleyed back, his palm shoved into the back pocket of some blonde's Daisy Dukes. "I can't believe I've never hit this place before."

"The locals swear by it. Even Bradley, who's a total taco purist, goes here," another girl chimed in. I tucked my chin down, putting my thumb ring to my lips, mouthing a prayer.

I hated when people looked directly at my face.

Especially people my age.

Especially people like Easton Braun, Reign De La Salle, and West St. Claire.

Especially when I knew they were going to have two possible reactions: they'd be grossed out by the gory scar under my makeup, or worse … they'd pity me.

Though it was probably going to be a mixture of both.

I tugged my ball cap lower. Their voices grew louder. The air around me rattled with rusty laughter and gauzy female screeches. The fine hair on the back of my neck stood on end.

"Oh, snap," Reign hiccupped, giving Tess a piggyback ride without breaking a sweat. "Before I forget. When we get to the truck, check out the chick who takes your order. Gail or Gill or whatever-the-fuck. The entire left side of her face is disfigured. Purple as a grape. Got a nice Rice Krispy complexion, too. Like, you can't *really* see all of it because she puts hella makeup on, but it's there. Apparently, people 'round here call her Toastie."

Reign didn't mean for me to hear it. He was clearly trashed. Not that it mattered. Bile rose up my throat. The sour taste filled my mouth. I was facing another take-the-bandages-off moment, and I wasn't ready.

Tess slapped the back of his head. "Her name's Grace, you moron, and she is super nice."

Easton glared at Reign. "Seriously? What's wrong with you, jackass?"

"He's right, though." Tess dropped her voice, forgetting the echo the vastness of the nothing around us created. "We have the same major, so I see her all the time. It's sad, because otherwise, she is *so* pretty. Like, imagine what it feels like to almost have it all. She can't even do any of the practical theater stuff, she is so ashamed of her face."

Tess was referring to that time I walked into an audition freshman year, and broke down in front of the director when he asked me to do my lines. It was very public, very embarrassing, and very much the talk of town for that semester.

"Aww," Blondie, next to Easton, put a hand to her heart. "That's so sad, Tessy. You're givin' me goose bumps."

"I wonder what happened to her," another girl murmured.

"Ground control to Major Shaw? Are you with me?" Karlie poked her head behind my shoulder to see what had turned me into a salt statue.

They stopped in front of us. I trained my face to appear calm, bored, but my heart was thrashing so violently inside my chest, I thought it was going to blast through my bones, cracking its cage in half.

I pinched Karlie's wrist under the window, signaling, *they're too late*, praying she'd let me send them away.

Karlie slapped a hand over her mouth, like the entire Kardashian clan had stopped by.

"Bro, we're serving 'em. We have plenty of ingredients left. You know Momma Contreras doesn't play when it comes to leftovers. Besides"—she pinched me back—"it's *them*!"

We lived in a small college town, where everyone knew everyone, our D1 football team was worshipped like a religion, game days were church, Easton Braun and Reign De La Salle were holy saints, and West St. Claire was God. We couldn't refuse them, even if they arrived at three in the morning and paid in human hair.

"Howdy, Grace!" Tess unloaded herself from Reign, drum-rolling the neon-teal truck as she scanned the menu under the window.

"Hi, Tess. Y'all havin' a good night?"

"Fab, thanks. Reign here says you have margarita slushies with gummy bears. This true?"

So many customers were disappointed by the fact we called them margaritas when there was no tequila inside. "Sure do. Virgin, though."

"Wouldn't expect anything else from you," Reign deadpanned, hiccupping again. The girls burst out in laughter. For the sake of keeping my job—and my butt out of jail—I ignored his jab.

Tess punched his arm. "Don't mind him. Can we have ten to go? And twenty tacos, por favor." She gave her shiny hair another toss. "Oh, hi, Charlie."

Karlie waved at Tess behind me, not bothering to correct her. I hated being the one working the front window, but Mrs. Contreras and Karlie insisted on it. They wanted me to get out of my shell, face the world, yada, yada.

"Soft or crunchy shell?" I asked.

"Half and half."

"Right quick."

I got to work, snapping and popping a pair of black elastic gloves. I started with the crunchy shells first. They were harder to work with. They kept breaking all the time, so I liked getting them out of the way. Grandmomma always said people were like tacos—the harder they were, the easier they broke. Being soft meant being adaptive, more flexible.

"When you're soft, you can contain more. And if you contain more, the world can't break you."

I felt everyone's eyes on my face as I shoved shredded lettuce, cream cheese, and Mrs. Contreras' homemade guac into the tacos' tiny mouths. Karlie flipped fish on the grill, bouncing on the soles of her feet excitedly.

In my periphery, I could see Reign shoving his elbow into some girl's side, jerking his head toward me.

"*Psst.* Domestic violence?"

"Arson," the girl suggested, trying to figure out how I got the scar.

"Bad plastic surgery," a third coughed into her fist. They all snickered.

Heat rose up the back of my neck.

Five more minutes and you're done. You went through physiotherapy, surgeries, and rehabilitation. You can survive these idiots.

Just when I thought things couldn't get any worse, West St. Claire finally decided to see what all the fuss was about. He took a step closer to the truck. His eyes zeroed in on the left side of my face, noticing my existence for the first time in the two years we'd attended the same college, even though we shared three classes. I swallowed, trying to push down the baseball-sized ball of puke in my throat.

I finished the crunchy tacos and started on the soft ones. West took another step, not bothering to conceal his open fascination with my scar. I felt naked and raw under his gaze and almost sighed in relief when his eyes tore away from my cheek, landing on the wanted sign. I chanced a quick glance at him. If he'd fought tonight, I couldn't tell. He looked relaxed and quiet. Tranquil, almost.

"Looking for a job?" Reign snickered.

"Seriously, Reign, zip it," Easton, who was probably the nicest of the three, barked.

West plucked the paper from the truck, balling it in his fist and tucking it into the back pocket of his jeans.

"Savage," Reign tutted, inching backward on a cackle, his face tilted up to the sky.

"Way harsh, West." Tess' voice lacked that same punishing bite she reserved for Reign. "Why would you do that?"

West ignored them both, turning his head to look directly at me. He rolled the candy stick in his mouth like a toothpick, giving me a look that crammed a loaded question into it.

Whatcha gonna do about it, Toastie?

I poured the margarita slushies in record time and tallied up the bill for Tess while Reign, Easton, and the rest of the girls scurried toward the edge of the parking lot to tuck into the food. West stayed by Tess' side, his eyes still stuck on my scar.

I braced myself for an insult, my shell hardening like a taco.

"So, I wanted to ask," Tess purred, taking his wrist and flipping it palm up so his inner bicep was on full display. "What does your tattoo mean? What does A stand for?"

My eyes betrayed me, and I stole a quick look to what she was talking about. It was a simple tattoo of the letter A. No special font or a design. Just one letter, in Times New Roman.

"Probably *asshole*," I muttered under my breath.

Both their gazes flew up to me.

Lord. I'd said it aloud. A soon-to-be dead idiot. What was I thinking?

You were thinking that he is an asshole. Because he is.

"Grace." Tess slapped her mouth. "For shame."

West spat the candy out on the ground, his slanted, fierce eyes on me. My head was dangerously close to exploding from all the blood rushing into it. After a long stretch of silence, he finally slapped two Benjamins into Tess' open palm, turned around, and walked away in catlike grace, paying for everyone's food and drinks. Tess rolled her eyes, handing me the money.

"Sorry about the want ad. West's got a bit of a mean streak. He's my work in progress."

"Ain't your fault."

I peeled the plastic gloves off and handed Tess the change. She grabbed my hand and gasped. Her unexpected skin-to-skin contact made me shiver. I wasn't used to being touched.

"Cool ring! Where'd you get it?"

"It was my momma's. Here's your change."

"Keep it."

I raised a skeptical eyebrow. That was one hell of a tip.

"You sure?"

She nodded.

"Screw him for acting the way he did. You know, West really gets a bad rep, but honestly, he is a big softie. He can be, like, super sweet when he wants to be."

I wasn't sold on West being anything other than a raging psychopath, but this was not a conversation I was eager to pursue. I wanted to get out of here, erase tonight from my memory bank, and binge-watch *Friends* reruns until my faith in humanity was sufficiently restored.

"All righty," I said robotically. "Thanks for stoppin' by and shoppin' at That Taco Truck."

Tess flashed me a dazzling smile and turned around, running toward her friends.

I followed her with my eyes. She cut between the golden dunes framing the parking lot, straight to her popular friends. They clinked their slushies together, laughing, talking, and eating. My gut twisted.

I could have been Tess.

Correction: I *was* Tess.

I guess that was the part I hated most about my life. I was once a Tess. Showing off my legs in tiny cut-offs. Hanging out with the likes of West, Easton, and Reign. Sitting on the back of their motorcycles as they did wheelies on the old dirt road at the edge of town by the water tower. Explaining to lowly mortals how the mind and soul of West St. Claire worked, letting them in on some exotic top secret.

I rolled down the food truck's window. When I turned around, Karlie squealed, barely containing her excitement. She high-fived me. My best friend was five feet tall on a good day. Tan and curvy, she had a round, gorgeous face laced with a constellation of freckles stretching from cheek to cheek. Once upon a time, when I was the designated Queen Bee of our school, I let her in with the cool kids. But that was four years ago. I could no longer offer her this perk.

"Easton Braun and Reign De La Salle, man. I'd like to be the pastrami between their buns." She fanned herself. "But West St. Claire was the cheddar on the taco. I think he fought today."

"He didn't look too beat up to me." I turned off the grill, taking out the cleaning products from the cabinet next to the fridge.

"That's because he wipes the floor with these guys. Though, I hear sometimes he lets them throw in a punch or two, just so people will bet on someone else. God help me, his *eyes.*" Karlie sucked on the remainder of her slushie, before dropping it in the trash. "They're, like, radioactive green. And you can forge metal with his cheekbones. Seriously, he could destroy my life, and I would literally say thank you."

I grunted, throwing water over the grill. It spat fumes in my face.

"C'mon. Give me the tea. The grill was too loud for me to hear anything. Did they say anything interesting? Any gossip?" She nudged me.

They said I was a freak.

"They were pretty tanked, so not much coherent conversation was going on. But they went gaga for the margarita slushies." I scrubbed the grill.

"Wow. Totally riveting." She rolled her eyes. "Do you think Tess and West are hooking up?"

"Probably. They'll make a corny couple, though. Their names rhyme, for crying out loud."

"Couple? Tess can dream on. West only does one-night stands. That's a known fact."

I offered a shrug. Karlie gave me an exasperated shove.

"God, you're the worst gossip ever. I don't even know why I bother. Last question: therapeutically-speaking, would you rather internet-stalk all the people in Michael Jackson's 'Black or White' video and freak out about how old they are today, or give Barbie a Joe Exotic mullet?"

"The latter," I mustered with a tired smirk, realizing how much I was going to miss her once she found a new employee to take most of her shifts. "I'd give Barbie a mullet, then dress her up as a cowgirl, put her in her Glam Convertible, and TikTok a video of her singin' Bratz Dolls Ate My Pet."

Karlie threw her head back and laughed. I peeked in her pocket mirror, which was sitting on the windowsill, checking my makeup.

The scar was mostly hidden.

I let out a relieved sigh.

The crunchy taco survives another day. Cracked, but not broken.

I got home at eleven. Grams was sitting at the kitchen table in her tattered calico housedress, the radio beside her playing Willie Nelson on full blast.

Grandma Savvy had always been an eccentric woman. She was the lady who went ham with her costumes each Halloween to welcome the trick-or-treaters. Who painted funny—often inappropriate—figures on the plant pots in her front yard, and danced at weddings like no one was watching, and cried watching Super Bowl commercials.

Grandmomma had always been quirky, but recently, she was confused, too.

Too confused to be left alone for longer than the ten-minute overlap between the time her caregiver Marla went home and I pulled into our garage.

I was three when my mom, Courtney Shaw, overdosed. She was lying on a bench in downtown Sheridan. A schoolboy found her. He tried to poke her with a branch. When she didn't wake up, he freaked out and screamed bloody murder, attracting half the school kids in our town and a few of their parents.

Word spread, pictures were taken, and the Shaws had officially become Sheridan's black sheep. By then, Grams was the only mother I knew. Courtney played a game of revolving doors with an array of tweaker boyfriends. One of them was my father, I assumed, but I'd never met him.

Grams never asked who my father was. She was probably wary of opening that can of worms and going through a custody battle with Lord-knows-who. The chances of my father being a respectable hard worker or a Sunday service attendee weren't exactly high.

Grams raised me like her own daughter. It was only fair now that she was not fully independent, I stuck around and took care of her. Besides, it wasn't like the job offers were pouring in from Hollywood and I was missing out on some huge career.

Reign De La Salle was mean, but he wasn't wrong. With a face like mine, the only roles I could snag were that of a monster.

I entered the kitchen, dropping a kiss on Grams' cloud of white, candyfloss hair. She caught my arm and pulled me down for a hug. I let out a grateful sigh.

"Hi, Grams."

"Gracie-Mae. I made some pie."

She braced the table, pulling herself up with a groan. Grams remembered my name. Always a good sign, and probably why Marla let her stay here by herself before I arrived.

Our house was a seventies graveyard, consisting of all the interior design atrocities you could find in that era: green tile countertops, wood paneling, rattan everything, and electronics that still weighed about the same as a family car.

Even after we redid big chunks of our ranch-style after the fire, Grams went to a Salvation Army thrift store and bought the oldest, most mismatched furniture she could find. It was like she was allergic to good taste, but as with all quirks, when they belonged to someone you loved, you learned how to find the beauty in them.

"I'm not really hungry," I lied.

"It's a new recipe. I found it in one of them magazines they have at the dentist's office. Marla came down with something, bless her heart. Couldn't even taste the dang thing. She wanted to try it so bad."

I sat obediently at the table as she slid a plate with a slice of cherry pie and a fork in my direction. She patted the back of my hand on the table.

"Now, don't be shy, Courtney. Not with your momma. Eat."

Courtney.

Well, that didn't last long. Grams called me Courtney frequently. The first few times after it happened, I took her to get some tests done, see what caused her forgetfulness. The doctor said it wasn't Alzheimer's, but to come again next year if things got worse.

That was two years ago. She hadn't agreed to go back since.

I shoveled a chunk of the cherry pie into my mouth. As soon as the pie hit the back of my throat, it clogged up and shot a message to my brain:

Abort mission.

She'd done it again.

Mistaken salt for sugar. Prunes for cherries. And—who knows?—maybe rat poison for flour, too.

"Fine as cream gravy, huh?" She leaned forward, resting her chin on her knuckles. I nodded, reaching for the glass of water next to my plate, chugging it down in one go. I glanced at my phone on the table. It flashed with a message.

Marla: Fair warning: Your gram's pie is particularly bad today.

My eyes watered.

"I knew you'd like it. Cherry pie is your favorite."

It wasn't. It was Courtney's, but I didn't have the heart to correct her.

I swallowed every bite without tasting it, down to the last crumb, pushing through the discomfort. Then I played a board game with her, answering questions about people I didn't know who Courtney had been associated with, tucked Grams to bed, and kissed her goodnight. She held my wrist before I got up to leave, her eyes like fireflies dancing in the dark.

"Courtney. You sweet child of mine."

The only person who loved me thought I was someone else.

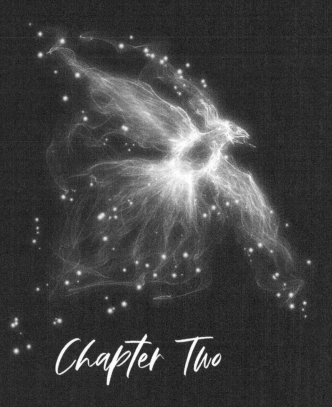

Chapter Two

Grace

THE NEXT MORNING, I ARRIVED AT THE FOOD TRUCK EARLY TO prep ahead of opening hour. Sheridan's Farmers' Market was open on Saturdays, which meant more competition, more food trucks, more human interaction and its byproduct—more war paint. I put so much makeup on my face on Saturdays, I gave party clowns a run for their money.

Silver lining: it wasn't rodeo day. I refused to do the rodeo shift. Not since a customer had compared my face to a horse and explained the stud would win in the beauty department.

Karlie was late, which wasn't out of the ordinary. Even though she was one of the most laser-focused, hard-working people I'd known, she could sleep through anything, a World War included. I didn't mind her slacking as much as I probably should. The Contrerases paid me well, provided flexible shifts, and Karlie had proven to be an amazing friend in the past four years.

I washed and cut fish, sliced vegetables, made the frozen

margaritas, and rewrote and hung the wanted sign on the truck. My best friend stumbled inside at quarter to nine. She wore big pink headphones and a tank top with Bart Simpson on it.

"Hola. Everything good?" She popped her watermelon gum in my face, taking off her headphones. "Rebel Girl" by Bikini Kill blasted through them before she turned off her music app. I shoved the tongs into her hands.

"Woke up feelin' somethin' bad is going to happen today."

That wasn't a lie. Waking up today, I'd noticed the flame ring on my thumb had finally succumbed to its old age, and half the flame had broken, leaving just the hoop and part of the flame.

It was a hundred and twelve degrees outside—so hot you could fry an egg on the concrete—and probably ten degrees hotter in the truck. Something about today felt different. Monumental, somehow. Like my future had been suspended over my head, threatening to thunder down on me.

"Today's going to be fine." She dropped her backpack on the floor, snapping the tongs in my face. "Fine, but busy. There's already a line outside. Better get your ass to your window, Juliet."

"If Romeo eats fish tacos at nine a.m., I'd rather stay single." I laughed, feeling a little more like myself again and a little less like the pitiful girl West St. Claire had made me feel I was last night.

Mrs. Contreras insisted on serving her special recipe fish tacos only. No Tex Mex in this food truck. We only did one type of taco, but we were the best at it.

"Ah, that's the angle Shakespeare didn't expand on. Romeo died of Juliet's fish taco breath, not poison."

"And Juliet's dagger?" I tossed Karlie an amused look. She pretended to shove the tongs into her gut like it was a sword, holding her neck as she fake-choked.

"Tongs can be deadly, too."

I opened the truck window with a smile, determined to push last night away from my mind.

"Good mornin' and welcome to That Taco Truck! How may I hel—"

The last word clogged up in my throat when I saw his face. A line of people trailed behind him.

West St. Claire.

My smile dissolved.

Why was he back?

"Is this about the tip Tess left yesterday? Because you can have it. Maybe buy some manners." My gut clenched, my mouth faster than my brain.

Why did I insist on getting socially murdered? Was I subconsciously suicidal? Either way, I didn't regret what I'd said. I doubted West wanted tacos or a civilized conversation. I knew going toe-to-toe with a guy like him was a bad idea, but he'd been cold and mean yesterday, and I couldn't help but call him out on that.

West looked like he hadn't slept all night. He was still wearing the same jeans and faded shirt combo, his steadfast, bored gaze making me feel like dirt. His eyes were bloodshot.

Wordlessly, West handed me a ball of paper. I immediately recognized it. My face clouded as I unfolded it. It was the ad he'd ripped from the truck yesterday.

"Already made a new one," I clipped, dunking the paper into the trashcan under my feet. "Anything else I can do for you?"

"Get the manager," he clipped.

It took me by surprise. First of all that he spoke at all. I'd never heard him talk before. His voice matched his looks. Low, smoky, and depraved. Second, it shocked me that he spoke to *me*. But most of all, I was surprised he had the audacity to boss me around.

"I beg your pardon?" I lifted an eyebrow. My good, right eyebrow. The left one didn't exist anymore. I penciled it in, though, and since I always wore my gray ball cap, people could hardly tell. The customers behind him lost their patience, shaking their heads, bouncing on their feet. Of course, no one actually *said* anything to West St. Claire. God forbid someone called him out on his BS.

"Manager. Also known as the person in charge of this truck. You slow?"

"No, I'm disgusted."

"Well, hurry up and get me off your hands, then. Call your supervisor."

His eyes were dead on mine. Up close, they weren't exactly green. They were a wild mixture of sage and blue, rimmed by dark jade.

He and his friends had had fun guessing what happened to my face last night. West had examined me like I was a circus freak. I'd felt like a caged three-headed animal. Desperate to bend the bars, pounce forth, and rip them to shreds with my pointy claws.

Back in reality, I smoothed the clinging nylon wrap sealing the guac in the toppings bar.

"Excuse me for being blunt, but the chances of you wantin' to work in this food truck are akin to the chances of my joinin' the Bolshoi. Now get on with your order or move along. I have customers waitin'."

"*Manager. Now,*" he repeated, ignoring my words. I felt my nostrils flaring with frustration. I'd heard he was intense, but experiencing it firsthand made me feel like someone had put my heart in a blender and forced me to watch it minced into a puree.

Karlie's face popped from behind me. She yelped in surprise when she saw him. "Oh my God. I mean, hi. West, right?"

Smooth. She would recognize him in Sheridan University's crab mascot costume.

He eyed her, not bothering to confirm his identity. Karlie stuck her hand out through the window. He pretended not to notice.

She drew it back to her side, snickering.

"I'm Karlie. We go to Sher U together. I'm the manager here. Well, her daughter anyway. How can I help?"

"I'm here for the job."

"Serious?"

"As a heart attack."

And just as deadly. Turn him away, Karl.

"Fantastic. You're hired," she chirped, not missing one single heartbeat.

A hysterical, high-pitched laugh involuntarily burst out of me. Karlie and West turned to me like I was crazy. Wait … they were serious? I looked between them, a chill rolling through my spine. An elderly woman behind West cleared her throat, waving at me as if I was the person responsible for the delay.

"You're joking, right?" I turned to Karlie.

She winced.

"I mean, we *do* need another employee …"

West jerked his chin behind my back, focusing on my best friend now. "Let's take this somewhere private."

"Hop on in through the door."

For the next few minutes, time moved sideways. Karlie and West scurried to the back of the truck while I stayed at the window, serving customers. Ten minutes later, Karlie came out of the truck, peeled off the want ad, and slipped back in.

"Congratulations! You have a new coworker," she sing-songed, shuffling back to the grill, flipping a piece of fish that was ten minutes past charred.

I ignored her, preparing tacos as fast as I could and internally convincing myself my life was not over and West St. Claire wasn't going to kill me as some part of an elaborate bet.

"Shaw, did you hear me?" The whitefish Karlie was flipping kept breaking into small, mushy pieces. I was hot, sweaty, madder than a wet hen, and full of dark, bitter sludge. I was pretty sure if I cut myself open with the knife I was holding to pierce the bag of shredded cheese, that's what I'd see. Black goo slithering from my veins.

"Loud and clear. I just thought you'd let me weigh in on this, seeing as I'll be the one workin' with your replacement."

"Hear me out. He is Sheridan's most notorious college hottie. He could bring a ton of customers to the truck. I couldn't say no, and I knew you'd be iffy about it."

"Right." I leaned forward, handing a customer his burnt fish taco with a fake smile. When I'd finished high school, I'd been on the fence about attending college. My instincts told me to hide from the world, slink back to the shadows and live in solitude. But I quickly learned that I didn't have much choice. I had to get out there and make money. Since I was already saddled with the inconvenience of showing people my face, I figured college was a practical, albeit cruel, solution to securing a decent job.

"He wants a job, does he?" I was on a roll. "I bet he desperately needs the money, seein' as he ain't cashin' in at the Plaza."

I knew West St. Claire made bank from those fights. Rumor was he'd made eighty grand last year at the Plaza, between selling tickets, taking bets, and charging a fortune for watered-down beer.

"I asked him about that. He said he needed to supplement his income."

"He needs to supplement his manners," I retorted.

"Why? Was he mean to you?" Karlie's brows slammed together.

Just thinking about last night infuriated me. I looked away, changing the subject.

"And anyway, what do you mean, you knew I'd be iffy about it?"

"Come on." She threw her arms in the air like we both knew the answer to that question.

"Come on, *what*?"

"Seriously? Fine. I'll go ahead and say it. But promise you won't get mad."

"I won't get mad."

I was *already* fuming.

"Well, the truth is, you tend to be intimidated by people, Shaw. Then you go and base your opinion of them on what you *think* they're like."

"Am not!"

"Do too. Look at you. You're livid because I hired someone you don't even know just because he's got a reputation. Guess what? We all have a reputation. Sorry, Grace, but it's true. I'm the brainiac know-it-all with the nineties obsession; you're the emo girl with the scar. We're all categorized. Stereotyped by our flaws and weaknesses. Welcome to life. It's a bitch and then you die."

Fearing I'd say something I'd regret, I kept my mouth shut. Karlie stopped tossing extra-dead fish, spun, and clasped my shoulders, forcing me to face her. She massaged my deltoids through my pink hoodie.

"Look at me, Shaw. Are you listening?"

I offered her a grunt.

"Maybe he is nice."

"Chances are he is evil."

I knew I was letting my insecurities get the better of me, but based on his looks, reputation, and social status, West St. Claire was a perfect candidate to ruin my life.

"If he's evil after the first shift, let me know and I'll give him the boot. No questions asked. Not even one." Karlie forced me into a handshake, making a one-sided deal with me. "You have my word. I know you think I'm starstruck, but to me he's just a fellow student lookin' to make an extra buck. I'm drowning in schoolwork and my internships are going to take the front seat once we finish this year. I need this. Now can you stop sulking?"

Unfortunately, Karlie made sense. West hadn't technically wronged me. If anything, he'd given me one heck of a tip and hadn't even asked for it back.

"Fine."

She grinned, turning me back to the line of people waiting for their food.

"That's my girl. Quick, tell me if you can see him in the parking lot. I asked if he could start today and watch me work the grill, but he said he had plans. Is he still around?"

I craned my neck, humoring her reluctantly. I spotted him straight away, the side effect of him being a head taller than the rest of humanity. He was leaning against his red 2016 Ducati M900 Monster, his Wayfarer sunglasses intact.

I recognized the girl with him, even from the back. Raven hair, endless tanned legs, and the same tiny shorts that couldn't cover a pencil. Tess. She talked to him animatedly, flinging her hair and giggling. They'd probably spent the night together. West didn't respond to whatever she was saying. He turned around, slapped a helmet over her head in one rough movement, buckled it around her chin, and hopped on the motorcycle. She slid behind him, snaking her arms around his torso.

He took one of her hands and placed it over his crotch.

"Yup. About to ride into the sunset, or closest STI clinic, with Tess Davis." I accidentally crushed a crunchy taco shell as they zipped through the parking lot, clouds of dust curtaining their figures.

Karlie made a face. "She always draws the best bull. I wonder who he'll do next?"

Hopefully his hand. We don't want any mini-Wests populating our planet.

I spent the next five hours listening to Karlie pondering West's taste in women, serving people, and obsessing over the disastrous turn my life had taken.

When I opened the truck's doors to leave, a pair of ballet shoes sat on the stair. I picked them up, frowning. They were around my size, brand-new, but out of the shoebox. There was a note stuck to them, scribbled lazily.

Better start practicing.

"What the …?"

My words from this morning bounced inside my head.

"The chances of you wantin' to work in this food truck are akin to the chances of my joinin' the Bolshoi."

West St. Claire had jokes.

Unfortunately, I had a feeling I was about to become his favorite one.

Chapter Three

West

Bzzz.
Bzzzzz.
Bzzzzzzzzzz.

My phone danced across my nightstand, falling to the floor, forming a jerky circle like a bug on its back.

I leaned down and picked it up, swiping the screen to turn off my alarm. A muffled shriek pierced my eardrum.

"Honey? Is that you? Larry! Come here! He answered."

Fuck. My. Life.

I'd been knocked out dead for ten hours, so it didn't register the monotone, wake-the-fuck-up sound of my alarm was also my ringtone.

For a split second, I toyed with the idea of hanging up then figured I'd filled up my asshole quota for this week yesterday by eating all of East's pre-prepared jock food. Biting my own fist to the point of drawing blood, I pressed my phone to my ear.

Here goes Nothing and its fucking asshole cousin, Calamity.

"Mother."

"Hello! Hi!" Mom cried out desperately. "Westie, I can't believe you answered."

Join the fucking club.

"How's it going?" I rolled sideways on the mattress, sitting on the edge of my bed. The clock on my nightstand said two in the afternoon. It also said I was a complete, goddamn moron who'd slept in again. Graduation was looming closer, and I knew I was going to get out of Sheridan University with my useless degree, but it would be nice to at least pretend I gave a damn.

"Nothing, honey! I mean, everything's good. Just fine. We wanted to check in on you. See how you were doing. Easton has been giving us updates, but we love hearing your voice."

"Is that him?" Dad sniffled in the background. I heard shuffling. Things knocked off a table. They were rabid with excitement. Guilt kicked in, followed by its loyal friend, Remorse. "Let me speak to him. Westie? Are you there?"

"Dad. Hi."

"It's good to hear your voice, son."

I pushed my feet into the Blundstones under my bed, dragging my ass to the bathroom. I took a leak and brushed my teeth as Dad launched into a story about how the guy who promised to help him fertilize his land still wasn't back from Wyoming, and that he'd lost another contract as a result. I got the subtext—I needed to send them more money before their electricity got cut off.

The sharp guilt I'd experienced a second ago dulled into numbness.

"I'm guessing the bankers aren't your biggest fans." I spat mint toothpaste and water into the sink, splashing water over my face. I didn't glance in the mirror. Hadn't faced myself in years—why start now?

"Oh, well, I mean … things aren't looking great, I suppose. But—"

I didn't let him finish.

"I'll send some money by the end of the day. Speak soon. Bye."

I hung up on him just as he started saying something. I grabbed my keys, jumped on the Ducati, and hauled ass to school. Eight minutes later, I strode into Lawrence Hall, to my two-thirty sports management lecture.

Late again, much to no one's surprise.

Luckily, Professor Addams (spelled with double-D, fitting for his man-boobs) was busy attempting to work this magical thing called an iPad. His head was down as he assaulted the screen with his greasy fingers, trying to make his slideshow appear on the white screen behind him. I slinked into the back of the room, sliding into a spot between Reign and East. Addams' slideshow finally popped into vision, and he let out a relieved cackle.

"'Sup." Reign fist-bumped me. He was making out with a random. She was mauling his neck while his hand was shoved inside her skirt.

East flicked the back of my head. "Late again. By the way, thanks for eating all my food."

"My pleasure."

Truly, it was.

"Dare you to do it again."

"You know I never turn down a challenge."

Everyone had laptops and notebooks out. Not me. I didn't bring a backpack. I showed up randomly whenever the threat of failing a semester seemed real. Professor Addams' voice rose from the bowels of the lecture hall.

"Mr. St. Claire, I see you decided to finally grace us with your presence."

I stared at him coolly, refusing to throw him a bone.

The girl next to Reign had the good senses to slap Reign's hand away from under her skirt as all eyes darted to us.

Addams leaned his thick waist against his desk, oinking as he pushed his glasses up his nose.

"Tell me, Mr. St. Claire, are you even faintly interested in gaining higher education?"

Truthfully, I wasn't. But this hellhole was far enough from Maine to lie low and do what I needed to do to keep my family from going bankrupt.

"Use your words," he instructed haughtily. "You do know how to speak, don't you?"

I smirked. I wasn't easily flustered. Came with the territory of being numb across the board. People couldn't touch me if they tried.

And they tried.

Often.

"Pursuing a degree seemed like a great excuse to leave the dump I lived in, and Sher U is pretty affordable for an out-of-state college. Jury's still out on the educational staff, though." I sat back, crossing my arms over my pecs.

"Burn!" Someone cackled.

"Holy shit," another student bellowed. "St. Claire is handing asses in the ring and out of it."

Laughs exploded from every corner of the room. Professor Addams' mouth slacked, and his cheeks turned flamingo pink. It took him a full minute to recover.

"Give me one reason why I should let you get away with what you just said to me."

"Because you were transferred here from an Ivy League university under mysterious circumstances, which no one cared to explore. Guess what?" I opened my arms theatrically. "I have all the time in the world. How is that for a full sentence for you, Professor Addams?"

"*Pfft.*" Reign raised his arm in the air, opening his palm, like he was dropping a mic.

"Savage to death." East chuckled.

"You think you're so clever, don't you, West St. Claire?" Addams huffed.

"Discipline me or let it drop. You're drawing it out." I yawned.

He turned back to his slideshow, shaking his head. *Idiot.*

Half an hour later, I strode out of class. Reign had his arm flung over the nameless chick, and East was scrolling through his phone, probably debating the girl he wanted to take out tonight. I decided to drop the bomb. Now was as bad a time as any.

"I'm starting to work at That Taco Truck tomorrow."

Technically, I was starting today. That Karlie chick was supposed to teach me how to work the grill this afternoon.

At first, there was no reaction. When I didn't expand on the matter, because it was pretty self-fucking-explanatory, Reign proceeded to snort-laugh.

"Umm, why the fuck?"

"Strapped for cash."

"You don't get enough juice from fighting?" He screwed up his nose. Reign had zero financial worries. When he wasn't playing ball, he was chasing tail. College to him was a string of parties and games, with hookups and pregnancy scares crammed in-between for dramatic relief. I, however, was busy paying my parents' loans, financing my own education, *and* saving up so I wouldn't have to go back home once I graduated this year.

Nameless Chick gasped. "That makes no sense. Everyone says you're loaded." I didn't answer. Getting dicked by one of my frenemies didn't make her a certified accountant.

"Do what you gotta do, man. Let me know if I can help." East hoisted his duffel bag over his shoulder, putting a lid on the subject.

"Maybe he's got the hots for Toastie," Reign mused. "And he's looking for leeway. I mean, she is smokin' once you put a bag over that face."

"The burn victim?" Nameless Chick flattened a hand over her chest. "Isn't it tragic? One of my sorority sisters knows her from high school. Heard she was in cheer and drama before she turned this way. She was real pretty, too."

I had no doubt I was going to knock every tooth out of Reign's mouth at some point in my life. He was a mean bastard and picked on people constantly. Anything to make his idiot friends laugh. His choice in female companion was obviously just as poor.

Reign cackled.

"Seriously, man, shut up." Easton collared him, swinging his body so he was an inch from crashing against the wall.

We reached the double doors of the entrance and split. Reign and East had practice, and Random Chick was off, probably doing random shit. I was about to head out when I heard shouting coming from the crack of the door by the exit.

"Fire! Fire!"

It was coming from the makeshift auditorium, where theater and arts rehearsed these days while they built a brand-new theater across campus grounds.

I burst through the doors.

They were rehearsing. *Phew.*

The door was ajar, practically inviting me to take a look. It wasn't like I had anything better to do. I had half an hour to burn before I met Karlie at the food truck.

I propped a shoulder over the doorframe, folding my arms. Tess was onstage, wearing a nightgown over a prosthetic pregnant belly, her hair pinned up, charging to the other corner of the stage, producing a wailing sound that could deafen a whale.

A fuckboy from theater was chasing her, clad in a wife beater, a cigarette hanging from the corner of his pinched mouth. He tried to sound Southern, but it came out like he had blisters the size of my balls on his tongue. I didn't know anything about theater, but I could recognize shitty acting when it hit me in the face with a shovel. No shade to Tess, she was a perfectly good lay, but I would buy the Hitler-is-still-alive-and-lives-with-2PAC conspiracy—logic and math be damned—before believing their acting.

My eyes drifted around the auditorium. The blonde girl from the food truck was there. Greer or Gail or whatever. *Toastie.* I spotted the back of her head. She sat in one of the back rows. Her white FILAs were propped on the back of the seat in front of her. Her long legs were clad in faded skinny jeans. She had the same pink hoodie and gray ball cap I saw her sporting at the truck. Her long, golden hair spilled across her back and shoulders, making her look like a Gothic angel.

Reign was about as perceptive as a can of Spam, but he wasn't off base. Greer-Gail was fuckable to a fault. Not that I was about to touch her. It had nothing to do with her face. Scar tissue never bothered me—my heart was 100% made out of that shit. But she had an attitude the size of Mississippi, and I had a strict no bitch-porking policy in place.

I'd left her the ballet shoes as a little 'fuck you.' Honestly, I had no idea what I was trying to convey with the shoes. I'd felt like an idiot when I bought them, and even worse after I'd left them on the food truck's stair. Whatever. Who cared if it was lame to put them there? I wasn't trying to woo her ass.

The director of the play, Cruz Finlay—another student who thought wearing a beret and a scarf in the Texas heat made him look artistic, as opposed to a complete moron—asked the actors to start the scene from scratch. I stepped deeper into the room so I could check out Greer-Gail-Whatever's face uninterrupted. All this talk about her scar, and I barely saw it, but she was so self-conscious about it, I was inclined to believe it was a sight.

I only got the right side of her face. The so-called "normal" side. Her eyes were glued to the stage. She mouthed all the words along with the actors, both Tess' lines and the dude's. Crazy thing was, they were reading from the pages, and she knew everything by heart.

It was pretty obvious Greer-Gail had a boner for acting, but I doubted she'd pursue it. Didn't take a genius to see she was all tangled up in her I'm-a-victim narrative.

"I don't want realism. I want magic," Greer-Gail mimed, echoing a third actress onstage, and I had a feeling the line applied to her more than anything else in the play. She seemed hella bitter about her own reality.

I was so fascinated by Greer-Gail reciting an entire goddamn play without anyone taking note, or even realizing she was there in the room, that it took me a second to notice the rehearsal was over.

"First run-through under our belt, and it is a complete and utter train wreck. Tomorrow. Same place. Same time. God." Finlay threw his hands up, peering at the ceiling like Lord Almighty had better shit to do than watch this crap. "Give me actors."

Or a punch in the face, I thought. *You can give him a punch in the face, too, and nobody will fault you for that, his parents included.*

"West!" Tess cried, hopping from the stage and charging toward the double doors. She discarded her fake belly on one of the seats, not breaking her pace. My stance was lax, lazy, and unflappable. Everyone's eyes turned to me. Tess made it sound like I'd just come back from a tour in Iraq. Greer-Gail swiveled her head. Our eyes met as Tess flung her arms around me, peppering kisses over my neck and cheeks.

I'd told Tess a one-time lay was the only thing on the table, and we'd had our first and last hurrah last weekend. She said she understood, but women rarely did. I removed her from my body, making a mental note to remind her we weren't a thing.

Greer-Gail offered no reaction as she watched us, but she didn't stop watching either. Her face was blank. Her eyes were a shade of blue I hadn't seen outside psychedelic paintings. Pale and arctic, like a snowflake. I had a feeling she allowed herself to look because she wasn't used to anyone noticing her.

Well, I did.

I noticed she was fucking glaring.

My eyes asked, *Did you get the ballet shoes?*

Hers answered, *Drop dead, asshole.*

I may have been paraphrasing, but whatever her eyes said, there was profanity in it.

Greer-Gail turned her head back to the empty stage, rearranging her feet on the seat in front of her. I was about to walk over and ask what the hell her problem was, but my phone buzzed in my pocket, just as Tess tried to pull me into the auditorium, blabbing about her role in the play.

I took my phone out of my back pocket.

Mother.

Seriously? Twice today? I hit decline, turned around, and charged over to my bike without a word. Tess knew better than to follow me. I got into my bank app and transferred whatever money I had in my account straight to my parents before heading off to see Karlie.

I'd live off ramen for the next couple weeks. Wouldn't be the first or last time.

I spent the ride resenting my parents and Tess and Reign and Professor Addams and even Greer-Gail-Genevieve.

And with every turn I took, the temptation to lean to one side, to throw myself off the bike, to veer off a cliff, was there, scratching at my insides.

A part of me still wanted to die.

To cease existing.

To stop taking care of my parents.

To stop pretending anything about this college experience mattered.

I just got real good at hiding it.

Even if it cost me everything.

Chapter Four

Grace

"**G**RACE, MY DEAR, WE NEED TO TALK."

Professor McGraw took a sip of her coffee from her *Eat. Sleep. Theater.* mug. I crept into her office the day after our first rehearsal, head down, shoulders hunched, ready for my verdict. I dropped my phoenix-themed JanSport under her desk, offering my best innocent, don't-know-why-I'm-here smile.

I *did* know why I was there.

"Have a seat." She pointed at the chair in front of her. I did. Professor McGraw was a willowy, fifty-something redhead with funky, polka-dotted reading glasses and fifties-style dresses. I adored her and wanted to believe she liked me, too. I was definitely among her more dedicated students. My theoretical grades were great, I was always happy to put in extra hours to tidy up after rehearsals, and my love for theater was genuine.

She began sifting through a pile of documents strewn on her desk, licking her thumb as she separated the pages. Her office was filled with posters of Sheridan University productions over the years. The university was known for producing classic plays and attracting people from neighboring towns. The profits went toward city council and improving the college facilities. A twinge of jealousy stung my chest as I scanned the posters while she searched for whatever it was she wanted to show me.

The Phantom of the Opera.

Chicago.

To Kill a Mockingbird.

My mouth watered as I stared at the pictures of the actors and actresses, smiling to the horizon, mid-act. They looked electric. Glowing. *Happy.*

Professor McGraw's voice pierced through the green cloud of envy surrounding me. She tapped a piece of paper with her fingernail. "There we are. I've been looking at the list of actors in *A Streetcar Named Desire.* I noticed your name was notably absent. Care to explain?"

"Oh. Yes. Of course." I shifted in my seat. The actors in the posters stared directly at me. Their judging gazes warmed my skin. "Lauren got Blanche and Tess is Stella. The other smaller parts were cast on the days I took my grandmother to Austin for an EKG. I did sign up for design and assistant stage manager. That's two roles." I stuck two fingers up, like she didn't know how to count.

Professor McGraw removed her reading glasses, closing her eyes and pinching the bridge of her nose. "We've discussed it, Grace. I cannot bend the rules for you anymore. Every student needs to get on that stage and show me what they're made of."

"Yes, ma'am. But I was hopin'—"

"I understand your circumstances, and I tried to cater to them for a couple years, but a part of earning a BA in Theater and Arts is *practical* acting. You haven't gone onstage since you started studying here. Exhibiting your ability as an actor is mandatory, not optional. No one expects you to be Meryl Streep, but you do need to show us something. I don't want you failing this semester, but I think if you don't take on an actual role in the play, you just might."

"But the play has already been cast."

"Ask Mr. Finlay to include you."

"Someone else will be losing their role," I argued.

"Someone else is not in danger of failing the final semester of this year," she volleyed back.

I knew Professor McGraw was right. All the other sophomores in theater and arts had already shown off their acting chops. Not me. I was going to be a junior next year, and I still hadn't set foot onstage. My legs wouldn't carry me past the threshold on auditions day. I tried but always ended up puking my guts out in the restrooms, or having epic meltdowns in my pickup.

This new play was no different. I wanted to take part. I truly did. But physically, I couldn't.

It wasn't that I wasn't good at acting. I was the star of every school play up until the fateful night that changed everything. The stage recharged and electrified me. But getting back up there after what happened seemed like accepting my new face and introducing it to the world, and I wasn't there yet. I didn't think I ever would be. Not that it mattered. I didn't want to become an actress anymore. That dream had been tossed into the trash along with a chunk of my face the night they brought me into the hospital. I wanted to work in theater, doing something that allowed me to hide in the shadows.

Director, producer, stage designer. Hell, I'd be happy working the concession booth if it meant being near the stage every day.

"Professor McGraw, please." I took in a ragged breath but still couldn't seem to fill up my lungs. "It's not just my face. I have other things goin' on."

Grams was having a bad couple weeks, but I didn't want to throw her into the mixed bag of excuses for why I hadn't signed up for the play. I was too busy trying to make sure Grams was alive and well to focus on school.

"Like what?" Professor McGraw leaned forward, knotting her fingers together.

"It's ... personal."

"Life is personal." She smiled. "You want another extension on your practical grade, I'm going to need to know why."

I couldn't bring myself to tell her about Grams. About her being paranoid, and forgetful, and needing constant care. Admitting Grams had a problem would force me to hear unsolicited advice, and I didn't want to put her in a home. Besides, portraying the woman who raised me as an obstacle didn't sit right with me.

I shook my head, stuffing my fists into my hoodie's pockets.

"Doesn't matter. I shouldn't have said anything. Sorry." I stood up, the chair scraping behind me with a screeching sound that clawed at my neck. "I understand you might have to fail me this semester, Professor McGraw. Obviously, I will respect your verdict regardless, but I'm hopin' I'll get an extension and take part in the next play, junior year. Would you let me know?"

She stared up at me, pity swimming in her eyes. I could tell she was disappointed in me. That she wanted this conversation to shake me into action.

"Will do. Is it really *that* bad?" Her voice dropped to a whisper.

You have no idea.

I shook my head, closing my eyes. I slung my backpack over my shoulder, turning around to leave.

"And, Grace?"

I stopped, my back still to Professor McGraw.

"Whatever your journey is, be certain you have someone to lean on when things get tough. Because they always do. Someone who is not your grandmother. Someone chosen, not a built-in family member. Someone who'd walk through fire for you."

I smiled bitterly. I only knew one person who would do something like that.

Me.

West arrived at the food truck five minutes early.

It surprised me that he showed up at all. I still thought it was some kind of trap.

I refused to accept this arrangement was real. That he didn't have an ulterior motive.

Standing closer to him than I had on Friday, when it was dark, I noticed he wasn't completely unscathed. He had a cut lip, a shiner on the verge of turning from purple to green, and a nasty nick running down his neck. He looked like he hadn't slept in years. I almost laughed at how different we were.

I would give up the world to have my unsullied face back, while he fought on a weekly basis, and rode a motorcycle, daring fate to take away his good looks.

Since I had Grams and Professor McGraw to stew over, I hadn't had time to properly freak out about working with St. Claire this evening. I'd even forgotten about the stupid ballet shoes. The minute West's face popped between the open doors of the truck, I rolled my hoodie's sleeve up my right elbow and jerked my chin to a stack of boxes waiting outside while cutting bell peppers into thin strips.

"Mind carryin' and unpackin' 'em inside?" I didn't bother to look at him.

Rather than commenting on my poor manners, or taking the high road and introducing himself properly, West lifted the heavy boxes that were stacked on top of each other like they contained air and not fifty pounds of guacamole, lemons, and fish. He arranged everything in the fridge under the window.

We prepped the food in silence, with him following my clipped instructions.

After food prep was done, West flicked on the grill and started roasting fish and bell peppers like he'd been doing this his entire life. His movements were relaxed and lazy, like a panther's. He was comfortable in this small food truck despite his size. I tried to be as invisible as I possibly could, sticking to my corner of the truck. I realized I hadn't been alone with an attractive guy in the same confined space since age sixteen, and that I'd missed the sweet, sticky current that hung in the air when it happened.

West was a space-hogger. He was everywhere, even when he was on the other side of the trailer.

Judging by the food prep, it didn't look like he was planning to put me through the nine circles of Dante's Hell, or if he did, he was doing a pretty crappy job of it.

We opened shop and served the customers trickling in, mainly high school and college students coming back from afternoon classes and practice, and a few working moms who opted out of making dinner. We didn't exchange one word, other than me asking him to do things and him asking me where certain ingredients were, both of us adopting our driest, least friendly tones.

West worked hard, never complained, and aside from missing Karlie and her nineties *this or that* questions, working alongside him was marginally pain-free.

"Is death by sweat a thing?" West drawled after hours of radio silence. He grabbed the hem of his shirt, using it to wipe his forehead. My whole body jolted at his voice, like he'd struck me. I was so used to wearing my oversized pink hoodie in this climate, the temperature didn't register anymore.

"It can be." I considered his question. "Dehydration comes to mind."

"No A/C?" He flipped a row of fish over on the grill, keeping them perfectly whole and bronzed.

I shook my head. "The ancient air-con that came with the truck costs thousands to repair, and Mrs. Contreras says it ain't worth it because the window's always open, so the cold gets out. She'd rather pay us above minimum wage."

"Well, I'd rather not die. Let's take the cut."

Was he for real? He'd been here for all of half a second, and he was already trying to make changes?

"There's a sayin' in Texas, St. Claire. Never miss a good chance to shut up. I suggest you make use of it now."

"Thanks for the tip. I'll be sure to dump it in the trash on my way out. And you're wearing a *hoodie*." He turned to face me for the first time during the shift. "Are you deranged?"

"I ain't hot."

"A liar on top of being prickly. You're the entire package, aren't you?"

Was anything coming out of his mouth not outrageous? I had a feeling if I asked, he'd say something shocking on principle.

"Okay. Fine. I'm a little hot, but I've been wearin' hoodies for years and it hasn't affected my work here one bit. Ain't my fault I'm good at things," I huffed.

"I'm good at things." He quirked an eyebrow, sticking a candy apple stick he produced out of nowhere into the side of his mouth, smirking. "They're just not resume-appropriate."

He handed me another stick from his back pocket. I shook my head, which, by the way, was painfully close to detonating from the sexual innuendo thrown my way.

He was riling me up on purpose, making fun of Toastie by acting like she stood a chance. *Talk to the fire victim about being hot ... that should be fun.* I could practically hear him and De La Salle plotting it together like two mega villains in a sleek spaceship, stroking look-alike black cats.

"Get used to the heat. Things get progressively worse. By June, we dab our faces with ice packs. July and August are a blur of heatwave headaches and suicidal thoughts. I suggest you get the heck outta here by summer break."

"Sorry to disappoint, but I'm sticking around for the summer. Better stock up on ice and find the local suicide hotline."

He sounded businesslike, dry, and tough as hell. But he did not sound like he wanted to murder me, which was good news, I guessed.

"That's a shame."

"Not for me." He rolled the candy stick in his mouth, dragging a rag across his station. I noticed he kept his space squeaky clean. "Home sucks."

"Where's home?" I slurped my slushie.

"Maine."

"How come you're not goin'?"

"Not many jobs available in Bumfuck Creek."

"Please tell me that's your town's real name."

"Wish it was." He scrubbed his jaw with his knuckles, dumping the rag on the counter. "That'd be the only good thing about it."

I looked away again, feeling crappy for assuming he made enough at the fighting arena when he'd first asked for the job. Who was I to make assumptions about his financial situation? I took his privileged asshole reputation and ran with it, even though it enraged me when people judged me based on rumors.

We hit a slow hour. The sleepy pocket between dinnertime to post-frat party munchies. Mrs. Contreras' policy was that we couldn't use our phones, unless it was an emergency call, so ignoring one another was pretty hard, seeing as we were each other's sole source of entertainment.

A few minutes later, West piped up again, "Mind if I lose the shirt?"

"Hmm, *what*?" I whirled around, glaring at him.

"I'm about to turn into a fucking puddle. Doubt I'd be much help liquefied."

"Uh ..." My eyes roamed the truck. "I'm not sure strippin' is the best course of action. For one thing, it's highly unhygienic."

"I'm not going to hold the tongs with my nipples," he said wryly. "Unless it'll get us more tips. In which case, I'm open to trying."

I let out a stunned, hysterical laugh. I didn't want to see his nipples, or any other part of him. In fact, I didn't want to acknowledge he had more of that bronze, muscular body underneath his clothes. It was bad enough the flawlessness of him was right in front of my eyes all shift.

"I was referrin' to your chest hair."

Stop talking about his chest. Stop speaking at all, Grace.

"Ain't got none," he said in a fake Texan accent I'd find insulting if it wasn't so accurate. He held the hem of his faded tee, raising it up to his brown nipples. His body was smooth, tan, and hairless. His six-pack was something out of an Armani underwear commercial. I wanted to trace the ridges between his abs with my index finger, which was extremely unexpected and laughable altogether.

I didn't crush on people.

Not anymore, anyway.

"Final verdict?" He dropped the shirt, waiting for an answer.

I felt myself turning crimson. I didn't want to look like a nerd and a prude.

"No."

"Let me amend: I was being polite. I'm taking off the fucking shirt, and, if I am being honest, you should do the same."

A second later, West's shirt was gone, and his six-pack was accompanied by defined pecs, Adonis belt veins, and the kind of back you wanted to marry. He turned to the grill and resumed his work. He had a faded purple-yellow welt on his lower back.

"Lookie here, Virgin Mary is still alive." He smirked when he caught me glaring.

I cleared my throat and looked away.

He moved past me, clapping my shoulder casually.

"Don't worry, sweetheart. For you to get knocked up, we'd have to at least hold hands. You're safe with me."

West St. Claire had touched me. *Willingly.*

My throat clogged up unexpectedly, the normalcy in his action making me feel like my old self for a fraction of a second. Not that I was bullied for having a scar. Not per se.

In some ways, people's reactions were far worse. Girls were nice to me in a fake, superficial, we're-cool-but-don't-get-too-close way. It was obvious I wasn't a competition to them anymore. Guys ignored me altogether. I confused them. I still had the same cheerleader body and long blonde hair, but I also had the scars, and they knew that whatever was wrong with the left side of my face bled underneath the clothes, to the rest of my torso.

At first, after the fire, I'd actually had the audacity to try to pretend everything was normal. To hatch the phoenix from its egg with a hammer. I went to the same parties, hung out with the same people. My peers set the record straight at supersonic speed. Through whispers, giggles, gasps, and rumors. My then-boyfriend, Tucker, whom I'd lost my virginity to, cemented the fact I was no longer my old self by quickly replacing me with Rachelle Muir, a fellow flyer. Everyone evaporated from my life like the sweat under my hoodie. The only people who stayed were Karlie and Grandma Savvy.

"*Hellooooo?*" a feminine voice drawled from outside the window. "Anybody in there?"

Yeah, me and my deranged, teenybopper thoughts.

I turned to the window. There were four high school girls in cut-off jeans, cowboy boots, and matching hats. They were giggling and elbowing each other, clutching their phones to their chests. One of them ordered a margarita slushie, while the others peeked behind my back, extending their necks.

"Is he there?" one whispered as I poured the drink.

"Yeah, I see him. Oh my God. *Ohmigod,* Kelly. He's like, freakin' gorgeous."

I handed Slushie Girl her change and drink, but the teenagers didn't budge.

"He's shirtless," the prettiest one, Kelly, who had long,

honey-brown hair and a nipple piercing outlined through her cropped white tee, gulped.

"Yup."

"Ask him."

"No, *you* ask him."

"Are you kiddin' me? You go."

"We had a bet."

"Shut up, you said you're not scared!"

My gaze ping-ponged between them. The rumor West St. Claire worked here had spread like wildfire. I was expecting this to be the norm from now on. Piles upon piles of fangirls knocking on our window, doing the whole *Oh, this? That's just me in my tiny bikini purchasing a taco after getting my hair professionally done, no big deal* spiel.

I didn't like the extra traffic to the truck, but there was little I could do about it, and it wasn't technically West's fault.

"Can I help y'all?" I grabbed my rag, wiping my station clean. They pushed one another, like cubs learning how to play. One of them finally snapped into action.

"Can we speak to West, please?"

"Sure thing. West?" I turned around, waving for him to come to the window. He frowned but complied. An unjust sense of possessiveness washed over me as he rested his elbows over the sill, leaning forward, and I got another glance at his body and that A tattoo on his inner arm. I wondered how Tess found the strength to leave his bed.

I wondered what sex felt like with West St. Claire, in general.

And that angered me to no end, because I couldn't possibly find West St. Claire attractive. He was everything I resented. Popular, handsome, and with a bright future. Just because he was strapped for cash didn't mean we had anything in common. He was going to soar and burst like a supernova once he was out of this small Texas town, and I was going to remain the ashes he left behind—the stardust that slowly descended the earth in his wake.

"Hiiiii, West." Kelly popped her bubblegum, twisting a lock of hair around her finger. My guess was she was a junior in high school. Total jailbait. I slinked into the depths of the food truck, something heavy pressing against my sternum. West may have proven to be a reasonable person to work with, but I still knew he was a jerk.

He flashed her a bored look, waiting for the punch line.

"My sister told me you work here. Anything you recommend from the menu?" She tapped her hot pink fingernail over the list of foods.

"Yeah," he said flatly. "Read it."

Her friends burst into giggles. She blushed, her lips flattening as she tried to take the humiliation in stride. West ran a hand through his damp hair. Every slight movement made his muscles flex.

"Ouch. Are you fighting tonight?"

He stared at her like she just grew a second hand and a pair of shiny, multi-colored wings.

"Just kidding. It's not Friday!" She pouted, nibbling on her lower lip. "Max says you're going pro next year. That true?"

He didn't answer. I knew he wouldn't. He wasn't big on words. West grabbed my slushie, spat his candy out, and sucked on the straw like it belonged to him, starting to retreat back to the grill.

"I … uh …" The pretty girl ran a hand through her tight curls. The pressure on my sternum grew. Trying and failing was the essence of soul shattering. It was exactly why I didn't want to take part in *A Streetcar Named Desire*. And she was experiencing it right now. "My friends and I had a bet. I said I could get you to give me a ride on your Ducati," she blurted out, flinching, bracing herself for rejection. West froze, turning around slowly.

"Why, that's a dumb thing to bet on." He smirked. Suddenly, his tone took a different, predatory lilt. Like she'd finally made a faux pas and it was time he set her straight. He was going to enjoy every minute of it, too.

"I was just thinking … I mean, *hoping*, maybe …"

Her friends began to cackle.

"He'd love to do it!" I jumped in, smiling at her brightly. I couldn't see her going through this. I hoped to hell she learned her lesson and wouldn't put herself in this position again, but I didn't want to see her walking away from here with her tail between her legs.

West's head twisted in my direction, his face turning from bored to thunderous in a heartbeat.

He lifted one thick eyebrow. I could practically hear him thinking, *what the fuck?*

I tried to communicate to him with the power of telepathy that he needed to do this. For her. For *himself*. His square jaw tightened. His eyes darkened. He didn't appreciate my interference—*or* telepathic abilities.

"Didn't know you were my pimp, Gray Cap."

He kept calling me Virgin Mary and Gray Cap, because he had no idea what my name was. The thought was depressing, but I held his gaze.

I didn't know why, but having him look at me didn't feel so horrifying. Maybe because he looked directly into my eyes, as opposed to being distracted by my scar.

"C'mon, she needs to save face," I whispered. The combination of 'save' and 'face' made my stomach churn.

West turned back to the girl. She looked like she was holding her breath.

"The answer is no. The humble pie is on the house and so is the free slushie." He handed her *my* slushie. I ground my teeth together. The girl took it, lowering her head dejectedly.

"Is it because I'm seventeen?" she asked, trying to keep her tone careless and flirty.

"*Sixteen*," her friend coughed into her fist.

"No, it's because if I indulge your underage ass, fifty schoolgirls will be lining up here tomorrow. I can't afford the gas, the trouble, or the pissed-off daddies. Not to mention, I'll get nothing out of this deal, since I don't mix with jailbait. I'm not Netflix. I'm not made for your entertainment. Now beat it."

"You givin' lessons in etiquette in your spare time?" I groaned, pressing the back of my head to the food truck's wall as I closed my eyes.

West kicked a crate around on the floor, moving it out of his way of the grill.

"Depends. You buying?"

I shook my head. "You were dang rude back there, St. Claire."

"I'm their parents' worst nightmare, the reason their daddies buy baseball bats and put on extra locks. They see me as an exotic animal, a rebellious phase. I'm not a pony they can ride in turns," he spat, sounding surprisingly heated.

"That's not what the rumors say," I mumbled, eyes still closed.

Now I was the one making sexual innuendos? What was I saying and *why* was I saying it? His reputation was none of my business. Not to mention, even I was starting to see Karlie's point. I was terribly out of line.

"Wanna know what the rumors say about you?" he taunted, but his heart wasn't in it. His tone was stony. Emotionless.

"No."

"Good, because you're not interesting enough to be talked about."

Turning my face to the window so he wouldn't see me blush, I dropped the subject. He was right. He was being objectified. If he were a woman, I'd be offended on his behalf. But because he was a guy, I assumed he enjoyed the attention. I also owed him an apology for bossing him around. For a lot of things, actually.

"I may have overstepped," I offered, after a few minutes of absent-mindedly scrubbing lettuce from the window crack with a rag.

He didn't answer. I thought maybe he hadn't heard me, or chose not to accept the apology, but then he spoke.

"I may have been a dickwad about that ad. I just wanted the job."

I turned around at the same time he threw me a smirk behind his shoulder.

It scared me to think Karlie was spot-on.

That I objected to working with him because I was intimidated.

That the world frightened me so much, I didn't want to do anything that forced me to take one step out of my comfort zone.

"I don't actually know your name." He turned off the grill, throwing a dishtowel over his shoulder.

"Grace." I cleared my throat. "You're Warren, right?"

We both chuckled at that.

"Wallace," he corrected.

"Cool."

There was a beat of silence, and then ...

"Truce, Grace?" He offered me his pinky. His raspy voice sent shivers down my spine. My whole body tremored. That couldn't be good.

I clasped my pinky against his, feeling silly and dangerously not unhappy.

"Truce."

When I got into my pickup, there was a message waiting for me from Karlie.

Karlie: Well? Do I need to fire him?

Me: He can stay.

Karlie: I KNEW IT. ADMIT IT. HE IS NICE. I KNEW HE WOULD BE.

I thought about his exchange with the girls. I wouldn't call West nice. Hell, I wouldn't even call him civilized. Fair, maybe.

Me: He is fine.

Karlie: Girl, he IS fiiiiiine. Just don't fall in love with him. That'd be a total cliché, and he is the type to break your heart.

Me: That's not a thing you need to worry about unless I'm a victim of a massive head injury, followed by a lengthy concussion. How's the school load?

Karlie: It's whatever. How's your grams?

Me: Surviving.

Barely.

I put my phone down on the passenger seat and closed my eyes.

When I opened them again, I saw West on the other side of the parking lot. He was sitting there on the curb alone, the dusk framing him in furious orange, red, and gold, next to his motorcycle. He chewed on his awful candy stick, blankly staring at nothing, deep in thought.

As I watched him there, I didn't see the most popular guy in college.

The sex god.

The illegal fighter.

I saw the loneliest boy I'd ever laid eyes on.

Sweet, confused, and lost.

And I thought, bitterly, he didn't even know that across the parking lot sat a girl just like him.

Chapter Five

Grace

THE NEXT COUPLE WEEKS PASSED IN A BLUR.
Between exams, attending lectures back-to-back and trying to keep up with my university assignments, I barely had time to breathe.

I'd ignored Professor McGraw's request to secure an acting role in *A Streetcar Named Desire*, biting my nails down to the bed each rehearsal as I envisioned her blasting through the double doors, kicking me out of the course publicly. This, of course, never happened. The reality was Professor McGraw hadn't gotten back to me with an answer on whether or not she was going to give me another extension on the performance part, which meant she fully expected me to contact Cruz Finlay for the role.

Which I didn't.

I felt like I was suspended in the air, my feet on the last inch of a cliff, bracing myself for a fall.

It didn't help that Grams was a handful. Marla said she was extra forgetful. That during her shifts she barely recognized her anymore, and that she was constantly in a sour mood.

Surprisingly, the one thing that *wasn't* a total disaster was working with West. Not that we'd become best buddies or anything. Ever since he'd started working at That Taco Truck, waves upon waves of new customers began knocking on our window. It had gotten so bad we had to put up a sign advising people they had to make a purchase in order to get a selfie with the Almighty St. Claire.

But Karlie was right. They *did*.

Twice, I'd had to call Mrs. Contreras to get more ingredients because we'd run out, and most days, we barely had time to breathe, let alone engage in small talk. But the shifts passed quickly, and by the time I went home, every bone in my body ached.

West worked with his shirt off the entire first week. The second week, he brought a portable A/C. It looked brand-new, and dang expensive. He pretended that it was no big deal that he'd just bought (*stole?*) an air-con that was probably going to save our lives. He put it smack-dab between us, turned it on blast, and stood beside it casually. It was the day I realized not all heroes wore capes. Some were clad in dirty Diesel jeans, Blundstones, and shirts that had seen better days.

Despite my unexplainable need not to like him, I had to mutter a quick thank you.

"What's that?" He cupped his ear, a mischievous glint lighting up his eyes.

Dang you, St. Claire.

"I said thank you," I murmured under my breath.

"Why, you're very welcome. Now you can stop ogling me. I feel objectified already."

It made me laugh so hard, I let out a horrifying snort. We both knew I'd avoided looking directly at his bare torso.

Lord. I'd *snorted*. In front of West St. Claire. Death by humiliation had never seemed so viable.

"I'm sorry. I sounded like a pig." I covered my face with both hands.

He threw a piece of fish at me.

"If you were an animal, what would you be?"

"A phoenix," I said, without even giving it some thought. My hand shot to my broken flame ring, turning it on my thumb. West nodded. I didn't know why, but somehow I had a feeling he knew exactly what I was talking about.

"You?" I asked.

"Koala. I'd get to sleep all day, but still be cute as fuck, so getting laid wouldn't be an issue."

"I heard koalas are actually pretty vicious. And stinky. And are prone to poop on people." I offered my useless knowledge of wildlife. Good thing I wasn't trying to flirt. Talking with hot men was definitely not my forte.

He considered this. "Well, that's just selling me the koala gig even more."

Other than *that* conversation, we were polite, but professional. I'd eased into the idea of us coexisting like treading into a dark, strange basement. There was no immediate reason to suspect I'd get hurt, but it was still scary.

I couldn't help but stare each time I noticed a new welt or bruise on his body. I never mentioned it, though. And the few times I saw him outside the food truck, at school sitting in the cafeteria or on the lawn by the fountain, or the grocery store, all we did was nod to each other and look away.

Two and a half weeks after West and I began working together, my life fell apart in a spectacular fashion, reminding me normal simply wasn't in the cards for me.

It was late evening. An unexpected graveyard shift after the Westival (West Festival) of the last few weeks. There was a spring fair two towns over, and every Sheridan citizen and their mother seemed to take advantage of the activity and drove up to Foothill to enjoy the rodeo, stale popcorn, candy floss, tilt-a-whirl, and bluebonnet blossom.

Fireworks blasted beyond the darkened yellow dunes. West and I watched them from the food truck window in childish awe, shoulder to shoulder. My phone buzzed in my hoodie's pocket. I checked the caller ID. *Marla.* I picked up, knowing she wasn't one to interrupt me at work unless it was important. I turned my back on the fireworks and ambled inside, pressing a finger to my ear so I could hear her through the explosions.

"Heya, Marla."

"Honey, I don't want you getting too worried, but I can't find the old bat. Ten minutes I've been lookin' for her, but I don't think she's home."

Marla talked about Grams with earnest disdain, which I'd learned to warm up to.

My breath caught in my throat. I leaned against the fridge, feeling my anxiety climbing up my toes to the rest of my body, like little ants.

"Did she look lucid to you last time you saw her?"

"She spent a whole lotta time in her room today, gettin' fancy. I thought maybe she wanted to go to the fair, so I let her do her thing while I cleaned up the kitchen, waiting for her to come downstairs. The radio was on—you know what her hearing's like—I must've missed it when she opened the front door. My car's still in the garage, so she couldn't have gone far. I'm going to look for her now. I just wanted to keep you in the loop."

"Thank you." My voice broke. Panic ran through me, and my blood turned cold. "Please keep me posted."

I killed the call and slammed my phone on the counter, letting my head drop. I wanted to scream. To break something. To lash out.

Not again, Grams. We've been through this dozens of times before.

The routine of looking for her everywhere, finding her at a neighbor's house or downtown—blabbing to someone incoherently—and removing her from the scene as I apologized from the bottom of my heart always wore me down.

I could feel West's sharp gaze on my back. He didn't say anything, but I knew he was watching me. A couple of customers showed up, asking for tacos, nachos, and slushies, and West served them, manning both our stations without making a big stink about it.

I looked down at my phone again and texted Marla.

Me: Where could she be?

Me: Can U check the shed, please?

Me: I'm going to call Sheriff Jones. Maybe he heard something.

I dialed up Sheriff Jones' number, pacing back and forth.

"Grace?" By the commotion in the background, he was at the fair with his family.

"Sheriff Jones? Sorry to call you so late. Grandma Savvy went missin' again."

"How long has it been?"

"Ah, a few hours." Probably less, but I knew he wasn't going to take it seriously. Grams went missing often and was always found a couple miles away from home.

"I'll call my guys. Grace," he hesitated, before sighing. "Try not to worry too much. It's always like that, isn't it? We'll find her before the night's over."

"Yes, sir. Thank you for your help."

I hung up, tears prickling my eyeballs. As always, I didn't let them loose. I hated this part. Where I had to beg people for help. I couldn't blame Marla. Grams had sneaked out of the house plenty of times while she was under my watch.

I sank onto an upside down crate, clutching my head in my hands.

"Is this an I-wanna-talk-about-it crisis or mind-your-own-fuck-ing-business crisis?" West grumbled above my head, sounding more annoyed than concerned.

The former.

"The latter."

"Thank fuck."

"Jerk."

"Let me know if that changes."

"You bein' a jerk? Fat chance."

"Don't insult the chance. It did nothing wrong." He wiped his sweat with the bottom of his shirt, still eyeing me in his periphery. I was an odd, out-of-place creature he couldn't decide what to do with. An unhappy female.

"I didn't insult the chance. I insulted *you.*"

"Still sarcastic. That's a good sign."

I needed to be out of this place and look for Grams, but the entire Contreras family was at the fair, and by the time one of them could come to replace me, my shift would be over.

Thirty minutes had passed without any news on Grams. I was completely out of it by the time West put his hand on my shoulder. It was heavy and warm and strangely reassuring. Like I was floating in the air, feet above the ground, and he anchored me back to gravity.

"That's enough of your sulking ass. Give me the keys. I'll close up and drop them in your mailbox. I don't know what crawled up your ass, but you should be focusing on pulling it out, not burning time here."

I shook my head, finding that all I needed to burst into tears for the first time since my hospital stay was him acknowledging something was wrong. People had stopped giving a crap. In Sheridan, I was just another statistic. Basket case grandmother, junkie mom. That was why Sheriff Jones hadn't even attempted to pretend he was going to leave the fair and help me look for Grams.

No one cared.

Hot, fat tears slid down my face. I wiped my cheeks with my sleeves, horrified that I was crying in front of him, and even more upset that I was probably smearing my makeup.

West regarded me with calm curiosity. Something in my gut told me he wasn't used to comforting women. He usually handled them when they were conveniently cheerful and trying to please him.

I shook my head. "I'm fine. Really. We only have thirty minutes left."

"Exactly," he bit out. "Thirty minutes is nothing. You've been as useful as a nun in a brothel since that phone call. Spare me the moping and get the hell outta here."

I eyed him from my spot on the crate. Was it irresponsible of me to consider his offer? I knew if Karlie and Mrs. Contreras were aware of the situation, they'd tell me to leave the food truck's keys with him, no doubt, but if something went wrong …

West read my mind, groaning. "Not gonna do anything shady. Give me your address."

I continued blinking at him.

He bit his inner cheeks, seething. "Not gonna come for your ass in the middle of the night either."

"Why should I trust you?"

"You shouldn't," he said, point-blank. "Trust is putting your optimism in another person, the very definition of being dumb. You should *believe* me because stealing from the register would get me nowhere. And because this is Texas, and there ought to be at least one motherfucker in your household with a loaded gun willing to blow out my brains if I decide to climb up your window uninvited."

It seemed crazy to hand him the keys. He'd been working here for less than a month. But desperate times called for desperate measures, and I was the very definition of desperate.

I had to find Grams. It was already late, and the more time had passed, the farther away she could wander off. Marla's shift was officially over, and running around in the middle of the night looking for Grams was above her pay grade.

"Okay." I grabbed a note, scribbling down my address. "Drop the money in Karlie's mailbox, then bring me back the keys. I owe you one."

He took the note, shoved it into the back pocket of his jeans, and kicked the door open, shoving me through it callously.

I stumbled toward my Chevy, struggling to control my flailing limbs.

It was only when I rolled into my garage that I realized what date it was.

Grandpa Freddie passed away a decade ago today.

Grams knew exactly what she was doing.

Where she was going.

She wanted to find him.

On my fifth circle around my block, someone flashed their lights behind me repeatedly, signaling me to stop. I kept walking, hugging my midriff.

I'd looked for Grams all over Sheridan. I'd gone to the cemetery first, thinking she would visit Grandpa Freddie's grave. Then I'd headed downtown, checked the local park, and called Mrs. Serle from the grocery store to ask if Grams had paid her a visit. I'd stopped by all our neighbors and friends. It was like the earth had opened its jaws and swallowed my grandmother whole.

I heard a motorcycle engine rumbling behind me. Seconds later, West appeared to my left on his bike, slowing down to match my pace.

"Dropped the keys in your mailbox." His voice was muffled through his black helmet. Red flames adorned it from either side, and I clutched the ring on my thumb, making a wish like my grandmother had taught me.

Please let me find you.

Hot air scorched my lungs. The temptation to collapse on the sidewalk and ignore all my problems was strong.

"Appreciate it. You have a good night now, St. Claire."

He didn't drive off, checking me out in his lazy, devil-may-care way. "Crisis still in motion?"

His motorcycle protested with small growls at the slow pace West forced it into. It was ten-thirty. I was sure he had plenty of places to go and people to see. People like Tess. Fun, uncomplicated, without the stipulations I came with.

"I've got it handled."

"That wasn't my question."

"Still my answer, though."

"Are you always so damn stubborn?

"Only on days that end with a y."

He hit the brake and hopped off the motorcycle like a tiger, tearing the helmet off of his face. His overgrown hair was damp, sticking in every direction in shiny chaotically chopped locks. I stopped, because it was the courteous thing to do.

A part of me thought maybe tonight it was going to be different. Maybe I wasn't going to find her after all. I'd never looked for so long. I'd never not-found her all over Sheridan.

"That's it. Talk to me, Texas."

"*Texas?*"

Did he just nickname me, or was I officially losing my mind?

He shrugged.

"You say Texan things. Like y'alls, and fixin' to, and right quick. You drop your g's like the English language wronged you personally."

"I salute to the place I come from, so what?"

"You're a small-town gal who probably skins squirrels in her spare time, sitting on a rocker on your front porch, chewing tobacco. Admit it, Texas, you're … *Texas.*"

"I don't like my nickname."

"Tough shit. It stays. Now, tell me what got your panties in such a wad."

I sighed, losing steam. "My grandmomma disappeared tonight. Just walked out the door and left her caregiver without sayin' where.

She's not very lucid, and ..." *About to give me a heart attack.* "Prone to accidents. I'm tryin' to find her."

"See?"

"What?"

"*Tryin'.*"

"Is that all you took from what I just told you?" I narrowed my eyes to stop myself from crying. I really, *really* felt like crying. It was on top of my to-do list, in fact, as soon as I found Grams.

He tucked his helmet under his arm. "Where could she be? Narrow it down for me."

"It's a decade to my grandpa's death, so I thought maybe I'd try the usual places. The cafeteria where they worked, the cemetery where he's buried, their old friends ..." I trailed off, feeling my eyes flaring as the penny dropped. "Oh."

"*Oh?*" He peered into my face, searching for clues.

"The diner by the highway. She could've gone there. It's where they first met. She worked the cash register. Grandpa Freddie worked the grill."

"Not shirtless, I assume." He clicked his tongue. But I was so consumed with my new idea, I forgot all about the coincidence. I snapped my fingers.

"Their first date was there. *Yes.*" I nodded. She'd told me all about it. How they'd stayed after their shift was over. How she'd dragged him behind the counter and kissed him senseless. "Grams would go there. Of course she would."

"Better haul ass there, then."

"Good idea."

I turned back, marching toward my house to get my Chevy, before stopping, my back still to West.

"*Crap.*"

"Hmm?" I could practically hear the grin in his voice. He hadn't moved an inch, knowing he had me in his pocket.

"It's outside Sheridan limits, about ten miles out. They closed the road for the fair tonight. The only way through is the old dirt road, and I can't drive there with my pickup."

My Chevy was my age, and just like me, not in pristine condition. Besides, it was more of a path, rather than a road. I didn't think the pickup would fit in there, in the first place.

Walking the dirt path wasn't a grand idea either. It was sand-wiched between cornfields. There were bobcats, coyotes, and all kinds of animals roaming about.

"We'll take the bike." West reappeared in my periphery.

"Since when are we a collective *we*?" I spun on my heel to face him, popping an eyebrow.

"Do you know how to ride a motorcycle?"

"No."

"That makes us a collective *we*. Geez, Tex, for a smart girl, you sure are kinda stupid."

He shoved his helmet into my hands. I caught the heavy thing but didn't make a move to put it over my head. I stared at him, dumb-founded. I opened my mouth to decline his crazy, albeit sweet, offer, but he raised his palm up, stopping me.

"Spare me the bullshit. You're in no position to turn me down, and I'm definitely not gentleman enough to insist on it."

"I'm sure you have better things to do with your time."

"No, I've got things more *fun* to do with my time." He tsked. "Nothing beats helping a friend in need."

A friend.

Something about the way he said it completely undid me.

I felt weak. Raw. I hated to be the recipient of his assistance.

If we were going to do this, I needed to give him a fair warning.

"My grandmomma is … a character," I warned cautiously.

"Thank *fuck*. Everyone else in this town seems to be clinically boring. Hop on." He slapped the leather seat of his motorcycle.

"Do you have another helmet? For yourself?"

West snatched the helmet from my hands, tossed my ball cap to the ground, and shoved the helmet over my head in one swift move-ment. He secured it over my chin, tugging the buckle.

He got on the bike and jerked his chin.

"Hop. The. Fuck. On."

I stuffed my ball cap into my back pocket quickly, ducking my head down. The helmet was unexpected heavy and squeezed the heck out of my cheeks.

"I don't want you to ride without a helmet."

I didn't want him to risk his life for me. Between illegal fighting and riding a motorcycle, he seemed to be doing a fine job trying to die all on his own. He didn't need my help.

He ignored my words, screwing his fingers into his eye sockets, shaking his head, clearly exasperated.

"Get on here before I fling your ass over it like a sack of potatoes. Fair warning: I won't be gentle."

I took a step in his direction, feeling my resolve cracking.

"And watch Christina's paint," he snarled.

"Christina?"

"After Christina Hendricks." He patted the shiny red neck of the motorcycle with his rough hand. "They're my favorite redheads."

"Good thing only one is stupid enough to let you ride her. And she ain't got a pulse," I deadpanned.

He stared at my helmeted head for a beat before throwing his head back and laughing with pure, electrifying joy that zinged through my veins, making my blood bubble. Watching the row of pearly whites inside his mouth confirmed my initial suspicion he had a smile that brought women to their knees.

Men too, probably.

I slid my leg over the seat behind him. My whole body quivered with anxiety and adrenaline. I'd never felt so scared and alive.

"Scoot forward," he barked.

I did. The engine rumbled like a feral animal beneath me.

"Now press yourself against me."

"That's more of a third-date move for me."

West laughed again. His laugh sounded throaty, smoky, almost foreign—like he was unused to being happy.

"It's either cozying up to the campus asshole or blowing in the wind like a deflating balloon. Your call, Tex. I'm going to get my fun in either scenario."

West St. Claire had the uncanny ability to do nice things and still act like a complete and utter jerk about it.

Reluctantly, I flushed my chest against his back, my head nestling between his shoulder blades. I closed my eyes and breathed, reminding myself I didn't have the luxury of being prudish right now.

"Wrap your arms around me, real tight."

I looped my arms over his body. I could feel the individual ridges between his six-pack, and my heart began to pound so fast I was sure he'd be able to feel it through his thin shirt.

We sliced the still air, shooting across the road like an arrow. West angled his body forward. I clasped him harder, stunned by the way we were balanced on his motorcycle, even when the concrete beneath us turned into gravel, and eventually, bumpy dirt. His shirt tossed about like a flag, and the biting rush of the wind against my skin took my breath away. Every inch of my body tingled with goose bumps.

"Get outta that head, Texas. Nothing good is going on there right now." The wind blurred his words. Fortunately, he rode slow enough that I could hear anything at all.

"If only I'd noticed the date, Grams would be home and safe," I murmured into his helmet. I was engulfed by his scent. Male and soap and sweet, heady danger.

I could get lost in that smell if I let myself. I wondered if that was how Grams felt about Grandpa Freddie. If his presence got her deliriously drunk with euphoria.

"Are you always so hard on yourself? Don't answer only on days that end with a y."

"It's my job to take care of her. She raised me."

"You can take care of someone without blaming yourself for all their problems."

"Clearly, you've never taken care of someone."

"Clearly, you're talking out of your ass," West countered, his voice turning arctic and biting. I'd obviously hit a nerve.

"My ass still makes more sense than your mouth," I ground out.

And just like that, he was back to laughing at my outrageousness. The fact I talked back to him.

"Don't know about that, sweetheart, but it's a great ass, so I enjoy listening."

He was so different from what I expected. Like he tucked his fun, lighthearted personality somewhere people couldn't find it to keep them at arm's length.

"Back it up, cowboy. If that's why you're helpin' me, you can drop me here and turn back around. I'm not that type of girl."

"What type would that be?" His tone turned sultry, taunting.

"The type to find herself beneath you because you gave her a crumb of your attention."

"On top of me works, too."

"Keep this up, and the only weight you'll be feeling is my pickup over your body."

"I'm playing, Texas. I'd never hit on you. I don't mix business with pleasure. Besides, I don't stick around beyond one hookup, and no offense, but you seem like a lot of work. This is a pure, altruistic favor I'm doing for a friend."

There it was again. *Friend.* It was the second time he'd called me that.

"It is?"

"Scout's honor. I don't expect anything back, other than your endless admiration."

"Why are you being so nice to me?"

I knew enough about West to gather he wasn't the sweet and helpful type, and this had nothing to do with the rumors. He was a sour-faced caveman on campus.

"Nice is a big word." We were edging closer to the intersection that had been blocked. I looked left and right, frantically trying to spot Grams. "I'm just not a complete piece of shit to you. Guess it throws you off-kilter."

"People aren't shitty to me," I protested.

"Let's agree to disagree."

"If you're talkin' about Reign and the girls you were with the other night, it's on them, not on me."

"It's on them that they're assholes. It's on you that you roll over and play dead."

"I don't remember you bein' so cordial either."

"No," he agreed, not a trace of apology in his voice. "Next time, you have my permission to pour slushie over my head and kick Reign in the nuts."

I was about to answer him when I spotted Grams. She was hard to miss, in her full, blue and red sequined evening gown, bright pink lipstick, and heels.

She had her hair fluffed and sprayed—*the higher the hair, the closer to God*—and she was holding the little clutch she carried to church every Sunday back when we still went. She crossed the road, on her way to the diner.

"Stop!" I shrieked.

He did, coming to a halt without slowing down. Mud sprayed around us, and I lurched forward, my chest colliding with his back. West snaked an arm around me awkwardly, catching me by the waist.

"Found her," I said breathlessly, dismounting from the bike. My legs were shaking. "Thank you. She's the one in the Diana Ross gown across the street. I'll get her home right away." I took the helmet off, knowing I must've left traces of foundation inside it, and planted it in his hands. I screwed my ball cap back on my head. "Have a good night now, West."

I ran across the road, nearly tackling Grams to the ground. She spun slowly at the thuds of my feet, the smile on her face collapsing into a frown when she spotted my approaching figure.

"Well, I'll be damned. What are ya doin' here, Gracie-Mae? You should be in bed. Tomorrow's a school day."

Grams swatted her purse against her thigh. Her forehead was damp from the long walk on the dirt road, her shoes caked with mud.

How old does she think I am?

"Just wanted to tag along." I came to a halt, an angelic smile plastered on my face.

"Sugar, I've got a date with your grandpa. Can't we do somethin' tomorrow?"

I shook my head violently. The smile on my face was as painful as a wound and just as tight. She thought Grandpa was still alive.

"Please. I *really* want to join you, Grams."

She opened her mouth, about to scold me again, when her eyes widened, lighting up at something behind me. I turned on my heel. My face immediately fell.

Please, Lord, no.

"Good evenin', Mrs. Shaw. How're we doin' tonight?" West swaggered toward us, a candy cane clasped between his perfect teeth, his bastard smirk on full display. The crinkles behind his shamrock eyes reminded me of Scott Eastwood.

I wondered what the deal was with the old-school candy. He'd always favored the same green apple flavor. "Fine weather, no?"

"Lovely." She fluffed her sprayed do, which remained as stiff as a rock. "I don't believe we've met before?"

Grandma Savvy extended an arm in West's direction. He plucked it, bowing his head and brushing her knuckles with his lips, temporarily removing the candy from his mouth.

"We haven't, much to my dismay. West St. Claire. I work with Grace."

"Why, she hasn't mentioned you, I'm afraid."

The look he shot me nearly made me giggle. He looked genuinely surprised. I had a feeling this was the first time a woman he knew didn't make him the center of her universe.

"That so?" He narrowed his eyes at me, sticking the candy back into his mouth, biting it until it crunched. I shrugged.

"Would you and Gracie-Mae like to join Freddie and me for a bite?" Grams asked.

It was half past eleven, and she looked a mess. Her feet must've hurt bad; she wasn't used to walking much. Besides, I really didn't want Sheridan University's baddest bad boy to spend one-on-one time with my chaotic grandmomma, no matter how shallow and ungrateful that made me feel.

"No!" I yelped at the same time West said easily, "Now, that's a plan."

Grams looked between us, raising an eyebrow.

"You kids need a minute to decide?"

My cheeks felt so hot I was surprised my head didn't combust. Dying of embarrassment would be cruel, but also welcome at this point.

"West just got off a shift. I'm sure he wants to go home."

"West can think for himself, and what he wants is a steak and good company." West pushed me aside crudely, rolling the candy stick in his mouth seductively, flashing a rakish, well-practiced smirk my grandmomma's way.

"Where're your manners, Gracie-Mae? The man's hungry, and he is asking to tag along, nice and proper. I raised her better than this, I swear."

"Don't doubt it for a second, ma'am."

West opened the diner's door for us. Grams strutted in first. He wiggled his brows at me, a taunting sneer on his face.

"Ladies first."

"What is wrong with you?" I bared my teeth.

He let out a long-suffering sigh.

"How much time have you got, kid?"

I punched his arm as I dragged my feet past the door.

He laughed.

He actually *laughed*.

Like the idea of me inflicting any kind of harm on him was ludicrous.

"Did you lose a bet?" I whisper-shouted as we fell into step together.

"Did you lose your fucking mind?" he countered, sizzling of quiet danger I couldn't understand how Grams didn't pick on. "It's just a meal, and your ass is not even on the menu."

"Don't tell me it's not weird that you want to spend time with me and my grandmomma."

I was Toastie, and she was a couple sandwiches shy of a picnic. Everybody knew that. Even if he hadn't, the last ten minutes had brought him up to speed, surely. Why was he going out of his way to befriend me?

"Not everything is about you, Texas. In fact, very few things are. It's a blessing and a curse, really. Knowing the world doesn't revolve around your sassy little ass. Sometimes a guy just wants a steak."

"I—"

He cut me off briskly. "Hungry. Outta my way. *Now*." He jerked his head, signaling me to move along.

Grams slipped into a red horseshoe-shaped booth, and we followed suit. A middle-aged waitress materialized to take our orders. She had a pink uniform with a black and white checkered collar and bleached hair.

Ronda's Roost was a twenty-four hour joint, catering mainly to truckers who passed by. There were only a handful of customers nursing filter coffee and cobbler. Grams asked for iced tea and chili, while West went for the Rajun Cajun club with double fries, milkshake, and an extra rare steak I would later learn was carved out of half a cow. I asked for fountain Diet Pepsi and a miracle. The waitress snapped her gum, cackling at my joke.

"Rough night, kiddo?"

"You could say that," I mumbled, narrowing my eyes at West across the table. He smiled easily, the stubborn glint in his eyes reassuring me he didn't mind my hostility one bit.

It was like he'd had a personality transplant overnight. Maybe he was having a mental breakdown or something, because he didn't resemble the guy I'd seen on campus for the past two years.

Surly, quiet, and grave. With an underlying current of darkness. He walked the halls, the Student Union, the library, and Greek row like he was a man waiting for lightning to strike him.

That bully, violent, quiet, simmering guy? The West in front of me wasn't even *related* to him.

Grams didn't act like Grandpa Freddie was there with us, so I guessed I *did* get my small miracle, after all. She leaned forward, rolling a coin into the jukebox and choosing "At Last" by Etta James. She was clearly enjoying the male attention, telling West about her time working at this diner.

"Let me tell you, ain't no grass grew under those feet during those days. Still, wouldn't change it for the world. That's where I met my husband."

"He must've been special." West smiled back at her, and I tried to remember seeing him smile at school. We took mixed media together, so I'd seen him plenty. I couldn't recall one time, which alarmed me.

"Boy …" She leaned forward, patting the back of his hand. "He was smart as a whip, dangerous as the Devil and twice as handsome."

Watching her happy made *me* happy, so eventually, I relaxed into the squeaky vinyl seat and let them mingle.

"So, Mr. St. Claire, are you courting my little Gracie-Mae?" she asked after a while, lowering her chin to examine him through her winged reading glasses.

I choked on my fountain soda, spraying it across the table.

West smirked, angling himself on the table across from us so he and Grams were almost nose to nose, his voice dropping to a whisper. "Can I be honest?"

"Honesty is the best policy."

"I'm not much of a commitment guy, Mrs. Shaw. Grace deserves a hell of a lot better, so that's one tail I won't be chasing. Besides, your daughter's not exactly my number one fan."

"Daughter?" Grams put her hand on her chest, giggling. "My dear, you've got it all wrong. I'm Grace's *grandmother.*"

"Why..." He shot me a playful smile. I wanted to murder him. He *knew* she was my grandmother. "I'll be damned. You look like Grace's sister."

"Baby sister, I assume," I sulked, sucking on my straw. He laughed good-naturedly.

The man was laying it so thick, I wished he could do my makeup.

Grams and West ate and fell into an easy conversation again.

They talked about the weather in Maine (according to him, it sucked), the food in Maine (same, save for the seafood), his family (West had more finesse than to say *they* sucked, but by his tight-lipped answers, I figured he wasn't close with his parentsg). By the time we were done, West promised to take Grams to the diner again, and soon, and she swore she would bake him one of her infamous pies. Since I wasn't a part of the conversation, I excused myself to go to the restroom to reapply more foundation. When I got back to the table, I saw West had taken care of the bill and was standing up to leave. Grams was caught in a lively conversation with our waitress, telling her about her days at the diner.

I winced. "You shouldn't have paid. Thank you."

He shoved his wallet into the back of his jeans, tugging at the chain link attached to it. Both his plates were squeaky clean, and he'd also polished off Grams' leftovers. He must've been starving.

"I ordered you a cab." He ignored my gratitude, his demeanor changing back to gruff sourpuss. "Lock the front door and put the key somewhere she can't find it."

"She's allowed to walk around the house," I protested for the sake of protesting. I didn't like that he'd told me what to do, even if I knew he was right.

He shot me a look. "Hide it where no one would want to visit."

"Where would that be?" I crossed my arms over my chest, spearing him with a stare.

"How 'bout your bed?"

He grabbed his helmet from his seat, tucking it under his arm. He kissed Grams' cheek goodbye and dashed off, not sparing me a glance. I watched him through the glass windows. He hoisted a leg over his bike, gunning it. Grams appeared beside me. We watched as the red light of his bike got smaller and smaller, until it melted away into a dot in the darkness.

"Be careful with that one, love. He's wilder than an acre of snakes." She coiled her arm around mine, patting my forearm. She was being normal, sweet Grandma Savvy again, and I wished I could have her just a little longer so I could tell her all about my life, my struggles, my relationships.

So I could get her sharp, Southern independent woman's input.

I thought about the girls who frequented our food truck window. About West's one-hookup rule. About his reputation and busted knuckles, and cunning, devilish smirks, and green, bottomless eyes that were carefully flat whenever he set them on someone else.

Grams was right.

My heart couldn't afford opening up to West St. Claire.

I was going to make sure the rest of my body was going to listen to it.

Chapter Six

West

"WEST, MY MAN, WHAT'S SHAKIN'?"

Max struggled to catch my steps as I breezed into the café. He panted like one of those rat-looking dogs who couldn't run from the kitchen to the dining table. He was a short, stout guy with a constellation of acne framing his jaw and coarse, ginger curls he insisted on trying to tame with hair products.

The combo made him unattractive to anyone with a pair of working eyes, which, sadly for him, was ninety-eight percent of campus population.

The idiot was best known for booking the fights at the Sheridan Plaza—and an eager collector of whatever leftovers East, Reign, and I didn't want in the ladies department during fight nights. Max got a nice cut from orchestrating my Reservoir Dog warehouse gig. He did the legwork; I did the fist-work.

He brought all his frat friends from Pike, Beta Theta Pi, and Sig Ep to the arena each week and had them shell out money for the bets, tickets, and beer.

Worked for me, since I was the one cashing in big at the end of each night.

"Get to the point, Max. We aren't shooting the shit here," I snapped.

I was on my way to the cafeteria, about to meet East. My phone danced in my pocket, as it did so goddamn often. I ignored it. I didn't need to look to see who it was—Mom—and what she wanted from me—more money.

Max clapped his hands together, practically skipping. He wore vintage Jordan Airs, a designer belt, and enough hair product to sculpt a fucking six-year-old. I got high from the fumes coming from his hair alone.

"Aight. Straight shooter, I'm digging it," he crowed. I ambled into the cafeteria, him trailing behind me like a fart. "I got a new gig for you. Could be sick. Something exclusive that doesn't come by every day. Lucrative as all hell, but super last-minute."

"Are you gonna spit it out?" I scanned the place for East. My best friend made me sandwiches every morning, like a doting little mountain girl with stars in her eyes, and brought them with him. I suspected he worried I'd die of starvation if he didn't take care of me. Maybe because he knew me well enough to know there was always going to be a small side of me that didn't mind dying.

That would have welcomed the post-death nothingness. I certainly didn't make an active attempt to stay alive, with my current habit.

"Tough crowd. Ever heard of Kade Appleton?" Max asked.

Appleton was a professional MMA fighter and a Sheridan native, who'd moved to Vegas about five years ago. He was known for getting suspended left and right for fighting dirty in the ring. The general consensus was he deserved to get punched in the face for a living. Every Sheridan resident who knew him growing up had a gory story about an animal he'd killed, a shotgun he'd pointed at someone, or a punch that made him send some poor bastard to the ER.

As far as hillbillies went, Kade Appleton was the poster child. I'd be surprised if he owned one pair of shoes.

"Turns out he's in town, and he is willing to fight you tonight if you're in. We still have the guy from Penn State lined up, but we can put him on the back burner for a while. Odds are against you if you pick the Appleton fight. I already made a spreadsheet." Max produced his phone, shoving an excel table in my face. I stopped midstride, whistling low when I saw the numbers.

One of the main issues I'd been facing since I started knocking people unconscious for a living was I smoked everyone I fought. Even when I let them get a jab or two to keep the crowd interested, I was competitive enough to never lose on purpose, and had some integrity left in me. This made for pretty shitty odds, and the money was drying up, since everyone knew I was going to win.

Kade Appleton was a professionally trained fighter, with a few championships under his belt. It made him a golden opportunity to roll in the big bucks.

A banana ricocheted in the air, bumping Max's chest and dropping at my feet. I looked up from Max's phone to the direction it came from, noticing East and Reign from across the cafeteria, slouched over a table. They waved for me to come over.

I started in their direction.

"Well?" Max followed. "What says you?"

"Count me in."

I slid onto the bench in front of East, who handed me a soggy-ass egg sandwich. I hoped his hookups were as wet as his omelets. He needed to lay off the oil.

"In?" East quirked an eyebrow. Reign was on the phone, his back to us. "In what? In love? Insane? Incapable of finishing a sentence?"

"He's fighting Kade Appleton tonight," Max volunteered, stars in his eyes.

East shook his head, his brows thundering.

"Fuck no. That asshole fights dirty and everyone knows it. His entire entourage is into shady-ass crap. It's not worth it, Westie."

I hated that he called me that. *Westie.* But I was also aware East was one of the only people on planet Earth I could stand, and more importantly—stood *me*. We came to Sher U together from our small town in Maine. Parting ways after everything we'd been through seemed wrong.

We lived together. We shared everything: Past. Present. Future.

There was no separating us at this point.

We were always East and West—wonder kids.

At least until I stopped being one.

I ignored East, taking a bite of my sandwich and pointing it in Max's direction. "Book the fight."

"Bro." East's eyes widened. Reign killed his call, boomeranging his phone on the table and tearing off a piece of grilled cheese with his teeth. "Afternoon, ladies. May I ask what got your corsets so fucking tight?"

"West is taking a fight with Kade Appleton tonight." East jerked his thumb in my direction, in a *check out this dumbass* motion.

Reign's eyebrows jumped to his hairline. "Holy shit. Personally, if I were suicidal, drowning in psychedelic drugs would be my death of choice, but whatever tickles your fancy, man."

"If you ever change your mind, I'd be happy to lend a hand." I took another bite of my damp omelet sandwich, trying not to miss my mother's Italian food. For all her faults, she could cook a mean-ass meal. Aside from the diner incident this week, I hadn't had a home-cooked meal in years.

"West is not suicidal," East said, more to himself than to anyone else at the table. He shot me a look. I shook my head. I had no plans to kill myself, but if I died, well, that would not be an unwelcome plot twist.

Reign laughed. "Seriously, though. You're actually considering getting into the ring with Appleton? Can I have your AirPods? Mine have enough ear wax to fill up a jar of mustard."

East kicked him under the table then proceeded to smash my shin in with his foot.

"East—I don't wanna hear it. Reign—I don't wanna hear *you*. Max—take a hike. I'll be there tonight. Spread the word. Make it worth my while."

"That's what she said," Reign jested.

Now both East and I punched his arm.

When I took the food truck job, I'd told Karlie Fridays were a nogo. She knew the score. She was one of the only chicks in Sher U, along with Texas, not to show up for fight nights. I liked that I could keep my food truck gig separated from my breaking noses gig.

Max scurried away. The table fell silent, before Reign cleared his throat.

"Jokes aside, there's a reason why Appleton is currently suspended from the MAF league. He was arrested last year for assaulting his girlfriend. The mother of his child. The photos of her face after the fact aren't something you'd appreciate seeing while eating. Just putting it out there."

"And his manager is notorious for arranging dog fights. He went to prison for it for, like, three years," East chipped in.

"That's right. Shaun Picker. Between them, they have a rap sheet longer than *War and Peace*." Reign pointed a finger at me with the hand that held his grilled cheese. "Which, for the record, I've never read, but I heard that like me, it is thick as fuck and not easy to swallow."

"I'm not marrying his ass, I'm putting it to bed." I scowled. "Look, this shit is settled, so you might as well change the subject." I lost interest in them and glanced around the cafeteria, looking for what, I wasn't sure, exactly.

I needed the money.

Desperately.

It was the cruelest type of irony.

Growing up, I'd always promised myself I wouldn't be that asshole who lived to work versus worked to live. Then again, I never was very good at keeping promises.

I grew older, I fucked up, made mistakes, and had to pay for them.

Nowadays, I was chasing paychecks like every sorry jerk I'd pitied as a kid, and I didn't even earn the money for myself.

Appleton was a fight I couldn't refuse. I was going to win. Even if I had to kill the bastard to cut a nice paycheck.

My phone buzzed in my pocket for the hundredth time today. I took it out, killed the call, and texted my mother.

West: Sending more money on Monday. Get off my case.

A voice message notification popped on the screen. I deleted it before I was tempted to listen to it. I looked up, between Reign and East. A flash of puzzled worry marred their faces.

"*Drop it,*" I stressed.

"You get into bed with Appleton, you might be dragging everyone else around you into a mess," Easton warned. "The man is basically a gang member. He operates like the mafia."

"If shit gets too hot, you know where the door is." I met Easton's stare steadily, my jaw tightening with barely contained anger. "Either way, I'm taking the fight."

Reign stood up, stretching lazily.

"All right, I'm dipping. East, I'll see you in practice. West—it was nice knowing ya. I'll be sure to leave some flowers on your grave and comfort your lady friends, who might need some bed warming at night." He bowed his head, grabbed his duffel bag, and dashed.

East watched Reign's back before fixing his gaze back on me.

"Are things that bad at home?"

He knew exactly why I was showing up in the ring every Friday, and it wasn't for the pride or glory. Yes, I was a competitive shit—it ran in my blood. Whenever I saw a challenge, I conquered it, but fighting would never have been my route in life if it weren't for what happened.

I shoved the rest of my sandwich into my mouth.

"You know my dad. He can't run a business to save his life. I can't let them lose the farm. They'll have nothing left."

East nodded. "I'm here if you need me."

Despite it being the fakest cliché I'd ever heard, I knew he actually meant it, and despite knowing he *couldn't* help me, it actually made me feel slightly better.

"Where were you last night?" He changed the subject.

"This Grace chick from the food truck had a crisis. She bailed early, so I needed to close shop."

I wasn't going to share Texas' business with East. Not because I had one decent bone in my body, God forbid, but because I was above town gossip. Besides, if I were in her position and someone spilled the beans about my fruitcake grandmother, I'd ream them out and use their remainders as decorations for a Christmas tree.

Texas sure didn't have it easy.

"Try again. You came back at one-thirty. I was still awake." East drummed the table, giving me a *busted* look.

"Grabbed dinner afterwards. Didn't realize you wanted to spoon."

"You don't eat out. You're too cheap to buy yourself a pair of god-damn socks."

That was fact as fuck. Buying everyone tacos and slushies a few weeks ago was a one-off. One of the chicks who'd accompanied us was the sister of a guy I'd sent to the ICU after a fight night. He was threatening to sue, and I needed to butter her up to convince him to drop the case. He did.

"Let's say I did hang out with the Shaw chick." I yawned provocatively. "What of it? I ate a steak, not her pussy."

"You never eat pussy," East noted.

That was also true. Eating a stranger's privates felt akin to licking a public toilet. I had no idea where their coochies had been, but considering this was college, and not a very good one, my educated guess was: *everywhere.*

"You never take anyone out either," East banged on, leaning forward, going in for the kill. "Dinner sounds *a lot* like going out."

"I didn't take her out. I *helped* her out."

"Funny, I don't remember you having a Superman complex."

"Once every full moon I feel charitable. Sue me, Braun."

"Bullshit, St. Claire. You've got your eyes set on this chick, and we both know why."

That really did it. I slammed my fist against the table.

"Do you have a point? If so, please get to it in this century."

It was just a fucking meal. Texas spent more than half of it shooting daggers at me with her arctic blue eyes and silently praying a bomb would land directly on the diner.

"I think you're interested." He wore his shit-eating grin. "Tell me she doesn't bone you up."

"She doesn't bone me up," I said offhandedly. "Even if she did, I'd never touch her."

Texas was attractive, but so were eighty percent of the girls on campus. And they came without the drama, complications, and detonated self-esteem. Bonus points: they didn't work with me. Hooking up with someone I had to see four times a week was a big fat no.

Not to mention, she almost certainly sucked in bed.

"That's what worries me." East scratched his smooth jaw. "Don't get her hopes high then watch them crash and burn. If you start giving her special treatment, she'll get ideas. You feeling me?"

Texas was too screwed-up about her scars to consider getting laid. That much was obvious. He had nothing to worry about. She was the one woman I couldn't get into my bed on campus, and despite my competitive nature, I was fine with that.

That was the thing about being on the fence with the whole life situation. I stopped caring and pursuing things I otherwise would have wanted and cared for. Life no longer had a taste, and a pulse, and colors.

Nothing charted anymore, and pleasure and pain were replaced with an overall numbness.

"It's all under control." I wiped my mouth with the back of my arm. "She's not my type."

"You don't have a type. You hate everyone." East balled his sandwich wrap and threw it in my face. I caught it midair. *Killer instincts.* I threw it back at him, getting his eye.

"Exactly."

"St. Claire. Wait up," a small voice squeaked behind me.

Feminine footsteps thudded behind my back. I didn't break my pace or turn around to see who it was, on my way to the campus gym. I'd never had my ass whooped in the ring, and I planned on keeping my unchallenged record intact.

Despite the vote of no confidence from East and Reign, I worked hard and was fully capable of annihilating Appleton with an arm tied behind my back.

"Geez, what's with you?" the voice behind me puffed.

Texas had never sought me out on campus before. She wasn't the kind to try to hang out just because we worked together, and it was fresh to have a girl who wasn't dazzled by my status, battle scars, or anger issues.

She fell into step with me, her fists shoved into her hoodie's pockets. Her winter attire looked out of place in the scenery of cropped shorts and short skirts. She wore the same ragged, gray ball cap, her long, blonde hair cascading all the way down to her lower back.

"You're ignorin' me." She squinted.

I didn't answer, still walking. It was important to distinguish we weren't BFFs. Just because I'd done her a solid last night didn't mean I cared. I was willing to lend a hand when she needed help, but we weren't going to sing "Kumbaya" by the fire or get matching Taylor Swift bracelets. East was right. I had to make sure she knew I wasn't interested, in the improbable case she had any ideas.

"Would you stop walkin'?" She threw her arms in the air.

"Eventually," I said with a biting tone. "When I reach my destination."

"Where to? Hell, I'm hopin'."

"Why go to hell when I can enjoy the same fine weather at the food truck, with an added bonus of your whiny ass?" I wondered aloud.

The air-con I'd brought didn't make much difference, but I stopped working shirtless, because Texas couldn't look at me when I had my shirt off, and I was tired of her talking to my boots whenever she addressed me.

It wasn't like me to banter, especially with chicks—*especially* with chicks I had no interest in watching taking my cock into their mouths—but for some reason, this girl brought the high school kid out of me. She was never above an immature, sarcastic remark, always down for a few verbal jabs, and I guessed both of us didn't care about impressing each other.

"Because you'd be a guest of honor there," she hissed.

See? Snarky with a capital S.

Then, out of nowhere, a sharp little elbow jammed into my ribs, exactly where I had a welt from last Friday's fight. I instinctively stopped, not because it hurt—even though goddammit, it actually did—but because I knew she knew exactly what she was doing, and that was a jerk move. Especially after I'd saved her ass yesterday.

She punched me in the kidneys, where she *also* knew I had a bruise. Then she hurled herself in front of me, blocking my path.

"What the fuck?" I inquired flatly, eyeing her like she was something I had to throw into the recycling can but was too lazy to pick up.

She flattened her lips, glowering. She looked like a five-year-old trying to be tough. I half-wished she'd take off the ugly-ass ball cap and show her face.

How bad could it be?

Pretty bad if they called her Toastie.

She examined my torso over my shirt, then went for my arm, punching it.

"Cut it out."

She punched my other arm.

Then my abs.

The little shit was trying to *fight* me.

In the middle of campus, with people strewn about on benches and the lawn, looking on. Everyone at the Student Union Building was glaring at us through the floor-to-ceiling window.

She swatted my chest and stomach. Sarcastic *and* insane. The latter was a new, unwelcome development.

I picked her up by the back of her hoodie, like a mouse from a tail, until her feet were above the ground. She was as light as a feather and just about as threatening. She kicked the air, trying—and failing—to punch my face. It was comical, seeing her going at me with everything she had and still not getting one shot in.

A curious audience clustered around us like a pre-cum stain on a teenager's underwear. I despised being watched. Could only tolerate it if people paid for the pleasure to see me in the ring. But she'd just made sure we were Friday afternoon's main event.

I took everything nice I'd thought about Texas back.

She was a massive pain in the ass.

"Let me down," she rustled, her balled fists shaking in my face.

"If I do, will you behave like a lady and not like a rabid animal?" I arched an eyebrow, speaking slowly and condescendingly to rile her up even more.

"You patronizing ass!" she spluttered.

"Wrong answer."

"You're such a jerk!"

"Bzzz. Wrong again."

"Screw you!"

I was growing impatient and bored. "Is that an offer, Texas? There was no need to be that aggressive. All you needed to do was ask," I drawled.

Texas was like the city of Troy. Her walls were high, thick, guarded, and not worth the conquest. Slipping in wasn't an option, and fighting my way through just to get laid went against my agenda toward women.

"You will *never* have me, St. Claire."

"Hold, I'll try to get over the heartbreak." I raised a finger and let a beat of silence pass between us. "Done. Now, if I put your ass down, will you eloquently explain why you're acting like a badger on meth?"

She folded her arms over her chest but nodded. I let her down. Everybody was looking at us from a respectable distance. They knew better than to get close and openly eavesdrop. I refrained from pointing out we were the center of attention. If I hated an audience, Texas goddamn loathed it.

Which was why it seemed downright nuts for her to major in theater and arts.

Either way, I couldn't ruin the chance of having her pass out. Something told me I wouldn't resist the urge to step over her and walk briskly to the gym without looking back.

"Listen." She let out a breath. "I don't mean to sound ungrateful—"

"But you're about to ..."

She snarled my way. "I swear to God, St. Claire, if you tell someone about last night ... about Grandma Savvy ..."

"Say no more," I sliced into her words again. "I won't."

She eyed me skeptically. "Promise?"

"I don't promise shit. Ever. That's a principle," I said firmly. "I have no plans to air your dirty laundry. But I'm not going to carve it out in my forehead to pacify your ass."

"That's a nice visual." She nibbled at the side of her lower lip. "You sure you're not open to that?"

I held back a grin. She was a weirdo. A curiously infuriating one at that. With an ass worthy of a poem by one of the twenty-first century's finest poets, Lil' Wayne.

"Your secret's safe with me."

There was silence. The charged kind. I glanced around, ready to be over with the conversation. "You're still here. Why?"

She took a deep breath, sloping her chin up. The sun was directly on her face, her silhouette burning like wildfire against the sunset, and I had the chance to see as much as I could of her scar. It wasn't just that her skin was darker around the area—somewhere between purple and pink—but the complexion was different, too. Raw and bumpy. The flesh stretched thinly across her bones, struggling to keep it all together.

She was right. That part of her wasn't pretty.

"I'm all ears." I leaned a shoulder against the red-bricked building of the Bush Art and Library Building.

"Stop helpin' me. I don't want your pity."

"You don't have my pity," I clipped.

"There's no other reason for you to go out of your way to be nice to me."

"Again, I'm not being *nice* to you. What makes you think I'd act any different if Tess or Hailey or Lara were in your situation last night?"

I may have made up the last couple names. I didn't know a Hailey or a Lara, though I was sure there were plenty of girls with those names attending Sher U.

Remembering chicks I rolled between the sheets by name wasn't my virtue. Face, maybe. Ass, probably.

"You're awful to everyone." Her eyes burned intensely. "I want you to be awful to me, too. Otherwise, I don't feel like your equal."

It felt like she pinched the back of my throat. Not that I wasn't awful to people—I know I was—but her constant crave to be normal threw me off guard.

In that moment, I wished I could smack some sense into her. Unfortunately, it was a firm red line I would never let myself cross. Because Grace Shaw sure deserved a few good spankings.

I leaned into her face, plastering my best see-if-I-give-a-shit smirk.

"Get it into your head, Texas: I'm not a good guy. I'm not here to save you. I'm not on some quest to make you get out of your shell and come out of this experience a stronger person or some other Dr. Phil bullshit. Just because I don't kick you when you're down doesn't mean I'm a standup guy, and you'd be wise to remember that. That awful enough for you?"

She stared at me, her face marred with disgust. Nothing I hadn't seen on my parents' faces a thousand times before. Just another Friday. Which reminded me—I had a fight today and needed to get my ass in gear. I grabbed her by the arms, picked her up, moved her away from my path like she was a traffic cone, and marched to the gym.

"You're a monster!" she bellowed behind me, her voice taut with anger.

I pushed inside the gym's door, ignoring her.

She wasn't wrong.

Kade Appleton was not a fucking walk in the park, that was for sure.

Unless that park was in Chernobyl.

He continually broke the few rules we had in the ring in his quest not to have his ass handed to him, which resulted in my being more beat up than I'd ever been the entire three years I'd been doing this gig.

I'd be lying if I said I minded. The floor was jam-packed with people crammed together, like worms pouring from rotten meat. Beer sloshed from red Solo cups all over the sticky concrete, which was filthy with blood, dust, and sex juices. The place hadn't been this crowded since I started attending Sher U. There was cheering, yelling, and whistling. Chicks sitting on guys' shoulders to get a better view.

At some point, the guys who sold the tickets ran out of stamp ink to mark those who'd paid. They had to doodle on people's hands with Sharpies. Max was on cloud nine. I could practically see the flashing pictures of him in a Hugh Hefner robe running through his Pornhub-infested brain.

It was a bloodbath in the ring. I'd popped Kade's nose in the first ten seconds with a mean uppercut to get people riled up, then kneed his face to make every blood vessel in his mouth gush like a fondue fountain. He'd managed to bust my lip and eyebrow open by getting two solid shots to my face minutes after. The mat beneath us was slippery, squeaking with every movement we made.

Reign and East were behind me, shouting unsolicited advice. My eyes stung with blood and sweat, and I was pretty sure I spat out a tooth ten minutes into the fight. I swayed, bumping into one of the cardboard boxes that marked the ring.

Kade and I circled each other. We were entering our fifth round. I'd never had a fifth round in my amateur fighting career, but Appleton was no spring chicken. I didn't find his size or technique challenging. I was just as good a wrestler and boxer as he was, and he figured it out when I cracked his rib before we even finished the first round with a kick that sent him flying like a kite.

Which was why he shoved fingers into my eyes, jabbed me below the belt, and tried other third-grade bullshit to slow me down.

Injured or not, I could still massacre the motherfucker.

"St. Claire! St. Claire! St. Claire!"

The chants vibrated the mats under my feet. Kade zeroed in on my face, his eyes already sporting two shiners. He had a face not even a mother could love (unless she was blind), with a nose that had been broken in the double digits, bug eyes, and nonexistent lips. His neck was as wide as some streets.

We were on opposite sides of the makeshift ring.

Max blew the whistle. "Fifth round! Make it count, gentlemen."

We approached each other in guarded stances. I dodged a few easy swings, ducking and bouncing on the balls of my feet, before going in for the kill. I sent a perfect right hook to the side of his head, knocking his lights out. I watched him falling down on the mattress Max stole from the college gym, his body bouncing on top of it.

He lay there, eyes shut, knocked out. The crowd exploded. I spun on my heel, gliding a hand over my bare chest to wipe off the sweat and blood. Reign cupped my cheeks, screaming in my face in ecstasy.

Max wobbled into the ring and took my arm, flinging my fist in the air.

Roars. Claps. More whistles. Not one to bask in attention, I was already halfway out of the ring when I heard a voice behind me.

"This is bullshit!" Kade's manager, a meathead called Shaun, blazed between the boxes, pointing at me. "Kade wasn't prepared."

"No shit." I plucked a bottle of water from a random girl who offered it to me, taking a gulp and splashing the rest on my face. "Next time I'll be sure to email him my game plan."

Easton elbowed me.

"The fifth round didn't start before you threw in that last shot!" Shaun bellowed, kicking something between us out of his way. His smoker's breath skulked into my nostrils when he jabbed his finger against Max's chest. "Pippy Longstocking over here didn't whistle."

"Umm, bro, I *did* whistle." Max positioned himself between us. "And Kade made a move toward West first. He tried to throw in at least a couple punches before the KO happened."

Shaun wasn't having it. Neither was Kade. As soon as Appleton swung up on his feet, he began shouting in my face, claiming he'd been set up. That Max hadn't blown the whistle, that I'd ambushed him. Throwing excuses around, seeing which one might stick.

An interested crowd molded around us, eager to see if we were about to start a second, free-of-charge fight.

Rather than hang around and argue to death with these suckers, I told Max I'd meet him in his "office" upstairs and cordially suggested Kade should go to hell where he belonged, and get a hearing aid and a pair of glasses on his way there, if he truly believed anything about the fight wasn't kosher.

Max's office was what was supposed to be the management floor in the mall that never came to be.

"You're not getting away with this." Appleton made a slashing motion at his throat. "Consider yourself a dead man walking, St. Claire."

"Dead or alive, I still rode your ass tonight, and I'm not the one limping out of here."

I cut through the mass of people cheering and slapping my back. The random chick who'd handed me water waved at me, smiling and batting her lashes at me. She had long blonde hair almost down to her ass, and her smallness reminded me of a certain infuriating little hick.

"Legal?" I breezed past her, not stopping. Her friends thrust her my way, giggling into their palms.

"About to turn twenty on August sixth!"

No need to get specific. My ass is not about to get you flowers.

I jerked my head upstairs.

"Really?" she squeaked.

"No talking."

"Okay. Sure. Totally."

That was three fucking words, but I let it slide.

"This ends here," I warned.

"I know. You're West St. Claire. Duh. My name is—"

I gave her a cutting look. She wasn't getting it.

"Sheesh. Okay."

Half an hour later, Max came upstairs, shaking his head and apologizing. I sent the blonde back down. I was pretty much out of it during our hookup, although I did remember going through the motions, showing her something of a good time.

My mind drifted to other things. My parents' relentless calling, Texas being impossible and difficult for no reason at all, and Appleton being a killjoy and a bad sport.

Max explained that Kade, Shaun, and a few other guys in his entourage had cornered him after the fight, making a big stink about his loss. He said he'd gotten them off his back by handing over some of his cut to settle the misunderstanding. It was Bullshit with a capital B. Everyone in that room knew Max had blown the whistle, including Max himself.

But if he wanted to pay them lip money, it was his problem, not mine.

Max handed me my cut. It was what I'd normally make in two months of fighting. He praised me for my form and good taste in women ("Melanie, huh? She's bangin'.") and sent me on my way. I was glad to get the night over with. It was late, I was sore from all the illegal jabs Kade had managed to throw in, and I had a morning shift tomorrow at the farmers' market.

I had no idea what mood I was going to find Texas in, but if she thought I was going to put up with her crap just because other people felt sorry for her, she was gravely mistaken.

I shuffled back to the Ducati, which was parked on the other side of the mall, hidden away from the throng who got in through the main entrance. I'd learned early on that Christina attracted star-fuckers and high school kids who wanted to hop on her and take pictures.

Christina was my one and only indulgence. I'd chucked her out as an expense, seeing as I played the role of someone who had their shit together. I couldn't afford having people dig into who my family was, get dirt about my life, find out I was as broke as a stick horse. So I pretended to be someone else.

Someone to fear.

Someone who had a sick ride and a sinister taste for fighting.

Ironically, pretending to be someone I wasn't only made me even more tired of living than I already was.

As I ambled to my bike, I heard rustling coming from the bushes behind me. I stopped, twisting my head. The rustling stopped. I turned back to Christina.

The swooshing resumed.

It sounded like people were whisper-shouting behind the scrubs.

I turned around fully now, cocking an eyebrow.

"If you've got something to say, come and fucking say it. See if you have any teeth left by the end of your speech."

Silence.

"Yeah, that's what I thought."

Deciding it wasn't my job to coax whoever waited for me in the bushes for another brawl, I got on my bike and drove off.

Once I got home, I crawled into my room and collapsed on my bed without taking a shower. I lifted my pillow, plucked a picture from under it and kissed it, rubbing my thumb over the person imprinted on it.

"Night, A. Sleep tight." I pressed a kiss to the photo.

I tucked the picture back under my pillow, hating that I was still breathing, living, fighting, *fucking*.

She didn't answer.

She never did.

Chapter Seven

Grace

"DEAR LORD, JUST BECAUSE I'M CLUMSY, THAT DON'T MEAN I have the Alzheimer's." Grams dangled her feet in the air, perched on the hospital bed. She moped like a punished child, glowering at the doctor like *she* was the one who needed to get her head checked.

The doctor who saw her, a middle-aged woman with cropped chestnut hair and a nose stud, scribbled something on her clipboard, frowning at the chart in front of her.

"No one is trying to suggest that, Mrs. Shaw. But since you're already here, and your granddaughter indicated you've missed your last two appointments, I think a quick CT scan can't hurt. We'll be able to get the results faster than if you book them later on."

"You're hollering down the well, Doc." Grams shook her head, her sweet Southern drawl taking a sharp edge. She glared between the two of us, narrowing her eyes with open suspicion. "I ain't doin' it. I burned my hand on the stove. It's a common mistake anyone could make. Y'all can treat me like an invalid, but that plan ain't gonna work. There's nothing wrong with my head. Nothing!" She knocked on her temple with her fist, as if this was solid proof she was in the clear.

The doctor and I exchanged looks. There was so much I wanted to say to Dr. Diffie. Things that would prove Grams exhibited advanced signs of Alzheimer's. But Grandma Savvy didn't allow for a CT, and I couldn't force her.

It didn't matter that Grams had burned her hand touching the hot stove—not for a fraction of a second, but for at least half a minute—until I burst into the kitchen, smelling the all-too familiar scent of burnt skin, realized what she was doing, and pulled her out of there, kicking and screaming.

It also didn't matter that her palm was now charred, red, and swollen, her skin peeling and blistering under the bandages.

And it definitely didn't matter that Grams blanked out on the night with West at the diner, and when I brought it up the next morning, she thought I was making up an imaginary boyfriend.

"You are a fine, smart girl, Gracie-Mae," she'd told me, giving my cheek a pinch and a shake. *"You ought to find a boy eventually. You don't have to make one up."*

Marla told me she'd been hearing Grams crying in her room when I wasn't home. That things were getting unbearably bad. I felt so out of my depth, I wished I could tell Dr. Diffie the entire story and beg her to tell me what to do.

Instead, I checked the time on my phone. It was close to nine. I was going to be late for my shift on farmers' market day. Crap. I'd texted Marla, asking her to take over in the ER, but also called Karlie and requested West's number.

Grace: It's Grace. I'll probably be twenty minutes late and won't make it to prep. I'll make it up to you. Sorry.

He didn't answer.

But of course he didn't.

He was a crass, rude son of a gun.

Although, you did ask him to treat you as horribly as everyone else, after he helped you out and even called you his friend repeatedly.

Never mind that. I knew I'd done the right thing. West and I weren't friends. He pitied me, and getting close to him was a terrible idea. This was for the best.

The only thing was, I wished he hadn't known how crappy my family life was, on top of having seen that ugly scar.

Marla rushed into the hospital room ten minutes later. Tufts of her bottle-blonde hair were still in rollers, hanging on her head like window washers on skyscrapers. She looked exhausted. I couldn't blame her. Grams had been deteriorating throughout Marla's two-year employment at a rapid speed. Marla was approaching her mid-sixties herself and hadn't signed up to assist women with special needs.

I jumped up from the bed opposite Grams and threw myself at the caregiver.

"Thank God you're here."

"Came as soon as I could, honey pie. What'd the old bat do now?"

"I can hear you!" Grandma Savvy shook her fist at Marla.

"I found her pressin' her hand to the blazing hot stove this morning. I had to pry her out of the kitchen kickin' and screamin'. She won't agree to a CT now." I dropped my voice to a whisper, staring at the floor, "What do I do, Marl?"

"Why, I think we both know the answer to that question," Marla said softly, squeezing my arm. She and Karlie had been trying to hammer it into my brain that Grams needed to go to a home. I'd thought if I made an effort, I'd be able to maintain her quality of life without sending her away.

She deserved to spend the remainder of her life in the house she'd built with Grandpa Freddie, where she'd raised Courtney and me. In the town she grew up in.

"I'll take over from here. You go work." Marla slid a Styrofoam coffee cup into my hand.

I nodded, taking a sip and saluting the cup in her direction. "Thanks. I don't know what I'd do without you."

"Prolly the same thing you're doing now, but much less efficiently. Now go."

Twenty-five minutes later, I parked the pickup by my house and sprinted down the road toward the food truck.

By the time I got to work, a film of sweat made my clothes cling to my skin. West was operating both our stations when I stumbled inside. There was a fifteen-person line by the window and two customers shuffling on the sidelines, complaining about an order West had gotten wrong.

Delirious from heat and panic, I peeled my hoodie from my body and threw it to the front seat of the truck, relishing the air on my damp skin in my white, short-sleeved V-neck. I shoved West out of the way from the window with my butt, taking over.

"I owe you one," I dropped my voice to a whisper.

"*Two.*"

"What?"

"Twice I've saved your ass, and it hasn't even been a month. Your favors are piling up real quick, Texas, and I'm going to cash in on them. Soon." He flipped fish on the grill, rolling a green apple candy stick in his mouth. It always made him smell delicious. Like Granny Smith and winter.

"Any chance you can stop bein' a prick today?" I growled, hiking the plastic gloves up my fingers.

"Not even the slightest," he said nonchalantly, but I thought I detected something else underneath his relaxed stance. An underlying exhaustion. The same boy I saw in the parking lot, staring at nothing, waiting for the day to end.

"Good talk."

"Communication is key, baby."

"I'm not your baby."

"That's a relief. You'd make me a no-show dad, despite my good principles."

Principles? *Ha.*

Luckily, we didn't have time to bicker for the next four hours. We worked nonstop before we sold out of everything. West St. Claire may have been a bad boy, but he was dang good for business.

When the endless line of customers was finally served, I took a deep breath, turning around and grabbing the edge of the counter behind me.

As soon as I looked at him—*really* looked at him—the air left my lungs.

"Holy crap. What happened to your face?"

His entire face was slashed up, like someone had put scissors to it and tried to cut him into ribbons. The scratches under his eyes implied that same someone had also attempted to gouge them out. He had nasty red, purple, and yellow bruises all over his neck, like he'd been choked, and his lower lip was double its usual size.

My guess was he bled buckets last night. He belonged in the ER no less than Grams did.

"Fell down the stairs," he said grimly. Sarcastically. Why did I think I was going to get a straight answer out of this guy?

"What's your excuse?" His hooded eyes drifted to my injured arm. I tilted my head sideways, not sure what he meant, before realizing I was standing there with a short-sleeved shirt and that he could see my *entire* purple arm.

I let out a frantic yelp, bolting to the passenger seat to grab my hoodie. I knocked a few pans and spatulas on my way and tripped over an empty case of soda. I fumbled with the hoodie, trying to get it on me as soon as humanly possible, but the more I tried to figure out if it was upside down or not, the more flustered I got.

Finally, West plucked the hoodie from between my hands, turned it inside out, and pulled it over my head, his movement flippant, almost lazy.

"There." He yanked my hoodie down, giving it a final tug, like he was dressing up a kid. "Nothing like a nice parka in the middle of a fucking Texan summer."

"It's not a parka." I wrapped my hands around my waist, shaking all over.

I couldn't breathe.

He saw my scars.

He saw my scars.

He saw my ugly, stupid scars.

Jarring, red, and bumpy, they were hard to miss, and I wondered if any of our customers had lost their appetite as I'd served them.

I was surprised I didn't throw up in West's lap as soon as he brought it to my attention. Maybe because he seemed so unfazed about it, and already knew so much about me, it wasn't totally shocking.

"Texas." His tone was low. Unruffled.

"I ... I ... I have to go," I mumbled, turning around, getting ready to bolt out of the truck. He snatched me by the arm, pulling me back in effortlessly. I jerked and cried, desperate to leave, to never face him again, but his clutch on my arm tightened, almost to a bruising point.

He backed me into the trailer, until I had no choice but to accept that I wasn't getting out of there before we talked it out.

Again, I found myself trying to kick and punch him.

Again, I *failed*.

He was now crowding me so close, his breath fanned my face as he spoke. I started screaming from the top of my lungs. Like he'd raped me. Like he was hurting me back.

"Calm the fuck down." He bracketed me with his arms, my back against the fridge. He didn't sound any less composed. "Or you'll leave me no choice but to slap the hysteria out of you."

I shut up immediately. I didn't think he would lay a hand on me—I already gathered he wasn't that type of guy—but I didn't put it past him to punish me in some other way.

I pretended to breathe in and out. The sooner we got this out of the way, the sooner I could leave.

"You done freaking out?" He raised an eyebrow.

"Sure. Totally Zen," I bit out, gulping greedy breaths. "May I have some of my personal space back now?"

West took a step back, allowing a sliver of space between us. He leaned against the counter, folding his arms. "So."

"So?" I huffed.

"You've got yourself a nice, angry scar."

He said it. He actually went out and *uttered* it aloud. Nobody had pointed out the existence of my scars before. Not to me, anyway. People usually ignored it. Pretending they hadn't noticed. Which was somehow even more uncomfortable for me.

"What's the deal with covering it up? We all have scars. Yours is just visible."

"It's gross." I swung my gaze to the ceiling, avoiding his stare. I refused to cry for the second time in a week, and I was definitely not going to let him see it.

"Says who?" he pressed.

"Says everybody. Especially when people around me used to know me as someone else."

As someone pretty.

"Sounds like a pity party to me. Should I bring anything? Snacks? Beer? Inflatable sex dolls?"

"Who said you were invited?" I was still focusing on the trailer's ceiling.

He snorted out a laugh, slapping a rag over his knee in my periphery.

I noticed West laughed a lot when we were around each other, but never at school.

I also noticed he was apparently insane, because he didn't seem bothered at all by his own dire state.

"You're making a big deal out of nothing. It's just scar tissue."

"It ain't attractive."

"It ain't unattractive enough to prevent me from wanting to tap your ass."

My mouth dropped, and I blinked rapidly, trying to figure out how, exactly, I was going to answer him.

He'd been throwing around the idea that he found me appealing every now and then.

I still thought he either said that sarcastically or because he wanted poor Toastie to feel better about herself. At least I'd stopped thinking it was De La Salle who sent him to breathe unfounded hope in me. West didn't seem like the type to answer to anyone, much less take direction and orders from others.

"Was that your idea of a compliment?" I hissed.

"No," he drawled, dead serious. "It's my idea of the goddamn truth. What is wrong with you?"

Something euphoric and warm clawed at my chest. It was the first time I'd toyed with the idea that he was telling the truth. We stared at each other wordlessly. I waited for him to explain why he looked like he'd been attacked by a pack of wolves. When he didn't, I arched an eyebrow.

"Speaking of not looking too hot …"

He clutched his heart, mockingly mourning my low opinion of his looks today. "You wound me."

"Apparently, I'm not the only one. Did you fight yesterday?"

West flipped two empty crates, one on my side of the trailer and one on his, and sank down. I followed suit. In a lot of ways, the food truck felt like our bubble. A snug confession booth.

The rules were different in the truck. Like we shed our primary skin, of our stigma and reputation and social status. Here we were simply … *us.*

"I fight every Friday." He popped his knuckles. His biceps flexed under his short Henley.

I looked away, clearing my throat. "No offense, but you can't tell me people come to see you on Fridays during football season."

"People go straight from the football field to the Plaza, get trashed, then wake up for college football. You Texans realize there are other sports other than football, yeah?"

"We try not to encourage other sports, as they tend to butt into the sports channels and water down the football. Do you always fight? Even when school's out?"

"Even if I have pneumonia and a broken rib."

That didn't sound like a figure of speech. It sounded like something that had actually happened in the past. He must have really needed the money. Or maybe he didn't care about dropping dead. I had a dreadful feeling it was a combination of the two.

"You normally don't look too worse for wear." I nibbled on my lower lip, my heart rate slowing down as the minutes ticked away.

So he saw my scars and knew about Grams. Big freaking deal.

"I normally fight with sane people. This time, my opponent was a bitch-ass coward who did everything short of pulling out a gun. Kade Appleton, man." He shook his head. "A dick from hell."

"You fought Kade Appleton?" My breath hitched.

Everybody knew Kade Appleton around Sheridan. I'd never met him, but I'd heard countless stories. He was a bully all throughout school, dropped out at sixteen, packed his stuff and moved to Vegas to fight. Word was he'd joined a gang while he was there. "What the hell is wrong with you? He's dubbed Appleton the Bad Apple in this neck of the woods. Do you *want* to die?"

"Not actively, but surely it won't be the worst thing in the world. All the cool kids are doing it. Kurt Cobain, Abraham Lincoln, Dr. Seuss …"

"West!" I hollered, slapping my thigh.

"Fine. I'm changing Dr. Seuss to Buddy Holly, but only because you're twisting my arm here."

When I shot him a sharp look that showed him I didn't find any of this funny, he jerked his chin toward me.

"Why were you late today?"

"Grams," I croaked, surprised with how naturally the truth jumped out of my mouth. It was liberating to talk to someone about her openly.

"She burned herself on the stove this morning. It was bad. I was with her in the ER until Marla, her caregiver, took over."

"Has she been diagnosed?"

I shook my head. "Not the last time I took her to get checked, but that was a couple years ago. She refuses to get another CT, and things have been gettin' pretty bad."

"She should be medicated."

"I know."

Not only that, but she should get more exercise and sunshine and scheduled activities. Marla could only do so much for her, and by the time I got home every night after school and work, I was too exhausted to give Grams everything she deserved.

West got up and made both of us margarita slushies. He dropped extra gummy bears into each of them and handed me one. We saluted at the same time, oddly in sync, taking greedy slurps from our drinks as he sat back down.

"Back to the scar thing." He motioned to his own face with his hand. "Is that why you don't go onstage? Because you don't like the way you look?"

He was referring to that time he saw me at rehearsal, mouthing all the words but staying far away from the limelight.

I felt the tips of my ears pinking. "It's more complicated than that."

"I'm a smart guy. Lay it on me."

"I haven't always been like this. I was kind of Miss Popular. I fought really hard to get where I was. My mom was a junkie who died when I was a toddler, and my father ... Well, I don't even know who he is. The one thing I always had goin' for me was my looks, as shallow as it sounds." I laughed nervously. "I was in cheer. I was in drama. I was *that* girl, you know. With the pretty Sunday church dress and dimpled smile, always camera-ready. I learned early on how to play the cards I'd been dealt. I thought I had the game figured out. But then ..."

"Someone flipped the table upside down mid-round and all the rules changed." West chewed on his straw, contemplating. "Same happened to me, so I know firsthand how bad it sucks."

"Oh, yeah?" I grinned, feeling dangerously comfortable around him. It was stupid. Like a kitten thinking it could befriend a tiger because they were vaguely from the same family. "You discarded your lifelong dream to become an actor because you experienced a traumatic childhood tragedy that has caused you to look disfigured beyond repair?"

He used the tip of his boot to shove my crate back. He scratched his temple with his middle finger. I laughed.

"What I mean is, the rules changed on me, too, mid-game," he clarified.

"I don't see how. You're still popular."

"I was Easton Braun-popular. Linebacker. Homecoming king. The obnoxious, wholesome, perfect, Tom Brady-type guy people lowkey suspect is secretly a serial killer."

I ran my eyes over his injured frame. I never would have guessed West played ball. That he had a sweet, straitlaced side.

"What made you switch to the dark side?"

"I became the sole provider in my family. Well, my parents work now, but they're mainly chasing bills."

"Oh."

Did I just say oh? Out of all the words in the English language, I chose this one? Really? Do better! "That's … rough."

He shrugged. "It is what it is."

"Do you have any siblings?"

He shook his head. "Just me, my parents, and a mountain of unpaid loans that keeps on getting higher. You?"

"Just me, Grams, and my in-the-gutter self-esteem." I smiled tiredly. "Yay us."

We clinked our drinks together.

Silence stretched between us like bubble gum, extending, on the verge of snapping. West was the first to put a needle in it. He slapped his rock-hard thigh.

"Now that we're even, let's clean up and get the fuck out of here. I've got shit to do." He stood, dumping his slushie in the trash.

He turned off the grill, getting ready to scrub it. I glared up at him, dumbfounded.

"What the heck is that supposed to mean?"

"You couldn't look me in the eye since I saw your arm, and I needed to counter-embarrass myself for you to feel equal again. So I indulged you. Shared a secret with you no one but East knows. But East doesn't count; we grew up in the same town and were born two days apart. He is practically my twin brother. My family is broke as hell, and I fight not because of the perks or the pussy. I need to keep a roof over my parents' heads. My mom needs her antidepressant meds, and, as you must know, healthcare is goddamn expensive."

I swallowed and looked down. I felt so pathetic in front of him, with the dementia-stricken grandmother and big-ass scar. But now that I knew his family was poor and his mother was battling depression, his life didn't seem like something to envy anymore. He wasn't untouchable, unreachable, or protected by an invisible glow.

"Your parents must be so proud of you," I grumbled.

"Not even a little." He let out a humorless laugh, dumping a rag into my hands, signaling for me to get off my butt and help. "But that's another story, and you'll have to show a lot more than scar tissue for me to trade *that* secret, Tex."

By the time I got back home, Marla had put Grams to bed. She was drained from today's trip to the emergency room. She wasn't used to spending so much time out of the house anymore.

I took a quick shower while Marla tidied up. Then I hugged her at the door, clutching her extra hard. "Thanks, Marl. You're a trooper."

"Don't mention it. Now tell me, whatcha gonna do, honey pie?"

"Probably watch Netflix and chill."

"Don't play dumb with me, sweets. I mean about the old bat. In the long run. This is not sustainable, sweetie. You must know that. You can no longer take care of her. I appreciate you did it through high school, but your grandmomma needs constant care. She is a danger to herself. And to others," Marla said pointedly, raising one eyebrow as her gaze drifted to the left side of my face.

I ducked my head down, rubbing the back of my neck.

"I'll think about it," I lied.

I wasn't going to think about it. There was nothing to think about. Grandma Savvy had raised me. She'd tucked me into bed every night, and kissed my boo-boos better. Sewn a replica of the prom dress I wanted because the original cost too much. She'd dedicated her entire life to me, and I wasn't going to bail on her when things got tough.

I just had to step up my game. Spend more time with her, shower her with more attention.

I was closing the door after Marla when a foot was shoved between the gap. The person on the other side let out a pained grunt but didn't remove their foot from between the door and the frame. My heart leaped in my chest.

The first thing I worried about was not having makeup on.

As opposed to, you know, having an axe murderer barge into my house un-freaking-announced.

"Who is it?" I demanded. The gap was too narrow for me to see them.

"Karlie. Secret code: Ryan Phillippe. Open up."

We didn't *have* a secret code, but this sounded like what we'd have if we chose one. My nineties-themed heart stuttered. I snorted, swinging the door open. My best friend wiggled her eyebrows with a sultry smile, a dripping bag full of takeout in her raised hand. Since our town only offered a diner, the food truck, and a pizza parlor, my guess was we were in for Italian.

Karlie knew I'd had a rough morning from our text exchange when I'd asked for West's number, so she'd shown up.

I yanked her inside, smothering her with a hug. She patted my back awkwardly.

"Anyone ever told you you're an amazing friend?" I ruffled her thick, dark curls with my breath.

"Everyone, and frequently. I come bearing offerings. Pasta, cheap wine, and gossip. We'll start with the food. Sound good?"

"Sounds *perfect*."

An hour later, we were lying on my living room couch in an advanced state of food coma, the TV flickering in the background.

I patted my stomach, staring at its hard roundness. I was svelte and small, and sometimes when I had a case of food baby, and my stomach would get all curved, I'd cradle it in front of the mirror and imagine myself as Demi Moore on *Vanity Fair's* cover (another favorite nineties nugget). Normally, it made me laugh. But tonight, a little buzzed from the wine, and a lot worried about my grandmomma, I couldn't help but wonder if I'd ever *be* pregnant. If I'd meet someone and make a life with him.

Typically, I shoved this kind of stuff to the back drawer in my mind. But ever since West stormed into my life with his battered body and broken soul, he'd jimmied that drawer open and flung out all its contents.

Lust.

Romance.

Longing.

And most dangerous of all—*hope*.

I wasn't sure if what he stirred in me was good and hopeful, or disastrous and shattering. Either way, putting my faith in someone who absolutely didn't want any type of relationship, and didn't exhibit much interest in staying *alive*, was both stupid and risky.

"What was that piece of gossip you wanted to tell me?" I nudged Karlie's shoulder with my foot, suddenly remembering.

Karlie shook her head from the other side of the sofa, her dark hair bouncing around her heart-shaped face. "Okay, so you know Melanie Bush? Small? Blonde? Blue eyes?"

"You've literally described sixty percent of Sheridan's student body." I laughed. "What about her?"

"So, my friend Michelle ditched our study group this Friday to go to West's fight against Kade Appleton. Apparently, it was brutal. The mats were so soaked with blood, they had to burn them in the junkyard afterwards. Anyway, so a fight almost broke out *after* the fight. Some of Appleton's people came at West, and he basically walked out on them, not giving two craps. But guess what he did on his way out?"

"What?" I tried to keep my tone light, but my spine stiffened, and

I felt the food I'd just consumed making its way up my throat. It didn't take a genius to know what direction this story was taking.

"He basically dragged Mel up the stairs, blood dribbling down his chin, slammed her against the empty elevator bank, and screwed her senseless. He was so out of it, Michelle said Mel wasn't even sure he was, like, conscious. Mel told her it was insane and carnal and hot as Hades. But that he didn't even look at her face as he gave her two orgasms."

"Wow."

I had to say something, so I went for a word that meant absolutely everything and nothing at all. *Wow* could be either bad or good. Shocked or sarcastic. *Wow* was also how I felt when my heart was crushed into miniscule dusty flakes.

"Get this—apparently, he's a weird lay. Mel said he kept touching her hair while pounding into her, and that he kept talking about Texas." Karlie screwed her nose. "What do you think our boy has against the Lone Star State? We invented Dr. Pepper, corn dogs, and silicone breast implants. That makes us undoubtedly the best state in the country."

"Right. So weird," I mumbled.

That was all I was capable of. Anything else, and my voice would have broken.

Texas.

He'd talked about Texas.

But it wasn't the state he was referring to, I knew, and a nauseating mixture of white-hot jealousy and euphoria washed over my body.

"Hey, you don't happen to have ice cream, do you?"

"Let me check," I offered, relieved to have an excuse to go to the kitchen and regulate my heartbeat.

I knew I was jealous, but I also knew I had no business being jealous.

West wasn't my boyfriend. Nothing in his behavior, banter, or personality made me believe he'd ever ask me out. If anything, he'd told me flat-out he'd never as much as flirt with me, even if he had found me attractive.

The only thing this story had proven was that he wanted in my pants—not heart—and I'd be wise to remember which part of me he was interested in.

Lord, I needed to get over this stupid crush. Fast.

I took a bucket of ice cream out of the freezer, plucking two spoons from the utensil cabinet. I stabbed the ice cream with one spoon, feeling a scream clogging up my throat.

My own foolishness infuriated me. So what if West wasn't an asshole to me? It didn't mean he wasn't an asshole period. He was to Melanie. I just needed to remind myself to stay away from him and take a step back.

Texas.

The man had some nerve saying my nickname while he was inside someone else.

I wanted to kill him. To throttle him. To …

"Shaw! Whaddup? Did you go make the ice cream from scratch?" Karlie hollered from the living room. I looked down and realized the ice cream wasn't so white anymore. It was flecked with scarlet drops of blood. *My* blood.

It was turning pink, sliding down the slopes of snowy vanilla mountains. I glanced at my hand. My mouth slacked. I hadn't used a spoon. I'd taken a dang knife from the drawer.

Quickly, I scooped all the tainted ice cream, threw it in the trash, and took out clean spoons.

"Comin' right up."

Crap. Crap. Crap.

I strode back to the couch with a Band-Aid Karlie didn't notice. She shoved a spoonful of ice cream into her mouth, closing her eyes and moaning.

"You know what we should do?"

Make a voodoo doll of West and stab it to death?

"Another *this or that* nineties quiz?" I asked in fake eagerness. She popped her eyes open, shooting me a skeptical look. I wasn't known for my enthusiasm.

"Duh, but we always do that. We should go to one of West's fights. Next Friday. It's Mom and Victor's shift, anyway. It would be nice to hang out. We never do that anymore."

We didn't. Karlie was wrapped up in her schoolwork and internships, and I was either working or spending time with Grams. But going to see West in action was the worst possible thing we could do together.

"Hard pass." I shoved ice cream into my mouth without tasting it. The whole night was tarnished by images of West screwing Melanie Bush against an elevator bank, and I didn't even know what she looked like. "Fight clubs aren't really my scene."

"Hot shirtless men thrashing each other is, though, right? Unless you're asexual. Or a lesbian."

"Guess I'm asexual."

Women really didn't do it for me.

"Come on. I knew you prior to you-know-what, and you were boy crazy just like the rest of us. Tucker, anyone?"

Eh, yes. Tucker. One of the very reasons I'd sworn off men in the first place. The way he'd discarded me the minute I'd lost my beauty still burned long after the fire wounds had healed.

Karlie and I established I would use a hammer as a Q-tip to clean my earwax before attending an underground fight. My friend went back home, which was right across the street from me.

I slipped under the covers, shoving the house keys beneath the mattress—like stupid West had suggested the night at the diner—so Grams couldn't wander off while I slept. So far, it had worked.

The last thing I thought about when my head hit the pillow was a fighter who had given up on himself.

Chapter Eight

West

O N SUNDAY, I CASHED IN ON ONE OF THE MILLION FAVORS Texas owed me and came in late to my shift. There had been a party on frat row the previous night. Parties were my idea of hell, but every now and again I tagged along when East rode my ass for being antisocial. He had the incorrect notion I would spiral into depression like my mother had. Sometimes I thought he also knew I was toying with the idea of gunning my bike straight into a tree or flinging myself off the water tower. I kept to myself throughout the night, cradling a bottle of moonshine and offering my I'd-rather-drink-straight-from-the-toilet face whenever people tried to strike up a conversation. The lowest point of the evening was being called out by some chick for asking her who she was when she approached me in one of the frat houses.

Apparently, we'd had sex on Friday.

And apparently, she found it fitting to tell everyone, short of the president, that we'd hooked up.

"Melanie!" she'd screamed. *"My name is Melanie. You'd remember if you let me introduce myself properly in the first place."*

Melanie whined about how she didn't think she was that forgettable. It surprised me, since I made a point of not asking girls for their names.

"And another thing, I'm not even from Texas, like you said. I'm from Oklahoma!"

What could I say? Chicks were an endless river of mystery I didn't want to dip my fucking toe into.

I ignored her, hitting the pool table with a few guys, talking NFL over her whining. At some point, Tess marched toward us and pulled Melanie (or was it Melody?) to the side, consoling her for the premature death of what was obviously a once-in-a-lifetime love story between us.

On Sunday, Texas was surprisingly silent and curt, considering Saturday had been spent spilling our guts out on the food truck's floor. I was way too hungover to find out what got her jeans in a jerk this time. She seemed to always find a reason to hate me. We hadn't exchanged more than five sentences, and that was fine by me. Her hot and cold games were getting on my last nerve.

By Monday, however, my patience with the universe wore off, and the urge to punch anyone within sight was overwhelming.

Not only did East wake up in the morning to find the seventeen unanswered letters my mother had sent me jammed in the bottom of our trashcan (*"What in the name, dude? Answer your mother!"*), but everyone still seemed to ride the weekend alcohol wave and showed up on campus hammered. The frat parties bled into Sunday and Monday, which meant half the students were in togas and J-Lo sandals.

They looked like Greek gods, if they came from Jersey Shore and carried extra pounds from an all-you-can-eat vacay on Olympus. It was all bullshit, anyway. Half those fuckers wouldn't find Greece on the map if it were highlighted with five different Sharpies. I made my way to my first lecture, determined not to kill anyone today.

The weekend's bad vibes still lingered on my mood.

I moseyed past Reign, his Sig Ep friends, Tess, the blonde deranged chick from Oklahoma—Melt-down-nie, as Reign had dubbed her after Saturday—and a few other girls. They were all hunched together, red-eyed, gossiping in the hallway. I was about to round the corner and get into Addams' class when I heard Reign howling behind me.

"Yo, Toastie! Did you fall from Heaven? Because your face sure is fucked-up."

The entire hall erupted in reverberating laughter.

I stopped walking, my hands curling into fists.

"Just kidding. Looking hot, baby girl!"

Another wave of laughter. Texas didn't respond. It took everything in me not to turn around and look at her face.

Don't fucking snap. She doesn't want your pity.

"C'mon, now, Toast. I'm not just buttering you up. Sex with me will set you on fire."

More laughter.

The flash of phone cameras as pictures were taken.

Snickers, cupped mouths, cell phones out.

Something inside of me snapped.

Sorry, Texas. No can do.

I turned around and charged toward him. He was still wearing his stupid toga and what looked like a crapped-on nest but was supposed to be a head wreath. His douchebag smile collapsed like a Jenga tower when he realized I was coming for his ass. I didn't check where Texas was. If she was even around. I tackled Reign with my shoulder, slamming him against the wall, bunching his toga in my fist. The fabric fell apart, pooling at his ankles, leaving a strap of white cloth draped over his chest. He was standing in the hall wearing nothing but his boxers. I grabbed his throat and raised him until his feet no longer touched the floor. My jaw ticked so hard I thought my teeth were going to snap out of my mouth one by one.

"Jesus, man!" His yelp was muffled as my palm crushed his air pipe. He brought his hands up and tried prying my fingers away from his neck, his knuckles turning white.

"*Itssaarrrjkk!*" he spluttered, foaming from the mouth.

I bared my teeth with a feral snarl. I wanted to scare him to death. To make sure he knew the next time he took a jab at Texas, he would be in a world of hurt.

"Work on your material, funny guy."

"She doesn't even *care!*" His eyes were bugging out as I put more pressure on his throat. I felt the delicate bones in his neck snapping as I pressed harder into them.

"Well, I do," I said quietly.

I could kill him. I knew that. I'd been aware of my ability to kill people for a while now. He wouldn't even be the first person who'd ended up in a body bag because of me.

But that was a secret I wasn't in a particular hurry to share with the world.

I got in his face. "I dare you to disrespect her again, Reign. I will break you into miniscule pieces then flush you down the toilet. A part of me half-wishes you'd be dumb enough to pick on her, just so I could finally end you."

"Bro, you're choking him," someone murmured to my left.

"He is turning purple!" This came from my right.

"Quick, somebody do something!"

The cries bounced all around me but never slipped under my skin. I watched as he turned colors, as his flailing subsided under my hands, as the realization he might not walk out of this alive crossed his face.

A few pairs of hands pulled me by the back of my shirt. East, Grayson, and Bradley plastered me against the opposite wall, away from Reign. I shot East a murderous look and shoved him away, launching myself at Reign again.

East pushed me back harder. "You almost choked him to death. What's wrong with you, man?" East panted, pinning me to the wall by my shoulders.

I threw a cool glance at Reign. He was slouched on the floor, gasping for air, and rubbing his neck, which was dark purple, a noose-like stain forming around his Adam's apple.

The crowd around us thickened, the buzzing of murmurs filling my ears. Texas stood at the back, clutching the straps of her phoenix backpack.

She looked at me like I was a traitor.

I was fed up.

With her.

With my family.

With the world.

I spun on my heel, marching in the opposite direction. She wasn't worth the trouble. I'd done as best as I could to help her out, but I was officially done. I couldn't afford a friend like Grace Shaw, even if I was interested in her company.

Which, for the record, I wasn't. Not anymore.

Too much drama. No, thank you.

I tramped my way into Addams' class. A part of me was sure Texas was going to run after me. Thank me. Apologize for being unreasonable.

Beg and cower like everyone else did.

Seek my unattainable affections.

When I was at the door, I glanced up at the hallway, expecting to see her face again.

She was gone.

"Whatcha thinking?" Reign nudged my shoulder with his foot later that evening. He plopped beside me by the kidney-shaped pool, taking a drag from his joint, the smoke rushing out of his nostrils in two thick streams.

Guess it was his version of an apology for what had happened in the hallway this morning.

I took a pull of my beer, dangling my feet in the lukewarm water. One look at his neck and I knew I had to own up for my part of the shit show, too.

Yes, he was an asshole, but I'd also almost killed him today. For a girl who didn't even want to be saved.

Damn you, Texas.

"I'm thinking I have really hairy toes," I said honestly, staring at my narrow, long feet.

Reign's shoulders trembled with laughter. He shook his head, kicking my foot with his in the water. "*Whoa*, man. You do."

There was a beat of silence. I was still seeing red every time I thought about him picking on Texas. I wasn't even sure why. She'd already established we weren't friends, and I'd told myself I wouldn't touch her.

It wasn't the first time Reign was being a yeast-infected dick to other people, but it was definitely the most persistent he had been.

"I wish I could get away with being like you." He drew circles in the water with his toes, which, I noticed, could use a trim, too. "You're the strong, silent type. You don't have to run your mouth to get noticed. I need to entertain. People expect me to talk shit."

"If this is you making an excuse for today, you better turn around and walk away before I drown your ass." I took another pull of my beer.

We were at a birthday pool party East had dragged me to. The birthday girl, who lived just outside Sheridan, had begged us to come, both on her face and to her party. Oil lord daddy. Parents out of town. It was a frat party on steroids. Everybody brought inflatable toys and danced poolside. Music blasted through a surround system that made the earth quake. There were ice bars and shot luges.

The birthday girl swaggered around in a pink and white bikini, high heels, and a Sweet Twenty-One sash. I'd come here to get rid of some of the stress with a quick lay, but as soon as my ass went past the iron-wrought gate, I realized I'd rather sit by the pool and glare at my hairy toes than pound into some nameless, faceless chick who'd whine about it later.

The cons outweighed the pros when it came to hooking up these days.

"Aren't you going to ask me why I did this to Goldilocks?" Reign asked.

When he gathered an answer wasn't in the cards for him, he soldiered on.

"I did it because I knew you like Toastie. Hell, my *dog* knows you like Toastie, and he lives in Indiana. That's why you went for Melanie, right? She basically looks like Toastie from behind."

If he called her Toastie one more time, I was going to hammer him so deep into the ground he was going to reappear in China.

"Long, blonde hair. Cute, round ass." He counted their similarities on his fingers. "You're pretty transparent, St. Claire. Guess I just wanted to give you a taste of your own medicine."

I sipped my beer. He was high if he thought I liked Texas. She was unbearable, other than the few times she'd made me laugh.

East plopped down to my other side, plucking the joint from between Reign's fingers.

"Are we having a heart-to-heart? Reign, are you finally coming out?" East beamed at Reign, who slapped the back of his head, laughing.

"I was just telling him I teased Toastie because he screwed Tess."

"Seriously?" I raised my fists to his face. Reign cowered, hunching his back with a wince.

"Shit, sorry. Old habits die hard."

"You'll die *easily* if you keep this shit up."

"Aw, I hate it when Mommy and Daddy fight." East took a drag, passing it back to De La Salle. "Seriously, though. That Toastie nonsense was so third grade of you, Reign. Taunt her ass one more time and I'll personally make sure Coach knows. He'll dump your ass faster than a shit after a laxative party."

"I already told West I'm done messing with her," Reign sulked. "My bad, okay? I'm going through a rough patch here."

"So, Westie knows you're into Tess?"

"He does now. Thanks for the spoiler." Reign rolled his eyes.

Was that what it was about? Fucking Tess Davis?

"You're welcome to Tess." I finished my drink just as a freshman leaned down toward us, her tits spilling over our faces through her Baywatch Red swimsuit, offering us a tray full of shots. East took three, distributing them between us.

"Nothing's standing in your way. Other than your ugly-ass face and shit-for-brains," I encouraged Reign in my own backwards way.

Reign shook his head.

"It's not so simple now. I wish you wouldn't have broken the bro code."

We clinked glasses and downed the tequila shots. I didn't remember Reign saying anything about wanting Tess, but I believed him, because I normally wasn't paying much attention to anything anyone said. And for the record—Reign had screwed about sixty percent of the campus population this month alone, so declaring what he had for Tess was love was pretty much on par with this Melanie chick getting butthurt when she found out I hadn't printed out our wedding invitations.

"Why's that?" East asked Reign.

"She's into his sorry ass now." Reign jerked his chin my way.

"Well, my sorry ass is not into anyone, so that's not gonna be an issue."

"You wanna tell me you're really not into Taco Truck Girl?" East poked at my rib. Someone cannonballed into the pool, splashing us. A girl. She tugged at our toes underwater playfully before slicing the surface, popping up like a slutty nymph. Reign splashed her back. *In love, my ass.* He wouldn't know love if it gave him a golden shower and totaled his Alfa Romeo, hurling it off a bridge.

East and I were still locked in conversation.

"Her name's Grace," I said curtly, because somehow it was important for me that these bastards stop referring to her by her scar or her job. "And no, I don't want her."

Especially after she froze me out at the food truck during our last shift and snubbed me in front of the entire school when I'd stuck my neck out for her.

East considered this.

"It's just that you haven't been your want-to-die-now-someone-hand-me-the-gun self since ..."

"Since?" I prompted.

"Since you met her."

My best friend was such a pussy I wanted to shut him up with a can of Friskies. I chuckled throatily. That was a good one. Me. A changed man. Because of a girl.

"For the last time, I've no interest in Grace Shaw."

"For real?"

More girls dove down to tickle our feet, trying to draw our attention. We ignored them.

"How many more times can I fucking say this?" I glowered at my best friend. "I can express it in a tribal dance, or Morse code, or maybe kicking your ass."

"Then you wouldn't mind if I ask her out, then?" East studied me carefully. I felt my jaw twitch. Out of all the chicks at Sher U, he wanted to fuck the one I was working with. I noticed Reign stopped splashing the girl in the pool, watching for my reaction.

I hitched a shoulder up. "Go ham. Don't forget to put a rubber on it. She seems like the type to lock you into marriage with a baby."

What did it matter? Texas wasn't going to go out with him if he were the only man left on planet Earth. She was probably a virgin. She didn't date, and she was wary of the football crew. Especially after Reign exhibited the manners of a fried chicken wing when it came down to her.

"So, let me get this straight." Reign grinned, enjoying the discussion immensely. "You'd kill anyone who disrespects her, but you won't date her?"

I plopped down into the pool, splashing water over my face.

"That's a good boy. Want your cookie now?" I snarled.

"Seems legit," Reign said sarcastically.

East joined me in the pool. I was done with discussing Grace Shaw. She'd hogged enough of my time, my life, my *thoughts*.

"So, Max says Appleton is talking mad shit about you." East squinted under the sun. That was news to me. Then again, I hardly kept tabs on what people said.

"He would do this to my face, but then he wouldn't have teeth to talk smack about me with."

"I bet Max is gonna try to arrange a second fight." Reign joined us, dipping inside the pool and coming out of the water, shaking his head like a dog. "Would you go for a rematch if it's on the table?"

"No way," East warned, flashing me a look.

"For the right price, I would kill Appleton, his meathead manager, and Max himself."

Both my friends laughed.

I did, too.

What they didn't know was I wasn't even kidding.

Chapter Nine

Grace

THEY SAY WHEN IT RAINS, IT POURS.

In my case, my week had been a thunderstorm wrapped inside a tornado.

It ripped away everything in my life, and all I could do was watch it swirling in the wind as I fell into the deep, dark depths of my own personal catastrophe.

"Honey pie, I'm so sorry. I know it's the worst timing possible for you, but please consider this my official resignation." Marla sat me down at the end of the week.

I was running on fumes at this point. West and I hadn't been talking at all during our shifts, Grams had gone on an odd hunger strike, still mad about the CT scan that never happened, and college life was a disaster of hushed whispers and sympathetic glances ever since West St. Claire had pretty much declared I was under his protection.

Everyone knew West and I weren't chummy, so they conveniently deducted he was feeling sorry for Toastie, his newest colleague, and wanted to make sure she didn't off herself.

He's the one who hates life, I wanted to scream in their faces. *He's the one who wants to die. Not me. I just want to be left alone.*

"You're quittin'?" I blinked at Marla, trying to keep my tone neutral. Marla nodded, gathering my hands in her oily, swollen palms and bringing them to her lips.

"*Retiring*. Movin' away. Pete found a great condo in Florida, just outside Miami. Real nice and fancy, and so cheap for what we're getting. We'll be close to Joanne, my daughter, and her little stinkers. It's been a long time coming. I ain't a kid anymore. I want to enjoy my grandchildren, and go on walks, and get fat with my husband."

Nothing about what she said was news to me. Still, I was irrationally upset. Not with Marla, of course. I could hardly blame her for wanting to better her own situation. But with the world. I depended on Marla, who at this point became more like family and less like an employee. She always put in extra hours and was on call twenty-four seven. Grams got along with her most of the time, and Marl never took any of her bullshit. Finding someone else was going to be a struggle. Marla was a Sheridan local, but not many people wanted to commute into my small town for work, and those who were willing to demanded to be financially compensated accordingly.

Even though I had some money put aside for medical bills for Grams, and her 401k payments kept us comfortable, I wasn't exactly in tall cotton.

"Oh, Marla, that's wonderful." I stood up, swallowing down my panic, tugging her into a hug. I relished the small, bittersweet moment in her arms, feeling the pinch of pain behind my eyes. "You deserve it. You worked hard for so many years. I'm so happy for you and Pete."

She reared her head back, patting my cheeks to make sure they were dry. I winced when she touched the scar tissue. It still felt raw. The skin was thinner than on my right, healthy side.

"Don't worry, Gracie-Mae. I'm giving you a two-month notice. Plenty of time to find a replacement."

I let out a breath. Two months *was* a good amount of time.

"Thanks. I'll start searchin' right away."

"Although, you know where I stand in terms of what should

happen next." Her mouth twitched, like she was fighting back the words that wanted to tumble out of her mouth.

"I know. Especially with the hunger strike." I bristled. Marla laughed.

"Yeah. 'Bout that. She's been slipping cracklins into her room when she thinks I ain't looking. And, well"—her laughter pitched higher—"I pretend not to look so she'll eat."

Shaking my head, I let out a relieved chuckle. "She's impossible. What am I going to do with her?"

"Send her to her home!" Marla snorted. "She'll thank you."

Sensing a big, juicy moment, Grams crept into the kitchen in her calico housedress and bunny slippers.

"What's all this fuss about?" She went straight for the utensil drawer, trying to yank it open. It didn't budge. I'd installed magnets on every drawer that contained anything that could be used as a weapon earlier that week, the stuff you used when you had toddlers. I couldn't take my chances. Not after the stove incident.

"Grandmomma, Marla just told me she will be leavin' us in a couple months. She is movin' to Florida to be closer to Joanne and her grandkids." I turned to face Grams. Her back was still to me.

"Shoot! What's this?" She wiggled the handle for the drawer, huffing. "I can't open it!"

"Grams, did you hear me?" I asked.

"What in the name ..." she muttered, ignoring the news—and me, still tugging.

"What do you need?" I rushed to her, eager to make amends after the ER incident. "I'll get it for you."

"What I need is to know how come I can't open my own drawers in my own dang house to get a spoon out for my tea!" She spun on her heel to face me, waving her hand in the drawer's direction. "Is this a part of your scheme, Courtney? To convince people that I have Lord knows what diseases? That I can't even open a drawer? You wanna put me in a mental institute? Is that it?"

This time, I didn't feel like playing her dead daughter anymore. It hurt too much.

"Grams, it's not Courtney. It's me, Gracie-Mae, and I don't want to put you in a mental institution."

"You want me to die there so you can take all my money and my house. So you can get high without anyone interruptin' you. I see right through you, young lady. All you ever cared about were those boys and the drugs."

"I just want you to get better," I gritted out. I was getting tired of this tango.

"Yeah, by diagnosing me with somethin' I don't have and putting me on a whole lotta drugs. Not everybody wants to be sedated. Just because you like drugs, doesn't mean they're for me."

"Grams." I put my hand on her shoulder. "It's *Grace*."

She pushed me. Hard. I stumbled across the kitchen, my back hitting the wall. A picture of my mother and me—the only one we had in this house of both of us—fell to the floor, the glass breaking.

It stung more than it hurt.

The humiliation.

The anger.

My helplessness in this situation.

I put my broken flame ring to my lips and whispered my wishes as Marla shot up from her seat, advancing toward my grandmother.

"Savannah!" The sharpness in her tone made the tiny hair on my arms stand on end. "Do you not recognize your granddaughter?"

Grams snapped her head toward Marla, her scowl melting into a sweet smile.

"What? Don't be silly. I know exactly who she is."

"You said Courtney," Marla countered.

"Quiet!" Grams raised her voice. "Stop challengin' my every step, both of you."

Marla walked over to me. "Go to school, honey pie. I'll be putting in some extra hours today. I promised your grandma I'd help rearrange her closet. All right?"

I stared at Grams but nodded.

I grabbed my backpack, keys, and wallet and dashed out. I waited until I was in my car before I let the first tear fall.

I thought about *A Streetcar Named Desire*.

Of Blanche's biting loneliness that seeped so deep she didn't even know what she was lonely *for* anymore. Blanche—like Grams—sat at home all day, her demons often her only companion.

I thought about the cruelty in giving someone freedom they didn't know what to do with.

Grandma Savvy always used to say, *if you're not scared, you're not brave.*

Right now, I was one out of the two, but for her, I needed to be both.

I sat at the back row of the theater, watching as Tess and Lauren butchered the roles of Stella and Blanche, respectively, during rehearsal.

Tess wasn't bad, but she kept overacting to compensate for her loss to Lauren for Blanche's role.

She also complained about it, often.

"Blanche has so much more meat! Stella is meek and timid."

"Grow up, Tess. Learn how to be graceful in defeat." Lauren snorted.

"I never lose," Tess replied, her tone taking an edge I'd never heard before.

Lauren tossed her hair and smiled at her serenely. *"That so? Then how come you're not on West. St. Claire's arm right about now?"*

Aiden, who played Stanley, wasn't exceptionally bad either, but he needed to tone down his frowning and glaring. He looked so constipated I worried people would throw Pepto-Bismol onstage instead of flowers at the end of the show.

About halfway through rehearsal, someone slid into the seat next to me. Peculiar, seeing as all the other seats were empty. Even though I didn't turn to look at him, I knew exactly who it was. It frightened me that I recognized him so quickly.

His scent of winter, candy apple, and alpha male. Wild and unique.

I balanced my feet on the back of the seat in front of me, trying to refocus on the actors onstage. I was still mad at West. Mainly because he'd screwed someone else last Friday while mumbling my nickname. But the official reason was him embarrassing me to no end by making a big stink out of how Reign had treated me. I'd sailed through college ignoring the odd taunt. Reign De La Salle was one of many idiots

I'd learned to overlook. West had redirected the limelight to my face again, and now everybody was talking about me—my story, my face, my hopeless future.

It was like high school all over again.

West draped his muscular arm over my headrest. His body language was indifferent, dripping confidence; he took something out of his front pocket—a small planner—and dropped it in my lap.

"Circle the date."

I ignored him, still glaring at the stage.

"When you're letting me out of the doghouse," he explained.

I pressed my lips together, resisting a faint smile, pouring metaphorical lava over the butterflies swirling in my stomach, taking flight upwards to my chest.

They were exactly the reason keeping my distance from him was a good idea.

The man had heartbreak written all over him.

"No can do. This planner doesn't go beyond mid-next year," I drawled, my eyes still trained on the stage. I didn't need to look to know planners didn't go beyond twelve months. Tess threw her head back during a scene, trying to steal Lauren's limelight.

The scene was cut due to the fact Lauren stumbled all over her lines.

"Dang it! She threw me off focus." Lauren stomped, choking the manuscript in her hand.

Tess parked her fists on her waist, puffing her cheeks.

"Nothing should throw you off when you're in the zone. I'm a method actor, Lauren. Untouchable once I get into character. I've been telling Professor McGraw for weeks that I should be Blanche. I was born for the role."

Secure in her stance she'd been robbed out of the role while Lauren tried to memorize her next few sentences, Tess' feline eyes began to wander the rows. They stopped and widened, a glint of excitement zinging through them when she noticed us. She gave us a wave.

"West! Grace! Howdy!"

I waved back. West jerked his chin forward, a barely noticeable hello, and cut his gaze back to me.

"What about probation?" he asked. "It's my first offense."

I shook my head. "Third. You've been gettin' on my nerves since day one."

"Damn you, woman, you think working with you is a picnic?" He bristled.

"I'm sure it's not, but I don't butt into your business and draw unwelcome attention to you," I pointed out.

"What am I charged with here exactly?" He rearranged his mammoth frame in his seat, his whole body angled toward mine now.

"You made a big stink out of what De La Salle said, and now I'm this pathetic emo kid who is at your mercy. You made me look helpless. Weak. A charity case." I turned my head, meeting his eyes.

The twinge in my chest became a full-on pull.

"So, you're mad at me for sticking up for you?" His eyebrows pinched together.

"I can fight my own wars."

"Bullshit. You've never once shown up for battle."

"That's none of your business."

"You *are* my business." He examined me, greatly enjoying the way my entire face turned pink under my makeup.

"I figured I am. I just wonder why that is. Did you need a pet project? I thought you had plenty on your plate already."

"Because you're my *friend*." His eyes narrowed into two slits of grim resolution. That was it. I was his friend, and I didn't have a say in this. "When someone disrespects my friends, they disrespect me. And *nobody* disrespects me. We clear about that?"

I turned my head to the stage, but only because I didn't trust myself not to launch at him with a hug. I'd never had anyone burst into my life, kicking the door down on their way in, and stick around after realizing how truly broken I was.

West was the first person to insist on being my friend, whether I was interested or not. It was uncharted territory for me. My instincts told me to push him away before he did the dumping, but every single cell in my body screamed to let him in.

He threw his arms in the air, exasperated. "Fine. You want me to back off? You got it. Either way, the asshole won't bother you anymore, so there's that."

"Woo-hoo. Thanks, Captain St. Claire." I fist-pumped the air mockingly. Now I had West's word he wasn't going to butt into my life. But I still wasn't placated. If anything, after the initial exhilaration of West seeking me out publicly at the auditorium, I was even angrier than before.

I knew exactly why—Melanie—but I couldn't tell him that.

"You realize you're being a bitch, right? You can't not-know that."

I knew I was being impossible, and it killed me that I couldn't stop. My shiny red self-destruction button was switched on, and I wanted to hit the bastard again and again with my fist, until there was nothing left of our friendship, so I could go back to being alone and invisible and safe in my bubble of nothingness.

His phone danced in his hand. He killed the call before I could see the name on the screen.

Melanie asking for a second round? Did you tell her you're a one-night kind of guy?

"What is this really about, Texas?" He raked his eyes over my face.

Cruz Finlay, the play's director, looked up from beside the stage and waved the script in our direction. "Excuse me, do you mind? You're distracting my actors."

"Your actors are distractin' us," I muttered under my breath. West snorted next to me.

"Grace. West!" Tess gestured at us again. "What's happening? Are y'all here for me?"

Tess was great, but she had the tendency to think the world revolved around her. Guess it grated on my nerves so much because I used to be exactly like her.

My stomach twisted into knots. If I chose to get flustered every time West received female attention, I'd go through a mental breakdown three times a day.

West stood up, jerking my arm, forcing me to my feet.

"Here for Texas. Now that I got her, I'll get outta your hair."

He saluted a shocked Tess and dragged me out the doors like a caveman. I didn't want to cause a scene, so I refrained from smacking his hand away. Once we were out of the auditorium, he pinned me against the wall, boxing me with his arms on each side of my body. His phone beeped again. He ignored it, angling his face down so his lips were dangerously close to mine.

The earthy, male scent of him seeped into my system. My heart beat so wildly I almost threw up.

"Let's try this again. Why are you mad at me, Texas? Don't give me the Reign excuse. I wasn't born yesterday."

"People are goin' to talk, now that you came to the auditorium and called me Texas in front of everyone. Hope you're happy."

He shrugged, unfazed. "The amount of fucks I give equals the amount of shit I give. Which is zero, in case you're wondering. Don't change the subject."

"You don't care if people think you are hookin' up below your league?" I taunted.

"I don't care if people think I'm hooking up with livestock. And you're not below my league. Now, I'm going to ask you this a third and last time—why are you mad? Answer carefully. There won't be a fourth chance. I'll flip you upside down and shake the answer out of you."

"You wouldn't." I scoffed.

His eyebrows shot up, a mischievous sneer curling over his lips.

Crap, he totally would. I deflated. "I'm not mad at you. I just want you to stop actin' like I'm a charity case. I've been doin' fine on my own, and I don't want the attention you bring to me."

He scanned me, looking for cracks in my façade.

Finally, he relented, pushing back from the wall. I felt the loss of him everywhere.

"If I stop bringing attention to your ass, are you going to go back to being relatively sane?"

"I *am* sane."

"Debatable."

"Tell me one thing that's insane about me."

"You wear hoodies when it's a hundred and twelve degrees out, you're nurturing an unhealthy obsession with the nineties, you think you're unattractive, you br—"

"Okay. Fine, I get it. I said *one.*"

He tucked a candy stick between his straight teeth, smiling like the Devil.

"I'm a competitive bastard. Once I start, it's hard to stop. Truce?" He offered me his pinky.

All I could think about was him kissing Melanie roughly as he'd unbuttoned her jeans, my nickname falling from his lips. My own lips stung, but I curled my pinky in his, almost laughing at how large his finger was against mine. It was the second time we'd done that. I liked that we had a thing.

"Ready to bail?" He nudged me.

"Bail where?"

"Austin. I just got a text from Karlie that the truck broke down and we don't have a shift. My schedule's wide open."

I frowned and checked my phone. Sure enough, I had the same text. Still, spending time with West outside work? That would be a big fat no with never-and-ever on top.

"No can do. I have rehearsals back-to-back."

"I don't know how to break it to you, but nothing is going to salvage this play. It's the worst thing to happen to Texas since the Jonas Brothers." West made an adorable face, a cross between genuinely sorry and sarcastic.

"Don't you dare hate on the Jonas Brothers. They're a national treasure." I wagged my finger at him, a giggle bubbling from my throat.

"That's a plot twist." He snatched my finger, tugging me toward him. "I pegged you for a My Bloody Valentine type of girl."

"I do know bands that were formed after the nineties," I protested.

"Prove it. But before that, let's hit the road."

With everything going on, it would be nice to unwind and take the day off. Besides, I'd already decided I wasn't going to fall in love with West St. Claire, and I'd been massively successful in not remotely liking guys before him.

What was the harm in one short trip to the city?

"You're twistin' my arm here." I sighed.

"I've been known for helping women discover their flexibility."

I scrunched my nose and shoved him away, savoring the hardness of his chest against my palm.

"Gross. I'll bring my backpack."

"Nuh-uh. I don't trust you to come back, and Cruz Finlay is one distraction away from a stroke. I'll fetch it."

He marched into the auditorium, returning with my backpack. He hoisted it over his shoulder as he flipped his keyring around his finger. I bounced on the balls of my feet, catching his long stride.

"Skipping. If I didn't know better, I'd think you are the h-word." He grinned.

"High?" I asked, still skipping to my displeasure.

Just stop. You're embarrassing yourself.

He laughed, slanting his gaze sideways, watching me. "No, doofus. Happy."

"I ain't happy."

"The shit-eating grin on your face begs to differ." He flicked my chin.

"You're rude."

"You're glowing."

I threw my hair over my shoulder, feeling unexpectedly pretty. My heart swelled, like it was soaked in water, and my whole body tingled.

"*Fuuuuuck,*" he drawled. "The sheer joy. Who even are you? Have I been catfished?" He stopped, picking me up from the floor and turning me sideways. He frowned, pretending to read something on my back. Instructions or a manual. He whistled. I kicked the air until he let me down, my giggles rolling out of my mouth uncontrollably.

We were doing a lot of touching—more touching than I'd done in the last four years, in fact—and the butterflies in my stomach were swirling and cartwheeling nonstop.

"Yup. You're the real Texas. I got the 2.0 version. Are you water-resistant?"

"Not at this time."

"Shame. I bet you're a sight in a two-piece."

"You're about to be cut into twenty pieces if you keep it up."

I felt like I was my old self again, and I didn't know why, but I thought he felt the same about himself, too.

That for some reason, we brought out in each other the previous people that we were and missed terribly.

We stopped by his Ducati. He took out two helmets, shoving one into my hands. This time, I turned around, ditched my ball cap, and put it on dutifully.

"Two helmets?" I turned back to face him when my helmet was on.

He shrugged. "Knew I was going to thaw your frigid ass."

"Are you always so confident?"

"Every second of the day." He spat out the apple candy in his mouth, putting his helmet on. "Are you always so nosy?"

"When I'm interested in something enough to explore it." I raised one shoulder. "While we're on the subject of my being nosy—what's with the apple candy? A bit dated, ain't it?"

"Not for me. Don't you have something that's nostalgic to you? A piece of your history that's close to your heart?"

Without meaning to, I brushed my fingers over my flame ring, feeling my throat working.

"I do, actually. This flame ring"—I lifted my hand—"belonged to my mom."

"It's …" He took my small, soft hand in his big, rough one, examining it. "*Hideous*. Anyway, the apple candy is it for me."

Feeling frisky, I grabbed one of them from his back pocket, where I knew he stashed them, and stuck it into my mouth under the helmet.

"It's … tasteless."

So tasteless, in fact, that I wondered what had him coming back to this specific candy, over and over again. Of course, if he wanted me to know, he'd volunteer the information.

West grinned, giving a lazy shake of his head.

I waited for him to mount the motorcycle then hopped behind him. He brought my arms to clasp his pecs. The engine roared to life. We zipped through the highway, bypassing a traffic jam, the desert wind licking at our bodies. I pressed against him, inhaling as much as I could of him. I loved wearing a helmet. It covered my face completely, giving the illusion I could be anyone. When I was like this, draped over a gorgeous man, my long blonde hair twirling, and all people could see was my body, it looked like I was normal. Just another girl going about her day.

No one could guess that my body and face were scarred.

That my grandmomma was sick.

That I was going to fail my semester this year.

The whole time, West's phone was vibrating in his pocket. I could feel it against my inner thigh. But I didn't want to chance ruining the moment by asking who it was.

We got to 2nd Street District, grabbed iced coffee, and walked around for a little while. The streets were crowded, booming with college kids and shoppers and blossoming flowerpots; light-decorated trees lined everywhere. The coffee shops poured with chattering youth. We talked about school and Friday night fights, and about my acting when West stopped dead on the curb and yanked my hoodie sleeve, causing a human traffic jam behind us.

"Jack. Fucking. Pot."

I looked up at the sign in front of us. It was a ball cap shop. I rearranged my faded gray cap self-consciously. I only took it off when I wore West's helmet or I was at home. He grabbed my hand, leading me inside.

"If you're going to hide your face under this thing for eternity, at least don't saddle me with the same old Nike logo. Keep shit fresh for me, Tex. That's the recipe for a good relationship."

"Fine, but you'll have to turn around when I try them. I must protect my virtue." I kept it light, shoving my fists back into my hoodie's pockets. We strolled between rows of hats. Unlike the street, the place was quiet. Other than a salesman in his late teens staffing the register, it was just the two of us.

"Not being seen is really that big a deal to you, huh?" West ran a hand over a dozen hats.

I thumbed through a stack of university-themed caps, shrugging.

"I like my privacy."

"You like being invisible."

"What's the problem with that?"

"That you're *not.*" He stopped walking, rubbing his knuckles against his chiseled jaw. "Let's compromise—I'll close my eyes every time you try a cap on and open them when you're ready. Trust me?"

"Why do you even care?" I stopped next to him, eyeing a baby pink cap with a cherry print on it. I was a girly girl and owned up to it prior to *The Fire*. I thought the cap would look super cute and wondered why I hadn't thought of buying a new one before. But the answer was obvious—I didn't think anyone was looking at me, and when they did, it was clearly for the wrong reasons.

"Texas, I can't even begin to tell you. The inside of this ball cap must smell like a used dental floss. I want you to own at least a dozen caps so you can alternate. Ball caps for weddings, funerals, parties, work, school …" His eyes caught the baby pink one I was holding. He grabbed it from my hand and slapped it against my sternum.

"Try it."

"Close your eyes."

"If I do, you can't turn around."

"Hey, that wasn't a part of the deal!" I protested.

"You were a cheerleader, right?"

"Yeah. Before—"

"What's the first thing they do in practice, before you make it to the team?"

I frowned, trying to remember. "Uh, trust falls?"

"Exactly. This is our trust fall. Trust I won't open my eyes."

"You told me trusting people is putting your optimism in the wrong place," I pointed out.

He twisted his face. "Don't listen to my ass. I'm just a fucking no-good punk who is only good with his knuckles."

"But …"

He put his finger to my lips. His eyes crinkled at the sides with a smile. I could tell it meant something to him. That I put my trust in him. Even if I didn't know why.

"I won't let you fall, Tex," he said quietly.

"Promise?"

"I don't promise. I never promise." He tsked. Wasn't that what he was doing? I wondered what made him so hell-bent on never promising even the smallest, most trivial things. "Try me."

The air was thick with silence as I considered his request. He squeezed his eyes shut. I took off my gray cap slowly, the adrenaline whooshing in my veins. I stared at him in shock, relishing the small liberating moment. I could practically feel his arms as I figuratively fell backward into them.

How he caught me.

How he kept his word and didn't sneak a peek.

I grabbed the pink cap. It wasn't bent on the sides, so when I put it on, West could still see a little more of my face than I was comfortable with. I secured it over my head, took a deep breath, and tapped West's shoulder to signal he could open his eyes.

"Decent?" he teased.

"Not by my standards," I mumbled.

His eyes fluttered open.

"*Whaddaya* think?" Even though it was only a cap, I motioned at my entire body, posing a-la Carrie Bradshaw in *Sex and the City*. It sounded stupid, but it felt like trying on a wedding dress.

He flashed me a lopsided, half-moon grin that made my knees weak, and whistled.

West reached for the cap and my heart stuttered. For a second, I could feel my body hitting the ground as he let go of me. But no. He didn't take it off. He bent it the way I liked it, so it shielded both sides of my face.

"You're beautiful," he said, his voice dropping low. "Cap's all right, too."

"Thank you." The softness in my voice jarred me. "And not cool, dude. If you bend it, you buy it."

"That's fake news. Ask any girl I've hooked up with."

I chuckled dully. I wasn't amused by the fact he was known for sleeping around.

"'Sides, we're buying it," he said flatly.

I turned around to change back to my old hat and checked the price, then proceeded to snort.

"For fifty-five bucks? You're kiddin' me."

"My treat."

"No." I shook my head. "You already got me dinner once. We can't make it a habit."

But he was swaggering to the register, spinning the pink cherry cap with his finger on his way there, not paying me any attention. I followed him, groaning. I knew he was going to do whatever he wanted.

"It's not a habit. It's a trade-off. I got you something I thought you needed, now it's your turn to get me something. How 'bout them apples?" He jerked his wallet chain (which my nineties heart had noted was very much in sync with my favorite era) and took it out, dropping a few notes on the counter in front of the salesman.

"Snap. You're West St. Claire. Sher U, right?" The guy's face brightened. They did a bro-shake.

"Saw your fight with Williams last year. You thrashed him. Is he still even alive?"

"Wouldn't bet on it." West stuck a green apple candy in his mouth, back to being his cocky, jerk self.

"You should go pro. You're the best fighter I've ever seen. You *go* there."

"You're a good kid," West said.

"Will you sign my cap?"

He did, and he also agreed to take a picture with the guy. We got out of the store in high spirits.

"So what do you think I need?" He was referring to our trade-off.

I tapped my lips, pretending to mull it over. "A genital guard."

He laughed. "You've got jokes, Texas."

"Hey, I wasn't the one who left you ballet shoes before I even knew your name."

West tugged his wallet back into his pocket, handing me the bag with my new cap. "You never acknowledged that. I wondered if it ever happened. I was starting to question my own sanity."

"You should do that regardless. But no, I got 'em. Still have them at home. Not sure what to do with them yet, but my poor girl complex wouldn't allow me to throw them out," I admitted, laughing. "Want them back?"

"Keep 'em. I'm not sure ballet is my field. I'm kind of a big girl." He feigned shyness, and I snorted, imagining him in a tutu.

After a quick cap change in an alleyway, I came back out with the pink cap. He catcalled me, and I swaggered past him, swaying my butt like I was some sort of femme fatale.

His phone buzzed again. He killed it.

"Aren't you gonna take that at some point?" I turned around and walked backwards, my eyes on him. "It's okay if you have better things to do."

"I don't have better things to do," he clipped, his mood changing back to sullen.

"Whoever is callin' might have somethin' important to tell you."

The more I thought about it, the more I realized a hookup wouldn't call him dozens of times a day. Worry settled in my gut. It was more serious than that.

"I'll be the judge of that. Your turn, Tex," he called out to me as I charged ahead. "Where to?"

"Ever had a Frito pie, *Maine*?"

His face broke into the goofiest, sweetest grin I'd ever seen. His eyes twinkled like fine jewels. I'd once watched a documentary about the fall of the Berlin Wall. Saw the thousands of people bringing hammers and bricks to it, demolishing it with their bare hands, glowing with triumph, buzzing with deep, dark ache. This was what I felt happened to my walls of defense the moment he truly flashed me a genuine smile. It was crumbling, brick by brick, as thousands of little Wests pounded their fists upon it, making it collapse.

"Can't say that I have." West tilted his head sideways.

"Let's get Christina, then. We have places to see. Frito pies to eat." He inclined his head, just as the last brick in my wall shattered.

"Lead the way."

"It's ... *odd*." West leaned back in his seat, dropping his fork directly into the Frito pie. I slapped a hand over my heart, gasping.

"Are you for real right now?"

He nodded, picking up his fork, dissecting the pie with a frown.

"What's in this thing, anyway? Beef, beans, cheese, enchilada sauce, tortilla chips, sour cream, corn, pecans ..." He started naming all the ingredients. "It reminds me of that time Rachel from *Friends* had two recipe pages stuck together and made that disgusting strawberry beef cake pie. You throw everything into this thing other than the kitchen sink."

"Oh." I smiled cheerfully. "The kitchen sink is there, all right. Right at the bottom. One layer away from the crust."

He burst out laughing. I signaled for the check and paid it. "Besides, I'll have you know, Joey liked that pie a lot."

"Joey liked eating everything. That was the joke."

"I take it you're a picky eater."

"Not really. Disgusting shit is where I draw the line." He scratched at his square jaw, giving it some thought. "And pussy. I don't eat pussy either."

I choked on my Diet Pepsi, spitting some of it back into my cup. "Excuse me?"

"You asked about my eating habits. Thought I'd be forthcoming."

"Why don't you …" I left the question unfinished. I never talked to guys about sex. Actually, I never talked to Karlie or Grams about it either. Marla was out of the question, for obvious reasons, too. It wasn't that I'd never done it. I had. When I was sixteen, with my ex-boyfriend, Tucker. But we'd never actually discussed it, and the experience was lackluster to say the least.

"Eat pussy?" He completed the question for me, enjoying my unease. "It seems like an intimate thing to do. I have nothing against pussies. Some of my favorite times were spent inside them. I just don't want to get too acquainted with ones who've been around the block. If I had a steady lay, well, that'd be a different story."

"Ever had a steady lay?"

He nodded.

"In high school. Ate her out for breakfast, lunch, and dinner. How 'bout you?"

"Same."

"Did he eat you out?" he asked, insultingly casual. I felt the tips of my ears growing impossibly hot.

"Yes."

"Did you reciprocate?"

"Of course. Equality for all, right?"

West sat back in his chair, his jaw ticking.

"Ever heard of positive discrimination? Whatever happened to feminism?"

I bit down on my lip, trying not to laugh. Was he actually *jealous*?

"I'm guessin' your oral sex rule doesn't apply to being on the receiving end?" I cocked an eyebrow. He smirked down at me, like he was proud that I was carrying the conversation without combusting into a thousand pieces of embarrassment.

"Correct. Never met a blowjob I didn't like."

"That's not very feminist."

"Hey, do you have any idea how many bras I've ruined in my lifetime?"

"And they say romance is dead." I rolled my eyes. He tugged my cap down. We were both incredibly at ease.

"Where to now, Tex?"

"Another Mexican dig," I said without missing a beat.

"*Another* pie?" His eyes flared in mock horror. "You're putting me through this again?"

"Sure am. Until you admit Frito pies are the best thing to happen to humanity since agriculture and language."

"Frito pies are the best thing to happen to humanity since agriculture and language," he deadpanned.

I laughed. "Nice try."

We got out of the restaurant and walked into the one next to it. He didn't like the Frito pie there either. After the third one I made him try, he got up from his seat and shook his head.

"No more Frito pies. It's against my human rights."

"C'mon, don't be so narrow-minded," I teased, catching his steps. My face hurt from laughing, and I wondered if it was because we'd had that much fun, or because I wasn't used to laughing anymore. "We were just warmin' up."

"I'm vetoing the pie." He shook his head, flipping his keys around his index.

"*Maine*," I whined.

"*Texas*."

I jerked his hand, but he didn't budge, soldiering toward his Ducati.

"Pretty please with a cherry on top," my purr turned flirty—raspy, even—as sixteen-year-old Grace took the reins over my mouth.

"Of course there'd be a cherry on top. You put everything else into this pie."

My heart, bloated with glee and soaked with laughter, began to deflate. It was nearing late afternoon. Truth was, I wasn't too hot on another Frito pie either. I just didn't want to leave. To go back to Sheridan. Let the West and Grace bubble burst. I wanted to continue being careless and happy. To feel beautiful—or at least not hideous—for a few more hours.

West stopped by the Ducati, handing me my helmet. I quickly changed from my cap to the helmet, shoving both my ball caps into the bag I was given by the salesman.

We rode back to Sheridan in silence, my hair whipping my neck and shoulders. When we reached Sheridan limits, West took a turn toward downtown, to Main Street.

"It's my birthday today," he said out of nowhere.

"What?!" I shrieked into his ear. My voice was muffled by the wind and helmet. "It is?"

He grunted, "Yeah."

"How old?"

"Twenty-two years young."

"Holy shit."

"Way to make me feel good about it, Tex."

"You bought me a gift on your birthday. This is all wrong. Stop. Stop right now."

He stopped by the Albertsons grocery store. I ran inside without taking off my helmet, then came back out with a bottle of tequila wrapped in a brown paper bag and some birthday candles. They were the cheapest kind, but better than nothing at all. I hopped back on, wrapping my arms around him.

"To Sheridan Plaza," I instructed.

"Have you started drinking without me? Why would I do that?" He whipped his head around, his stormy eyes zeroing in on mine through his helmet.

"I've never been there," I admitted hoarsely.

He tore his helmet from his head, the engine still running, and scowled. I was lucky I still had my helmet on, because West St. Claire's face so close to mine, his lips a breath away from my mouth, was the definition of seduction. A film of sweat made his tousled, gold-brown hair stick to his temples and forehead and his carved cheekbones glow under the sun.

"You're shitting me."

I shook my head.

"You grew up in Sheridan and never been to the Plaza?"

I nodded.

"Fine. But you're not allowed to go there by yourself. Promise me."

"*No promises.*" I wiggled my eyebrows, throwing his rule back in his face. "Tit for tat. Why don't you want me to go there?"

"The place is a cum dumpster."

"Isn't that where you hook up with all your lady friends?" I kept my tone light.

"Hence why it's a cum dumpster. It's no place for a lady." He pushed his helmet back on and kicked his foot forward, getting back on the road.

When we reached Sheridan Plaza, West parked at the back, leading me inside. The ground floor was empty, save for a few soggy mattresses, cigarette butts, and red Solo cups strewn about. We took the concrete stairs up to the second floor. The left wing, which was probably meant to be a food court, was vast and empty. There were gym mats scattered around, framed by crates and boxes to create a ring, with enough space around it to contain at least a hundred people. The right wing of the floor consisted of small rooms that were supposed to be the stores, where there were yet more mattresses in each small alcove. Like filthy individual motel rooms. No wonder people liked coming here. The place was a makeshift brothel.

West showed me around quickly, clasping my hand in a punishing grip, like the vibes in this place could suck my tender soul straight into hell. He held the paper bag with the tequila bottle in his free hand.

"That's basically it. Third floor is management. It's where our offices are," he said, not a trace of sarcasm in his voice. I snorted.

"Do you work nine-to-five?"

"More like sixty-nine." We took the stairway to the third floor.

The minute I saw the elevator bank in front of me, my smile collapsed. He couldn't see that, since he had his back to me.

So that was where he took all of his hookups.

Where he and Melanie melded together into one.

I needed to say something to change the subject, quick.

"What do you wanna do? When you graduate this year?" I swiveled to face him, clearing my throat.

He ran a hand through his hair, the A tattoo in his flexed inner bicep taunting me, reminding me how little I knew about him.

"Sharp change of subject. Guess I haven't thought about it."

"Don't you have any preference? Ideas? Aspirations?"

"No, no, and no." He stopped, turned his back to me, and lifted his arms in the air. "I don't want to talk about the future. Trust fall, Tex. *Catch.*"

Before I knew what was happening, his body swung toward mine. I let out a little wheeze, opening my arms to try to clasp him. *Crap.* I needed more time to prepare. He was heavy. *Really* heavy. I fell right along with him, crushed by his weight, and winced, bracing myself for the cold concrete behind me. But when he fell on top of me, his whole body pressed over mine, I realized there was a mattress behind me that blocked the fall.

That's why he'd done it.

He knew I didn't have time to catch him, but also that we'd both fall onto something soft. He'd just wanted to see if I'd *try* to catch him. *Damn this man.*

I cackled, shoving him off of me. He rolled around, popping the tequila bottle open. He was about to take a swig, but I snatched it from his hand before he could.

"Not so fast, birthday boy. I would like to make a toast."

He sat up, listening intently. Seriously. He looked like a curious kid all of a sudden, about to be given a very important lecture about his favorite subject.

It broke my heart to see him hungry for my words, because it was clear he didn't want to celebrate his birthday. He didn't do anything with his friends and didn't bother telling me about it until later today.

In fact, he was planning to work a shift at the food truck.

For some reason, West St. Claire wasn't very happy he'd been born, and knowing that nearly undid my soul, breaking it to pieces.

"I would like to make a toast to a very special friend of mine, who, despite my being stubborn and sometimes a handful, is always there for me." I tried to keep my tone casual, but I was pretty emotional, re-alizing all the things I said weren't an exaggeration of the truth.

West rolled his eyes. "Get to the part where you talk about me, you little shit."

I swatted his shoulder. "I don't care what the entire universe says about you, West St. Claire. I don't care that you are a fighter and you ride a monster named Christina and that you're a man-whore. To me, you're just a cool guy who always does the right thing, and that's enough. No." I felt myself flushing. "It's more than enough. It's every-thing. Happy birthday, jerk-face."

I tipped my head back, took a swig of the tequila, and passed it to him, embracing the burning sensation slithering down my throat. We stayed on that mattress for two whole hours, drinking and talking. The conversation was all over the place, ranging from our childhoods to football, TV shows and music, then books. The more we drank, the less we made sense, until we both had two completely separate conversations at the same time.

By the time we finished the bottle, it was dark outside. The Plaza got surprisingly chilly. We were both perched on the mattress, our arms brushing, staring at the ceiling.

"Know what I feel like?" I asked.

"Pushing me away for no fucking reason other than your heighten sense of self-preservation?" he asked dryly. I snickered. Touché.

"Some real Mexican food to soak up all the alcohol."

He picked up the empty tequila bottle, squeezing one eye shut as he stared into the bottom of it. "You mean, like fish tacos and tortilla chips?"

"Exactly."

"Don't know where we can find something like that 'round here."

We exchanged knowing grins. It wasn't right, and it wasn't okay, but it made perfect sense. Hell, we'd broken so many rules today, one more wouldn't kill us.

And really, Mrs. Contreras would never find out.

"Are you thinkin' what I'm thinkin', birthday boy?" My grin widened.

"I'm thinking Texas just got a whole lot more fun."

We staggered into the food truck, locking it behind us, keeping the window shut. I turned around and pressed my index to my mouth.

"*Shhh!*"

"We're both quiet, dummy." He gave my neck a squeeze, chuckling as he brushed past me.

West flicked on the light and turned on the grill while I cut vegetables. I prepared soft tacos, stuck the birthday candles on them, and lit them up. Since the truck had come back from the shop, we were a few ingredients short, like sour cream and guac, but we were too drunk to care.

I butchered the song "Happy Birthday," somehow missing all the notes, and let West blow out the candles.

"What did you ask for?" I rubbed his arm, placing my chin on his shoulder as we both watched the thin trail of smoke curling up from the candles.

"If I tell you, you promise not to dig into the subject?"

"Sure."

"I mean it, Tex. I don't want you going girly on my ass. The only reason we're here is because you're *not* that person."

"Spill it out, boy." I laughed.

"I asked to never want to die again."

My throat clogged up, and it got all quiet, but I kept my word, not pressing the issue. "Then I'll wish for that, too," I said softly.

We sat on the floor and ate broken, distressed tacos while I asked him *this or that* nineties questions. I decided not to dig into why West befriended me anymore. Instead, I'd run with what we had going and see where it took us.

I hadn't been this happy in years, and that had to count for something.

West was in the midst of explaining to me why fanny packs were boner killers when someone rapped the window outside the truck.

"Hello? Anybody there?"

We both fell silent, staring at each other with wide eyes, mid-bites. I clasped my lips together, stifling a laugh. I rarely got drunk anymore, and I forgot how giggly I turn once I get tipsy.

"Hey, the lights are on," the man outside the truck said. Gravel crunched beneath his shoes as he rounded the truck. He was probably trying to peek inside through the window cracks. "Open up, y'all."

I slapped a hand over my mouth, trying to contain my laughter, but a small horrifying snort escaped my nose. West's eyes broadened, and he grinned big.

I covered my face, mortified that he'd heard, my whole body shaking with silent laughter.

"Look at the truck," one of the two people outside said, muffled. "It's shaking. Are you thinkin' what I'm thinkin'?"

"I'm thinking if what you're thinking is true, they're definitely not going to open up for us, Rick, and I ain't eatin' no food from there either."

They thought we were having sex! Oh, Lord. I let out a second, uncontrolled snort, unable to hold it back, tipping backwards. West pounced on me, pinning me flat across the floor, straddling my waist and pressing his hand over my mouth to silence me.

Our tacos were discarded around us, and all the air left my lungs as I watched him on top of me, his groin pushed against my belly. Nothing about what he did was meant to be sexual. He just wanted me to shut the hell up so we wouldn't get in trouble. We weren't supposed to be here, and if Mrs. Contreras found out, she'd probably fire us both, her affection toward me be damned.

Still, my whole body came alive, and a small moan escaped me as his delicious weight pushed against me. I felt my nipples puckering against my bra. The friction against its fabric every time I moved made my mouth water. His thighs were so strong and muscular, I wanted him to hike up, unzip himself, and put his penis in my mouth.

West curled his fingers around my lips. I resisted the urge to lick his palm. I could feel his skin, rough and salty, against my mouth. He leaned deeper into me, engulfing me everywhere, so heavy I could barely breathe. His eyes were dead-set on mine. I wasn't laughing anymore. The people outside kept trying to look into the truck, flashing their phone's flashlights inside, decorating West's face with soft slivers of light.

Both our hearts thudded wildly, so fast I could hear them, almost see their imprints through our shirts.

The crunching became quieter, and the sound of crickets outside the truck enhanced. They were leaving.

West leaned all the way down, propping my ball cap sideways, resting his forehead over mine. Our chests bumped into one another with each violent breath. He closed his eyes. The tips of our noses touched. A heady, strange feeling overcame me. Something told me I was going to replay this moment in my head for years to come.

He removed his hand from my mouth and tugged on an electric cord next to us, turning the lights off.

Pound, pound, pound, went my heart.

"Texas." His whisper blanketed me, making me feel fuzzy and warm.

"Maine." My voice was thick, strange. Not mine.

The truck was so dark I couldn't see anything. My eyes were glued to what I imagined was the curve of his lips, and even though my brain told me a kiss was the worst possible thing that could happen to our friendship, the rest of me rebelled, desperate to feel his mouth on mine.

"Today didn't suck." His breath tickled my face.

I swallowed, losing my ability to speak. "No, it didn't." My lips moved a breath away from his.

"My birthdays usually suck," he explained.

"Oh."

I had officially stopped showing any signs of intelligence. I blamed his proximity. It made me drunker than the actual tequila.

"Texas," he said again.

"Maine?" I shook with anticipation.

"Permission to do something really fucking stupid, yet acutely necessary right now?"

My heart flip-flopped in my chest. I wasn't even sure what he was asking, but I was darn sure what my answer would be.

"Granted."

"Happy birthday to me." His mouth descended on mine in the pitch black.

Every cell in my body blossomed and sang. I arched my back, my mouth falling open to accommodate his tongue. The brush of his lips against mine sent a shiver down my spine, and I growled, the blood in my veins sweet and sticky.

West's phone buzzed to life again. He pulled away quickly, breaking the trance we were in. He scrambled up to his feet, turning the light on, and I followed suit, gathering the discarded taco pieces as he turned his back to me and finally picked up the call.

"Yeah?" He sounded short of breath. Flustered. He was pacing now.

I busied myself, throwing the broken tacos into the trash, my eyes wandering discreetly to his jeans, detecting the outline of his erection. It was long, thick, and inviting. It was good to know that he was driving me mad, but that I was capable of doing the same to him.

Oblivious to my perverted thoughts, West turned around and ran a hand through his messy hair, giving me his back once again.

"Been busy."

Pause.

"Just hanging out with a friend."

Pause.

"Yeah, a she."

Pause.

"Because there's nothing to tell. She's just a friend. As I mentioned in my previous fucking sentence. You should do more memory puzzles, Mom. Give your brain a little workout."

Ouch.

"Feels about the same as last year." He let out an icy, impersonal chuckle. "Anyway, gotta run. Say hi to Dad from me. Bye now."

He shoved his phone into his back pocket and turned around, his cool, collected expression making me feel like I was a complete stranger. Like the entire day hadn't happened.

"Ready to hit the road? I don't know if I'm good to drive, but I'll walk you home." His jade eyes were hard as diamonds, and there was not even a hint of the warmth that swam in them a second ago.

"Was that your mom?"

I didn't think I'd ever heard anyone talking to their mother so impersonally. As someone who grew up without a mother, I always watched the interactions my friends had with theirs carefully. The bickering, the exasperation, the vein of love running between them in an invisible cord.

The closeness varied, but there was always this underlying, built-in familiarity that wasn't there between West and his mother.

"Yeah." He helped me clean up the floor, going about everything quickly and efficiently, avoiding my gaze. Whatever that phone call had meant, it had thrown him off-kilter. "My friends know better than to try to celebrate my birthday, but my mother still tries."

Why didn't he celebrate his birthdays?

And why had he chosen to share this one with *me*?

I knew I wasn't going to get any answers. Not tonight.

I rubbed his arm with a smile. "Wanna say hi to Grams?"

"Are you kidding?" He scoffed. "Only reason I hang out with your sorry ass is to get close with Mrs. S."

West

And the Idiot of the Decade Award goes to …

Me.

It was going straight to my fucking open arms.

Kissing Texas was by far the craziest thing I'd done since moving to … well, *Texas.*

She'd been drunk enough to let it happen, and I was dumb enough to piss all over my rules.

My unlikely savior was my mother. The second I'd heard my phone ringing, I remembered.

Remembered why I was here.

Why I'd never go back to Maine.

Why I didn't do girlfriends or serious relationships or had a plan for the future.

East was right—I liked Grace Shaw, and if I didn't keep my hands to myself, I was about to drag both of us into a clusterfuck she didn't deserve and I had no idea how to get out of.

No promises, no disappointments.

That was my motto in life.

Grace and I walked side by side. She was still buzzed, bouncing around and talking animatedly. She was cute with her little pink cap and blonde hair. A part of me couldn't wait for the moment she'd see past her own insecurities and open up. Guys would start asking her out the minute she stopped giving them the don't-get-close signals. Another part of me wanted to skin each and every one of those motherfuckers and make drum kits for orphans out of their flesh. They didn't deserve her. I didn't know who 'they' were per se. Just faceless, hopefully dick-less dudes.

"…said she might not let me pass this semester. Which is actually frightening. But I can't go onstage. I know there's some good special effects makeup, but what's the point in that? Everyone would be trying to drill a hole through my makeup with their eyes to see my new face. The play would take the backseat, and my freaky new face would be the talk of town. No, I can't go onstage. Not without the ball cap. Which, let's admit it, isn't really an option," I heard Grace explaining in the background, and fuck, I'd blanked out again, this time thinking about what it'd have been like to finish that kiss. To have more than the quick peck we'd managed to slip through before I got a phone call.

"Who?" I asked as we reached her doorstep.

"Professor McGraw." She stopped by the low gate leading to her house. "You wandered off, didn't you?" She reached to stroke my hair to one side, trying to make it resemble something neat. I'd only cut it every few months, and even that only happened when East literally sat my ass down and put scissors to it.

I groaned, looking away. Girls touched me, constantly. Giving me head, kissing me, groping me, riding me. But it'd been a hot minute since anyone had touched me like *that*. With care instead of lust. No one since Whitley had, anyway.

The door swung open and an older woman breezed out, swinging her purse over her shoulder. "Honey pie, I saw the porch lights turning on. I left you some food in the microwave, if the old bat didn't get to it yet. Sorry I don't have time to wait till you take your shower. Pete's coming down with somethin'. No time to piddle. Call if you need me."

"Thanks, Mar." Texas reached on her toes to hug the woman. We both walked up to her porch. Marla clapped my shoulder on her way to her car in hello.

"Treat her nicely, boy, or I'll be sure to acquaint you with my shotgun."

Fucking Texas.

"I'll entertain Mrs. S while you get a shower," I offered Grace as Marla took off in her Dodge. The shotgun remark passed over her head like Marla had offered me tea.

"Oh, it's fine. Really." She blushed under her makeup.

"That's a statement, not an offer. Move it." I pressed a hand against her lower back, close enough to her ass to get my mind rolling. My dick strained inside my jeans, and I couldn't wait to get home and rub one out.

Texas bolted upstairs to the shower, and I strolled into the living room, making myself at home. It looked old, but the foundation around it was pretty new, which told me all I needed to know. There was a fire here, and parts of the house were remodeled.

Savannah was sitting on a recliner in front of the TV, knitting something that looked like a never-ending scarf. Her eyes were blank, her mouth pressed into a thin line of discontent.

I sat in front of her. "Hey, Mrs. Shaw. Remember me?"

She looked up from her twelve-foot scarf, above the rim of her glasses, then dropped her gaze back to her knitting.

"Of course I do," she said, her tense expression relaxing. "You're my husband, Freddie."

Ten minutes later, Texas was out of the shower, and I was one hundred percent sure her grandmother had dementia. Mrs. S spent the time I'd been watching over her asking me about people I didn't know and apparently worked with, recited entire conversations we hadn't had, and treated me like I was her dead husband. This wasn't an act. She had no clue who I was.

Grace came down the stairs, taking them two at a time, wearing an oversized, long-sleeved shirt she used as pajamas. Her legs were bare, and my eyes licked them greedily. Her legs were perfect. Tan and long and athletic. I could easily visualize them wrapped around my waist.

But I didn't.

Because we were JUST FUCKING FRIENDS, as I kept forgetting. Maybe I needed to stick a Post-It note to the insides of my eyelids. *Just* and *Friends*.

My pupils finally slid up to the rest of her. She was wearing the ball cap, and her face was full of freshly applied makeup.

We playing it like that, huh, Tex?

I stood up.

"Thanks so much for doin' this. I really appreciate it." Grace threw her arms around me when she reached the landing, giving me a squeeze. Her tits pressed against my pecs. She wasn't wearing a bra.

West Junior made a mental note to do her more solids if she repaid us in hugs. She led me back to the front door, her polite way to tell me to get the fuck out.

"What's with the makeup?"

"What's with the screwed-up relationship with your parents?" she ricocheted back to my court, opening the door for me.

Touché.

I flicked the back of her ear. "For the sake of full disclosure, if you cage in on me tomorrow at school, I'm going to hurl your ass into the fountain and scrub every inch of that face clean of makeup."

She grinned. "I ain't doin' that no more. Pinky promise." She gave me her pinky. I wrapped her pinky in mine and pulled her into my body, kissing her unmarred cheek. She gasped. I drew back, smirking back at her before she had the chance to freak out.

I stepped down her porch stairs, feeling surprisingly light, even though it was my birthday, and my birthdays were the worst days of my life.

I stopped at the last squeaky step, turning around, knowing she was still at the door.

"Hey, Texas?"

She rested her forehead against the door, smiling at me sleepily.

"You should open up a little."

"So should you."

"I think I am."

It was the first birthday in the last five years where I'd actually cracked a smile. Which was insane to think about. It made me feel guilty as hell. No wonder Mom, Dad, and East had called me all day. They probably thought I'd finally offed myself.

That this time I had a deer-on-the-road moment I managed to seize.

Grace bit her bee-stung lower lip in a way that told me she was fighting one of her make-the-world-melt grins.

"I think I am, too."

Chapter Ten

Grace

I WAS CLEANING UP THE AUDITORIUM, DOING MY JOB AS A STAGE assistant, the evening my first phoenix feather finally peeked out of its ashes.

It was the day after my almost-kiss with West. Tess and Lauren were the last to leave, after staying late and rehearsing some of their scenes together. Lauren was still struggling to get all her lines right. She blamed it on a recent breakup with her boyfriend Mario. Tess had been working the angle of passive-aggressively coaxing her into convincing Professor McGraw to switch roles. She argued that Stella didn't have as many lines and her role wasn't as emotionally draining.

"Seriously, Lor, just tell Finlay and McGraw you've got too much on your plate. Switch to Stella. You'll get an A+ and would only have to memorize half the lines."

I tidied up around them, moving the mop around their feet. They both waved me goodbye, with Tess' eyes lingering on me a moment too long, as if noticing my existence for the first time. I had no doubt it had everything to do with West snatching me from the auditorium the other day.

After I finished mopping, I rearranged all the props backstage, hanging the costumes on the racks.

Humming "No Me Queda Más" by Selena to myself (because: '90s and Selena were *double* the win), my thoughts wandered to West. Specifically, to his relationship with his parents. He was angry, that was for sure. He'd been cagey about them, but from what I'd pieced together, they were struggling financially, and he was breaking his back trying to help them.

About to turn the lights off, I paused on the threshold between the stage and the backstage, peeking through the burgundy curtains. I loved the stage's floor. It was my favorite. It was full of scratches and dents, from actors and dancers wearing it down over the years.

Beaten and broken, it was still capable of creating the greatest magic.

Without really meaning to, I found myself taking a step toward the center of the stage, swallowing hard.

"You need to open up."

West's words tickled the bottom of my belly.

Another step.

"Don't roll over and play dead."

The next one was my grandmother's.

"If you're not scared, you're not being brave."

Before I knew what was happening, my feet hurried across the stage.

Tap, tap, tap.

My heart accelerated, my mouth dried up, and my breath stuttered in my throat.

I stopped and stood there, in the middle of the stage.

Alone.

Brave.

Scared.

But undefeated.

I took off my pink ball cap, took a deep breath, and let out an earth-shattering scream that pierced through the walls and made the entire place shake. It lasted long seconds before subsiding, its last echoes still dancing in my lungs.

I smiled and bowed to the rows upon rows of empty red velvet seats.

I imagined the auditorium full of people. They were clapping and cheering for me, rising to their feet in a standing ovation.

I felt a little part of my phoenix peeking out of the ashes.

Not an entire wing, but one lonely perfect feather.

It was red. The color of my scar.

It reminded me of myself.

"There's a fight this Friday. I thought maybe you changed your mind about coming." Karlie was plopped on her bed next to me, her nose stuck in a textbook.

I scrunched my nose, hugging her pillow to my chest as I leaned against her headboard. "Why would I change my mind?"

"For one thing, rumors travel fast, and Tess has been telling everyone West freakin' St. Claire whisked you away from the auditorium last week. People think you two are bumping uglies now. The one interesting thing to ever happen to us in, like, five years, and you forget to tell me about it." She rolled her eyes, turning a page in her textbook and running a marker over an entire paragraph. "I'm five seconds away from dumping your ass, Shaw. You're a bad best friend."

I laughed, throwing the pillow in her face. "There's nothing to tell. We're just friends."

"Riiiiiight. And denial is just a river in Egypt."

"I'm not in denial."

"Not even a teeny-tiny bit?" Karl dropped her textbook in her lap, pinching her fingers together, looking at me through the gap between them with an impish grin. There was no point telling her about a kiss that hadn't happened and was promptly branded as a mistake by West before he backed out of it.

"I swear, it's totally platonic. He is a commitment-phobe who loves variety. I'd be an idiot to fall for a guy like that."

I am the idiot who is halfway there.

"You don't choose who you fall in love with."

"Maybe, but you do choose how to act on things," I countered.

Karlie rearranged her limbs, sitting crisscrossed on her white duvet, leaning against her poster-filled wall. Pearl Jam and Third Eye Blind and Green Day. Her room was a nineties shrine, including a Discman on her nightstand, Beanie Babies on her bed, and an old-school see-through phone.

Karlie was born at the end of 1999. The last day of the year to be exact. December thirty-first, at eleven fifty-eight at night. That made her obsessed with the era, and whatever Karlie liked—I loved. It was the natural, courteous thing for me to do to join her obsession for moral support.

"Look, I'm studying how to become a reporter, and call it an investigative knack, but I ain't buying what you're selling, Shaw. The reality is you're both single, and hot, and you spend a *lot* of time together." She popped her watermelon gum in my face.

"He also spends a lot of time inside other girls, like Melanie and Tess," I murmured.

"True, but I've never seen him hanging out with them one-on-one." Karlie grabbed her textbook, placing it back in her lap and highlighting the bejesus out of it, her eyes glued to the page. "And it's been a while since Tess. Just remember what I said, Shaw. He might be nice, but he's trouble."

"Actually ..." I sat up straight, feeling bizarrely protective toward West. "He's not trouble at all. He's really nice. The other day, he noticed Marla went home before I had a chance to take a shower and watched over Grams for me for a few minutes."

"That's why I'm reopening the invitation to go to his fight on Friday." She flipped another page in her textbook.

"Because he is nice to me?" I blinked, confused.

"No, because he is putting up a front. He is on his best behavior at the food truck because it's a different environment, but he is still a beast."

She rolled her eyes when I didn't respond.

"Look, aren't you curious to see if your friendship is just a food truck thing or goes beyond it?"

Curious? I was *rabid* to find out. My communication with West at school was nonexistent. He'd taken my request not to draw any attention for me extra far and didn't even acknowledge me when we passed each other.

It was like I didn't exist to him.

A part of me didn't want to find out what we were outside of our bubble, but a bigger part of me realized I had to find out whether I was a convenient friend he kept in secret and was ashamed of or a person he considered his equal.

"Fine," I bit out. "I'll go to the fight."

"Yes!" Karlie pumped her fist in the air. "That's my girl. Now let's get slutty clothes to distract him."

"Wait, didn't you say dating him is a terrible idea?"

"Dating? Yes. Teasing? No. It is high time you realize you're hot shit, Shaw. And if West St. Claire is the guy to make you realize it, I'm all for it."

I grabbed one of her pillows, pressing it over my face and yelling into it in a mix of horror and excitement.

"Quick. If you could bring one thing back from the nineties, what would it be—Blockbuster or hot Keanu Reeves?" Karlie tapped my knee.

I dumped the pillow on the floor, my eyes nearly bugging out of their sockets. "Excuse you! Keanu Reeves is still bangin."

Karlie threw her head back, laughing. "Ding, ding, ding. That was a test. And you just passed with flying colors."

I stared at myself in the mirror, unable to stop myself from grinning like a loon.

Ten tons of foundation?—check.

Catlike eyeliner?—check.

Blow-dried hair?—check.

Sparkly pink lip gloss and a matching ball cap?—check.

Tiny, long-sleeved, black mini dress that showed off my legs?—triple check.

Karlie's honks blasted through my bedroom window, signaling her arrival. I bolted downstairs, my heart flipping desperately like wings. Grams was sitting in the living room, knitting and listening to a Johnny Cash record. She was having a good day, thank the Lord, but I still asked our neighbor, Harold, to check in on her a few times tonight.

"Church's out, Grams!" I hollered as I picked up my small clutch. I was dressed for a fancy club or a restaurant, not a fighting ring, but I couldn't help myself. It was the first night I'd gone out since I'd given up on having a social life, and it was a big deal for me.

Grandma waved her hand up in the air without lifting her eyes from her knitting.

"You be careful, Gracie-Mae. And if you drink, please give me a call. I'll pick you up."

I stopped dead in front of the door. She spoke like the old Grams. The coherent one. My throat burned with tears.

"Thank you," I said softly. "Karlie's the designated driver. She'll have a dry night, and so will I."

"Contreras blood runs true. Karlie took after her momma. She's a real good kid." Grams nodded approvingly, taking a sip of her tea.

Why couldn't she be like this all the time?

Karlie honked again, and I nearly jumped out of my skin.

"All right! I'm off!"

"Ta-ta. Oh, and Gracie-Mae?"

"Yeah?" I paused, halfway out the door.

"Come back home when the first streetlamp goes on. Curfew's at six-thirty, young lady."

It was already nine. My smile collapsed, and the dull ache in my chest resumed.

Not completely lucid after all.

"I'll be sure to do that, Grams."

We got to Sheridan Plaza ten minutes late and spent fifteen minutes driving around looking for a parking space. Karlie had to drive extra slow because there were clusters of people marching toward the Plaza, laughing, drinking, and making out. I hadn't realized the fighting ring was that big an event in Sheridan. Friday Night Lights had nothing on this thing.

I knew West wasn't the only guy who fought—there were about five fights every Friday—but he was always the main event and the reason tickets sold like hotcakes.

On our fourth round trying to find a parking space, a senior jock signaled Karlie to roll her window down. She did.

"Y'all gonna run outta gas if you keep circling the lot. Park wherever you can; they don't give out tickets around here, doll."

Karlie flashed me a disapproving glance.

"I didn't know your boy was *that* popular."

"Stop callin' him my boy," I half-asked, half-begged. I couldn't allow myself to believe it.

"You're right. If you date him, I will punch your tit. Your heart's too good for this guy, Shaw."

We parked and stabbed the dunes with our high heels, ascending toward the Plaza. We paid at the entrance—twenty bucks a pop, by no means a cheap night out—and proceeded inside.

There were dozens of people crammed into the second floor. College age crowd, but also a few randoms who were clearly in high school or way past twenty-five. Everybody was holding red Solo cups, chatting and laughing as two shirtless guys fought in the ring. They were clearly just the warm-up act, because nobody paid much attention.

There was no sign of West or his friends.

"I'll beer us." Karlie tilted her head toward a dude who stood behind a few crates, pouring keg beer into cups.

I nodded. "I'll go find West, wish him good luck."

"No canoodling." She waved a finger my way.

I saluted her before wandering about, scanning for his face. Realizing he was nowhere near the ring, I strolled toward the small bare rooms with the mattresses. At first, I peeked into each of them, trying to spot West. But after encountering a guy jerking off, half-dressed, as two cheerleaders licked each other, I passed them swiftly, not looking sideways.

Groans and moans rose from the mattresses in the coves. I hated this place. Absolutely despised it. And with every single second that ticked by, the possibility I was going to find West with someone else became more and more real. I wanted to be sick. Why had I thought it was a good idea to come here?

He warned you not to. Called it a cum dumpster. You are not even welcome here.

I was about to turn around and run for my life when his gruff voice came from behind one of the concrete walls.

"You need to give it a rest," West growled.

"Question is, do you give Tess a rest?" another voice—Easton, I assumed by his neutral, sensible tone, countered. "You know, between rounds."

There was a burst of male laughter and the sound of beer cans cracking open.

"Don't tell me you're still tapping her ass?"

That was *definitely* Reign De La Salle speaking. My stomach churned and twisted. The guy was a total tool.

"Relax, asshole. You know I never tap it twice. Although, I'm not opposed to fucking her every which way if you continue getting on my nerves."

"Is that a threat?" Reign screeched.

"Nah, it's a promise."

"You don't make any promises," Easton pointed out. That much was true.

"For an ass like Tess', I'm willing to make an exception."

I stumbled backwards before I heaved and threw up. A sharp stab of jealousy cut me open. I bled out so many dark feelings, my head was spinning.

Wariness. Distrust. Heartbreak.

Lord, why did it feel like my heart had been blown to the sky? He hadn't even kissed me, and I was already scarily possessive toward him.

Dashing back toward the ring, I glanced behind my shoulder to make sure they didn't see me.

"Shaw! There you are!" Karlie jumped into my vision, holding two Solo cups in her hands. She pushed one into my palm.

"I made sure the guy opened a brand-new beer and poured it in front of me, so it's not spiked or watered down. Well? Did you find lover boy?"

"I did," I hissed. "And without gettin' into detail, lover boy loves having sex with Tess, so I guess now we know where I stand."

She gasped, a glint of curiosity lighting up her eyes. "You caught them together?"

"No, I overheard him declaring his intentions toward her."

"Told you he was bad news."

"You also told me to come here." I sighed.

"True." She shrugged. "We've never done this before, and I really wanted to see what all the fuss was about."

I shouldered my way to the first row of viewers as Karlie trailed behind me, changing the topic to her workload at school. I tried to tell myself that it was better that way. West wasn't mine. His body belonged to everyone else, and his heart was unreachable to anyone on the planet, himself included.

The fight in front of us came to an end.

Then the drumrolls came.

Max Riviera stepped onto an actual soap box and cupped the sides of his mouth.

"And now, ladies and gents, to our main event. Knox Mason against the one and only. The man, the legend, the panty dropper who gives King David a run for his money"—he allowed a comical pause in which people snickered—"*WEST. ST. CLAIRE!*"

People pumped their fists in the air as both men entered the ring. West's shoulder brushed mine, the familiar scent of winter and male trickling into my nostrils, but he didn't notice me. I clutched my Solo cup to my heart.

Karlie elbowed me. "Well, if nothing else, it'll be fun seeing him getting bitch-slapped a time or two."

"West's goin' to annihilate the poor guy."

But I was wrong.

West didn't annihilate Knox.

He dang near killed him.

Every time Knox tried to throw a punch, West dodged it and countered with something to knock his opponent out for five to eight seconds. A kick. A jab. Sometimes he grabbed the dude—and there was a *lot* of that dude—and threw him on the mat WWE style, for funsies.

Fighting wasn't a sport to West. It wasn't even a hobby. It was akin to him changing his sheets or brushing his teeth. Just another mundane act that didn't require any special effort. His body language was bored, languid. At some point, when Knox was on the mat folded into himself, holding his stomach and shaking in pain, West turned around and strolled in my direction. His eyes skimmed over the audience like he was looking for something—probably his fling for the night—and halted on me.

Everything stopped.

The room went quiet.

Or maybe it didn't, but I certainly blocked all the background noise as his eyes widened, first in shock—and then in anger. His brows drew together. Every muscle in his body tightened.

Now he was looking like he was ready for a fight.

"What the fuck are you doin—" He began with a low, gravelly hiss so dark and depraved it sent chills down my spine, but he never got to finish the sentence. Knox took the opportunity and threw a hook to the back of West's head. It snapped sideways from the impact, and blood began to trickle out of his mouth. I yelped. West swiveled on his heel, and with a swift kick to the liver, followed by a sucker punch to the side of his face, sent Knox across the ring. The fighter hit a few crates, rolling around several times before falling headfirst onto the mat, undoubtedly knocked out.

The crowd burst with cheers and whistles as Max ran toward Knox and crouched down, counting to ten.

West didn't bother staying in the ring to be announced as the winner. He charged toward me like a bat outta hell. I stumbled back, bumping into people as I tried to retreat. A tanked guy behind me burped, shoving me into West's arms carelessly.

"Dang, St. Claire's horny tonight. Usually he waits until he splits the cash with Riviera."

"Whoa," Karlie whispered, her eyes growing impossibly large.

I was now tucked firmly in West's arms, courtesy of the drunk guy. West shoved me back with open disgust, looking at me like I'd committed the worst crime on planet Earth.

"Who let her in?" He let out a roar that ripped through the air and made everybody take a collective step back.

Gingerly, the guy who'd sold us the tickets took a step forward, lifting his arm. "I … I did, bro. I recognized them from Sher U?"

West's eyes were still on me when he spoke. "You're fired."

"But I …"

"*Fired,*" West repeated with icy venom.

My eyes burned with humiliation, and my entire face was so hot I felt dizzy with anger. "You promised not to draw attention to me," I gritted between my teeth, barely a whisper.

West threw me an impersonal glance, *tsking.* "I don't promise.

I told you not to come here. The moment you stepped foot in my realm—you fucking asked for attention, and now you're going to get the wrong kind of it."

"You're unbelievable."

"You're un-fucking-welcome."

"Too bad you don't own this place." I shrugged, trying to look nonchalant and hating the eyes on me. "I'm staying. In fact, I'm going to go top off my drink. So if you'll excuse me ..."

Metaphorically picking up the scraps of my pride, I turned around and began marching to the other side of the floor, knowing Karlie would follow.

Guess I'd gotten my answer. West and I weren't friends. Not even close.

The crowd parted for me, mesmerized glares following my movements, when I was snatched and lifted in the air from behind.

"You big pain in the ass."

West scooped me up, fireman-style, hurling me against his shoulder as he dashed up the stairs to the third floor. "Management" as he called it.

"Where are you taking her?" someone in the crowd yelled, laughing.

"Giving her a good spanking, then hurling her out the window."

Rage pulsated in my bloodstream. Not only was he screwing other people on a weekly basis, but he thought he owned me in some way. Picking me up, ordering me around, making me feel like a reject publicly.

I rained fists on his back and shoulders.

"Let go of me, you asshole."

He ignored me, climbing up the stairs. It scared me, just how light I was to him. He breezed up, like I was nothing more than a six-pack of beer.

I heard Karlie crying out my name and saw Reign and Easton blocking her way up with polite smiles. It looked way rape-ier than it actually was, and, knowing West and I weren't going to do much more than fight, I felt inclined to give my best friend a secretive thumbs-up, indicating that I wasn't going to die in his hands.

"Karlie will call the police," I said anyway, pulling at his hair now.

Lord. I was behaving like a wild animal. At the same time, I didn't want to be alone with him. I knew I'd yield to temptation. Take whatever he'd offer me.

"Shut up," he snapped.

"Not until you let me down."

"No thanks. Enough people have done that in your life."

"Who the hell are you to judge?"

"The only person to notice your existence."

"I don't want you to!"

"You don't have a fucking choice in the matter, and, unfortunately, neither do I."

He put me down with my back flat against the wall. He popped what looked like his dislocated elbow back into place with expertise, the sound of bone clicking back into place filling the air. I winced. He acted like it was no big deal.

"There are two ways for you to get out of here. Through the stairs or the window. They depend on how you're going to cooperate in the next few minutes. So I suggest you answer my questions and keep your sassy comments to someone who appreciates them. Question one—what the hell are you doing here, Tex?"

He bared his teeth like a beast.

I folded my arms over my chest, trying to hide my raw nerves with a smirk. "Enjoyin' the fight. Pickin' up a hookup, if I find someone interesting. Why? What do you care? We are nothing to each other."

"Wrong." He got in my face. I had a feeling even he had no idea why, exactly, he was so furious with me. "We're not nothing. You're my friend, and I told you I don't want you anywhere near this garbage place."

"This garbage place is *yours*."

"I *am* garbage. You're not. We don't play by the same rules."

I threw my head back and laughed, hurling my arms in the air for good measure. "You don't get to dictate the rules for me. My life is my business, not yours. I wanted to be here. And guess what?" I felt vindictive and completely out of control. Adrenaline was pumping in my veins, hard. All I wanted in that moment was to hurt him in the same way he'd hurt me. Beyond repair. Rip his heart out of his chest and watch it bleed in my fist. "I might go and find a hookup tonight. I think it is high time. There are so many people to choose from here. I get why you like it at the Plaza." I whistled, making a show of looking around me. "It's a great place to get laid."

His jaw tensed, his brows pulling together as his eyes narrowed at me.

"If you think you're going to come into my club and get fucked by anyone who is not me, you've got another thing coming."

"Why not? You do it all the time. Whatever happened to your feminist streak?"

"I don't pick up chicks here."

"Of course you don't." I smiled.

He ran his fingers through his hair, letting out a sigh. "Not recently."

"Define recently, West."

"Keeping tabs?"

"People talk. So, Melanie wasn't recent?" I couldn't help myself, even though I hated how pathetic I sounded.

His lips thinned. "Melanie was before my dick and I had the awkward conversation in which it told me it was dead-set on you."

"What about Tess?"

"What about her?" He looked momentarily confused.

"Was she before or after you and your dick sat down for the big talk? You said you weren't opposed to havin' sex with her again tonight."

Lord. I was admitting to eavesdropping on him. West's face hadn't changed. It was still a stony mask of brutality. He was trying hard not to snap.

"You ... you *idiot*." He closed his eyes, exasperated, rubbing at his forehead. "I wanted to rile Reign up. He's got the hots for her, and I'm still pissed about the way he treated you."

"No. *You're* the idiot," I screamed in his face, not caring if people heard us. I stabbed his chest with my finger. "You are mad at me and you don't even know why. At least I know why I hate your guts. You keep givin' me mixed signals. Kissin' me, but not goin' all the way. Why is that, West? Is this Grace-is-pretty thing just an act? To help my self-esteem?" I chuckled bitterly, but there were tears coating my eyes. I could feel them.

Now it was his turn to bark out a dark laugh.

"You think I care about your self-esteem? Gimme a break, Tex. You're not that important to me."

I didn't even bother to be offended, because I knew whatever came out of his mouth was a lie. Everything we felt toward one another—good and bad—spun together into something that was bigger than us.

He took a step back, giving me a silent once-over. I knew I looked the best I ever had since he'd met me, but his expression didn't give anything away.

"What do you want to hear? That I have dreams of lowering your pretty blonde head down inside the food truck, unzipping myself, and making you deep-throat me until you choke on it? Would it help if I admitted that I want nothing more than fucking you six ways from Sunday? That I would devour your ass in a heartbeat, if it wasn't for the fact we're both majorly fucked-up—sorry, Tex, it's the truth—and I'm getting out of this shithole as soon as I get my BA, and I don't do serious relationships? Because you seem to know all that. You *know* why I didn't kiss you.

"Tess, Mel, those chicks … they know the score. I don't know them. I don't *care* about them. The aftermath, once my dick is out of their holes, is none of my business. I can't kiss you, Grace." He shook his head sadly, taking another step back. "I can barely even fucking *look* at you."

I was losing him. I knew that. And for the first time in a long time, I wanted to fight. The phoenix in me pushed through the sand, struggling under its weight, revealing more of its magnificent feathers. I rubbed at the broken flame ring on my finger, tipped my chin up, and gave the most seductive smile in my arsenal.

"It's okay to be scared."

His jaw locked, his Adam's apple bobbing with a swallow.

"I'm not scared," he said drily. But I knew him well enough to feel the undercurrent of anger rising up to the surface, dimming his green eyes.

"Sure you aren't." I picked up my little clutch that had fallen from my hand while we were fighting, hoisting it over my shoulder, preparing to leave. "And I get what you are sayin'. It really is a bad idea to get involved. But that doesn't mean I'm goin' to be a saint. Too chicken shit to start somethin' with me? No problem. I'll go downstairs and find me a nice Southern boy lookin' for commitment. One who won't get scared when things get serious. One who would be happy to make the promises you are so frightened of. A guy who …"

He pounced on me like a panther, causing my back to smash against the wall. I let out a cry, but he shut me up with his lips as his mouth crashed on mine with punishing force. He grabbed the pink ball cap he'd bought me and tossed it to the floor. I shook my head in protest, but he held me still, his strong fingers clasping my jaw in a bruising grip.

"How about you let me take a nice good look at you, Texas? You talk a big game, but when it's time to show up, you're too wishy-washy for my taste. Want a dirty hookup with the town's favorite fuckup? You got your wish. Now open up." It was a cruel demand, not a request.

I pressed my lips together, looking up at him under my lashes, waiting for his next move. I felt naked without my cap, and I hated that he watched me so intently, devouring me with his eyes.

I kept reminding myself I had a lot of makeup on, and that it was very dark. He couldn't see much. I shook inside his arms like a leaf but met his stare.

"Having a change of heart?" I tried to taunt, my tone fragile, torn apart.

He smirked sinisterly, looking like Satan himself. "I'm not like you, Texas. Once I make up my mind, it's a done deal."

He darted his tongue out, tracing the seam of my lower lip ever so slowly. His hot, wet tongue felt like crushed velvet, leaving shivers in its wake. My whole body quaked, every inch of my skin turning into goose bumps that started spreading on the crown of my head, trickling to the tips of my toes. Every nerve ending in my body was on fire.

I was on fire.

And this time, I wanted to perish in his arms.

"Who is chicken shit now?" he whispered into my mouth, teasingly coaxing it open with his expert tongue. I slammed my eyelids shut. His mouth was too much. Too warm. Too inviting. Too perfect.

The smell of him—apple candy and sweat and alpha male—made me press my thighs together. I felt a damp spot of need settling on my panties. I was so wet I wanted to cry.

"You're going to break for me, like you always do, so you might as well do it with some of your pride intact," he rasped into my lips. "Because once I decide to kiss you, nothing is going to stop me. Least of all your ass."

The nerve of this guy.

My lips were still locked together. I let my eyes flutter open, my blues challenging his greens.

He laced his fingers through mine beside our bodies, his thumb rubbing my flame ring knowingly. He brought the ring to his lips and whispered into it, his eyes still on mine.

"I wish Gracie-Mae would let me kiss her silly."

He noticed.

Noticed I whispered wishes into the ring. Noticed the little broken flame jewelry was my own candy apple.

I wondered what he thought happened to my face. It shocked me that he hadn't asked once since we became close.

"Now, if you don't open up and let me kiss the shit out of you in the next three seconds, Tex, I'm going to never try again. As I said, I never turn back on my word. Three. Two. O—"

I opened up for him.

His tongue found mine immediately, stroking it greedily. It was my first kiss since Tucker. This kiss tasted like beer and Granny Smith and *West*. And West, I realized to my horror, tasted like home.

I knew, with a clarity that made my gut coil into itself a thousand times over, that nothing and no one would taste like him.

He pushed his chest against mine, and we both groaned, surprised by the force of the kiss. West propped his knee between my legs, shamefully grinding his hard-on over my stomach. He was throbbing, jerking behind his jeans.

It was a molten, passionate kiss. Something I'd never experienced before. A mixture of wild and raw.

I couldn't tell exactly when our lips disconnected from one another, but his hands were still on my cheeks after it happened. He brushed his nose against mine, up and down, in a way I found impossibly soothing. I tried to take in a ragged breath, but I found that my chest was so tight with emotions, it was hard to draw oxygen into my lungs.

"We're playing with fire," he croaked.

I nodded, my eyes dropping from his gaze to his mouth. I wanted more. I didn't feel ugly in his arms, even when his hand touched my scar.

"I've walked through fire before, so I know what I'm getting into." My voice shook around my words, but each of them tasted like redemption and change. Like *rebirth*. "I'm willing to pay the price."

He closed his eyes, inhaling sharply, like it pained him to hear this. "I should walk away," he said, mostly to himself.

"I'm not too proud to follow," I admitted.

"If we go this route, it has to be casual, Texas. It has to. I can't do promises. Or relationships. I'm as far from boyfriend material as humanly possible."

"You don't know that," I argued.

He smiled sadly at me. "Trust me, baby, I do."

Something in his eyes told me that he had a good reason to make that statement. I grabbed his hand and turned it over so his inner bicep was to me.

"Who is A?"

I was already jealous of her. I wanted to be A. I wanted his undying devotion and heartbreak. I wanted to have the power to ignite the celestial turmoil she'd put him through.

He took a step back, putting space between us.

"She's the one, isn't she?"

He looked away, down to the floor. "No promises," he warned steely. It felt like he'd severed my veins and was watching me bleeding out. "It's casual or nothing."

I picked up my ball cap, slipping it over my head. I hoisted my clutch over my shoulder again. "I need to think about it," I said honestly, starting for the stairs.

He grabbed my wrist, stopping me. "Think about it tomorrow. Be with me tonight. *Please*."

I glared at him.

He growled, shaking his head, exasperated with both of us.

"Look, I promi—" He stopped himself, clearing his throat. "I give you my word I'll keep the cobwebs on your pussy intact. But you're all dressed up, fucking smoking, and it's probably the first night out you've had in a long time. Let's get a little dirty."

I looked at his tan fingers curled around my wrist. Big, but gentle. I couldn't refuse him. I couldn't refuse him if the world went up in flames—which, for me, it had.

I had no excuse for what I said next.

I knew I was reaching for the poison, taking a generous sip.

"I'll give you tonight," I said quietly, knowing he'd already taken much more than we both had bargained for.

We raced downstairs to the second floor. Other than our friends, everyone else had left.

Karlie was chatting up a cute frat boy with sandy hair and Nordic features named Miles by the beer station. Reign was flirting with Tess in the corner, even though her eyes darted past his shoulder, our way, as soon as we came into view.

Max was perched on his soap box, counting money, and Easton was messing around on his phone.

West went directly to Max while I tugged at Karlie's dress, telling her I was going to split and hang out with West.

The smile Miles had put on Karlie's face evaporated in supersonic record. "Whatever happened to *just* friends?" She frowned. "I was worried *sick* about you. I kept wondering if I imagined your thumbs-up or not."

I shifted weight between my legs. "You didn't imagine it. And I promise, it's just casual, so …"

"You don't do casual."

"I *can* do casual. I'm not allergic to it. I just haven't tried it before," I argued.

"And what better person to do it with than the most infamous, popular man on campus, who happens to break noses for a living? I see no potential complications at all." She gave me a skeptical look that was supposed to bring me back to my senses.

Clearly, I did a good job hiding how far gone I was for this guy.

"Karl, *please*." I pulled her into a hug, trying to melt her reservations away. "It's just fooling around. No feelings involved. Weren't you the one who told me the ends justify the means?"

"I take it lover boy is no longer all about Tess," she grumbled, patting my back without much enthusiasm but starting to come to terms with the idea. God bless Mrs. Contreras for creating this supreme human being. I didn't think I could survive a second without Karlie in my life.

"We cleared that up."

"Ah-ha. Is that what you kids call it these days?" She pulled away from me, giving me a stern, motherly once-over.

I laughed.

"I'm half-worried, half-morbidly curious. You better call me with all the details."

I felt myself blushing.

West reappeared by my side, looking cold and apathetic. "Ready, Grace?" He tucked a thick stack of cash into his front pocket.

Grace. Not Texas or Tex. I nodded.

West jerked his chin toward Karlie, Miles, Reign, Tess, and Easton in goodbye.

"Where're y'all headed to?" Tess called out, sticking her hip out.

"Giving Grace a ride home," West flat-out lied.

"Wanna hang out afterwards?" Tess smiled brightly.

"I'm good."

We crossed the road to the food truck silently. There was an unspoken agreement upon where we were going. It just felt right. That Taco Truck was our safe haven.

I unlocked the door and pushed it open, sneaking in first. West locked the door, leaning against it, his hands tucked behind his back, flashing me a rakish smirk.

"Oh, how the mighty have fallen." I propped myself against the opposite wall of the trailer, smiling back. "And to think your famous first words were you were never going to touch me."

"Well, Tex, I'm not sure I *will* be touching you," he teased. "But you're still going to come so hard you won't be able to walk straight tomorrow."

I slid down the wall. He slid down the door. We were facing each other, on opposite sides of the truck. Maybe not touching each other was a good idea. I was already in too deep.

"Nice panties," he commented, his hungry gaze dipping teasingly between my legs. I flipped him the bird. My legs were pressed together, and I was hugging my knees.

"Nice try. You can't see my panties."

"Black cotton. A little white pearl at the center. Interesting symbolism." He licked his lips, his eyes trained between my legs. I gasped, prying my knees open and leaning forward to check. I did remember wearing black panties, but not the pearl …

"Hey …" I felt myself frowning.

West burst out laughing. His throaty voice reverberated in the trailer, in my head, in my *chest*. "Figured you'd coordinate."

"You owe me a peep show." I looked back up at him, pushing my lower lip into a pout. My heart was pounding like a maniac.

"Your wish is my command." He unbuttoned his jeans, his eyes trained on mine. He wanted to see if I would freak out. If I would kick him out of the truck. I did neither.

He shoved his jeans down his butt, but only enough that his gray briefs peeked out. I could see he was fully erect under the waistband. His penis was so thick, I could make out the individual veins snaking through its length.

He stroked himself through the fabric of his underwear.

"Your turn," his voice was strained. "Trail your pussy lips with your finger for me, Tex."

I momentarily stepped out of my anxiety, solely focused on the way his hands stroked his manhood. He had great hands. Large and rough.

Running my index over the seam of my sex through my panties, I panted. I dropped my head against the wall, letting it loll back and forth.

"Push a finger into yourself through the fabric," he instructed, watching me intently. There was something potently hot in watching West watching me doing this to myself. I did as he asked. He grumbled, closing his eyes, now pulling and yanking at himself through his briefs.

"Take it out," I said.

There was a pause.

"You sure?"

"Yeah."

He let his penis spring free from his boxers. It looked like a giant, raging leech pressing against his stomach. I'd forgotten what penises looked like. Not that I'd seen more than one in real life.

"Pull your panties to the side so I can see your pretty pussy." He tugged at his own length harshly. I liked the way he said the word *pussy*. It sounded just dirty enough without being degrading somehow.

I bit my lip. "I'm not … camera-ready down there."

He chuckled. "A little on the wild side, cowgirl?"

Lord.

"I wasn't expectin' a photo shoot."

Why was I encouraging this metaphor to continue? His laughter danced inside my stomach, but his mirth didn't stop him from growing even more swollen and hard inside his palm. His penis was way bigger than Tucker's. Tess and co should be given some sort of a prize for accommodating it. Or maybe medical care. Possibly both.

"Hundred bucks says it's gorgeous," he murmured.

"How would you know?" My mouth practically hung open.

"It's attached to you."

"Genitals aren't often described as gorgeous."

"Your dirty talk game is weak, Tex. Less talking, more showing me your snatch."

I nudged my panties aside, knowing full well what he was seeing wasn't a porn-worthy vagina. There was a plume of fine, baby-blond hair covering my opening. It was trimmed, but not completely removed. I opened myself with my fingers, exposing my pink insides.

"Oh, fuck." He closed his eyes, pumping harder before focusing on me again. "Rub your clit for me, baby."

I didn't have to be asked twice. Especially as it looked like he was liking what he was seeing. A lot. I flicked my clit in circles, watching a pearl of pre-cum gracing the crown of his penis. My tongue swiped my lower lip. Why was this the hottest thing I'd ever done with a guy, even though I'd gone all the way with Tucker?

Because you never wanted Tucker half as much you want West.

"Texas." His voice was hoarse. Like he could barely contain all this. I knew exactly what he was feeling. My orgasm crept in on me like a giant wave rolling ashore.

"Hmm?"

"Can I scoot closer?"

"Yeah."

He dragged his butt across the floor. We were now rubbing ourselves, his penis directed at me, our hands and arms brushing together with each shallow stroke, our knees bumping into one another. It was so dirty and fun. It was everything I should've been doing during my college years and missed out on.

West swiped his thumb over his pre-cum and used it to lubricate himself as he went even faster. His forehead dropped to mine. We were closer than ever before, and now my hand bumped into his penis every time I rubbed myself.

"Coming." His lips moved over mine. The pleasure taking ahold of my body made me delirious. I shook all over.

"Me too."

I watched as hot spurts of white cum shot from his penis, just when every muscle in my body tightened. We came together, but kept on rubbing, tugging, and moaning.

A full minute after, we still had our foreheads pressed together. Our lips on one another. Our arms hung on the floor like they'd fallen from our bodies. We grinned into each other's mouths. Everything around us was sticky and damp and smelled of sex.

"That was …" I drew in a breath. "*So* far away from hygienic. Way worse than you working shirtless. If health and safety dropped by, they'd kick our asses."

He toppled backwards, laughing his butt off.

"If Mrs. Contreras was here, she'd hang us in town square," he agreed.

"We don't have a town square," I pointed out.

"She'd have made one." He leaned back toward me. "Whatever, I had a good run."

"Short one."

"Not too short for me." His eyes glittered.

I slid my gaze down, reached for his half-mast shaft, and swiped a finger over the crown. He shuddered and hissed at my touch. I stuck out my tongue, touched my cum-filled finger to it, giving it a thorough lick.

"Hmm." I closed my eyes, covering my whole finger with my mouth.

He groaned, yanking me into his embrace. We hugged, my head tucked under his chin. He drew circles over my back with the tips of his fingers.

I had no idea what we were at this moment, but it was definitely more than friends. There was intimacy there, no matter how much he tried to deny it. But pushing him to do something he clearly wasn't interested in wasn't fair for him or me.

"Promise me you won't regret this tomorrow morning," he whispered.

I closed my eyes, feeling a fat, warm tear sliding out of my right eye.

"No promises."

Chapter Eleven

West

STUBBORN RAYS OF SUN POURED FROM THE CRACKS OF THE FOOD truck's window, making my eyelids sting. I shielded my face from the sun and rolled over on the floor. When I didn't bump into a small body, I opened my eyes.

No Texas.

I sat up straight. The Clorox scent around me told me everything I needed to know—Grace had wiped last night out of the trailer and scrubbed it clean while I was passed out. Question was—did she wipe it from her memory, too?

I couldn't blame her if she had. I basically gave her my old no-strings-attached shtick. By scrolling all the way down my bullshit verbal contract and signing on the small print, she'd agreed to never ask for anything other than a dirty fuck. The tragic part was, I hadn't even had the balls to fuck her. Even though, in all probability, I could have.

But I knew screwing her was going to mess with my resolve to leave her alone.

And I really, *really* needed to leave her alone.

My fascination with this chick had gone too far, and it was time to back away. Unless, of course, she'd agreed to do this casually, then fuck my logic and fuck my promises to myself. I was going to have her any way I could.

I got up from the floor, looking around me. The scent of steaming brewed coffee and freshly baked croissants filled my nostrils. I spotted them immediately on the counter, right next to a note.

I grabbed the note first—already a bad sign. Ninety-nine percent of men would reach for the food first.

I had to go take care of Grams (it's the weekend and Marla is off).

Take care of yourself. I turned your phone alarm to half an hour before Karlie and Victor start their shift.

—Texas

I grinned to myself like an idiot. I had no indication that I looked like an idiot, but I sure felt like one.

Stuffing her note into my back pocket, I dug into the pastry and coffee on my way out of the trailer. I was glad I didn't have a shift today. All I wanted was to take a shower, catch up on more sleep, and maybe hit Tex up later today, see if she wanted to hang out. I spent way too much money when we hung out, on stupid shit like designer ball caps and Frito pies, but it was always worth it. It recharged me. Made Fridays a little more bearable. Or should I say—a little *less* hellish.

Which reminded me—I needed to send a text message to everyone who worked at the Plaza, warning them Grace Shaw was banned for life from our fine institute. One less problem to worry about.

I whistled on my way to the Ducati and spent the ride home replaying the moment she licked my cum from her finger until my mental tape was stuck. My dick stirred against the hard leather seat, which was unfortunate and un-fucking-comfortable, but unthinking about it was a waste of a fucking good memory.

I was pretty sure even if I died at the ripe age of a hundred, reaping many memories along the way, this would still be the moment to flash before my eyes before I finally kicked the bucket.

I parked in front of the rundown house East and I had rented, taking off my helmet and striding toward the front porch. I stopped as soon as I saw her.

What the hell was *she* doing here?

My blood simmered in my veins, threatening to melt my whole damn body into a puddle of anger. My molars were a nanosecond from turning into dust, and I could feel my jaw squaring. I put an apple candy between my teeth, not bothering to take my sunglasses off. "Caroline."

Normally, I'd call her Mother, but I was too pissed for that. She looked a mess. Her mom-jeans and outdated yellow blouse were wrinkled. Her hair was completely gray now, and she wasn't even that old.

I walked past her. She darted up from the front stair of my porch, following me like a puppy. I hated myself for treating her this way. But I also hated *her* for putting me in this position.

"What brings you here?" I jingled the key in the keyhole, my back to her.

"You haven't answered any of my calls recently."

I could see her wringing her fingers in my periphery, looking down, like a punished kid. My mother was the world's greatest hugger. Even more than Texas, who I noticed was into hugging her friend Karlie, and her grandmother, and hell-knows-who. Finding the strength not to hug her own son after five years must've killed her.

"Finally, your father told me I should get on a flight and check that you are okay. Your wellbeing is more important than money, obviously."

"I'm okay. You can go now." I pushed the door open with my shoulder. It creaked in protest. I walked in. She followed me hesitantly, knowing I wasn't above kicking her out. She didn't have a suitcase. *Good.* At least she wasn't planning on staying long.

She looked around the room. There really wasn't much to see. It was a two-bedroom house, small and in desperate need of fixing. The living room consisted of a couch and a TV. The kitchen had a retro orange table with four plastic chairs. The gray-yellow wallpaper was peeling, torn at the edges. That was what you got for getting the cheapest place available in Sheridan. And that poor bastard East went along with me. He couldn't see me doing this to myself without sticking by my side.

Speaking of …

I turned around and flashed my mother a scowl. She knew exactly what I was asking. She raised her palms up.

"Of course I tried to check if he is home. I guess he stayed out last night."

Translation: East got tail and never bothered hauling his ass back home.

"Surprised you dragged your royal ass here. East keeps you up to date with my BS."

I avoided my parents so often, East had resorted to calling them weekly, just to let them know I was still alive. He gave them a curated version of my activities, taking out the underground fights, dirty hookups, and public feuds with professors.

"I don't want to bother him too much." Mom reached to try to fix my collar.

I swatted her hand away.

"Shame you don't extend this courtesy to me."

I got into the kitchen and grabbed milk out from the fridge, drinking straight from the carton. Mom took a seat at the table, trying to shrink into herself and take as little space as possible.

"You haven't been home since you started studying here."

"You're not telling me anything I don't know." I wiped my milk moustache with the back of my hand, shoving the carton back into the fridge and slamming it shut. I took a seat across from her. She wasn't leaving before grilling my ass. Might as well get it over with.

Mom put her hands on the table, staring at them, not me. "How do you like it here?"

"I like it fine."

"Very up-and-coming, isn't it? Nice town."

"Fucking lovely."

"Think you want to stay here after you graduate?"

"I don't think past what I want to have for dinner."

I was careful not to ask anything about how things were back home. It felt like a slippery slope that could lead to an actual conversation.

"We miss and love you so much."

"Bet you love the weekly allowance even more." I cocked an eyebrow.

Her big brown gaze sprang up from her hands then scurried to the peeling wallpaper. Her eyeballs were coated with a thick layer of tears.

I sighed, sprawling on the chair, folding my arms over my chest and staring at the ceiling.

"What's up with you, anyway?" I grumbled.

"I'm doing well, thank you for asking. Better, on all fronts. Still on the meds. Still working at Walmart. I got promoted last month. I'm a cashier now. It's a nice environment, and I get to go out, talk to people."

Her fingers were inching to touch mine. I wanted to throw up.

"I make my own money now." She puffed her chest out, gaining more confidence. "Things are not as bleak as they look, Westie. We'll get out of this mess soon. But we never expect you to help us financially. It's not on you."

Only it *was* on me. It was my fault they were in this situation in the first place. Mom finally put her hand on mine, leaning toward me.

"Let's go out downtown. I want to buy you soap and shampoo and new shirts. Maybe get you a nice haircut. I want to see the town you live in. Do the whole mom-thing I didn't get the chance to do when you first moved here. Please, Westie?"

Her fingernails clawed at my skin, so desperately they nearly produced blood.

She wasted the hard-earned money I sent her by booking herself a surprise flight. Then suggested we'd go on a shopping spree.

My knee-jerk reaction was to call her out on it, but I knew if I threw her out, it would bite me in the ass in the form of East giving me hell. Also, I would feel guilty.

Spending time with my mother was so low on my to-do list, you couldn't find it unless you read that whole shit through. Still, even I recognized taking her out would be less soul-crushing than sitting here with her, one-on-one, and face the artillery of questions and attempted hugs she would no doubt throw my way.

"What do you say?" A hesitant, synthetic smile spread on her face. It looked wrong. Like a wonky picture on a bare wall. I knew what she looked like when she smiled for real.

I still remembered, even if vaguely.

I squeezed her hand in mine and felt the pressure dissipating from her body, all at once, as she dragged me in for a hug.

"Whatever."

An hour later, we were out on the town, carrying approximately a thousand nylon bags full of socks, shirts, toiletries, and groceries. My hair was trimmed into an actual cut. Buzzed at the sides, longer at the top.

I felt rich, in a screwed-up, poor boy way.

I wasn't used to getting new shit. My socks were so holey I stopped wearing them about six months ago, and when my shirts became too faded to have a distinguished color, I dealt with the problem by wearing them inside out.

Soap and toothpaste I *did* use (life sucked badly enough without actively preventing myself from getting laid), but I always went for the cheap crap you could buy in bulk at the dollar store, or better yet—hit a party or two during the weekend and raid the bathroom like it was Target.

Mom didn't spend a lot of money by any stretch of the imagination, and one hundred percent of that money came from *me*. Still, the new shirts and briefs made me feel like one of those nerdy chicks in movies, who got a makeover consisting of an entire new wardrobe and a personality implant while she was at it.

Who the fuck was I?

What the fuck was wrong with me?

The answer was clearly everything. Everything was wrong with me. Because I'd started imagining Tex laying her angel blue eyes on my new briefs, admiring how pristinely white they were. Yesterday, her innocent gaze made me feel like we were doing something dirty. And dirty was a realm in which I'd thrived.

Then I remembered another hookup probably wasn't in the cards for us.

I'd told her flat-out I could only do casual, but she wasn't a casual type of girl. She said she'd think about it, but really, it was a no-brainer.

Couldn't blame her. She deserved a whole lot more than my delinquent ass had to offer.

"How about I make dinner?" Mom looped her arm in mine when we pushed the door open, back at my house.

"Pretty sure neither of us can afford a restaurant meal after this, so go ahead," I muttered.

East was there, lying on the couch in his boxers, texting. He welcomed us with a loud fart.

"'Sup, Sir Crabs-a-lot?"

"Easton Liam Braun!" my mother screeched, and I let out a genuine laugh for the first time today. When East heard her shriek, he jumped up from the couch so fast he nearly made a dent in the ceiling.

"Mrs. St. Claire." He flashed his good boy smile, hurrying into his bedroom. He hopped back into the living room with one leg in his sweatpants, the other still out, and wobbled in her direction. She sucked him into a viselike grip that was supposed to be a hug, peppering his cheeks with wet, motherly kisses. I glanced at his crotch. He had a semi. He was probably sexting someone. Fucking gross. I made a note to punch him in the face until his nose curved out of the back of his head for touching my mom while he was aroused.

"You look wonderful, Easton. You're doing a fine job here. Your momma is very proud." She pinched both his cheeks and tried to make them wobble, but East's baby fat was long gone.

Now would be a good time to stop touching this pervert, Mother.

The thought was so natural and funny and old-West, as opposed to the newer, miserable version, a pang of nostalgia hit me.

"Sure am trying." He bowed his head in fake modesty.

Mom gave him one last peck on the cheek. "Well, you're succeeding. I'm making pasta and meatballs. You boys are going to be my little helpers."

"Yes, ma'am." He flashed me an eager grin. And just like that, it was like when we were kids all over again.

For him, anyway.

Mom made the best meatballs and pasta in the universe, a fact I would defend with my last breath, no matter how fucked-up my relationship with her was.

I was half-French from my dad's side, half-Italian from my mom's.

My height and size were from my mother's family—the Bozzelli men towered to six-five on average and were built like tanks. I also got the olive skin from her. But I had Dad's hair and pale green eyes.

The recipe definitely worked in my favor back when I was still in the business of conquering women as an Olympic sport.

"I'll let you two catch up in the kitchen." East clapped both our backs, already retreating back to his room. Not only was he a shithead, but he was also a traitor—leaving me with her, knowing that I avoided her at all costs.

"I'll go buy some wine and bread. Give me a shout when dinner's ready."

Stuck in the kitchen with Mom with nowhere to hide, I listened to her small-town gossip. When she realized she'd been talking for twenty minutes straight without getting any type of response, she stopped, still stirring the tomato, basil, and garlic sauce in the pot.

"But enough about me. Who was that *friend* you spent your birthday with?"

I was sitting at the kitchen table, cutting lettuce into miniscule pieces for the salad. "Just a chick."

"She must be special to acquire your friendship."

I hated when she did that. Acted like she gave a shit. My mother wanted me to meet someone. Become someone else's problem. Guess it was inconvenient for her to check in on me daily to see I hadn't offed myself/killed someone/started a cult.

In her eyes, I wasn't above doing all three.

"It's just someone from work."

"Does she have a name?"

"Yes," I drawled. "Don't know many people without a name."

Even I had one. Never mind that my parents had named me after a fucking cardinal direction.

Downplaying my relationship with Grace wasn't lying per se, but it didn't feel right either. Whichever way I looked at it, we were tight. Definitely tighter than I was with Reign or Max or any other oxygen-wasters on campus who thought I was their buddy. The fact I wouldn't shy away from riding Texas' ass like a cowboy didn't help matters.

I was considering dropping the food truck gig to avoid her altogether.

Mom bit down on her smile, childish glee radiating from her.

Half an hour later, food was ready: salad, spaghetti with meat balls, garlic bread, and red wine. The last two were Easton's courtesy. The three of us gathered around the creaking table. Mom rushed the grace part so we could tuck in, and I was finally able to somewhat relax.

The doorbell rang.

We all glanced at each other. East knew better than to invite people over when I was around. I was notoriously misanthropic.

"Who could it be?" Mom asked around a bite of pasta.

"Only one way to find out," I muttered, pushing my chair back and walking to the door. Our peephole wasn't working. Some punks filled it with wax before we moved in. I had no choice but to open the door and trust it wasn't an assassin sent by Kade Appleton. Recently, I had a weird feeling I was being followed.

It wasn't.

The person who stood at the door was far less welcome than a serial killer.

Grace.

What was she doing here?

She wore a stripy long-sleeved shirt, skintight jeans, and her timeless FILAs. Her ball cap was screwed on top of her head, lowered down, serving as her invisibility cloak.

"Hey." She smiled at her feet. Both my dick and I gave her smile a standing ovation. I wondered how many brain cells I was going to be left with by the time this chick was done showing me all of her mundane facial expressions.

"What's up?" I clipped.

"You forgot your wallet in the truck. You weren't picking up your phone, so Karlie called to let me know. I thought I'd swing by and drop it off."

She took out my wallet from her back pocket, handing it to me.

"She asked me why we were there in the first place, why it smelled like cleaning products. I told her we went in to get slushies and spilled some. I think she bought it."

Then, I think she's an idiot.

Also: *Goddammit.* How had I not noticed my wallet was missing before? Oh, that's right. I was too drunk on watching Grace masturbating to care where my fucking limbs were, let alone my wallet. Then my mother treated me to clothes and groceries (albeit with the money I transferred to her earlier this month). I hadn't had to take out my wallet once today.

I plucked it from her hand and moved to close the door in her face.

"Thanks. Catch you later, Tex."

"Westie?" Mom called out behind my shoulder, peeking outside to see who it was. She rested a hand over my shoulder. "Aren't you going to introduce me to your friend?"

Fuck. My. Life.

Both women sized each other up in the way females did, grinning simultaneously, as if unearthing some rare secret. Grace did a little wave. I almost forgot that behind the sarcastic minx I wanted to shut up with my reproductive organ was a polite, Southern belle just ready to burst out at the first sign of a worrying momma.

"Howdy, ma'am. I'm Grace Shaw."

"Caroline St. Claire, West's mother. Such a pleasure." Mom ditched any attempt to act like a civilized human and jumped Grace's bones in a suffocating hug. Texas, of course, returned the favor, squeezing her right back.

I opened the door all the way, even though if it were up to me, I'd rather slam it in both their faces.

"Why, you must join us for dinner!" Mom exclaimed. It didn't take a genius to do the math. Texas was The Chosen One whom I'd spent my birthday with.

She was my so-called redemption.

Antidote to my poison.

The one Mom had been praying for.

"Oh, I wouldn't want to impose." Grace blushed, batting her eyelashes and tucking her chin down. She was hiding her scar. Smart girl.

If Mom saw her face properly, the shit show train would officially get off the rails and head straight off the cliff.

My mother and Grace in the same room was my idea of a nightmare, for too many reasons to count.

"Nonsense! We would love to have you. Westie doesn't have very many friends, and I'm dying to hear more about his life on campus."

Mom was now pulling Grace into the house, even when the latter dug her heels at the door like a cat approaching a full tub. Caroline St. Claire would lock the poor girl in a glass room, if it meant making sure she'd dine with us.

Texas shot me a *sorry* look. It was the first time she was here. She looked around, her aqua eyes big and exploring. I normally didn't feel embarrassed about where I lived. And it wasn't that Grace's house was going to hit *MTV Cribs* anytime soon. Still, I hated that my brokenness, my *poorness*, was right up in her face.

When Grace entered the kitchen, Easton stood up and greeted her while Mom took out another plate and utensils. We all sat down and tucked in. I avoided eye contact and all attempts at conversation.

My mother, of course, was in full Spanish Inquisition mode.

"So you work with Westie?" she asked before Texas took her first bite.

"Yes, ma'am. At a food truck just down the road from here."

"Do you go to Sheridan University, too?"

"I do. I major in theater and arts."

"Then you must know our Easton well."

"Sure do. He's got himself quite the following." Grace nodded, and I wanted to stab my own chest with a fork. "West too." She shot me an apologetic smile.

"Really?" Mom's brows knitted incredulously. "Is he known for anything on campus?"

Making people bleed.

Texas didn't even flinch.

"He is quite popular with the ladies."

"Always has been. Why, sweetie, you can take off that hat now."

Being handsy as all fuck, Mom took it upon herself to remove Grace's ball cap, tossing it to the counter behind her shoulder. "I want to take a look at your pretty fa—"

She never got to finish the sentence because Grace let out a squeak that sounded like an injured animal was trapped inside her throat.

Then there was silence.

A whole fucking lot of it.

Utensils cluttered on the plates. Easton sucked in a breath. The red, angry, ragged skin under Texas' makeup told a horror story that wasn't dinner-table appropriate.

It wasn't that Texas' face still wasn't caked with enough makeup to open a Sephora, but even through it, you could see the Freddy Krueger complexion she desperately tried to hide.

Both Grace and I shot up from our seats in unison, reaching for the ball cap. She pawed it first, slapping it over her head with shaky fingers.

Mom cleared her throat, clutching her fake pearls. Easton looked down.

I tried to block away the disturbing fact that Grace Shaw was stunning. Because she absolutely fucking was. With her ball cap down, and her face in full view, the magnificence of her was like a punch to the gut.

"I'm so sorry. How did you ..."

I'd known Grace Shaw for months and refrained from asking about her scar. My mother had known her for less than fifteen minutes and already felt comfortable digging in.

"I mean, when did that happen?" Mom finished.

"That's none of your goddamn business, and you have no right asking her that," I roared, knocking my fist against the table. Every single thing on it bounced up in the air, and my mother let out a cry.

Easton jumped up from his seat and asked Grace to help him open another bottle of wine, even though the one on the table was half-full.

They both disappeared to the living room while I pierced my mother with a deadly stare.

"What the fuck are you thinking?" I hissed, my rage barely containable.

"I ..." Her voice shook, and she looked at me like I was about to hurt her. "I didn't think."

"Damn straight you didn't."

"Westie, I swear, I would never …"

Easton and Grace slid back into the kitchen. He dragged his chair closer to Grace. Mom was shooting worried glances her way, her eyes wide and bottomless with emotion.

"Why," Mom said shakily, to inject some words into the awkward silence, "I wish I had dessert to offer you, Grace. How about some coffee, though?"

"She doesn't want any coffee," I snapped, getting up from my chair. The last thing I wanted was for my mother to talk to Texas. I couldn't afford Mom telling Grace my big secret. My this-is-why-he-is-so-fucked-up reason. "Grace was just leaving."

I quirked an eyebrow and scowled at Texas meaningfully.

Her eyes were two pools of shock, but I didn't let myself look away.

Hurting her hurt me, and I deserved all the pain in the universe.

"Certainly," I heard Grace say tightly. She stood up, reaching to hug my mother. "It was lovely to meet you, Mrs. St. Claire."

"You too, sweetheart. And again, I'm so sorry."

"Let me walk you out." Easton grimaced.

I knew I looked like a world-class jerk, but I figured whatever mess I'd created was salvageable with Grace. If I apologized and explained myself, we could still hang out and work together.

If she found out the truth about me through my mother, however, she wouldn't be able to look at me again.

East and Grace walked to the door. My mother swiveled in my direction, her face twisting in horror. "The poor girl."

"You were the one who took off her hat," I said flatly.

"You kicked her out. I've never known you to be this cruel."

Have you ever known me at all, Mother?

"Know what else is cruel? You showing up here. Barging into my shit like we haven't been strangers for the past goddamn five years. Making me pasta and meatballs for the first time in half a decade doesn't make up for all the time you haven't showed your face, Caroline. And before you give me the I-distanced-myself-from-you bullshit"—I raised my hand to stop her, because I knew what was coming; her mouth already hung open, ready to fire back—"*You* were supposed to be the responsible adult between us. *You* were supposed to reach out to me. I send you money each week. Do me a fucking favor and pay me back by never contacting me again."

Her eyes were full of tears. Her lower lip shook.

"Yes," she breathed. "That's right. You are helping us out financially. Doing what, exactly? Can you remind me? TA, was it?"

I could tell she was burning on the edges of hysteria.

I'd told my parents I was working as a TA, making money doing some tutoring on the side. They bought it because I had a natural knack for math and statistics, but as time went by and the money got *really* good, they must've been having their doubts.

"Didn't know money's this good in TA," Mom said.

I threw her a patronizing smirk. "You would if you'd ever gone to college."

"I didn't have that opportunity." Something dark and depraved that reminded me of myself crossed her features. "You know that."

"That's right." I snapped my fingers. "You were knocked up with me by seventeen, right? Great fucking life choices. Please, give me more advice about how to run my shit."

I shouldered past her to my room. She chased me, an angry scream ripping from her throat. Easton was still outside. Asshole probably used the opportunity to *walk* Grace home, now that he'd finally taken notice of the fact she was beautiful.

And you gave him the OK to ask her out. Nice going, moron.

"West! Please!" Mom was at my heel. I slammed the door in her face. Then opened it again, realizing I didn't get the chance to deliver the final verbal blow.

"Get out of my house." I pointed at the door. "You had no right using the hard-earned money I send you every week to buy a plane ticket. Splashing on me with my own money doesn't pass as good parenting either."

I grabbed one of the shopping bags from the floor, turning it upside down and emptying it at her feet. Shirts and socks rained down in a heap of cheap fabric. I thundered toward the door, opening it for her, pointing out.

"*West.*" Mom still stood at the hallway, her knees buckling. She sent a hand to the wall to right herself. She looked helpless, small, and out of sorts. Problem was, she was *always* hopeless. For years, she'd been the recipient of help, never giving any back. For years, my parents gave me nothing, and I gave them everything.

But even everything, I'd come to understand, wasn't enough.

I was fed up with living like a beggar, walking into a cardboard-framed death trap every Friday, and not even getting some privacy. Not only was I handing over my money to them, but now I also needed to give them affirmation that everything was dandy.

"*Out*," I roared, feeling my lungs quaking in my chest as I brought down the roof.

She ran out of my house like a timid mouse. I watched her from my spot at the threshold, panting like I'd just run a ten-mile course. She jogged all the way to the top of the street, then took a right turn, toward the only bus station in this ghost town.

I slammed the door, throwing a punch from hell to the wall beside me.

Maybe it was for the best that everything with Grace blew up to the sky.

She was scarred.

But me? I was *screwed*.

Chapter Twelve

Grace

EASTON GAVE ME A RIDE BACK AFTER WEST KICKED ME OUT, since I'd walked to West's place.

He was trying to talk about football and college the entire time, but all I did was move my mouth over my flame ring, making wishes, like Grandma Savvy had taught me when I was stressed.

The worst part was I didn't even know what I'd done wrong. I'd popped in to drop West's wallet off and warn him that Karlie knew we were at the food truck the night before. I'd lied to my best friend to keep both our butts out of trouble.

I figured his mother dropped in unannounced, since he hadn't mentioned it, and also because he looked like he was more than happy to fling himself off a cliff. I tried to make it as painless as possible, answering all of Caroline St. Claire's questions. I even tried not to make a big fuss out of the ball cap incident, even though I could feel my anxiety sucking the air out of me, sinking its lethal teeth to the soft side of my throat.

Was it my scar that embarrassed him?

Was it my general Grace-ness? The broken ring and the cap and the long sleeves? My strangeness stuck out in Sheridan, Texas like a stripper in a nunnery.

Or was West simply in one of his dangerous moods, and I was just one of his many casualties?

Whatever it was, dwelling on it wasn't going to give me any answers. West St. Claire didn't deserve my sympathy, and that was that.

Easton killed the engine when we reached the truck, turning his face to me. "Westie likes you."

"He's got a weird way of showing it," I managed to mutter, staring straight ahead.

"He does," Easton agreed easily. "It's uncharted territory for him. He either hates people or is indifferent to them. You confuse the heck out of him."

"He confuses the heck out of me," I retorted.

"You know what we need to do?"

"Kill him with fire?" I muttered.

Braun snickered, tilting his head as he examined me in a different way. Not just a sob story, but a fully formed person.

"Funny, he always goes for the agreeable ones. You're a little fighter, aren't you, Shaw?"

I rolled my eyes. I was getting tired of hearing how West always went for girls who were the exact opposite of me. I didn't need the reminder.

"You were saying?" I prompted. "About us needing to do something?"

"Oh, yeah." He snapped his fingers. "Press him where it hurts most."

"And where would that be?" I finally turned to face him, too.

The grin on his face scared me.

"His heart."

I'd seen West once on campus after *the* dinner. We'd ignored each other dutifully. He strode past me, remaining committed to his Grace Shaw Doesn't Exist policy, while I pretended I hadn't seen him either. He was quiet and curt on our two shifts together. I thought about confronting him, then figured if he was in no hurry to apologize, there was no desperate need for me to work things out either.

So, I gave West the cold shoulder right back.

It wasn't like I had time to sit and ponder over boy stuff, anyway. The day after the dinner with Caroline St. Claire, the local news channel announced that Sheridan's one and only bus station was going to close down by the end of the month.

Which meant potential caregivers for Grams would have to get here by car.

Which meant I had to pay them gas money, too.

Which was money I certainly didn't have.

That was what I'd been focusing on to take my mind off of West: looking for loopholes and ways to hire a caregiver for Grams who'd be able to commute here as cheaply as possible.

I was hunched in front of my laptop in my room when Marla rapped on my door, sticking her face in the gap between the wood and the frame.

"Honey pie? Whatcha doing?"

I clicked on the X button on the website I was surfing—*Care4You*—and sat back.

She scrunched her nose. "No luck, huh?"

I cracked my knuckles, shaking my head. There was no point in lying. I supposed Marla knew it wasn't easy to find her replacement, but I wasn't ready for another Find a Nursing Home lecture.

"Don't worry. I'll figure it out."

She nodded, entering my room and closing the door behind her. Uh-huh. That couldn't be good. Just when Grams was beginning to eat regularly again, after figuring out she couldn't sneak cracklins to her room for eternity.

"There's something I need to tell you." She perched awkwardly on the edge of my bed.

"Yeah?"

"The old bat has been refusing to go out on our walks. She is not getting any physical activity. I think she is depressed."

"Depressed?" I echoed.

"Ya know, down. Whatever those psychiatrist people call it. I don't think it's a phase. This rough patch is not going to go away, honey pie.

I've seen this happenin' over and over, taking care of folks her age. She needs to be medicated. Properly."

No shit, I wanted to scream until my throat parched. *I can't drag her butt to the doctor's office.*

But I just smiled, as I always did, nodding.

"Thank you, Marla. I'll handle it."

A few days later, Professor McGraw called me into her office again.

"I'll make it swift." She breezed into the snug room, her signature scent of incense and honey wafting behind her. She took a seat in front of me, entwining her fingers together.

"I decided not to give you an extension on the performance part of your exam this semester, Miss Shaw. Which means, you'll have to find a way to get into *A Streetcar Named Desire* and actually go on-stage, or you will be failing my class this semester. Mr. Finlay is well aware of the situation. I've spoken to him, and he said he is looking forward to sorting this out with you. I'm sorry, Grace, but consider this a favor from me to you. You must face your fears and move forward. Getting on that stage will liberate you. Whatever happened to you …" She shook her head, closing her eyes. "You cannot let it define you. Or stop you. Not anymore. Anxiety is a hungry beast. Feed it, and it will grow. Starve it, and it will die. This is my final decision. I'm sorry."

Later that day, I had a shift with West. Working alongside him wasn't ideal, but in order to dodge shifts with him, I'd have to tell Karlie all about what had happened at dinner, and I wasn't prepared to recite the humiliating scene aloud.

West had been acting weird throughout the shift. Glaring at me every so often, spacing out, opening his mouth to say something then thinking better of it. I stuck to silence, broken only by monosyllabic, work-related requests. Whenever there was a lull between human traffic, I got on my phone and looked for caregivers for Grams. There was also a typed-out message waiting to be sent to Cruz Finlay.

Hi. It's Grace Shaw. Any chance of landing a last-minute role in the play? ☺

Finally, West spat it out. "Look, I'm fucking sorry, okay? Jesus Christ." He growled as if I'd showered him with wordless accusations. "Regardless, I think maybe it's for the best if we don't mess around anymore."

I didn't even look up from my phone.

He'd spent the entire week ignoring me, only to give me a half-assed apology, stuffed into a clichéd breakup line?

"Messin' with you again was never on the menu," I lied, my eyes still on my phone.

"Fine. Okay. Good."

He nodded to himself. For the first time since I'd met him, he looked a little out of sorts. Kind of pitiful, actually. He offered me his pinky, blocking my view to my phone.

"Truce?"

I turned around, giving him my back and not bothering to take his pinky in mine.

A cold war was still a war.

West

The week after Mom's visit slithered like a slimy sci-fi monster out of a sewer.

As soon as Mother got back to Maine, she resumed her hourly phone calls, sending me two emails a day on average. She apologized a thousand times. For blindsiding me, tossing Grace's cap, asking too many questions, and sending too many emails. She owned up to everything that went down between us ever since I was seventeen. Tried to explain.

None of it mattered. The damage had been done. I kept sending money, but I dodged her calls.

Things went from bad to worse. Before I'd seen her face, I could pretend we were okay. But after the dinner blowup, there was no denying whatever had been left of my family was dead at the root. Rotting, sullied, and irreparable.

The cherry on the shit cake was the Texas situation.

The girl, not the state.

Though damn, the state got real hot, real fast.

I'd screwed up with Grace, not only on the day I'd kicked her out, but in the days after, when I couldn't look at her face. I was so embarrassed.

By the time I gathered the courage to talk to her, it was too late. She treated me like I was air. She'd gotten so good at ignoring me that week, sometimes I questioned my own existence.

Then I put on my big boy pants, owned up to my behavior, and apologized.

And what did she do? Looked the other way.

On our third shift working together since the disastrous dinner, Karma had finally reared its spiked dildo and decided to shove it up my ass—lube-less.

I was minding my own business, flipping fish on the grill, low-key envying them for the state of their nothingness, when I heard something dropping on the gravel by the window.

"Oh, hey," Grace's voice purred.

I didn't turn around to see who the customer was, still locked in my fort of quiet rage.

"Hi," Easton answered back.

"Do you want to speak to West?" she asked.

"Nope. Here for you."

My head flew up and I turned over my shoulder, my guard rising twelve feet. East was there, fresh out of the shower after football practice. His blond, damp hair stuck out in different directions on purpose. He wore a sleeveless surfer shirt that showed off his bulky arms.

What the hell was he doing here?

East met my eyes behind Grace's shoulder. He gave me half a shrug, as if to say, *You said it was cool if I hit that. Remember?*

I turned back to the grill, drawing a breath.

188 | L.J. SHEN

"*Me*?" Texas asked.

"Yeah."

"Okay, what's up?"

"I realized I forgot to do something when I gave you a ride home the other day."

Pick up some loyalty from the closest drug store, jackass?

"And what was that?" Grace asked, her voice turning suspicious. I liked that she didn't fall at his feet. She was immune to the charms of men in general.

"I forgot to ask for your number."

Motherfucker ...

"Why would you need my number?"

I couldn't help but grin to myself. She wasn't one of his teenybopper star-fuckers. Faith in humanity: partly restored.

"So I can ask you out."

"Ask me out?"

Ask her out?

"Yeah. Been meaning to do it for a few weeks now, but Coach has been on our case like a drill sergeant. Scrimmages, you see. Thought maybe you'd wanna grab a bite or something? Go to the movies? There's a new Kate Hudson film coming out this weekend."

"And you like Kate Hudson films because ...?" She left the question hanging in the air. My back was still to them. I was torn between wanting to snicker at her indifference to East's persistent flirting and bashing my best friend's (scratch that—*ex*-best friend's) head against the gravel.

"I don't like Kate Hudson films, Grace. But I do like *you*. And you're a woman. And women tend to like her, for whatever reason. That clear enough?" East asked.

I swung my head again, glaring at him. He didn't look at me anymore. His eyes were focused on Texas. What was the shithead trying to prove, exactly? That he could date someone I was interested in? That I liked her?

Even if I did, I didn't date, and he damn well knew that.

Grace drummed her fingers over the toppings bar. "Wouldn't it pose an issue for your roommate, seein' as we work together?"

"No. I asked him. Three times, actually."

"And he doesn't mind?" She didn't sound surprised.

Turn around and look at me, goddammit. Then you'd see I'd rather see my balls eaten by a tiger than watch you go out with someone who isn't me.

"Yeah. Ask him yourself."

"No need, we're not really on speakin' terms at the moment." She paused. "I accept."

Aw. Bet it hurt. Too bad he hadn't listened when I told him that she didn—

Hold on.

She accepts?

I opened my mouth to say something, but nothing came out. I had no argument against what was happening here and no grounds to stop them from dating. Technically, I had told Easton I wasn't interested in Grace. And, also technically, they were both single. I had no pull on either of them.

And that drove me nuts.

They exchanged numbers while I quietly fumed. Then he had the audacity to stick around and chitchat. Ten minutes into his riveting story about how Reign almost sprained his ankle victory dancing after a touchdown a few weeks ago, I sauntered to the window, parking my elbows on the sill, shoving Grace aside.

"Sorry, pal, this truck's not Bumble. Care to evacuate yourself before we get more customers?" My tone was casual. Bored.

Easton shrugged. "My bad, man."

"Don't come back unless you want to buy something."

"Duly noted. See you at home?"

"Where the fuck else can I go after work?"

"Yikes. Someone's touchy."

"Get the hell outta here."

He did. I slinked back to the grill, knowing damn well Grace's burn-in-hell gaze was scorching holes in my back.

My self-restraint lasted three minutes, after which I offered her my unsolicited input.

"Shit, Tex, didn't peg you for the naïve type." I let out a sardonic chuckle. "Easton Braun only does casual, in case you didn't know."

"Who says I don't do casual?" She rolled down the window,

closing shop. Was it that late? Guess time flew when you fantasized about new and creative ways how to kill your childhood friend.

She still had her back to me. "I did casual with you, and lo and behold, I'm alive and intact."

"*Texas*," I warned.

She whipped around, the wounded look on her face gutting me like a rusty hook.

"Don't call me that. Don't you dare act like we're cool with each other."

"Tell me what it'd take to change that."

I couldn't believe the words coming out of my mouth. I wasn't supposed to care. Caring wasn't on the menu anymore.

Not about my parents, my hookups, my so-called friends …

"Be a decent human?" she offered sarcastically.

"Anything within my capabilities?" I cracked a joke, testing my audience. She slammed her gloved hands over the toppings bar, starting to clean each individual container.

"Why did you say yes?" I asked. I should've just let her stay for coffee when Mom had been here. Bit the bullet. Had my secret spill out. Then spent the rest of my life trying to win her approval back when she realized what I'd done.

"Why not?" she huffed.

"You don't like Easton."

"I didn't like you either. Then I did, for a while. Opinions change. *Constantly*."

Something weird and unwelcome happened in my chest when she said that.

Candy apple dipped with poison.

Good news: She liked me.

Bad news: I'd fucked it up.

"You'll regret it," I warned. But I didn't know that. East could step up this time and take her seriously. Then what? I couldn't watch them together. I couldn't even imagine her holding hands with someone else.

"Maybe." She bypassed me, holding a silver container as she headed for the trash. "But I regretted ever knowin' you, too, and know what? I still survived."

Chapter Thirteen

West

"I T'S CONFIRMED—APPLETON WANTS A REMATCH." MAX plopped down in front of me in the cafeteria, clutching his lunch in his greasy fingers.

I was trying to figure out what the fuck was in the sandwich I'd purchased five minutes earlier from the canteen. I'd spent a good portion of my time on earth hating on Easton's soggy omelet sandwiches; I hadn't considered cafeteria food was far worse.

But Easton's sandwiches weren't on the menu for me anymore. Having them would require talking to Easton, and as of the last three days, we were officially beefing.

At first, my ex-best friend had the audacity to act like nothing had happened.

He'd tried to talk to me about football, then about a few campus rumors, then about how Tess had been going around telling people she got her Tarot cards read and apparently, she'd been told she'd marry a guy from Maine.

I adopted Grace's strategy and treated him like he was air.

I'd live off mud and ingrown nails before speaking to the traitor. Even when he pointed out that I'd given him explicit permission to date Tex, I didn't relent. He'd obviously pursued her to piss me off.

Mission accomplished—I was toeing the line of decapitating him.

"A rematch?" I elevated an eyebrow, scanning Max like I needed to scrub him off of the bottom of my boots. "Last time we fought, he and his friends blackmailed you, if I'm not mistaken."

I was *never* mistaken.

Max chuckled, ruffling his mane of fuzzy red hair, which re-minded me of those metal pads people used to clean industrial skillets.

"I mean, yeah, but I still made three times more than I would on a normal night. You win some, you lose some, right?"

I slam-dunked my sandwich into the trash, opting to pluck a bag of Cheetos from Max's hand. He made no move to reclaim it. I popped it open and threw a Cheeto into my mouth, eyeballing him.

"Asshole tried to claw my eyes out."

"Yeah, he was a little desperate to win. Had something to prove." Max stroked his pimply chin. "But the pay would be at least double this time. Emotions were running high last time. Word of mouth alone would allow us to up our charge on the tickets, and that's with-out concessions."

I did the math in my head. The number made my mouth water. It was high enough for me to be able to pay off my parents' loan, which was currently suffocating the hell out of them.

I'd finally get them off my case and give them what they'd always wanted—enough money to start over. Bonus points? I'd be out of their lives for good.

Sure, Kade Appleton was about as honorable as a used thong, and I was pretty certain he'd been following me around town, or at least sending someone else to do the dirty job for him, but I'd taken down guys three times his size, while I was in various levels of intoxication.

"Heard he's been running his mouth about me," I said.

"Can't say he hasn't. Ever since he lost the Vegas gig, he's been a bit of a Bitter Betty. Fighting is all he really knows how to do."

He was pretty good at whining, too.

"What's in it for him?" I jerked my chin toward my bookie.

"His pride," Max crowed, throwing his arms in the air. "You anni-hilated him. Knocked his lights out for thirty seconds straight. Then he argued and fussed about it like a pussy."

The 'like' had no business being in that sentence. He *was* a pussy. End of story.

I finished Max's Cheetos and cracked open his can of Coke, tak-ing a gulp and running my tongue over my teeth.

"I'm gonna have to set some ground rules."

"Such as?"

"Record the whole thing, so the asshole won't make excuses when I obliterate him."

"That's fair. I'll pass on the message."

"And winner takes all."

"All the money?"

I crushed the empty Coke can in my fist, tossing it into the trash without aiming. "You'll get your bookie cut."

I'd done some digging after my fight with Appleton and found out just how much of a shady jackass he was. Blackmail, dog fighting, stalking, and domestic assault took a huge chunk of his internet pres-ence. But the money was too good to pass up. I didn't mind breaking a rib or two. Hell, dying wouldn't be so awful either. It wasn't like any-one around truly gave a crap.

"One last thing—no funny business this time. If I catch him try-ing to shove fingers into my eye sockets, mouth, or ass, I'm breaking every bone in his body. No exceptions." I pointed at Max.

He nodded, his tongue almost lapping out. A rabid dog after a meaty bone.

"Sure thing. So, can I tell Shaun it's on?"

Shaun. I remembered the useless sack of muscles. He looked like every murderer in an eighties movie. A flashback of the moment I got out of the Plaza and heard murmurs from the bushes assaulted my memory. I pushed it away.

And so what if I was being followed? The outcome of the fight didn't make much difference to me. If they killed me before the fight, tough luck. If not, at least I'd be able to detonate his ass, take the money, give it to my parents and throw them out of my life for good.

"Make it happen." I rapped the table between us, getting up to leave.

I had a feeling this was going to implode.

Luckily, I didn't care.

I showed up to work fifteen minutes early. Karlie was there, standing in Texas' station, filling the bar with sour cream, guacamole, and fajitas. I slouched off my backpack, scowling at her ass.

"What're you doing here?"

What I'd meant to ask was, *where in God's name was Texas?* Had she stopped taking shifts with me now?

I'd apologized. What more did she need? Chocolate and flowers?

Chocolate and flowers. My brain had officially left the building. My dick, however, was in the house and calling all the shots. I wasn't buying anyone chocolate. Or flowers. Or matching purity rings, goddammit. Tex was just a friend. All I wanted was to have her back as one and, if possible, not get asked by Easton to be the best man at their wedding. Unless he wanted his bride stolen.

Karlie looked up from the sour cream she was pouring, sweeping her intelligent eyes over me. "Grace got the day off."

"I can see that. Why?"

She set the empty sour cream container aside, wiping her hands over her turquoise *That Taco Truck* apron.

"I'm sorry, how is it any of your business?" She elevated a manicured eyebrow. That was a good question. I wasn't entirely sure how to answer that. I just knew it *was.*

"I'm guessing she shared details about our last hang out with you," I quipped.

"You're guessing correctly. A few days late, but I'm now in the loop."

"And I'm guessing you are not deeply impressed with me at the moment."

"Also correct. Wow. It's your lucky day. You should be buying lottery tickets right about now." She blew a raspberry.

"You're fucking hilarious, Contreras."

"And you're a fucking douchebag," she quipped back.

"Tell me something I don't know."

"Are you sure?" She smiled tauntingly. "'Cause I got a few things I know that might be of interest to you and will spoil your mood."

I immediately saw what she was getting at.

I turned around, locked the door, then folded my arms and leaned against it, staring her down.

"Is this supposed to scare me?"

"Only if you don't tell me where she is."

I had an inkling Grace had gone out with Easton. I also had an inkling Easton was getting murdered tonight by yours truly.

"Get comfortable. Because I ain't gonna do that."

"I'll give you free tickets to the fight next Friday."

"Oh my God, really?" Karlie put her hands on her heart, squeaking. Her smile dropped immediately. "Hard pass. The beer is gross and you're not that important."

I racked my brain to figure out what a girl like Karlie might want in return for information. The answer was obvious. *Dick.* She wanted to hook up, like everyone else in college. She was with Texas' crowd. Meaning, she hung out with Bible-thumping virgins who treated the other sex like they were mythical creatures, only to be admired from afar.

Of course. A Bible-thumping girl would go for the whitest, most middle-class guy on campus. I remembered the night Karlie and Grace came to see me fight.

"I'll throw in a good word with Miles Covington."

"You don't *know* Miles Covington."

"He's my errand boy."

He wasn't, but I knew him well enough to get him to take her out if need be. Hell, for the right price, I'd have him marry Little Einstein.

She rolled her eyes, her shoulders dropping with a sigh.

"Well, it's not really a secret, anyway. I just wanted to mess with you." She excused herself.

I leaned forward, giving her my full attention.

"She went to the movies." Karlie jutted her chin out. "With Easton Braun."

There was only one movie theater in this godforsaken town.

I turned around and dashed out, bailing on my shift.

"Hey! Where are you going?" she hollered after me. "I can't do this on my own!"

"Have a little faith," I yelled back.

I was getting the fucking girl.

Whether I deserved her or not.

When the teenager with the retainer and unfortunate dad bod asked me what movie I wanted to see behind the box office glass, I pointed at the one with Kate Hudson on the poster.

"M—Mona Lisa a—and the Blood Moon?" he sputtered, pushing his thick glasses up the bridge of his nose.

"Problem?" I drawled.

The kid shook his head, his shoulders quaking with a suppressed laugh. He was about to get a front row seat to *How to Lose an Eye in Ten Seconds* if he wasn't careful.

I grabbed the ticket and got into the theater forty minutes into the movie. It was early afternoon. Who took a girl to a movie mid-day? A pretentious little shit like Easton, that was who. He'd probably promised to have her back home before curfew.

I went up the stairs, scanning the mostly empty seats. I spotted them in one of the back rows, huddled together, sharing popcorn.

I lumbered up the stairs, taking a seat beside Grace, essentially sandwiching her between Easton and me. Their eyes didn't waver from the movie. Collateral punishment for my shitty behavior.

I could practically hear East snickering in my ear.

"Here to team-tag Blondie?"

He hadn't even said that, and my fingers curled around the armrests, almost snapping the damn things.

Nothing about this was familiar territory for me.

I'd never had girl problems before.

My philosophy had been as follows: if they wanted to hook up—great; if not—no problem. The two relationships I'd had in high school were easy. My girlfriends had been physically pleasing and cool to hang out with. But I never felt like I could kill anyone who looked their way. And it was starting to feel like, in Grace Shaw's case, I had the tendency to get very jealous and very possessive anytime someone as much as breathed her way.

"I was an asshole," I piped up finally, my voice rough.

Grace popped two popcorn kernels into her pink mouth, blinking at the screen under her ball cap.

"Fine. *Am*. I *am* an asshole, happy?"

"Amp it up, man." Easton tsked, snickering into a fist full of popcorn. "I'm not hearing you owning up to it. I wanna see you sweat. Maybe throw a *Notebook* quote in."

Suddenly, I knew exactly what this was. My best friend wanted to prove a point. To show me I cared for this girl.

East pushed, and he'd pushed far, not because he wanted to tap Grace's ass, but because he wanted to kick mine into action. I'd been lying to myself since the day I'd met this chick.

A faint smile rose on Texas' lips. They were a nice pair of lips. Pale and pillowy, the bottom plumper than the upper one.

"He's right," she teased. "A quote from *The Notebook* would make everything better."

"Shh!" someone a few rows below growled.

The Notebook, they said? I'd watched it a thousand times with … *never mind.*

My jaw ticked, and I ignored the rapid pulses in my eyelid. "You got a taste for humiliation?" I scanned her coldly.

"Tit for tat," she tutted. "You humiliated me. It's only fair that I witness you squirm."

Damn this girl to hell. I closed my eyes and took a deep breath.

"I could be whatever you want. Just tell me what you want, and I'll become that," I said quietly.

It might not have been verbatim, but it was damn close. She shivered in her seat. Easton threw his head back, his entire body quaking with silent laughter. He wasn't going to be so happy when I got back home later tonight to pull out his toenails with tweezers while he watched.

"I'm sorry I shoved you out the door the other day. It was shitty, and rude, and out of order. It wasn't because I didn't want you there. My mother and I don't get along—as you can tell from my ignoring her constantly—and I didn't want her to say something that would offend you. Which, ironically, blew up in my face."

In my periphery, Easton's body was now practically shaking in his seat with laughter. He got up. I spat the apple candy in my mouth into the cup holder between us before it snapped in two.

"I'll leave you two lovebirds to it. Westie, don't be … uh, *you*, basically." Easton excused himself, clapping my shoulder on his way out. He skipped down the stairs, merry as a stoner at a dispensary.

Grace turned to face me. Again, I found myself cursing the douchebag who'd invented ball caps. I could hardly see her face.

I took her pinky in mine and squeezed. She let me. She tipped her chin up. Those damn summer sky eyes were going to be my undoing. I'd always been an ass man, but those eyes did to my dick what no ass on planet Earth could.

"Tex."

"I hate you."

"I know. Tex?"

"Next time you're a jerk, I won't be so forgivin'."

"Duly noted. *Tex*?"

"We can be friends again, but this is your last chance."

"Tex!"

"*What!*"

"Fuck friendship. I miss your lips."

Her shoulders eased, like she'd released a breath she'd been holding. "They missed you, too." Pause. "The rest of you, not so much."

This girl gave as good as she got.

And she got a whole lotta shit from the world.

I grabbed her cap and flipped it backwards as I dove in for a kiss. Even through the coat of popcorn salt, she tasted warm and sweet and soft. Always so fucking soft. I sucked her lower lip into my mouth, nibbling on it until she moaned and gasped, clutching my shirt.

My eyes were so heavy lidded, I could barely keep them open, but I still didn't fully shut them. She was gorgeous like this, in the dark, the blue lights of the screen dancing across her face. I wanted to ink this moment into memory, because I knew I *would* screw it up eventually.

I was going to lose her.

But at least I was going to *have* her first.

This was going to be temporary.

And painful.

And worth it.

The only thing that had changed between today and yesterday was my acceptance that the train wreck had left the station and was now heading toward a sizzling pile of explosives at a rapid speed.

I wanted Grace 'Texas' Shaw.

Wanted in her pants.

In her mouth.

In every hole she possessed (apart from the urethra, maybe).

I wanted her mean jokes and pure heart and dazzling eyes, and that bumpy scar that felt like silk under my fingertips.

Her skin was a continent of explorations I wanted to unveil, and kiss, and nibble. To learn her stories—her fears—by tracing my lips along all the places of her that hurt once.

She slid her fingers into my hair, producing small throaty noises that made all my blood rush south. Our kiss was feral and deep, our tongues twirling together. I'd never enjoyed kissing so much. Normally, it was just a pit stop on my way to my final destination—Boneville.

But I could kiss Texas to oblivion and back, without coming up for air. My thoughts sounded like a dated Hallmark card, but that didn't make them any less true. Or any less goddamn disturbing, for that matter.

Her hand slid across my pecs, down my six-pack, her fingers curling over the first button of my jeans.

"Wanna get out of here?" Her lips traced mine as she spoke.

I unglued my mouth from hers, studying her face. She looked sober, and I was one hundred percent positive she didn't want to go to the concession booth for more stale popcorn.

"I only have one condition," she warned.

Was it the moon she wanted me to give her? I was open to that. I'd give her the sun, too. I just needed a little time, and maybe a loan or two.

And definitely good life insurance.

"Lay it on me."

"I don't want to become one of your Tesses or Melanies. No one-night only rule for us." She shook her head. "I want you to treat me with respect and care. I know we're casual, but …" She sucked in a breath, her voice dropping along with her gaze. "For me, it means something. To open up again. Promise you won't break my trust, West."

It was the drunkenness of the moment that made me do it.

Forget about my oath to myself. Piss all over my promise not to make any promises.

All I thought about was being inside Grace. To drown in her purity, hoping some of it would rub off on me.

"Promise."

The word rolled out of my mouth before I could stop it, tasting like ash. I couldn't take it back. It was there, between us. Alive, swelling, and growing by the nanosecond, pressing against my sternum, making it hard to breathe.

Promise.

Promise.

Promise.

Remember what happened the last time you made a promise?

Grimacing at my own stupidity, I took her hand.

"Let's dip."

Twelve minutes later (yes, I counted), we were in front of Texas' house. Marla had just finished her shift, skipping down the porch's steps, pushing a cigarette into her mouth and lighting it up.

"That's all she wrote, kids. Have fun and keep your hands to yourselves. You especially, St. Claire."

Grace stood on the first stairway leading to her doorway. The sunset smeared across the sky in pink and orange around her, making her look like a fallen angel.

Apparently, I was now taking note of the fucking scenery *and* waxing poetic.

I wanted my balls back, but I wanted them slamming against Grace's pussy even more.

"Do you want to come inside?" She jerked her thumb behind her shoulder after Marla left.

"Any man who tells you differently is buying expired condoms in bulk." I leaned against Christina casually, trying hard to pretend I didn't care, when I'd already proven to be so far gone for this chick I wasn't even in the same zip code as my fucking brain anymore.

It took Tex a second to get it.

She wrinkled her nose. "No bulks for you, huh?"

I shrugged. "Call me old-fashioned, but I like to treat my companion to a good time that includes no-strings-attached or unexpected trips to the pharmacy."

"Such a fine gentleman."

"So I've been told."

"And to think I always pegged you as a surly ass."

"I am."

"Not with me."

She wasn't wrong. Maybe that was why I couldn't keep away from her, even when every bone in my body (other than my bone*r*) begged me to.

"You remind me of how I was before." I pretended to wipe invisible dust from my Ducati to do something with my hand.

"Before what?"

"Before everything."

We stared at each other. Church bells rang in the distance. She took her ball cap off, clutching it between her fingers in her lap. Even though no words were spoken, I knew she was inviting me in.

I took a step.

Then another one.

She didn't stop me.

By the time I got to her, my toes touching hers through our shoes, we were both breathless.

"I don't know what we're doing," she croaked, tilting her face up. It was the most I'd ever seen of her face. Still full of makeup, but sans the ball cap, the sun sinking its claws inside her skin.

I took her hands in mine.

"Let's find out together."

It was the first time I'd been inside Grace's room. Her grandmother sat in front of the TV, half-napping, half-cursing at VH1 for their poor video clips choices. She looked about as static as the sound coming from the monitor, but pointing it out to Grace seemed counterproductive. Not only for the blood-filled salami between my legs, but also because Tex seemed adamant not to send Mrs. Shaw to a nursing home.

Texas' room was exactly what I would have expected from Grace Shaw before her scars: peach-colored walls filled with pictures of herself with her grandmother and groups of smiling, wholesome friends. White embodied linen, pompoms, and tickets to plays and movies she'd gone to pinned onto a board along with handwritten letters. It didn't escape me that her room was in fairly good condition and probably redone after the fire.

She'd wanted to keep being the person she'd been before.

Had hoped that would be the case, which made her tragedy so much more painful.

Grace Shaw was the exact opposite of me.

I tore apart everything that resembled my life pre-tragedy. She held on to hers for dear life, refusing to let go.

I stood in her room, waiting for her to come upstairs while she checked in with Mrs. S. She appeared at the door holding two glasses of iced tea. I didn't know when or how, but she'd managed to put even more makeup on her face between the time we rode home and now.

Tex went ham with the foundation. It looked like she had an extra face, and I couldn't imagine it was better than the real thing. Plus, that damn ball cap was on again.

We stood there staring at each other.

"Hi," she said again, nervous. "Maine."

"Texas."

"How do you like our weather?"

What the fuck were we talking about? I was only half-sure.

I swallowed. "It's very fine."

I took a step closer.

She stayed put.

I took another step closer.

The swell of her breasts rose as her breath hitched. I was throbbing so hard, I felt my pulse in my dick.

I reached for her, tossing her ball cap to the floor.

I felt like that John Mayer song they played to death on the radio a few years back. "Slow Dancing in a Burning Room." Everything was urgent, yet agonizingly slow.

We were toe-to-toe now. She didn't back away. I clasped her chin between my thumb and index, tilting her head up.

"Trust me?"

She nodded, her throat bobbing. I caught her lips in a blistering kiss. It was deep and slow and methodical and different from every kiss I'd ever had. I curled my fingers over the hem of her shirt, jerking her close, until we were flush against each other.

Grace kissed me back, gasping, trying to catch her breath. When her fingers fumbled for my zipper, I raised her shirt, one inch at a time. I wasn't nervous about what was waiting under it. But I knew she didn't feel the same.

When I hiked her shirt up to her ribs, Texas stopped my hands from climbing upward, slapping one of my hands away. I raised both my palms up in surrender. She broke the kiss off, taking a step back.

"Sorry." She chuckled. "Maybe …" She hugged her midriff, tucking her left cheek shyly to her shoulder. "Maybe we can just do it with our clothes on? I mean, you can take yours off. And I'll take off my pants, obviously …" She closed her eyes, turning beet-red under her makeup. "You won't mind, right? I guess you hardly have time to undress your hookups at the Plaza …"

"*Don't*," I barked, feeling my nostrils flaring. "Apples and oranges."

She winced.

Deciding to change tactics, I toed my boots off, then my socks. I pulled down my jeans and briefs in one go, standing in her room completely naked from the waist down. Just me and my raging hard-on, both of us staring pointedly at her.

Her eyes widened.

"Umm, okay? This was sudden …"

"Shirt off, baby," I ordered in a low growl. A tone I was familiar with, that was all me. She narrowed her eyes at me.

"I told you it made me uncomfortable. Why do you insist on it?"

"Because you're under the impression whatever I'm going to see is going to be a turn-off for me, and what better way of proving how mistaken you are than by showing you." I pointed at my throbbing cock. It was purple and swollen. So erect, I doubted I had blood left in other parts of my body. Hell, if I cut my wrist open, I'd probably bleed bone.

"That's not an experiment I'd like to take part in."

"Then I guess you'll have to flick the bean to get off." I crouched—yes, without my goddamn pants on—making a show of picking up my jeans.

"Wait!"

I froze mid-action, smiling to myself with my head bowed down.

"You won't … we won't do it if I don't show you my scars?"

I straightened my spine, licking my lips as I took off my shirt, now standing butt naked. That was better. Nothing felt quite as emasculating as standing partly naked in front of someone (though buying one midday showing ticket to a Kate Hudson flick came in close).

The things this chick makes me do.

"That's right. Tit for tat. I'm naked. You're naked. That's the equation."

She stared up at the ceiling, shaking her head. "It ain't pretty. The left side of me anyway."

"Every part of you is lickable. Nothing is going to change it. Especially your battle scars. Now get naked before I faint from lack of blood."

She hesitated before removing her shirt in one rapid flick. She unclasped her bra then squeezed her eyes shut, wincing as she awaited my verdict, standing very still in front of me.

I stroked my cock, drinking in every inch of her torso. Her stomach was flat, her tits pear-shaped and bouncy. Her nipples were tiny, perfect for my mouth, and pebbled. The left side of her body was marred from the fire. Uneven, angry stains of red and purple wove across her skin like a painting.

Everything about her was honeyed and smooth and fuckable to a fault.

I advanced toward her while her eyes were closed. With every step I took, her breathing became shallower, until I was standing beside her.

She stopped breathing.

So did I.

I bent down, taking the nipple of her left, marred breast between my lips and sucking it deep into my mouth. She moaned, her hands shooting to clasp my head. I dropped my forehead against her collarbone, my cock pulsating between us, begging to get in on the action.

Down, boy. Not yet.

"If you tell anyone about this, I'm goin' to kill you." She drew me closer to her uneven nipple. A shade darker than her right, healthy one and a few inches larger due to scar tissue. I gave it the royal treatment. Kissed and licked and tugged softly with my teeth, running the tip of my tongue around the areola and blowing on it. She shuddered, thrusting her breasts in my face. Her entire body was arched and ready.

"About what? Your scar, or sucking your tits?" I moved to her other, "normal" nipple. I was half-crouching, and my quads were on fire. But I wanted her to see just how much she turned me on. Which reminded me …

I took her free hand, the one that didn't try to yank out my hair, and circled it around my cock.

Still hard as a rock and just as intelligent, considering I made you a fucking promise I'm definitely going to break.

"Both," she croaked. "Lord, you're so hard."

"You're so beautiful. And so fucking insane," I murmured to her flesh, now alternating between her tits, kissing and massaging, getting acquainted with them.

We're going to become the best of friends, ladies, my kisses said. *And spend a whole lot of time together.*

I hoisted her up so her legs wrapped around my waist and carried her by the ass to her twin bed. I eased her down to the mattress, not breaking the kiss as I unbuttoned her jeans. She stroked my dick, up and down, her hands unsure but eager. I wondered how much experience she had in the sack. The fact she wasn't a virgin didn't mean jack shit. I didn't know anything about her ex-boyfriend, other than the unpromising fact he hadn't stuck around after the fire.

He was—you guessed it—on my growing list of people to kill if I ever went berserk.

Grace kicked her jeans down her ankles. I stroked the outline of her pussy over her white cotton undies, a violent shudder racking through my body.

So this was what being horny felt like. I must've mistaken bored and restless for desire until now, because nothing I'd ever experienced came close to this moment.

Her hand moved faster over my dick. I yanked her underwear sideways, dipping one finger in while kissing a path down her throat. *Soaked.* I began thrusting two fingers into her, working her up, knowing I couldn't keep the foreplay up much longer without coming.

Her hot mouth was on my jaw, sucking and nipping. My tongue was on her scars again, lapping, biting. I was rough. I was confident. I didn't treat her like a china doll. A precious, fragile thing to be handled with care and pity.

I treated her like someone I wanted to fuck until my dick fell off.

She moaned, "More."

I slid another finger into her, pumping as her hisses became louder. Greedier. She dropped her hand from my cock and clawed at her bed, pushing her face into her pillow to stifle a little scream, her hips bucking into my hand, demanding more.

"West, please."

"Please, what?" I licked my way down her belly button, dipping my tongue into her perfect innie. My mouth watered as the scent of her became more prominent. I wanted my lips on every inch of this girl, so next time I saw her, I could look at her and think—*I know what she tastes like. Everywhere.*

"If we don't do it right now, I might explode," Grace said.

"I'll spare you the trip to the ER."

I rose to my knees, took my wallet out of my back pocket from my discarded jeans on the floor, grabbed a condom, and ripped open the packet, sheathing myself as one of my hands fondled her blemished tit. For some reason, it appealed to me even more than her milky white side. It turned me on, seeing how much she'd been through. How she'd come back swinging, strong and feisty. A survivor.

I sank back down, my body draped all over hers missionary-style, angling my cock toward her center. I drove in an inch at a time, hissing at every fraction of movement. She held my waist, sucking in a breath. We both watched as I slid in. She was hot and wet and damn snug.

Swear to God, I'd never wanted to be in Texas more than in that moment.

It was only when every inch of my cock was inside her that I looked back up at her face again and saw her biting her lower lip, stifling a giggle.

Which … wasn't the usual MO for chicks who were under me.

I frowned. "Something funny?"

"It's you." She shook her head, her face glowing with mischief. "You look like you are on a mission. You should see yourself. So focused. So concentrated."

I glared at her, not sure how to react.

"When I saw your, eh, *thing*, in the food truck, I was ninety-nine percent sure I never wanted it inside me. It seemed too big. Too threatening. But you make me feel so comfortable. Thank you."

I dropped my head to her shoulder, giving it a quick kiss. Essentially, she'd just told me my dick wasn't *that* big.

"Stop talking," I ordered.

"Why? You're so adorable."

She called me adorable while I was *inside* her. Was I ever going to recover?

"Fuck you," I groaned.

"Please do."

"On it."

I began moving inside her. Holy shit, did she feel amazing. Sex always felt damn good. But with Texas, it wasn't just better, it was … *different*. We fit.

With each thrust, I felt my balls tightening and tingling, my dick throbbing and pulsating. She shivered in my arms, and I knew she was close, too.

C'mon, Tex. Come before I do.

I wondered since when did I care. I wasn't a complete jackass. I made sure it was fairly good to the person I was with. Oral aside, I ticked all the boxes—foreplay, strumming their pussy like it was a violin, kisses in sensitive spots, et cetera, et cetera. But I never cared if they hit the big O. Not as long as I knew the happy customers would recommend me to their friends.

With Texas, I cared.

"West. Oh. Lord." She grabbed my face and lowered my head. I kissed her roughly, my fingers finding her clit between us and rubbing in circles.

Come, or I will have to die from cum poisoning.

"Are you close?" I groaned.

"I'm ..." she started, but then flinched, froze, and every muscle in her body tensed like she was having a stroke. She clenched around me so hard the rest of my body had no say in what happened next. I felt my cum shooting into the condom as I experienced the most intense orgasm I'd ever had.

She spasmed around my cock.

"Comin."

Thank. Fuck.

"Me too, baby. Me too."

Grace

I had sex.

With a boy.

Here was the real kicker—I enjoyed it. I even climaxed once.

Fine, twice.

All right, *thrice.*

Who would have thought?

Not me, that was for sure. The carnal need in me to feel another body against mine, warm and alive, blew up like a hand grenade the minute West put his lips on my marred nipple and didn't even flinch.

I tiptoed my way to the living room in an oversized shirt after spending the past three hours with West. It took us ten minutes to recover before tearing at each other again after that first time. I'd suspected we could have gone all night if it wasn't for West running out of condoms.

Grams was asleep on the couch, snoring softly, her lips pinched in stern disapproval. I scooped up the tiny woman like she was a toddler, carrying her up to her bedroom. It was probably a weird visual to an outsider, but I'd gotten used to it over the years.

Savannah Shaw had the childlike quality of not waking up when she was put to bed. I'd been doing it for a while now. Even before Grams began losing touch with reality. When she still worked two jobs to support us. She'd always fall asleep on the couch. At first, I'd woken her up so she could go to bed—our sofa was narrow, tattered, and itchy—but she'd always wake up for good and end up cleaning the house, doing the dishes, or folding the laundry. With time, I mastered the art of carrying her to her room and tucking her in.

After I put Grams in her bed, I went back to my room. It was dark, hot, and damp, the scent of sex and man lingering in the air. The iced tea glasses I'd brought hours ago remained untouched, framed by little pools of sweat on my nightstand. West was sprawled in my bed, his arms tucked behind his head, his eyes trained on my ceiling, which had been freshly painted four years ago. He was shirtless, his lower parts covered haphazardly with my blanket. I took a mental photo of him like this, in my territory, calm and content.

My gut wouldn't let me believe this picture-perfect moment would last.

He patted an invisible space next to him. "Join me, Tex."

"You're not leavin' much room." I ran my eyes along his frame from the doorway. A lazy smile spread over his face.

"Guess you'll have to get on top of me, then."

It was still mind-blowing to me that he looked past my scars. Of course, he hadn't seen the true extent of their ugliness under my makeup, but they were still there nonetheless. I slid on top of him, bracketing his waist with my thighs, squeezing as I ground over his erection through my blanket.

He groaned, kneading my butt cheeks.

"Pretty sure my dick's got skid marks at this point. Up for a fourth round?"

"We ran out of condoms." I laughed throatily.

"I'll pull out."

"Are you insane?"

"Horny. Which must be technically the same, because I've never suggested that in my entire life."

"We're not doin' that."

"Why not? I'll be fast."

"You're really selling this to me." I rolled my eyes.

He laughed. "Fast to pull, not to finish."

I ran a hand over his forehead, cheeks, and chin, leaning down to kiss the tip of his nose. He was perfect. Every single part of him. Unmarred, smooth, and striking.

"We'll do it again soon. And be safe about it," I whispered.

"Promise," he demanded, covering my hands with his on his chest so I couldn't move. I thought about the promise he'd made me earlier tonight. To never break my trust.

"Promise." I smiled.

We snuggled after that. I lay on top of him, skin-to-skin, my ear pressed against his pec, listening to the steady drum of his heart. I thought he fell asleep as the room grew dark.

Then he spoke. "Are you ever going to tell me what happened to you? And no, I'm not asking because I saw your scars today. I'm asking because you act like it never happened, yet you let that shit define you. Every. Single. Day."

My breath caught in my lungs. *Here we go.*

It was one of the reasons why I hadn't gotten close to anyone since what happened. Avoiding the questions, the confessions, the ugly truth behind the uglier scars. But didn't West deserve a bit of honesty after everything we'd been through?

He did make a promise to me, even though he'd sworn to never do that.

I opened my mouth, not sure what was going to come out of it.

"Nobody knows exactly what happened the night of the fire."

His chest flexed beneath my head, like I'd knocked the air out of him.

"Rumors around town spread like wildfire, but nothin' had been confirmed, and I'd like to keep it that way. That's why I don't advertise it."

Plus, reliving the worst night of my life wasn't exactly my favorite pastime.

I twirled the flame ring around my finger, watching it intently, and suddenly hating it with a passion.

Hating Courtney for never giving it to me in person.

For not being there when the bandages came off.

For not taking responsibility for what she'd created—*me.*

West stroked my hair. My yellow and gold locks fanned across his bronzed skin. It looked beautiful. Like the sunset.

He should marry a blonde. The thought came out of nowhere, clogging up my throat. *Like who, you?*

"There's not advertising it, and there's not acknowledging it ever happened. I've known you for months, and you haven't mentioned it," West said.

I closed my eyes. "What do you want to know?"

"Everything. I want to know everything, Tex."

One more tiny breath.

One last kiss to his chest.

Then I dove in, telling him what only Karlie and Marla knew.

"It was just another night. A Tuesday, actually. It always surprises me, how the days that reshape and change our lives forever start so ordinary and unassuming. Grams was workin' two jobs at the time. Her day job was at a cafeteria in a middle school in town, and her afternoon job was helpin' out at the local grocery store. But she still insisted on cookin' me homemade meals and being there for my cheerleadin' gigs and my plays. She was exhausted. And forgetful. All the freakin' time."

I took a deep breath, pushing through the details. It was like going uphill in the midst of a snowstorm.

"I had a boyfriend at the time. His name was Tucker. He was a football player. Popular, handsome, comes from a good, known family here in Sheridan. He stayed the night that day. He stayed the night often, but when Grams came home, he'd slip out through my bedroom window, so by the time she woke me up in the morning with waffles, he wasn't there wrapped around me. She called him The Octopus," I recalled, a small smile tugging at my lips. "Since the day she found him in my bed, our limbs were tangled together."

"We can skip the parts where other guys touch you," West grumbled.

"The window was rusty, so it made a cracklin' sound I'd gotten used to."

I felt him nodding, but he didn't say anything. My chest hurt. Each word that passed through my mouth felt like chewing and swallowing glass.

"I was asleep when it happened. Grams came home, probably late. She fixed herself some gin and tonic, lit a cigarette, and sat downstairs. Finished her drink and went up to her room.

"The worst part was that I heard the crackling sound, after the cigarette ember caught and moved across the couch, but I was so tired, I thought it was the sound of the window when Tucker sneaked out, not knowing that he'd left an hour before Grams came home."

The memory was fresh and real, the scent of the fire assaulted my nostrils, my lungs filling with black smoke. I could see what happened next vividly behind my eyelids. I opened my eyes in the dark, my heart galloping against West's chest. He secured his arm over my back, pressing me so deeply against him, I thought I was going to drown in his body.

"I'd only realized what was happenin' when I started coughin'. I sat up in my bed and looked around. Something was wrong. Smoke rolled from the door crack. The room wasn't that foggy, but the clouds that seeped in from under the door were dark and hot. I jumped out of bed and called for Grams. Her room was at the end of the hall. I got out of my room and saw that the fire reached the second floor. It was dancin' across the top stairway. I swear it looked like it was taunting me, West." My words tripped over one another. A lone, fat tear rolled down my cheek, landing on his bare chest. The second it hit his skin, he groaned, almost like he'd sucked all the pain out of me and felt it in his bones.

His lips brushed the crown of my head. "You don't have to continue."

But I wanted to. For the first time, I wanted to get this off of my chest. To cleanse myself of the burden of knowing the truth and keeping it from the world.

I took another breath, soldiering on.

"I ran to Gram's room and dragged her out. We couldn't jump out. There were rosebushes directly under her window, and Grams had a bad hip. Besides, she was fast asleep. I shielded her with my body, wrapped her around like a human blanket, then charged back to the hallway. By the time we made it out of her room, the second floor began to collapse, like a stack of cards. A part of the wall warped on top of me. It pressed against my left side. Hard. For a few seconds, I couldn't move. We were crushed against a wooden plank, and the plank was on fire. I felt my face, my shoulder, my arm meltin' away. I was sure this was it for me. That I was already dead."

Another tear fell on his chest. I remembered thinking being dead still had some life to it. I could still hear things and feel pain.

"I fainted. Probably from the adrenaline and pain. What woke me up was Grams. She was wide awake and screamin' bloody murder, crushed beneath me, but safe in my arms. Her voice kicked me into action. I wanted to save her, no matter the cost, like she'd saved me when my momma ..."

Left me at her door.

Ran away with her tweaker friends, never looking back.

"I grabbed Grams with the remainder of my strength and got us both out. I remember what I did when we were finally out of the house. Just when it started folding into itself, like in the movies, the flames dancing so high, they tickled the sky. I rolled on the grass, screamin'. It was damp from dew, and soothed my burnin' skin. By then, there were a few ambulances and fire trucks parked in front of our door. My downfall had an audience. Everybody came out of their houses to watch. Including Mrs. Drayton, who got out with her three-year-old son, Liam, clutched in her arms. He'd asked her aloud, '*Mommy, why does Grace smell like toast?*'"

I closed my eyes again.

His chest caved beneath me.

Toastie.

That was how the name stuck. Eden Markovic overheard Liam say it, and passed it on to Luke McDonald, who told all his friends, who told their parents, who told everyone at church.

Even when they didn't say it to my face, they still said it behind my back. I knew every single person in Sheridan heard the tale of how I rolled around on the grass like a dog in heat, shouting like a mad-woman as my face melted away in front of an audience.

The ungraceful fall of Grace Shaw, who'd almost slipped from the deadly claws of the screwed-up future her mother had given her. *Almost.*

"Texas …" The rawness in West's tone snapped me out of reliving that moment.

I shook my head. I wasn't finished. "Wanna know the worst part?" I licked the salty tears around my mouth.

"I thought I already did."

I smiled bitterly. He had no idea.

"When Grams woke up at the hospital, she was very confused. She didn't remember anything. Not even the part where I got her out of the fire. I don't think she had dementia back then. I think she just blanked out, or maybe it was the first raindrop in what was going to become a thunderstorm. Either way, I was on life support and unconscious when they asked her what happened …" I stopped, forcing myself not to break. Not to scream.

I wasn't there when she'd given them her version of the story. I'd been busy fighting for my life as my inner organs failed, a few rooms down from her. "When they asked her what happened, she said her granddaughter must've tried smokin' one of her cigarettes and left it unattended downstairs. She didn't remember causing the fire. Still doesn't. She thinks it's my fault. And … well, I let her think that, because it doesn't matter. By the time I woke up, everybody made up their minds, and the insurance company accepted her version of things. It was a done deal. The fire was my fault."

That was the story Grams offered Sheridan, and the townsfolk ate it up.

Grace Shaw, daughter of Courtney Shaw, the infamous, late junkie, played with fire and got burned. After all, she must've inherited Momma's flavor for trouble.

"Really, it was her fault for trying her grandmomma's cigarettes. What kind of kid does that?"

"An utterly irresponsible one. And it took away her best asset—her beauty!"

"Try only asset. Poor Savannah Shaw can't catch a break. First, her daughter. Now, her granddaughter. She ain't nothin' short of a saint, yet both of 'em broke bad."

I heard it all.

With my ball cap on, my oversized clothes, and my head down, I was barely recognizable. Completely invisible. And hard to miss when you were out on the town, eager to gossip.

I lived in a town I hated, among people who were suspicious of me, with no chance at escaping, because I needed to take care of my grandmother—who'd started the fire she'd blamed me for.

West cupped my cheeks—even the tainted one—and forced me to look up at him.

I blinked away the tears, holding my breath as I awaited his verdict.

He kissed my forehead, his lips lingering on my skin, then said the most stupid, outrageous, beautiful, awful, touching thing anyone had ever told me.

"I'm grateful that Tuesday went down the way it did." His voice was scratchy. Thick. "Because the worst day of your life gave me the best version of *you*."

Chapter Fourteen

Grace

THE NEXT DAY, I WALKED THE LENGTH OF LAWRENCE HALL toward its cafeteria, hugging my textbooks to my chest. I thought about how weird it was that so many things had happened in the same week.

West had begun to work at the food truck.

The rehearsal for *A Streetcar Named Desire* had started.

And because our university auditorium had been under construction ahead of the big show, fifty percent of my classes had moved to Lawrence Hall—where West spent most of his time—until the end of the semester.

Normally, I wouldn't have seen him too often. We were on opposite sides of the university, in different buildings, in different cafeterias, even different sections of the parks.

Suddenly, our lives were entwined everywhere.

An arm snaked through the narrow gap of the men's restroom, yanking me inside.

My back hit the wall with a thud.

West's face popped into my vision. He boxed me, running his nose along mine, his hot breath wafting over my face.

"Texas Shaw. Fancy seeing ya here."

"Well, you *did* drag me in here." I clutched my books to my chest tighter, still unsure whether I was delighted or annoyed with his gesture. Yesterday, after the post-orgasm fog had dissipated and West had grabbed his stuff and left, I wondered what on earth I was doing. What were we?

A couple?

Friends with benefits?

A gorgeous, obnoxious, colossal mistake?

I gave him access to my everything—secrets, body, deepest, darkest thoughts—and I didn't even know where we stood. It irked me. A part of me wanted to claim him as mine, but another warned me I wasn't ready for the gossip that came with it. To the questions and whispers and self-doubt, when the world would no doubt remind me Sheridan's best would never truly settle for its worst citizen.

West's lips latched onto mine. He grumbled into my mouth as he pried my lips open, thrusting his tongue inside. I whimpered, my textbooks dropping on the tiles between us. A warm surge of pleasure pooled in my womb. Lord, the man knew how to use his tongue.

When he pulled away, it took me a few seconds to find my voice again.

"You owe me three textbooks. I'm not pickin' these up."

He looked down and laughed, kicking them aside.

"On it."

"How can I help you, St. Claire?"

"Why, I'm glad you asked. Suck me off after our shifts tonight," he said briskly.

"No can do. I have to look for caregivers for Grams."

He gave me a look I didn't like. It was the same look Marla and Karlie offered me. The one that told me I needed to look reality in the eye and start looking for nursing homes. They were more affordable in the long run, they'd accommodate her situation, force her into medicating, and she'd lead a more active lifestyle. I knew all that, but I couldn't help but fear she'd never forgive me.

It wasn't what she wanted.

At least, it wasn't what she *thought* she wanted.

"I'll help you out."

"You will?" My eyebrows shot up.

"Sure."

"Why?"

"Why?" He tapped his lips, leaning into my personal space, making a show of thinking about it. "Because I want to spend time with you. Ideally horizontally."

I punched his shoulder. He pretended to stumble back, holding on to his "injured" deltoids.

"Horizontally, huh?" I rolled my eyes.

"Vertically too. How are your oral skills?"

"You're not about to find out anytime soon. Tit for tat, remember?" I wiggled my eyebrows, feeling so normal my heart swelled. He swaggered back to my side, slipping his hand under my shirt and kneading my left breast, dragging his mouth from my collarbone to my neck.

"Speaking of tits, I missed those."

"Such a romantic."

"I can be anything you want me to be." He grinned mischievously. "Other than a unicorn. I can't be that."

And truly mine, I thought bitterly.

I stumbled out of the men's restroom, making a stop in the girls' restroom to apply the makeup he probably ruined in his quest to nibble on my face, then went into the cafeteria, on the lookout for Karlie.

My best friend was sitting with a bunch of her brainiac friends, crouching over thick textbooks, arguing heatedly over something. West was three tables down, with Easton, Reign, and the football crew. Guess all was well between West and Easton, now that the latter was out of the picture and West and I were finally happening.

Easton raised a hand and winked at me good-naturedly.

Reign look the other way, avoiding my gaze.

And West? He flat-out ignored me.

I moved quickly, sliding into the seat next to Karlie, giving her arm a squeeze and disregarding the pang of disappointment prickling my chest. He didn't even say hi.

"Hey, Karl! You having a good day?"

She started talking as I sneaked another look at West. He wasn't looking at me. He was talking to Tess, who parked her hip on his table, schmoozing while flipping her raven hair.

He is not your boyfriend, my brain reminded me.

My heart, however, wouldn't listen.

West and I quickly fell into a routine.

During the days, we'd be in college, acting like we did not exist to each other. So much so that people had stopped wondering if I were under his protection, and judging by our scene the night I showed up at the fight club, started talking about how we were archenemies. This made me even less popular—I was now officially the idiot who got on West St. Claire's bad side—but now no one could accuse West for drawing attention to me.

I knew it was exactly what I'd asked him for, and yet, I couldn't help but hate it when we passed by each other, training our faces to be cool and blank. Then again, the alternative of people knowing about us, and judging and whispering and talking about just how much I didn't deserve the greatness that was West St. Claire, wasn't really an option. I didn't need a reminder to the fact most people didn't think I deserved him.

On the days when we had shifts together, we'd work, laugh, talk, then head over to my place. He'd entertain Grams while I showered, reapplied my makeup, did the laundry, and made dinner. Then the three of us would eat together before I put Grams to bed.

Grandma Savvy adored West. He was charming, polite, and rolled with whatever mindset she was in. If she talked to him like he was Grandpa Freddie, he played along. If she recognized he was West, Gracie-Mae's friend from the food truck, he'd be himself. One day he even pretended to be Sheriff Jones. Though I wasn't impressed when he tried to carry on his charade as sheriff when we slipped into bed and he began ordering me around.

After dinner and putting Grams to bed, West and I would lock ourselves in my room and explore each other. Sometimes we were slow and leisurely. Sometimes fast and desperate. But we always clung to each other a moment too long, and every time we said goodbye, I watched his back from my window, knowing he was taking a part of me with him.

West made no effort to conceal where he stood about Grams. He wanted me to put her in a nursing home but recognized he wasn't going to succeed where Karlie and Marla had failed.

That didn't stop him from trying, though.

He would drop leaflets and brochures for nursing homes in Austin and its surrounding areas in my mailbox and on my desk. Twice, he had asked to use my laptop and left the window open on a website for places that came highly recommended for people in Grams' condition. Whenever I talked to Marla and West was in the kitchen, and she told me how Grams wouldn't want to leave the house or visit a doctor, he'd flash me a look.

I knew he was trying to help. I was running out of time to find a replacement for Marla.

Fridays were the worst.

I never went to his fights. Doubted they would let me in after he'd lost his temper on me the last time—plus, one time was quite enough. Seeing him bleed wasn't my jam. I hated it, even though I understood why he did it.

Friday was the only night we spent apart. We made up for it every Saturday after work. I'd make sure I kissed away every bruise and welt, spent extra time licking his wounds and worshipping every inch of his aching body.

I was falling for this warrior of a man, who fought to get his family back on its feet. Literally.

There were only two things that took away from my sheer glee at having him to myself.

One—I still didn't know what we were. Where we stood.

And two—I started to wonder whether he ignored me on campus because I asked him to or because he was embarrassed. It was one thing to play, suck, and bite on my marred skin in private when we were in my room, running his fingers over my bumpy flesh as he pounded into me, beads of his sweat dripping down my imperfect flesh, and another to publicly endorse me as his girl.

I tried to tell myself that West wasn't the give-a-crap type of guy. He couldn't care less about his own popularity and what people thought of him. But that didn't always work.

Even though it drove me nuts, not knowing what we were, I refused to ask him. I didn't want to be one of *those* chicks. The needy, submissive types that flocked to him so often. One of the reasons West was attracted to me in the first place was because I refused to throw myself at him like everyone else in this college town.

As for him ignoring me at school? As much as I hated it, I didn't want it to change. I still didn't want people talking about us. I was still scared of the uproar it could cause.

The first hint that we were more than just friends with benefits came on a Tuesday night, of all days. I was on the phone with our electric company over an unsettled bill I knew I'd already paid. I was cooped up in the kitchen, going over the bill with the customer service representative. Grams kept tapping my shoulder, saying that she wanted me to help her get in the shower.

"Some daughter you are, Court. Your momma's asking you for help."

"Give me a sec … ah, *Momma*." I patted her hand distractedly. West was leaning against the fridge, watching us with his arms folded over his chest nonchalantly. He hated when I pretended to be my mother, even though he pretended to be whomever Grams thought he was at any given moment. He explained that it was different. That he hadn't been raised by her, didn't care if she remembered him or not.

"What? No, I don't … this is not true. I have the reference number for the transaction. Of course I paid."

"*Lord, Courtney! I stink!*" Grams boomed over the representative's words on the line. "Help me."

I was getting flustered. I couldn't afford to pay the bill twice. Grams kept moping around me, getting in my face. I dropped my forehead to the kitchen counter, closing my eyes and drawing a breath.

"Hold on a moment … Momma," I murmured, more to myself than to Grams. "*Please.*"

"Come on, Savannah, let me help." West stepped in, and I turned around, my phone still pinned between my shoulder and ear, glaring at him hard, as if to ask, *are you out of your mind?*

222 | L.J. SHEN

Grams, however, seemed content with his idea, linking her arm in his.

"You don't mind helpin' an old gal, do ya', West?"

She remembered him and not me today? *Fun.*

"Ma'am, it'd be my pleasure."

"No peekin'."

"Wouldn't dream of it, Mrs. Shaw."

They tromped out of the kitchen before I had the chance to object. Grams could manage a shower most days—I'd put a wooden chair under the water spray and all she needed was to reach for the shampoo and soap—but it was vital she had someone in the bathroom with her in case she fell.

West would have to see her naked. To help her in and out of the shower. *Lord.*

Ten minutes later, I had settled the bill with the electric company and taken the stairs to the second floor, two at a time. I peeped into the bathroom through the cracked door, not making myself known.

West was leaning against the sink, his back to the shower, telling Grams about one time when he gave his mother's blind cat a shower when he was four. Behind him, Gram cackled in the shower breathlessly, sitting on her wooden chair, enjoying the stingy stream of water on her back, running a sponge over her arm.

"Lordy! You couldn't have. Christ, I would've whooped your butt good if I was your momma."

"She wanted to, Mrs. S. Trust me. The only thing standing between her and whooping my ass was my speed."

That made her nearly topple over with laughter. I smiled, my chest tightening, something warm rushing through every blood vessel in my body.

As if sensing my presence, West's eyes shot up and met mine.

He smiled, but didn't comment on my snooping.

"All right, I'm ready. Hand me my towel, young man!" Grams swiveled in the chair, turning off the water. West plucked the towel from the hook and handed it to her, his eyes still on mine.

She patted herself dry, and when she had secured her bath towel around herself, he helped her to her room while I slipped back into mine, letting them have their moment.

Half an hour later, I tucked Grams into bed and made my way back to my room.

I found West plopped down on my bed, tossing one of my old pompoms like a ball in the air, catching it every time. I sat at my study, powering up my laptop and logging into Sheridan University's website to see if Professor McGraw had answered my latest email. My guess was that she hadn't. She'd been ignoring my pleas ever since she'd made up her mind about not letting me pass without taking part in the play. But I never could send that text message to Cruz Finlay. Standing on-stage was just something the phoenix in me wasn't capable of. Not yet.

"Tex?" West grumbled behind my back.

The whooshing of the pompom flying up and down in the air soothed me. It was something Tucker might have done. Back when I was still normal.

We all remember how that ended, right, Grace? So don't get your hopes high.

"Yeah?"

"You ever gonna take off your makeup in front of me?"

I blinked at my screen, forcing my pulse to keep beating at a normal pace.

"Why are you asking?"

"I've seen every inch of your body up close, and I'm still here. I've never seen your face bare, though. Don't you think that's weird?"

"Nope." I typed away on my keyboard. "I don't feel comfortable showin' my face to people."

"Karlie has seen it. Marla too."

I said nothing. He wasn't Karlie. He wasn't Marla either. He was the boy I loved—really loved, wasn't just infatuated with—and I didn't want him seeing me at my ugliest.

The realization that I loved him didn't shock me, nor did it freak me out. In the back of my mind, I'd known it to be the truth for a while.

I was in love with West St. Claire.

Madly. Wholly. Obsessively, even.

He was the most complex man I'd ever met—sweet, caring, kind, responsible. But also violent, aggressive, offhanded, and cruel.

And I couldn't get enough of him. I shook with fear from the thought that we were going to end at some point. He was going to graduate and move on, and I was going to stay here and mourn his loss.

"All I'm saying is, I want to kiss your face without it tasting like a wall."

"Speakin' of …" I swiveled in my chair, feeling my walls building up. "Don't you think it's unfair you know what happened to me, but you never told me what happened to *you*?"

I had no doubt West wasn't about to share his darkest secret with me. Nothing had changed on that front. He still wouldn't pick up the phone whenever his parents called—which was often—and became cagey whenever I brought up his old life in Maine.

"Life isn't fair," he clipped.

"Ah-huh. That's what I thought."

"You don't want to know."

"Why?" I asked, turning back to my laptop, pretending to type on my keyboard in an effort to appear casual. In reality, I was fully invested in the conversation. Of course I wanted to know. I was hungry for whatever information I could have from him. The only thing stopping me from asking Easton about what made West the way he was, was my loyalty to the man on my bed.

"Because you won't be able to look me in the eye after you hear what I've done. Topic closed."

The whooshing of the pompom stopped. My chest was knotted with anxiety. I'd already figured whatever happened to West was vastly different from what happened to me.

My battle scars were external, on the surface.

His were internal, but cut deep.

He was disfigured inside, perfect outside. A lethal combination.

"Reign is throwing a party this Saturday. You're going."

I spun my head around, spearing him with a deadly glare. "Reign's an asshole."

"Reign is harmless. And you're going to have to face people at some point. You're going," he said again, calmly.

"Why would I go there?"

"Drink. Dance. Be a normal college chick."

"I'm not a normal college chick," I pointed out. "And the only friend I have would never go with me. Karlie has three study groups over the weekend. Are you crazy?"

"Not that I know of, but I wouldn't rule it out completely. I've been known to do some pretty fucked-up shit. I'll pick you up at eight."

"Wait, you want to go *together*?" I slanted my head sideways, feeling my eyes widening. We never did anything together outside of my house. Outside of my *bed*. Unless I included the food truck, which I really couldn't, because we were both paid to be physically present there at the same time.

West helped me with Grams, but I always thought of it as a kind of barter. Him looking out for me the way I looked out for him.

He sat up. "Yeah, together. Are you unfamiliar with the concept?"

"I … I didn't think we were …" I tried to articulate the part that confused me, although in truth, it was all of it. "Together-together."

So eloquent, Grace.

"You didn't think we were together-together?" he repeated, dumbfounded.

"Why would I? You keep telling me it's casual."

"Casual shit still counts for something."

I smiled bitterly. "Then consider me bad at math, because I don't think it does."

"Wait, am I your fluffer?" A cocky gleam zinged in his eyes.

"Fluffer?" I spluttered.

"You know, the person who jacks off porn stars or gives them half a blowie so they'll get hard before the shoot. Someone who fucks the issues out of you, so that by the time Prince Charming rides into town, you'll be ready for him?"

He said that with a smile, but I could tell he wasn't joking. I was surprised he'd even suggest that, considering he was the one who went on and on about his no-strings-attached rule.

I reared my body back, narrowing my eyes at him. "No, you're not my fluffer. But you said you only do one-night stands."

"Yet here you are, dozens of nights in, still thoroughly fucked," he deadpanned, like I was stupid.

"You ignore me at school."

"You mean, like you explicitly asked me to?"

Were we arguing or declaring our feelings toward each other? I was confused.

"I know. But it still makes me feel weird," I admitted. "Maybe you should stop ignoring me."

"Maybe I should. Let's start with me taking your ass to Reign's party this Saturday."

"Fine. But I refuse to socialize."

"Ditto." He leaned over, fist-bumping me. "That's why I'm bringing you along. At least I'll get a hookup out of it. East's been riding me hard about showing my face in public."

So that was why he was going to a party. Easton was nagging him to get himself out there. West had the reputation as someone who was usually above social gatherings.

He picked up the pompom he'd discarded on my bed, tossing it up to the ceiling again, one hand tucked behind his head, smirking.

"Shit, Texas. Looks like you and I are going on a date."

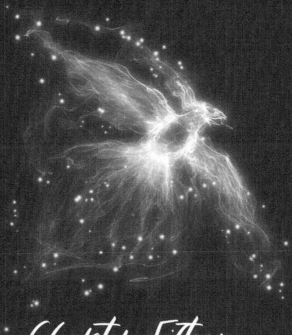

Chapter Fifteen

Grace

"It's not a date," I insisted to Karlie the following day as we both walked out from the lecture hall, heading toward my pickup. "Easton forces him to go out. We're probably goin' to stand in the corner and sulk together."

But even as I said it, I didn't really believe it. I didn't want to make my best friend feel left out. West St. Claire and Karlie Contreras didn't hang out with the same crowd, and the last thing I wanted was for her to think I was ditching her for the cool kids, even though, in all probability, she was studying or working on Saturday and wouldn't be able to make it anyway.

Karlie examined me skeptically. She knew West and I were having sex. On the one hand, I could tell she was excited about me finally coming out of my shell. On the other, I could also see why she was worried I'd get hurt. West didn't scream steady boyfriend material. Heck, he didn't even whisper it.

Karlie stopped by my pickup, balancing her laptop case against her waist.

"Don't drink anything unless you pour it yourself and keep your phone with you at all times. Just stay safe, okay?" It sounded like a warning more than a request.

"How do you mean?" I eyed her.

She shifted her gaze sideways, like her eyes would reveal something she didn't want me to know.

"Remember the day you went on a fake date with Easton Braun and I told West where you were?"

I remembered. I knew Easton had only taken me out to put West in his place. I'd played along, because I didn't want to lose West as a friend. If that was what he needed to snap back into place—a reminder that I wasn't disposable—I was ready to prove it to him.

"Yeah?"

"Well, West said he'd hook me up with Miles Covington if I spilled the beans about your whereabouts. It wasn't why I told him, of course; I knew you wanted him to know. I just wanted to see him sweat. I forgot all about West's agreement with me. But then Miles *actually* asked me out."

"Isn't that awesome?" I blinked at her, not following. "Miles is a great guy, and you seemed to be into him when we were at the Plaza."

Karlie's eyebrows furrowed. She looked at me like my phone was off the hook.

"You know I stand no chance with the guy. He just asked me out because West told him to. Miles said he didn't want to get on West's bad side. Your precious boyfriend is the campus bully we always stayed away from when we were kids. He's playin' everyone like a puppet master. I don't know, Shaw. He seems to have too much power 'round here."

"Karlie, he just wanted you to meet a nice bo—"

"It's not just about Miles. I heard West has been messing with the wrong crowd. Taking fights with dodgy people, mixin' up with criminals. Stuff like that. There's plenty of rumors going around, and I don't want to say anything that's not true, but I don't think I realized what kind of trouble he was when I hired him."

The roles were now officially reversed. I was all for West, and Karlie thought we should be wary of him.

"Don't go cagey on me, Karl. What do you know?" I asked.

She gnawed on the side of her fingernail, torn between wanting to tell me and avoiding a fight. "I heard he arranged a second fight with Kade Appleton. Know the guy? He's a local. Allegedly beat his pregnant girlfriend to a pulp and got kicked out of an MMA league for it. It was all over the news."

West told me Appleton didn't play fair. I nodded faintly. My paper heart wrinkled into a ball of sorrow. He'd tell me, wouldn't he? West told me everything.

Other than what matters.

"I'll ask him about it."

"Tell him not to do it. If he messes with the wrong people, and you are associated with him, you could get in trouble, too."

"West's smarter than messin' around with criminals, and he'd never put me in danger."

"West is fearless, and stupidity is bravery's mistress. Recklessness is its wife, something else he has in abundance."

She was, of course, right. I knew that. I popped the driver's door open.

"Don't worry. West is a good apple."

A green candied apple.

And possibly a poisonous one, too.

"Did you agree to a second fight with Kade Appleton?" I asked West when we were on the Ducati, on our way to Reign's party. Hot wind swirled my yellow hair. I wore another long-sleeved mini dress. White with pink dots, paired with hot pink heels. I took a risk in wearing lacey sleeves. If people paid close attention, they could see some of the scars on my left arm. But I felt wild and beautiful next to West. A full-fledged phoenix, stretching out its golden wings, flying sunward, with glittering specks of fire in its wings.

West turned his head back toward me, but all I could see through his helmet were those smoldering, earth-scorching eyes that shone like beacons in the dark.

"Where'd you hear that?"

"Doesn't matter. Is it true or not? I don't want you gettin' in trouble."

He whistled low, making a show of downplaying the entire thing. "You sound like my mother."

I sound like your girlfriend, you hopeless brute.

We cut through the assortment of stores on Main Street. The Albertsons grocery, little café, and pizza parlor. There wasn't a soul in sight. Everyone worth knowing was currently at Reign's frat house. Karlie was right. This definitely wasn't our scene.

"Just answer the question, West."

"And if I am?"

"Then I'll have to ask you to kindly withdraw from the fight on the grounds that he almost killed you last time."

"I won the match."

"Half-dead," I quipped, trying to keep my temper in check. "How do you expect me to sleep at night knowing you're goin' to fight some bastard who beat up his pregnant girlfriend?"

"I don't expect you to sleep at all. I expect you to wait for me with a beer until I'm done whooping his ass, preferably spread eagle, with a bow over your neck."

"Are you fightin' him or not?" I bit out, not half-entertained by the visual. I had a feeling that if Kade Appleton were given another chance at fighting West, he'd use it to kill him.

I felt his muscles going rigid under my fingertips. He was angry. Tough luck. I wasn't going to let him risk his life to cut a paycheck. It was our first real argument as a couple. Even though it made me nauseated, I stood my ground. Maybe that was why West refused to fall in love. Because when you loved someone, and they hurt you, it felt like your soul was shredded to tiny ribbons.

"I'll tell Max the fight's off," he clipped, just as he parked in front of a red-bricked Georgian building with white columns, hoisting one leg over Christina. "Now get off my case, woman."

We headed to the door, shouldering past clusters of partygoers while I tried to recall what had made me think it was a good idea to come here. My eyes roamed the people around us. The more I drank them in, the colder my blood ran.

West had left out one little detail about the party—it was *anything but clothes* themed.

Girls were strewn on the front yard's lawn, sheets of bubble wrap swathed around them like strapless mini dresses, secured by fashionable belts. They all waved and blew kisses to West as we passed them, shooting me inquisitive looks. A herd of guys who'd taped fluffy animals to their genitals manned the front doors. They fist-bumped West when we got to the entrance.

"Yo, St. Claire. Wassup, wassup, wassup."

"Move," he grumbled, snatching my hand quickly, like I was a parcel he needed to dispose of. One of the guys held up a hand.

"Sorry, man. You know the drill—no rules, no party." One of them pointed at a sign on the door.

Get naked or get goin'

A tall blond guy scanned me head-to-toe, crunching an empty beer can in his fist.

"That's a nice piece of ass you got there, St. Claire. Need help undressin', baby girl?"

West flashed him a look that sobered him up instantly.

"I will smoke your ass and use the rest of you as munchies if you so much as look her way again," West drawled, icy venom leaking from his words. His grip tightened on my hand, almost punishingly, like he hated to be put in this position. "Now move. The. Fuck. Away."

"Whoa. Sorry. Didn't know she was your actual girl." The blond guy blew a raspberry. They stepped aside, and we ambled in, fully dressed.

A bunch of dude-bros slid on top of a king-sized mattress down the wide stairs to the landing, using it as a sleigh, wearing cardboard boxes as diapers.

West tugged at my hand as we moved through the rooms, stopping at the kitchen for booze. He handed me bottled beer and popped another one open for himself. I took a sip and leaned against the kitchen island, looking around me.

"Having fun yet?"

"Immensely," I bit back with as much sarcasm. From the corner of the room, we spotted Max. A cheerleader-type was draped under his arm. "Sixteen Years" by Vandoliers blasted through the speakers, and I wondered who was in charge of the playlist and if I could marry them.

The girl next to Max jerked his arm and pointed at West, obviously begging for an introduction.

"Gimme a sec." West squeezed my shoulder and walked over to them, leaving me behind. I took a pull from my beer, watching the three of them, feeling something heavy pressing against my chest.

He was going to bow out of the fight for me.

It made me feel important, and beautiful, and not at all casual.

When West got to Max, the freshman jumped up and down, asking my boyfriend for a selfie. He stared at her like she was a nuisance, but agreed, sending her away as soon as she was done. He and Max huddled in the corner of the room, speaking with their heads down.

"Howdy, Grace. Cute outfit. I guess for you, being dressed in anything short of a windbreaker is naked." Tess sashayed over to me, clinking her beer with mine. She was wearing an elaborate dress made out of real roses dipped in black, which left little room for imagination or modesty. By her hooded eyes and the sway of her body, I could tell she was drunk.

"Hi, Tess. How's it goin'? How's the play comin' along?"

I was present at every single rehearsal, so I knew it'd been going pretty horribly. She and Lauren were bickering nonstop. Tess was clearly still wounded by the loss of her favored role. As for Lauren, I had to agree she wasn't the best option for Blanche; then again, I really didn't think anyone in my class measured up to Vivien Leigh.

"It's goin' real well," she slurred, dragging her words heavily. "Hopefully there'll be scouts coming in for the premiere. Otherwise, I wasted a perfectly good time of my life for nothin'."

I smiled, ignoring the slash of jealousy ripping through my chest. "I'm sure there will be many scouts there."

She leaned against the island. We both looked on at West and Max. She let out a loud, un-Tess-like hiccup.

"So nice you started hanging out with Westie. Who knew working together would earn you a friendship, aye?"

I didn't correct her assumption that we were just friends. I knew she liked him and rubbing it in wasn't my style. Besides, she was clearly skunk-drunk.

I liked Tess, despite her shortcomings. She reminded me of the old me. Sweet to everyone, no matter how they ranked in popularity. She was also part of the Friendly Visiting Program, where students had weekly visits with elders in the community. I knew, because Grams had told me Tess had been visiting her friend, Doris, since her freshman year at the university.

"He's great."

"He really is. I just think it's so unkind that people are making up all these rumors about y'all being a couple. I swear, college folk just live for the drama. Men and women *can* be just friends. We're not animals, you know!" Tess let out another hiccup, putting her beer to her mouth.

I knew there was bait to be taken here. West was arguing hotly with Max in the corner of the room.

Tess didn't wait for me to contribute to the one-sided conversation. She took my silence as an invitation to continue. "When I heard you guys were an item, I was like, no way. You know I've always rooted for you, Grace. There's something about you that really resonates with me. You live with your nana, right?"

"Yeah."

She nodded briskly. "My grandparents raised me, too. I still visit them every chance I get. They're down in Galveston. Anyhoo, I told people they should mind their own business. That you and Westie are just there for each other. I mean, you're too smart not to know that if he takes you to his bed, it's just because he feels some sort of way about your …" She shot me a sidelong glance, flinching. "Life story."

"Life story?" I decided to play dumb, smiling sweetly. "I'm not sure what you mean, Tess. I had a great childhood, right here in Sheridan."

She put a hand over her heart. "Bless your heart, you wouldn't, would you? I sometimes don't see things for what they are when I'm in the situation, too. What I mean is, Westie's had it pretty rough. He seems banged up about something. He needs someone to make him feel good. Helpful. I don't know about you, but I'd never lower myself to the position of being someone's pity-girlfriend."

"Pretty sure you would lower yourself to any position possible, if it involved havin' West." I put my beer on the counter behind us, no longer worried about how I came off, and pushed off of it.

West was right—it was high time I put people in their place.

Parking a hand over my waist, I turned to Tess fully. Her smile wilted like the roses wrapped around her body. But I was on a roll. For the first time in years, I felt secure in my place.

"I know what you think when you look at me, Tess, and it's not that I take good care of my grandmomma. You're thinkin', *thank God it didn't happen to me.* You value your good looks and hold on to them. Well, let me tell you, sister, one day you are goin' to wake up and find out you're not the prettiest girl on campus. Or at your workplace. Or—know what? Even in your household. Your beauty is just one brief chapter in your history book. Nothin' but a sweet, elusive lie. Elegant wrapping paper, wrapped around a mysterious gift. And while it is true beautifully wrapped gifts are more appealing to the eye" —I cocked my head sideways, giving her body a quick, cold scan—"I'm sure whatever I have to offer under my wrapping paper's worth more than your ugly words tonight."

I straightened my spine, tilted my chin up, and walked away. Through the wall mirror in front of me, I could see Tess standing behind me. Mouth agape, face pale, heart shattered. She watched as I made my way to the bathroom. I waited in line, taking out my phone and texting Karlie.

Grace: Tess Davis just heavily implied West is only with me because he feels bad about my scars.

Karlie: Right. Because St. Claire is big on charity. What a dumbass.

Standing up for myself didn't feel half-bad.

Ten minutes after waiting in line, it was finally my turn. The bathroom door finally swung open, two giggling girls skipping out of it, sniffing and rubbing their noses. I was about to close the door, when an arm shot behind me, prying it open.

"No way, Jose. You're goin' to wait in line just like all of u—" As I yanked at the handle, a large, dark figure shoved me into the bathroom, locking the door behind us with a soft click.

I stumbled backwards and turned around to face the towering man, my back bumping against the sink.

"Jesus Christ, West. Ever heard of knockin'?"

"Rings a bell. That's another word for whacking, right?" He crowded me, pinning me against the sink. My hands shot to the basin behind me. My heart was doing Olympic-level acrobatics. His chest was flush against mine, his eyes hooded, dark, and full of desire.

"Been looking for you." His breath stroked my face. Apple candy and sawdust and the man who could destroy me without laying a finger on me.

"I figured you weren't done with Max, so I excused myself to the powder room."

I was pretty sure this place was indeed full of powder, but not the kind ladies used as makeup.

"Did you tell him?" I asked breathlessly. He gave me a curt nod, grabbing the back of my thighs in his calloused hands.

"Broke his heart, and bank account, probably, but I did it. Tess looks a mess." His mouth fluttered against mine teasingly as he hoisted my legs up to wrap around his narrow waist. "Tried to catch me on my way here, asked me if we were banging."

"She did?" I felt my lips puckering. "What'd you tell her?"

"To mind her goddamn business."

"What did she answer?"

"Didn't stick around long enough to find out." His nose brushed the side of my neck, his mouth traveling down my skin.

"She insinuated you're pity-bangin' me," I explained, ignoring the ribbons of pleasure each of his kisses unfurled inside me. "Said she'd never lower herself to this position. I told her I was pretty sure being on her knees was her favorite position."

West dropped his head back, laughing in his low, feral baritone. "Nice claws, baby. Can't wait to feel them on my back."

"I may have a face even a mother can't love, but when it comes to dishin' it out, Tess Davis has got nothing on me."

His laughter rang in my ears, bouncing on the walls around us.

"You're hot as shit, Tex, but that smart mouth." He cupped my face, giving me a little peck. "One day it's going to get you into trouble. Better wrap it around my dick as penance."

He tossed my ball cap into the sink, licking a path from my forehead down my nose and to my chin. I shivered with goose bumps, giggling and swatting him away.

"Watch the makeup, St. Claire. Also, what the heck are you doing to me?"

"Showing you what we are." His voice turned strained. His tongue rolled down the column of my neck, leaving a delicious shiver in its wake. His teeth grazed the collar of my dress as he continued dipping south, dropping to his knees, his rough paws seizing my waist, locking me in place. I let out a small whimper when his face was parallel with my groin. He nuzzled the hem of my mini dress, hiking it up so it gathered around my midriff. My white cotton panties were soaked, and I could smell my own arousal filling the air. He kissed my center through the fabric, closing his eyes and drawing a long, hungry breath. He groaned into my sex. Every bone in my body rattled with anticipation.

"Hi, Grace's pussy. It's me. West. We meet again."

My eyes bugged out, and I looked down at the crown of his head.

"Actually, we haven't met face-to-lips yet. I usually send my errand boy your way. You might know him—tall, thick, accompanied by a couple nuts?"

I bit down on my lip, trying not to laugh. He continued, undeterred.

"But there's a pressing matter we need to discuss, so I figured we should talk it out. Mind if we lose the panties?"

When my lower set of lips failed to answer him, he looked up, wiggling his brows.

I gave him a curt nod. "This is weird, but I'm excited to see where you're going with this."

He slid my underwear down, brought his mouth between my folds, and parted them with a wet lick. A hot surge of pleasure shot up my spine, and I grazed his rumpled hair with one fist, holding on to the sink tighter with my other to keep myself upright.

"Lord."

"All right, Grace's puss, here's the deal. Your owner isn't sure what we are to each other, and she's been not-so-subtly hinting at that recently, so I took her out to a party. Know what happened next?"

Instead of waiting for my sex to answer him, he used the tip of his tongue to circle my clit, using his fingers to pry my folds open, stroking my opening before dipping one finger into me. My hips jerked, and a sound I didn't recognize fell from my lips.

The bathroom door rattled with a sudden pounding.

"Hey. Get outta there, assholes. I wanna take a leak!"

West ignored the person on the other side, sucking my clit,

pumping lazily with his lips while fingering me. My knees buckled, and he threw one of my legs over his shoulder, angling my hips so his fingers hit a deep, sensitive spot inside of me.

I panted like crazy, dropping my head back, my mouth falling open. "Oh, Lord."

I could feel myself tipping over the edge, hitting the big O, when he suddenly stopped, removing his finger from me and licking the length of my pussy leisurely, like he hadn't a care in the world.

"Anyway," he continued in his matter-of-fact tone, "as I was saying, Grace isn't sure we're the real deal. What do you think I should do in order to show her I'm serious about her?"

I tugged him by the hair to look at me, snarling.

"Make her come."

"Using third person now." He arched his brow. "Does getting eaten make you lose IQ points, Texas?"

"Keep teasing me, and you'll be losing your head!" I bared my teeth.

The door rattled again. "Jeez, open up!"

West's lips wrapped around my clit again, and he pumped his finger faster inside me. I shattered into a million pieces, crying out as spasms ran up and down my body, every inch of me on fire.

West continued latching onto the lips between my legs until my climax dwindled. He rolled my panties up, then kissed my center through my underwear again, peppering the gesture with a smile and a pat.

"Good talk. Next time Grace and I have an issue, I'll come directly to you."

He rose up to his feet, took my hand, and pulled me into a bear hug. I shook in his arms and didn't even know why. Something about what had happened was emotional for me. Maybe because West had told me he didn't go down on women normally. That it meant something to him. I buried my head in his shoulder.

"Do you know what I wanna do right now?" he murmured into my hair.

"What?"

"My girlfriend. I want to do my girlfriend right this second. Ready to roll?"

"I was born ready."

West got out, wiping his glistening mouth with his forearm as he shot the stunned guy on the other side of the door an indifferent, go-screw-yourself smile.

"Sorry, sweetheart. The tampons are in the bottom drawer. All yours." He gestured to the open door mockingly.

I followed behind him, and we dashed out, practically skipping our way to Christina the Ducati.

Chapter Sixteen

West

Max: Sorry, bro. Shaun says fight's still on. I tried everything I could. I swear.

Max: He said he'll let you off the hook if you take the financial blow and compensate. Interested?

Well, that gave the word *fuck* a whole other, less pleasurable meaning.

I'd agreed to take the fight with Kade Appleton prior to hooking up with Grace. Now that I wanted to bow out of it to keep her ass pacified (and presumably myself alive), Appleton, who'd agreed to all of the rules I'd dictated to Max some weeks ago, called me out on it and came back to the negotiation table with an ultimatum: pay up the losses or fight.

Nothing about what he asked made sense. We'd lost zero money since we hadn't sold any tickets yet. Hadn't even officially announced the fight. Still, reasoning with Appleton and his manager was like trying to teach a toad linear algebra.

West: Tell him to go to hell.

I tucked my phone into my back pocket at the food truck. The fight was getting closer, and I didn't want to lie to Grace about what was going down, but I sure as hell wasn't going to pay the bastard with money I didn't have either.

"What's with you?" My girlfriend flashed me a crooked smile, rubbing my arm. We were closing up for the night. I dropped a kiss to her ball cap.

"Nothing. Just Max being Max. Can Marla stay with Grams a few minutes more? I want to grab a bite before we head home."

Home. I was half-living with Grace at this point. Luckily, East was too busy dipping his dong in every other female on campus to mind my absence. I'd barely seen him at Reign's party. I needed to sit Texas down and tell her what was up with the fight, with no interruptions.

"I'll check." She moved from the open window to the fridge, putting away some containers. I'd leaned over to roll the window down when I noticed movement in the dark. Two pairs of eyes twinkled from behind black ski masks, staring back at me.

Male.

Large.

And goddamn threatening.

I heard the soft click of a gun as the hammer cocked back.

"Unlock the door"—the cold barrel pressed against my bare wrist—"unless you want your precious arm blown off."

The mask muffled the voice, but the order was clear.

I took a step back, holding my hands up. The desire to smash their heads together was strong.

"I'll hand you the money through the window," I said evenly.

And your ass later, when I figure out who you are.

Grace stiffened in my periphery, her breath catching.

"We know you're not alone. Open the damn door," the man said.

"You want money, be my guest. You want access to the girl, you're going to go through me. Friendly advice—you aren't gonna like it," I hissed.

There was no point pretending Texas wasn't there.

The man raised his gun, firing one bullet. It grazed my shoulder and lodged into the metal roof of the truck like gum. Adrenaline pumped in my veins, and my fingers itched to take action. Not doing shit when provoked wasn't in my DNA.

I was going to fucking end them, given the chance.

"Unlock. The. God. Damned. Door."

Grace saw the blood and cried out, rushing to the door and unlocking it with shaky fingers.

Fuck, baby. No.

The masked men didn't waste time. They burst into the trailer, flipping everything that wasn't drilled into place upside down. I shoved Grace behind me. She dug her phone out of her pocket. While I handled asshole number one, asshole number two grabbed it from her hands and tossed it to the driver's seat. Asshole number two then headed straight to me. Neither of them made a move toward the register.

My attacker tried throwing in a punch. I dodged it, crouching down. I sent a jab from hell to his torso. The sound of his rib cracking filled the air. He folded in two, saliva dribbling from his ski mask.

"Motherfucker!"

I grabbed his friend by the collar of his shirt and hurled him across the trailer, away from Grace. There were too many people inside the truck. But I knew the guy I tossed around had the gun. I pounced on him, prying the gun out of his hand and throwing it out the window. I raised my fist, about to knock his lights out, when his friend grabbed me by the back of my shirt and smashed me against the fridge. They both climbed up to their feet, throwing me down, and started kicking me in the ribs, shoulders, and head.

Texas' shriek pierced through my ears. I had a flashback to when she'd told me it was her grandmother's scream that made her find the Samsonian strength to fight back.

She jumped on one of them, trying to shove him away from me. "Leave him alone!"

Why didn't they take the fucking cash and leave? But the answer was clear—they weren't here for the money. They were here for *me*.

I grabbed one of the guys' legs as he was about to smash it into my face and pulled him down with me. He struggled to clamber up, and I used the opportunity to bracket him with my thighs. I grabbed a can of refried beans and smashed it against his face. His nose broke with a pop.

Crack.

I hit his forehead next, watching as his ski mask soaked with blood.

Crack.

Next, I smashed the can against his mouth, hearing his teeth cracking. Soon, I pounded into his face with the can so furiously, I was pretty sure there was nothing behind that mask but a pool of blood. All I saw was red—and the threat of someone hurting a person I cared about.

Not again, bastards. Never again.

The guy he'd come with was trying to crawl out of the trailer, moaning in pain. Somewhere in the distance, I heard Texas yelling hysterically. At first, I thought she was upset about my getting injured, but then her voice became sharper.

"You're killing him! West, stop! Please! Lord, stop this!"

Her arms wrapped around my neck, pulling me away from the bastard. She collapsed on top of me, her forehead sticking to mine. Our hair matted together with sweat. She was sobbing.

I pushed to my feet and gathered her into a hug, kissing her cap.

I knew she was frightened, and that a huge reason for that was my reaction. The guy underneath me was unconscious—maybe dead—lying in a pond of his own blood. The other guy was grousing, reaching for his phone.

I kissed the tip of her nose.

"Gimme one sec."

I turned around and walked over to the moaning attacker, pressing my boot over his fingers around his phone and hearing them snap. He wailed. I tore the ski mask from his face in one go. Two brown eyes blinked back at me. I recognized the guy. He'd been with Appleton's entourage the night we'd fought.

Taking off the other guy's mask would achieve nothing, other than freaking Grace out even more. I already knew who they were and why they came here.

The man shook all over, his teeth chattering. I leaned forward, whispering in his ear, "Tell your boss I said hi, take your fucking friend with you, and never, ever come back."

I threw the ski mask over his face, turning around back to Grace to give them time to get the hell out. Having them here when she called the police—and she undoubtedly was going to do that—wouldn't do me any good. Just uncover my list of highly illegal actions, including the fight I was still preparing for.

Grace struggled in my arms. "Wait, let me get my phone. I need to …"

I held her tighter. "You need to calm down first."

Idiot One carried Idiot Two out to the dark, his uneven stumbles on the gravel giving away the fact they were both going to be in crutches tomorrow morning.

"We should call the police." Grace frowned, fighting against my grip.

"You sure?" I bought more time, letting them run away. "They didn't take a dime."

"Are you kiddin'? We *have* to tell the cops. Or at the very least bring it to Mrs. Contreras and Karlie and see what they want to do about it. Look at you. You're all banged up."

"Baby." I took her hand in mine. The floor was slippery with blood. The place was going to be a bitch to clean up. "They were just a couple punks looking for trouble."

"They had a *gun*, West."

"They didn't use it."

"They shot your shoulder."

I glanced down at my shoulder, pulling at my collar to see the damage. The skin was red and angry, but my guess was the bullet hadn't even grazed my flesh properly. It was just heat.

"I'm fine."

"You're not takin' this seriously. Is there something you know about this that I don't?" Her eyes narrowed at me.

The more she knew about Appleton and his doings, the more she was involved. And she couldn't be involved. It was my shit to fix. From now on, I was going to keep the thing with Grace even more under wraps. Both for my sanity and her safety.

Canceling the fight wasn't an option anymore, but as long as Appleton didn't know of her existence, he couldn't hurt her.

I was going to see it through, thrash the jackass, take the money, and push him out of my life for good.

"You're right. Let's tell Karlie and Mrs. Contreras. They need to know."

By the time I said that, the bastards were gone anyway.

It was just semantics.

But it bought me more time.

A couple hours later, I was in Grace's room, freshly showered. That wooden chair Texas had put in the shower for her grandmother turned out to be mighty handy tonight. Every muscle in my body screamed in pain when the scorching needles of water pounded over my flesh.

I lay down half-naked on her bed, which smelled like honey and shampoo and her pure, unique scent, texting Reign and East in a group chat. There was no point adding Max. Sucker was about as helpful as a bag of Skittles during Armageddon.

East: It's Appleton. Of course he's behind this. It's got his name all over this kind of operation. I told you not to take the first fight, @West.

Reign: You can't not-retaliate. You're going to look weak.

East: @Reign are you high?

Reign: Of course I'm high. We're off-season. What kind of question is that?

East: Why poke the bear?

Reign: Because it's already wide awake and tried to put its dick in West's wife.

Reign: (I'm paraphrasing here, West. Nobody is trying to put their dick in Grace. Thought I'd clarify, since you're supremely pussy-whipped these days).

There was nothing I wanted more than to go directly to Kade Appleton's house and smash everything within sight, including his goddamn face. As it happened, I couldn't even TP his front yard. I couldn't do jack shit. I needed to keep my head down and make sure Grace remained a secret.

Because Grace was my weakness.

And Appleton thrived on exploiting others' weaknesses.

West: No retaliation. He'll answer to me in the ring. Which reminds me—Grace cannot know about the fight with Appleton.

Reign: How can you keep this from her? Shit's gonna sell out in a day.

East: Your friend here is not wrong, Westie.

West: I'll tell her closer to the date. She's got a lot on her plate. She doesn't need to worry about this too.

Between finding a caregiver for Savannah, and potentially failing a semester, Texas didn't need to worry about me. My plan was to spring it on her the day before the fight. Explain why I had to do it, even though I'd tried to get out of it, and assure her it would all be over in less than twenty-four hours. That way, she'd worry about me for a day, not weeks.

East: I'll tell Max to keep the ticket sale on the DL.

West: Appreciate it. How're things going with Tess, @Reign?

Reign: They aren't. Her lady boner is still firmly directed at you.

East: She'll come around.

Reign: And on my face.

East: Amen.

I wasn't Tess' number one fan after she'd been bitchy to Tex, but I was all for her hooking up with Reign. The faster she landed in the idiot's lap, the less she'd bother Tex.

East: Talked to your folks recently, @West?

West: Negatory.

East: You're the worst.

West: But I'm the best at being the worst.

I'd just sent them a few pictures of my new shiner and welts when Grace entered the room, patting her blonde hair dry with a towel after coming out of the shower. Her face was full of makeup, as always. I'd been with this chick for a while now and still didn't know exactly what she looked like under all the foundation.

She was still freaked out, but fairly pacified since we'd called Mrs. Contreras and given her the rundown of what happened. We'd had to wait for the cops to arrive to give a bullshit statement before being promptly sent home. Mrs. Contreras was there, too. She went back with Sheriff Jones to the station to file an official report.

Texas collapsed beside me, kissing my wounded shoulder. I tucked her under my arm and gave her neck a soft bite.

She closed her eyes, her little breaths tickling my jawline. Her fingers trailed circles around the tattoo on my inner bicep.

"Who were you texting?"

"East and Reign."

She cleared her throat. "That it?"

"Who the fuck else?" Had she missed the memo that I wasn't exactly a social butterfly?

"Tess?" she asked quietly.

I snorted, stroking away ribbons of gold hair from her face. She looked so much like an angel, sometimes I wanted to run a hand over her bare back just to make sure she didn't have wings.

"Green looks good on you, Tex."

"Remember the first time we met?" She strummed my hair with her fingers, like I was a violin, her head tucked under my arm.

Of course I remembered. It was the night I'd lost the bet to Tess and bought everyone slushies and tacos. Tess and I had probably looked chummy that night. It was the same night I'd bent her over the Ducati and fucked her raw in the junkyard, barking at her to mind the paint. It made sense that we were cool with each other. That was how guys operated—we were nice to chicks we wanted to bang, until we banged them.

The morning after I'd twisted Tess' gymnast ass like a pretzel, I gave her a ride home and got rid of her number. I was crude enough to make a stop at the food truck for the job interview, to make sure the position wasn't taken.

"Vaguely," I lied, mostly because it was pathetic to admit most of what I remembered from that night included Grace, not Tess. "Why?"

"Tess asked you what the tattoo on your bicep meant while I served you."

My heart stopped beating for a second. She proceeded with caution and determination.

"What does the tattoo mean, West?"

I knew I had to tell her. That if I didn't, she'd think she and Tess were in the same category. They weren't. Tess was a one-night stand, and Grace ... Grace was an every-night lay. A girlfriend. The first girl to mean something to me in a long while. She ought to have known that.

"A stands for Aubrey. My baby sister."

"You said you're an only child." I felt her eyes fluttering open, her lashes flapping over the side of my chest like little butterflies.

I sucked in a breath. "No. I said I have no siblings. And I don't. She died when she was six. I was seventeen at the time."

"Oh." The quiet around us was so loud, I wanted to rip down the walls with my bare hands just to hear the crickets outside. "I'm so sorry."

What could I say to that? *Thank you?* I hated thanking people who didn't help me. Being sorry for my loss didn't bring Aubrey back.

"How?" she asked.

I felt my split lip reopening as I bit down on it. "Car accident."

"Were you in the …?"

"No," I snapped. The wound of her death was too raw for me to pick at it. "There you have it, Tex. Something you know and Tess doesn't. No one does. Well, other than East. Can we stop talking about it now?"

She didn't answer. Rightly so. I was being a prickly *sonovabitch* again.

A ten-minute silence stretched between us. I hoped to hell she'd never bring Aub up again, but knew that in all probability, she would.

"You okay?" I asked finally, when I felt her going under, surrendering to sweet slumber.

"Yeah."

I knew it was a lie.

I still took it.

Grace

A for Aubrey.

It didn't mean anarchy or asshole or any of the things I'd guessed as I'd tossed and turned in the nights we were just friends, trying to read the impossibly mysterious West St. Claire.

Aubrey. What a beautiful name. The pieces were finally clicking into place, creating an exquisitely tragic picture.

West had gone through one of the greatest losses one could experience. His parents were broken after losing their daughter, possibly being in the car when it happened, possibly even being the *reason* why the accident occurred in the first place.

West was trying to help them back on their feet financially, but he still hadn't forgiven them for Aubrey's death.

Yes. That was what happened.

I clutched onto my boyfriend extra tight that night.

Loving him with every piece of my heart … and a little bit more.

Chapter Seventeen

Grace

"**P**ROFESSOR McGRAW WANTS YOU IN HER OFFICE. PRONTO." Lauren, AKA Blanche, greeted me by my pickup truck first thing in the morning. Her voice was hoarse, like she'd spent the entire month going through seventeen packs of cigarettes a day; she swathed a scarf over her neck, even though the concrete hissed and sizzled with heat beneath our feet. I wobbled out of my Chevy, making my way straight to Professor McGraw's office, thinking, *Oh boy, that can't be good.*

McGraw was waiting for me, her hands folded over her desk.

"You want redemption, Grace Shaw. To be a phoenix. Everything about you screams it—your bag, your flame ring, your tragedy. You carry yourself in the hallways, taking as little space as possible, waiting for the change to happen. But in order to turn into a phoenix—you have to fight for it. To take flight. Well, it's your lucky day."

I darted an eyebrow up, curious. She was bang on about everything, but I hadn't realized people were paying attention to me at school at all.

It was only recently that I'd stopped feeling like a timid bird.

"Poor Lauren has just been diagnosed with vocal cord nodules and is down for the count. We need a new Blanche, and you need a role to save your semester. I formally put down your name, and Mr. Finlay is in full agreement you should take the part."

I opened my mouth, but she rushed in before I could add anything, shaking her head.

"As you probably know, Tess Davis has been pursuing the role actively. She is extremely disciplined, but I think, seeing as she's been vying for this role for so long, if I give it to her, students might think they can bully their way into getting things around here, and I just won't have that. The premiere is in less than a month. Please don't tell me you're unprepared. You know these lines by heart—can recite them in your sleep. Cruz has been paying attention to you during rehearsals. He's been having doubts about Lauren for a while now. As you may know, she struggled with the manuscript."

People had noticed me. The thought made something bloom in my chest.

"I know the lines," I said quietly, trying to process all of this as I sank into the chair in front of her.

Blanche was the main role.

The golden opportunity.

The crust on the biscuit.

I would get to salvage my semester. Probably ace it. Anything short of a full-blown disaster would do wonders for my grade. The thought of going onstage without my ball cap made me shudder ... yet it didn't make me cower.

I'd done this before.

Taken off my ball cap.

Thanks to West.

Dozens of times, actually.

I could do this.

The realization nearly knocked the wind out of me. I could do a fine job portraying Blanche. I'd read the play so many times, my brain bled out my favorite lines every time I fell asleep. In my dreams, the old me—the *me* without the scars—stood on that stage, playing alongside Marlon Brando.

I was going to do this.

I was going to save my year and overcome my stage fright.

"Say something." McGraw cocked her head, blinking at me. "I don't like all this silence. Are you or are you not going to sub in for Miss McCarthy?"

I pressed my lips together, biting down on a huge smile.

"It would be my honor, Professor McGraw."

"Ah, finally!" Her red lips twisted in a motherly smile that put a thorn in my heart. "And so the phoenix rises!"

An hour after my meeting with Professor McGraw, Cruz Finlay gathered the entire play's cast in the rehearsal room at Lawrence Hall, making the official announcement. Lauren stood beside me, dissecting the threads of her scarf with a pout. Professor McGraw had assured me Lauren's work thus far would go toward her overall semester score and that she would still pass, which was a relief. As much as I wanted this opportunity, I didn't want to see Lauren fail.

"Shoot! That's such bad news for your throat, Lo. So, I take it Blanche's role is now up for the taking?" Tess shot Lauren—whom she'd actively tried to kill via voodoo dolls and death stares throughout the academic year—an apologetic smile.

"Actually, no." Finlay rearranged the beret on his head. "Someone else has already got the role. Y'all, say hello to your new Blanche—Grace Shaw!"

People golf-clapped, glancing between Lauren and me for official permission to celebrate the announcement. I ducked my head, feeling my cheeks blush.

Lauren rolled her eyes. "Oh, for goodness' sake, a little more enthusiasm, folks!" She hugged me, leaning forward to whisper in my ear, "You totes deserve it. I saw how passionate you were about this project from day one. I'm glad it's you, Shaw."

"Thank you."

"Right on, Grace! Glad to have you on board." Aiden, my co-star, gave my shoulder a squeeze.

Soon, people lined up to hug and congratulate me. Tess wasn't one of them. I was hardly surprised. Even before the news broke about my role as Blanche, she hadn't been happy about West and me.

West. I couldn't wait to tell him about my role. He was going to be over the moon. Karlie too. And Grandma Savvy …

If she remembers who I am today.

"All right, I've got two back-to-back lectures and a wax appointment. See y'all at four o'clock. Be here and be queer!" Finlay finger-waved to his cast, swaggering up the stairs and out of sight. Everyone trickled out in clusters, chatting and laughing among themselves.

I lifted my head, coming face-to-face with Tess, who like me had stayed behind.

Her lips were pursed, her eyes clouded with anger. Disappointment marred her face with streaks of blotchy, red stains.

"Wow," she breathed.

I smiled politely.

"Congratulations, I guess. Not sure where it is going to get you—it's not like you're about to win any Tony Awards with this … with this …"

"Face?" I completed the sentence for her gently. "So you keep remindin' me. Let me give you a piece of advice, Tess. If you can't change the outcome of somethin', let it go."

"I just think it's so unfair. So … so selfish!" Tess threw her hands in the air, her shoulders slouched. "Historically speaking, the actress to play Blanche always soared and skyrocketed from obscurity. From off-Broadway shows to the West End, school plays, and even movies. Have you ever watched *All about My Mother*?" She slanted her head, throwing me a doubtful look. I couldn't say that I had, so I offered her a shrug.

"That's what I thought. The whole movie starts with the mother in the story. She is enamored with the actress who plays Blanche. Her love toward Blanche leads to terrible tragedy. Blanche is magic. Iconic. I was *born* to be her. And you …" She sucked in a breath. She buried her face in her palms, giving her head a desperate shake.

"You've already taken West. Look, I get it. You won. He's yours. I don't even care anymore. But you can't take away Blanche, too. Please,

Grace. This role can be it for me. It could open so many doors. For you, this is where it's going to start … and end. You don't even want to go onstage. Been avoiding it for as long as I've known you. You'll never do anything with your acting career, and even if you wanted to, you have no chan …"

She looked away from me, knowing that she'd overstepped again. I knew the rest of the sentence. She began to pace the length of the room, her muscles long and tight.

"I'll give you Stella's role. I'll hook you up with my agent. We could help each other! Yes!" She snapped her fingers together, beaming. "It's going to be amazing. We'll fix each other's crowns. You know I've always been on your side."

Did Tess really think just because she wasn't actively mean to me, she'd been doing me a huge favor? I felt my fists clenching beside my body.

"No can do, Tess. In life, you have to let other people have their win. Failure builds you up or breaks you down. It's your choice what to do with it."

I uncurled my fists, tipping my chin up as I examined her beautiful, yet painfully vacant face.

"You're going to take everything from me, huh? Not gonna stop until you break me?" she murmured.

"Are you kiddin' me?" I seethed, losing patience. "You have the entire world at your feet. Everything I have—this role, West, *life*—has come to me after twice the work you put into things."

"Exactly!" Tess growled with frustration, waving her hands around in front of my face. "Exactly that, Grace. Everything you'll ever achieve will be hard-earned, if even possible, in the world of acting. It's clear Professor McGraw gave you this role to cut a corner and let you pass. I'm the one who gets screwed over here. I'm the one who is losing the role of her life."

The worst part was I knew Tess truly wasn't a horrible person deep inside. She simply wanted all the things that I'd happened to accomplish. Up until this year, until West and Blanche happened, she was the nicest to me out of all my peers.

Until I was no longer invisible to everyone else.

Until I became her competition.

Until I *won*.

"Tess," I whispered, narrowing my eyes. "I'm sorry you feel that way. But I'm not goin' to give up the role to appease you. I won't give up on my boyfriend either. I hope you come to your senses and realize you're better than this." I jerked my chin in her general direction. "Have a good rest of the day. I'll see you at four."

Turning around, I walked away, feeling her eyes on my back, like a rifle's lens.

Nobody warned me what was going to happen when the phoenix finally burst up from the ashes, ridding its glorious, red-tipped wings of the heavy dust.

That there would be other monsters and creatures to fight along the way.

That despite having its freedom, there were still battles ahead.

And that all of them would be bloody.

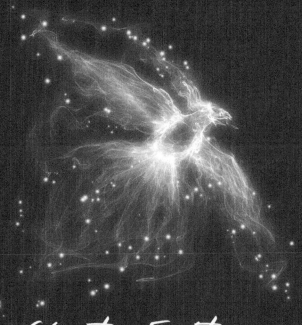

Chapter Eighteen

Grace

AFTER A TENSE REHEARSAL WHICH CONSISTED OF TESS moping and quarreling with Finlay over every minor thing—the stage's lighting, the late hour, her coffee-stained manuscript, and even the dang weather (*"It's too hot, can't we continue tomorrow?"*) I made my way to my pickup, emotionally drained.

I was so exhausted that I resorted to texting West the good news about my role, which I was growing more and more excited about. I didn't have it in me to pick up when he called. I couldn't muster the enthusiasm that the conversation deserved. I promised myself I'd bring him a hearty sandwich tomorrow, made from scratch, and tell him about what had happened with Professor McGraw at length.

I parked in front of my house, walking in to the sound of a commotion upstairs. My back stiffened. Marla was yelling, and the persistent rattle of a wooden door echoed through the house.

"Open up, you old bat. I ain't asking again. I'll call Sheriff Jones and have him kick this thing down. You're puttin' yourself in real danger here!"

Lord, what now?

I dumped my backpack at the landing, racing up the stairs. Rounding the corner to the hallway, I spotted Marla pounding her fists on the bathroom door, her face flushed and hair a mess. Her fists were pink and swollen.

"Savannah!" Her roar almost blew the roof to the sky. "Open up right this second!"

The sound of water whooshing from the other side of the door filled my ears.

"No!" Grams' voice jangled like a coin in an empty piggybank, hollow and screeching. "You ain't fooling me no more. You want to lure my sweet, sweet Courtney back to drugs. I'm not opening up. I don't know you, miss. If anything, *I'm* going to call Sheriff Jones and have him come arrest *you*. This is my property! I may be old, but I sure know my rights."

It wasn't the first or even fifth time Grams didn't recognize Marla, but it was the first time she'd actively resisted her.

"What's goin' on?" I asked, placing my hand on her shoulder.

Marla wiped the sweat from her face, shaking her head. When she turned around to face me, I could tell she'd been crying. Her eyes were shiny and puffy.

"I can't do this anymore, honey pie. I'm so sorry. I just can't. Your grandmomma is ..." She shook her head, pursing her lips to stop herself from bawling. "She's not doing well. And keeping her here, undiagnosed, is not doing her any favors. You sending her to a nursing home is not about doing what's convenient for *you*, sweetheart. It is not a selfish act. I wish you'd understand this. At this point, you're doing the poor woman a disservice by keeping her here. She is no longer in a position to make her own choices. She ain't lucid, and she belongs in a place that can accommodate her needs twenty-four seven. Grace ..." She choked, her chin wobbling with the impending burst of a wail. "No one is going to accept this job. And that is something *you* must accept."

I gave Marla a quick hug and sent her off, then hiked up my sleeves to pound on the door.

The water had begun to leak through the door crack. My breath hitched as I watched the thin sheet of water sliding down beneath my FILAs, making its way to the hallway. Was she filling up the bathtub?

I didn't know how she managed to lock Marla outside. She wasn't supposed to be there alone. Ever.

You were supposed to swap out the doorknobs that could be picked from the outside, a little voice inside me fumed. *You kept telling yourself Grams was incapable of being so reckless. Of doing something so dangerous. Another lie you fed yourself about her.*

"Grams," I called out in my softest voice. "It's me, Gracie-Mae, your grandchild. Please open the door so I can help you."

"Gracie who?" she asked with a suspicious huff. "I don't know any Gracie-Mae. The only family I have is Freddie and my Courtney, and she's in trouble, because riffraff like yourself are trying to sell her drugs. But I'm not going to let it happen anymore. It ends now. Right, Courtney, baby?"

Who was she talking to?

Dear God, how bad was she?

But I already knew the answer to that question. I just pretended it wasn't so.

I grabbed the door handle, giving it a shake. When that didn't work, I slammed my palms flat against the wood desperately.

The water kept pouring, slithering down the stairs now. Just like the night of the fire, but in reverse. She was going to drown. I couldn't let it happen. I feared even if I called West or Sheriff Jones, by the time they got here, something bad would have happened.

"I'm comin' in!" I announced, angling my shoulder toward the door and taking a step back. I used all the momentum I could muster and crashed into the door with the side of my shoulder.

Other than possibly dislocating it, nothing happened.

Crap. Crap. Triple crap.

"Grams!" I hit the door, gasping. No answer.

I thrust my shoulder against the door again, trying to pick at the door handle, the sting of tears coating my eyes. I fumbled to take out my phone, calling West while continuing my attempts to open the door.

"Tex," he answered after the first ring. "What's up?"

"I need you to come here. Grams locked herself in the bathroom, and the water's runnin'. It's *everywhere*, West."

"On my way."

I heard him getting up and the sound of his wallet chain, the jingle of his keys as he scooped them up, and the crunching of his boots on loose gravel.

"I worry you are going to be too late …" I choked on my words. I should have never left her alone. Marla couldn't take care of her on her own.

Then, what? Do you want to drop out of college and dedicate your life to taking care of someone who you make miserable and doesn't even remember you half the time?

I heard him revving the Ducati, but he didn't hang up.

"Do you have your debit card handy?"

"Ah, I don't have a card," I mumbled, blushing.

"Any cards in your wallet? Costco? Health insurance?"

"I have my library card," I swallowed.

"Is it plastic?"

"Yes."

"I'm going to walk you through unlocking the door. Get the card."

"Okay."

I ran back downstairs, holding the phone while he was on speaker, and hunted for my wallet in my JanSport. It took me three times before I managed to produce the library card, my fingers shook so badly. I sprinted up the stairs again, positioning myself in front of the bathroom door. The water reached the ground floor, and terror flooded through me.

I could hear West riding, the wind blowing about. His phone was tucked inside his helmet, the way I saw him doing dozens of times.

"Got it?" he asked.

"Got it."

"Slide the card between the door and the frame, just above the lock."

I did as I was told, my breath stuck in my throat.

"Now, tilt the card toward the door handle and try to bend it between the lock and the frame."

"On it."

I wiggled the card back and forth, feeling the lock latching and unlatching, but not all the way. My raw nerves shot a signal to the rest of my body, making me tremble. The heavy swishing of water in the bathtub on the other side of the door made me want to throw up. And then …

The door clicked, sliding open, just an inch. I flattened my hand on it, bursting in. Grams was in the bathtub, completely clothed, the water at her chin-level. She stared me down, awake, her eyes murky.

She looked like she wanted to shoot me.

"It's open!" I cried into the phone with relief, dropping the device in the dry sink. I launched toward Grams. She swatted me away, her hand heavy with water. I turned off the water immediately.

"Get out of here, you Devil's child! Get out of my house! Out of my life!"

I stopped dead in my tracks.

"Look at your face!" she hissed. "*Monster.*"

I patted my face, realizing that sometime during my efforts to unlock the bathroom door, I'd discarded my ball cap. "The Devil has touched you, and now you are marked. Ugly and tainted, inside and out. You're here to take my Courtney, aren't you?"

"Grams, no. You don't know—"

"I do know." Her voice was low. Eerily calm all of a sudden. "Grace. *Gracie-Mae.* Quite the nuisance you are, Gracie. You were the reason she ran away. Did you know that? You were too much. Too loud, too whiny, too demanding. When she gave you to me, I looked at you and all I thought about was that I'd got myself a raw deal. A granddaughter for a daughter. I never wanted you. You took her away from me. *You.*" She pointed a shaky finger at me, her nostrils flaring, her lips turning blue, along with her ever-paling skin in the cold water. She was going to catch pneumonia, and I needed to get her out of there, but I couldn't stop her stream of words. "You no-good Devil's daughter! My only consolation is, God has already done the work for me. Punished you with this face. Paid you back for all your sins!"

She tilted her head up to the ceiling, smiling, as if touched by an invisible ray of sun. She pressed her eyes shut, a bitter chuckle leaving her mouth. "They all think that you did it. All of them. No one knows our little secret, Gracie-Mae. No one knows what I did that night."

There was a loaded pause before she went in for the kill.

"I did it on purpose. Left the cigarette next to my nightcap and let it catch. I didn't want to live anymore. Didn't want you to either."

A feral scream tore through my throat. I launched at the old lady, gripping the hem of her dress and hurling her out of the bathtub, dragging her out to the hallway and into her room to dry her up. I dumped her onto the flowery linen of her bed like a sack of potatoes, throwing a towel over her and patting her dry. She fought me, but I still took care of her.

Me and my ugly face.

Me and my dead mother.

The broken flame ring seared my skin, and I wanted to dump it on the floor and stomp on it a thousand times. Grandmomma was wrong. It never granted me any wishes. It just reminded me that I was an unwanted child.

Grandma Savannah blamed me for all of this. For Courtney crumbling down. For the Shaw household following in her footsteps. I was the responsibility Grams had been saddled with, a dead weight, someone she wanted to get rid of.

We wrestled on her bed, me on top, tears blurring my vision. I was almost done drying her up when I felt a strong hand on my shoulder.

"Go, Tex. I'm taking over."

"But I ..."

"Go."

I turned around, running away, not daring to look him in the eye and see what was there. Everything about me was complicated and disheartening, and I wondered, for the millionth time, why West had stuck around when he could have had something so much better with any of the beauties who worshipped the ground he walked upon.

Selfishly—oh, so selfishly—I locked the bathroom door and took a shower, ignoring the filled bathtub not a foot away from me. There were soaked towels on the floor, toothbrushes, and soap scattered everywhere.

I focused on scrubbing every inch of myself clean under the scorching water, shedding the god-awful day from my body—my ugly, scarred face included.

Then I tiptoed to the hallway. I heard West behind Grams' door, soothing her quietly to sleep, an unwarranted arrow of jealousy ripping through my heart.

I should be the one being comforted in his arms. He is mine.

I slinked into my room before the urge to start a catfight with my elderly, Alzheimer-suffering grandmother overtook me.

I put my jammies on and collapsed on my bed, staring at the ceiling. The tears ran freely down my cheeks. For the first time in years, I didn't try to stop them.

After Grandmomma's soft snores filled the hallway, I listened as West stomped about the floor. I heard him cleaning up the bathroom, mopping the hallway and the stairs, and going down to the kitchen to brew some coffee.

Listening to him living, *breathing*, existing in my realm by my side, was reassuring. He was a godsend. I couldn't have handled Grams on my own tonight.

Eventually, it sounded like he ascended the stairs, put the two mugs of coffee down on the floor outside my room, and pressed his forehead against the door from the other side.

It scared me how well I knew his body language. The way he carried himself around my house. I could practically envision him doing all that.

"Open the door, Texas."

In my haze, I'd forgotten to reapply my makeup. I didn't want to face him. Not when I knew he'd heard all the ugly things Grams had said about me while the phone was on. It was bad enough that I was atrocious, without anyone seeing me.

I'd been broken many a times, but never quite like I had been today.

I didn't answer him.

"I want to see your face."

The urgency in his voice startled me. He sounded choked up, on the brink of something I didn't want him to go through.

"Okay. Give me five!" I swung my legs sideways on my bed.

"*Bare.*"

I stopped dead in my tracks, halfway to my desk to pull out my makeup kit.

262 | L.J. SHEN

Fear glided up my spine like a deadly snake, wrapping its length around my neck, choking my breath.

"You don't know what you're askin'," I said thickly, throwing his words back at him. I still remembered how he thought I wouldn't be able to forgive him had I known what he did to make him the way he was.

"Fucking try me."

"You heard her. I'm ugly. The Devil's daughter."

"You're beautiful. My girlfriend," he countered.

"She wanted to kill us …" I broke down, sobbing, still standing in my room aimlessly. It took him a moment to answer me.

"No. She was confused and vindictive. She wanted to hurt you. She never wanted to kill you. The fire was an accident."

But there was no way either of us could know. The truth of the matter was that I was never going to be able to ask lucid Grams this question. It was too painful for everyone involved.

I stepped toward the mirror on my study and blinked back at myself, catching a glimpse of what West was about to see in a few seconds. There wasn't a lick of makeup on my face. My history—my tragedy—was written all over it, like a scream.

The melted complexion of my left side. My slightly crooked left eye, a tad smaller than my right one due to the scar tissue pulled around it after the reconstructive surgery. The missing eyebrow. The purple … *everything*.

Gingerly, I moved toward the door. I put my hand on the handle and threw it open before I lost my nerve.

West and I stood in front of one another silently.

I watched him watching me. He took it all in, gulping every inch of me. His eyes ran the length of my left side, inking it to memory.

He cannot unsee what he is seeing, I reminded myself. *From now on, every time he looks at you, with or without makeup, this is what he will see.*

West's expression didn't give away what he was thinking. I felt my insides collapsing like a demolished skyscraper imploding and knew that if he chose to walk away from me, my phoenix wasn't going to be able to fight its way past the ruins.

But he didn't walk away.

He took a step into my room, raising his hand. He traced his fingers over my scars so gently that I wanted to cry, staring into my eyes, gazing at my naked soul. His fingers were trembling. I snatched his hand and kissed it. One of my tears caught between his index and middle finger.

"Listen to me carefully, Grace Shaw. You're the most beautiful girl I've ever seen in my entire life. When I look at you, I see a fighter. I see resilience and strength and defiance that no one can touch. You take my breath away, and no one—and *nothing*—will change that."

I closed my eyes and opened my mouth to speak, but nothing came out. I tried again, searching for my own voice. I didn't know what was going to come out of my mouth.

The truth, I supposed. The most vulnerable secret a person could tell.

"I love you. I'm terrified of loving you, but I do, nonetheless," I admitted gruffly. "Have since the moment you helped me find Grams that terrible night, not letting me refuse the help I so obviously needed. My heart is in your fist."

He kicked the door shut behind him, diving in for the kiss to end all kisses.

It was the kiss that rewrote our history.

A kiss that made me feel like the most beautiful girl in the world.

A kiss that tasted like victory.

"I won't break it."

West

The kiss tasted like a lie.

I'd said I wouldn't break Grace's heart, but I could already see myself doing it.

As I undressed her.

Made love to her.

I needed to put some distance between us. Kade Appleton had

been watching me, I knew. And almost living at her house put a target on her.

When dawn broke, I grabbed my stuff and made my way home.

I was waiting at an intersection when a helmeted man on a Harley came out of nowhere and crashed into me. I was thrown off my bike, hurled onto the middle of the road. Luckily, there weren't any other vehicles at butt-crack o'clock.

I twisted on the gravel, hissing as I held one of my hands tightly with the other. I'd landed wrong and could already tell I'd broken at least two fingers. The sound of heavy boots on concrete came thudding toward me, and I looked up to see who wore them.

When he reached me, the man leaned down, crouching to my eye level, bracing himself on his knees. There was nothing I wanted more than to tear the helmet from his face and introduce his nose to my fist, but I couldn't move.

"Nice little girlfriend you have there. Shame if somethin' happened to her, eh?"

He turned around and walked away, back to his Harley.

I had to keep Grace safe, no matter the cost.

Even if it meant losing her.

Chapter Nineteen

Grace

A WEEK INTO REHEARSALS FOR *A STREETCAR NAMED DESIRE*, and even though Marla had been agitated and West had been mysteriously distant (and sported some seriously freaky-looking fingers, presumably after his last fight), I knew I had one thing going for me:

I was thriving onstage.

True, the amount of makeup I required to actually *go* onstage was sure to make me go bankrupt, but the ball cap was off, and I enjoyed being Blanche. Being trapped in her head was a lot like being in Gram's head, I assumed. Confused, but smart. Sweet, but feisty. Lost, but found.

I'd decided not to think about the things Grams had told me that day in the bathtub. Something I'd told Tess resonated with me—if I couldn't change something, I had to let it go. Even if my grandmother truly believed I was the source to all of her woes, I couldn't change it. Not now. Probably not ever.

Finlay salivated over my performance at rehearsals, and Lauren was always sitting a few rows from the stage, cheering and clapping whenever I nailed a scene.

Even Tess had simmered down. We weren't exactly friendly, but she was professional and made a point of not throwing any more crappy remarks my way.

We were in the midst of an early morning rehearsal, so close to the night of the premiere I could almost touch it, when we took a ten-minute break. I scurried backstage and grabbed a drink of water, talking to Finlay and Aiden after crushing the scene in which Stanley rapes Blanche.

Tess swaggered up next to me, talking to Kelly, the producer.

"Seriously, I'm so happy I started dating Reign. He is so there for me, you know? I just don't need complex right now." She flung her hair to one shoulder.

If it was meant for my ears, she was wasting her breath. I hoped she and Reign were happy together. However, if she thought dating someone who had been mean to me would throw me off-kilter, she was wrong.

Finlay continued talking to me as Tess sighed dramatically behind my back. "I really couldn't see myself dating someone so dangerous and imbalanced like West. This answers-to-no-one gig just gets old at some point, you know?"

Yeah, I was sure her decision had nothing to do with the fact West had ignored her repeatedly since they'd hooked up.

"I mean, look at him, going on a second fight against this Kade Appleton guy next Friday. Who does that? Only someone with a death wish. No, thank you. I like to sleep at night knowing my boyfriend is in one piece. Even Reign tells him he should back out of the fight. But it's a well-known fact West cares about money more than he does about the people in his life."

My mind filled with red fog as her words sank deep into my stomach, settling in there like rocks.

He took the fight after all.

He had lied to me.

I'd asked him … No—I'd *begged* him to promise me that he wouldn't pull any of the crap he fed to other girls on me, and he did.

He made me a promise, and he'd broken it.

"I need to … I need to go …"

Finlay, who was midsentence, closed his mouth, frowning at me in confusion. I grabbed my JanSport and rushed out of the auditorium. It was probably an eyeful for Tess, who must've known I wasn't privy to the information she'd fed me. If any of it was even true.

Maybe she just wanted West and me to fight.

There was only one way to find out.

I burst into the hallway, looking around frantically, expecting to find West in the sea of students. This was the building he had most of his classes in, so it made sense. I scanned the ocean of heads, but couldn't see him. I didn't even know if he was on campus. Sher U wasn't exactly small and consisted of a few different faculties. I took out my phone and hit dial on his name.

Straight to voicemail. I tried again. Same outcome. I texted him.

Grace: Call me. It's urgent.

Pushing the double doors open, I searched for him outside. By the fountain. At the gym. Then headed to the cafeteria. I wanted to strangle him. Now I knew how his parents must've felt. I was about to head out of the cafeteria, get in the pickup, and drive to his house when I noticed a head of auburn curls in the corner of the cafeteria.

Max.

My legs carried me to him, my mind focused on one thing—preventing West from getting into the ring next Friday. *Next Friday.* That was why he was so agitated this week. Lord help me.

Max was chatting up a pretty girl, leaning over the wall she was plastered against. I tapped his back. He turned around slowly, his smile vanishing when he saw my face.

Feeling's mutual, pal.

"Uh, hey?"

"Hi. I'm Grace Shaw."

"Okay," he said as he pushed his sunglasses up his head. "How can I help you, Grace Shaw?" He made a show of repeating my full name, like it had been dumb of me to introduce myself like that. The girl next to him snorted.

"You're West's bookie, right?"

His chest broadened boastfully, and he flashed me a grin.

"That's right. You're his flavor of the week, right?"

I ignored his jab.

"I'm here to ask you to stop the fight on Friday from happenin'."

"Excuse me?"

"You heard me." I narrowed my eyes. "I don't want him in the ring with Appleton."

"West's a big boy."

"He's also not doin' the smart thing here, and we both know that."

"He's about to make more money than he made in a year and a half, so with all due respect—and I have none toward you because I don't actually know you—we'll agree to disagree."

I opened my mouth to answer, but he shouldered past me, forgetting about the girl he was leaving behind. He wanted to run away from this conversation before it got ugly, not knowing it was too late for that. I followed him.

"Now, I suggest if you have issues with the fight, you take it up with him personally. I'm not his momma."

I caught his wrist in a death grip, every bone in my body burning with anger. He stopped.

"If you let this fly," I bit out every word, my teeth clenched tightly together as I spoke, "I'll go to the authorities with this information."

As soon as the words left my mouth, I knew they were the wrong ones. Max stilled. The chatter around the cafeteria halted. Disaster hung in the air, fat and swollen, ready to blow in my face.

No one snitched on Max and West.

No one had informed the authorities about the Sheridan Plaza parties. For years.

That was the rule.

And I'd just threatened to break it.

Max turned slowly to face me, but it was West who made my heart leap in my chest. I saw him galloping from the entrance in my direction, Easton and Reign on either side of him. His eyes skimmed the room, and when they found what they were looking for—me—he headed straight in my direction.

The first time he'd acknowledged my existence at school since we started dating, and I had a feeling I wasn't going to like it.

Someone had tipped him off about my public argument with Max.

West knew what was happening.

Knew I knew about his fight. About his lies.

But I wasn't the one who was supposed to feel the way I did. Angry, flushed, and scared. He'd broken a promise. He had a lot to answer for.

West came to a screeching halt in front of me, all bronzed muscles and barely contained fury. I took a step back and reminded myself that this was the same man who worshipped me between the sheets every night. Who acted as a caregiver to my grandmother when I broke apart. Who *cared.*

"Is there a problem here?" His voice dripped ice. He stared me down like I was a complete stranger again. Devoid of any emotions. I took a deep breath.

Really? That's how you talk to me in public?

"There is, actually." I tipped my nose up. I spotted Tess in my periphery, behind West's back, standing next to Reign. They were pushing and whispering to each other.

"I told you not to tell her. He didn't want her to know." Reign groaned, and Tess shrugged helplessly, looking humbled for the first time since I'd started dating her crush.

"You lied to me, West. I asked you about taking a fight with Appleton, and you flat-out lied."

The crowd surrounding us was thickening. People murmured and nudged each other in awe. The unshakable, imperial West St. Claire was having his ass handed to him—and by Toastie, no less. Next thing they knew, pigs would be able to fly, too.

"No one manages my business other than me." West flashed me his teeth.

"Think again. I do. I care, and I don't want you to get hurt."

My spine was ramrod straight, my voice stoic. Broken promise or not, I couldn't let him kill himself for money.

"You're my boyfriend. I have a say."

The room sucked in a collective breath. I'd outed us without his permission, but rather than feeling embarrassed and shy, all I could feel was the blazing flame of anger.

I smiled serenely, pretending like the gasps and shocked glances didn't hurt.

"Yup. That's the truth, folks. West St. Claire is my boyfriend. Who would have thought, right? Different folks, different strokes, I guess."

I turned back to West. "I told Max you can't do the fight."

"I can." He took another step in my direction, an ugly sneer smearing across his gorgeous face. "And I *am*. You have no pull with me on this, so I suggest you go back to your little play, *Gracie-Mae*."

Did he just call me Gracie-Mae? Like Grams did?

I took a step back, feeling my expression collapsing. But West, apparently, wasn't done humiliating me. For some reason, it was important for him to shatter everything we were and leave nothing but broken pieces.

"And to make shit clear: you're not my girlfriend, sweetheart. You're just another notch in my never-ending belt. Just because I slept with you more than once doesn't mean you're going to wear my ring on your finger. The facts don't care about your feelings, and fact is, you mean nothing to me. I screwed you because I'm screwed-up, yes." He half-shrugged, letting all our time together roll off his back. I couldn't breathe. Easton, behind him, buried his face in his hands, but even he didn't stop West from saying all those things to me. I had a feeling he knew if he stepped too close, West was going to rip his head off.

"Wanna hear the truth? The big secret?" West air quoted the words with a chuckle. "Fine. I'll humor you. When I was seventeen, my sister, Aubrey, died in a fire. The fire was my fault. She died because of me. For a while, when I looked at you, all I saw was redemption. I thought fooling around with you would give you the little pick-me-up your self-esteem had needed. But you were never more than that. There, I said it. Now get off my fucking case, Shaw."

He turned around and left, leaving me with the flashes of phone cameras, chortles, and laughter.

All eyes were on me.

No ball cap. No boyfriend. No pride left.

Easton and Reign ran after West, trying to catch his step. Through my shock, I could see Karlie shouldering past the crowd, making her way toward me.

"Get out of my way! Out! I'm coming, Shaw. Stay put. *Oof!* Passing through! Make way!"

I was too numb to move.

I stood there, frozen in place, while Karlie stomped on feet and elbowed ribs to get to me in record time.

Tess was the first to snap out of her reverie. She was still standing closest to me. She jumped forward and placed her body in front of mine, covering me completely. She put her hands on her waist, huffing haughtily.

"Jesus, jerks much? Give the girl some space. What the hell are you looking at? Never seen a couple fighting before? Shoo! Shoo!"

I didn't feel anything.

Not gratitude.

Not sadness.

Not anger.

Nothing.

"I'm going to make sure y'alls fancy iPhones are going to be smashed, or worse, if you don't take a hike right now!" Tess' voice boomed.

The dense ring of people finally shuffled sideways. Karlie snatched my arm, pulling me away from the throng.

"We have to make sure these videos don't leak," she barked at Tess, who nodded, biting down on her lip. She looked guilty, her cheeks flushed pink. As she should be. She wanted to hurt me. She just hadn't been sure how far things were going to go.

"I'll talk to Reign and East right quick. They'll throw their weight if need be."

Karlie nodded. "Text me."

"I will."

"Come." Karlie wrapped her hands around me. "Let's take you home."

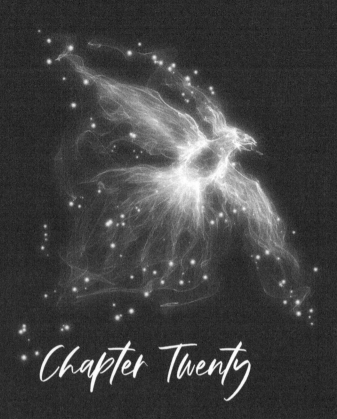

Chapter Twenty

West

Then.

"P**ROMITH TO MAKE ME WAFFLES TOMORROW MORNING?**" *Aubrey stood in the kitchen doorway, pouting. I poured a Costco bag of tortilla chips into bowls. East was setting up red Solo cups on the kitchen island after lining up bottles of liquor. My girlfriend, Whitley, was hanging up a stupid birthday sign on the wall.*

Happy 17th Birthday, West!

Honestly, I thought it was exceedingly lame to have a birthday sign when I was the one throwing a party, but I let her have her way. Figured if I played my cards right this evening, I could get a blowjob out of it.

Birthday plus being an agreeable boyfriend? That equaled more than good sex. Getting head was nothing. I should think outside the box. Ask for anal. Or maybe a threesome.

"Westie?" Aubrey was tugging at my shirt now, pulling my horn-dog brain from the orgy I was throwing in my head. I looked down at

my six-year-old sister. We had a huge-ass age gap, but I loved her to death. She blinked up at me with her big green eyes, smiling her partly toothless grin. Her two front baby teeth were gone now—I'd pulled them out myself when she was too chicken to do it—and she looked adorable. Aubrey was self-conscious about her teeth. When I took her to the carnival the other day, I had to blacken my two front teeth for solidarity purposes. The grin on her face was worth all the shit I got afterwards from the football team who saw me there.

"Yeah, Aub. I said it before and I'll say it again—you keep inside your room all night, and I'll make you waffles in the morning."

"Wiv chocolate chips and apples on the side. Freshly cut."

"Yupsters."

"And chocolate milk."

"Bet on it, lil' sis. Just don't come out of your room."

My parents had gone to visit Aunt Carrie, who lived about forty minutes south. They were supposed to have a relaxing poker night, but they drank a little too much and called to ask if I could watch Aub until tomorrow morning, when they were sober enough to drive. It was the first time they'd left us alone together. I said it was cool and, of course, picked up the phone immediately to summon a spontaneous birthday party.

East and Whitley were coming in and out of the garage now, busting more snacks open, dividing them into bowls and clearing the large furniture from the living room to make space for the people who were going to be here any minute.

"Pinky promith?" *Aub asked, wiggling her tiny finger up in the air.*

I put the tortilla bag aside and turned to face her, crouching down to her eye level.

I took her pinky in mine and squeezed.

"Pinky promise, Aub."

She threw her arms around my neck, squeezing me close. She smelled like green apple candy. She was addicted to that shit to a point our parents wouldn't let her have anything sweet anymore. I knew she hid a stash of apple candy sticks under her bed and nibbled on them when nobody was looking.

I knew, because I was the one who gave them to her.

"We're going to have the best morning ever!" *she exclaimed.*

It was the last time I saw my sister smile.
It was the last time I saw my sister at all.

"Westie? Westie, wake up."

I groaned, rolling from my back to my stomach in my bed, my eyes shut. I was shirtless, with only my boxers under my quilt. That wasn't an issue. Aub had seen me shirtless plenty of times. But I knew Whit, who slept right beside me, was shirtless, too. And that was something Aubrey had never seen before. I wanted to open my eyes and see exactly what my little sister was seeing, if Whit was at least covered by the quilt, but couldn't for the life of me crack my eyes open.

I shouldn't have drunk so much last night.

Things got wild fast. The strip poker had turned into shots poker when all of my friends were butt naked, and after consuming at least seventeen shots—one for each year of my life—I passed out. Luckily, it was after Whit and I went for a quickie in my room. But I didn't remember either of us bothering to put our clothes on.

"Westie? Puh-leaseeee," I heard Aubrey's little squeaky voice.

"Not now, Aub," I managed to croak out.

"But you promithed!" she whined. I stirred in my bed, trying to pry my goddamn eyes open and look at her, but failed. My eyelids felt like they were fifty pounds each. My body ached like every motherfucker within town limits had walked all over it. Back and forth.

"Yeah, well, I'll make you pancakes in an hour."

"Waffles!" she shrieked at my blasphemy. "And it's already ten o'clock! Mommy and Daddy should be here any minute, and you know they don't let me eat waffles."

I knew damn well they wouldn't. Aub had cavities in her milk teeth from all that green apple candy, so they were taking extra precautions to make sure her new teeth weren't going to rot. That was why waffles were a big deal for her. And I fully intended to make her those goddamn chocolate-chip waffles with fresh apple on the side. I just needed another hour or so to feel human again. Was that too much to ask?

"Give me thirty …" I mumbled, my eyes still closed.

"They'll be here by then!"

"Then I'll take you to the diner tomorrow. Promise. You'll get a milkshake out of it, too. We'll say we're going ice skating."

"I want waffles now. Not tomorrow. Besides, what's a promith anyway, if you don't keep it?"

"A lie?" I creaked sarcastically. I was nasty when hungover. I laughed at my own lousy joke. My mouth tasted bitter. In all of Aubrey's six years, every time we did a pinky promise, I always delivered. I never broke my promises. But I couldn't for the life of me fulfill this one. I was too hungover to move.

"You're such a ... a ... butt sniffer!" Her voice broke midsentence. I knew what she sounded like when she was about to cry, and she was definitely heading there.

"C'mon. Aub ..." I tried opening my eyes again. I couldn't—again. I heard her little feet thudding quickly on the carpeted hallway. She probably went back to her room to hate me privately. I tried to reassure myself. It was fine. I'd take her tomorrow—no, fuck it, this afternoon—and make it up to her. We'd hit the ice rink, then go to the Pancake House, and I'd let her order enough waffles to clog every artery in her body.

"Babe?" Whit moaned from beside me, throwing an arm over my pecs. "Was that Aubrey? Is she okay?"

"She's fine. Go back to sleep."

We both did.

The way I remembered it, about two hours had passed before I woke up, but in reality, it couldn't have been more than forty minutes. The scent of something burning filled my nostrils. Food burning.

Or plastic burning?

Fabric burning.

Flesh burning, like at the butchers.

No. It was all of the above.

I blinked, trying to sit up. It felt like my head weighed a ton. I wanted to punch my own face for drinking so much. Whit was still asleep beside me.

I sniffed, looking around. Everything looked fine. Normal. Well, other than the smoke skulking from the hallway and into my room.

What the …?

That was all the adrenaline rush I needed to sober up. I jumped out of bed like my ass was on fire, charging down the stairs, taking them three at a time. Something clearly was on fire. It just wasn't my ass.

"Aub? Aubrey? Aubrey!" *I screamed so hard and loud, I didn't even wait for an answer. The smoke was racing up the stairs as I descended them. By the time I reached the landing, I was standing in a thick cloud of black-gray smoke. I grabbed a shirt I'd thrown on the lamp yesterday night and pressed it against my nose. The air was scorching, and I couldn't breathe without coughing.*

The heart of the fire was in the kitchen, so that was where I went.

"Aubrey!" *I kept calling, shouting, begging. There was no answer. When I got into the kitchen, I had to stumble back. The fire almost reached the living room, and since there were carpet and wallpaper, it spread fast.*

"West? Oh my God! West!" *I heard Whit behind me. She was running down the stairs.*

"Get out. Now. Whit!"

"West, I'm naked!"

"Out!" *I ran into the fire, not giving a shit if I burned to death if it meant saving Aubrey.*

"Where's Aubrey?" *I heard Whit ask. I didn't reply. I fanned the smoke with my arm, trying to recognize anything beyond the curling flames.*

Once I did, I wished I were smart enough to never think I'd stood a chance to save her.

There was an exposed hook on one of the cabinets in our kitchen. It used to be a door handle, but I'd yanked it out accidentally weeks ago and never bothered to fix it. My mom gave me grief about it, saying it was a health hazard. That someone could get injured.

"My pants get stuck in this thing on a weekly basis, Westie. You have to do something about it. Aubrey can get a nick."

I hadn't listened.

I should have.

The toaster was placed right above that cabinet with the hook.

And this time, it wasn't my mom's pants that got stuck in it—it was Aubrey's shirt.

I saw Aubrey's body under the hook, the remainder of her little jacket still wrapped around the exposed hook.

Fuck.

Fuck.

Fuck.

I ran to her. If I could save her—good. If I couldn't—I didn't deserve to live either.

I got so close to the fire I felt its echo burning my skin. I grabbed her jacket, but it felt empty. Light. Her tiny body was limp in my arms. I tried to pry her off the hook, feeling my eyes stinging with smoke and tears and fuck, fuck, fuck.

"Aubrey, please!" My voice broke. "Please, baby. Please!"

I was yanked back, my fingers still wrapped around her jacket. I fought the force that dragged me back. Kicking, screaming, and clawing at the arms around me, blind with rage and hate. The hatred facing inward made me delirious. I'd made a promise to my baby sister, and I'd broken that promise. I was so busy getting drunk yesterday, I hadn't even thought to take her into consideration. The one single time my parents gave me the responsibility of keeping my sister safe overnight while they were out, I failed them.

I failed her.

I failed myself.

I screamed until my lungs burned. Whoever grabbed me threw me on the snow and ran back inside. From my position in the front yard, I saw someone else running after them, screaming.

Dad. He saved me and went back for Aubrey.

Mom. She went inside with him to try to save someone, him or Aubrey, I couldn't tell.

A piercing wail broke above my head. I knew it was Whitley, but I couldn't turn around and look at her. In fact, my body couldn't move at all.

I was no longer drunk.

I was stone-cold sober.

And facing the harsh consequences of my actions.

In the days after the fire, I found out a few things.

For instance, I discovered that the reason the toaster caught on fire was because someone had thrown bottle caps into it, and Aubrey, who didn't know this, pushed two chocolate-chip waffles from the freezer into its jaws, trying to make herself waffles.

Afterwards, the insurance investigator (or whoever the hell he was) explained to us that she'd tried to escape, but couldn't, because her Barbie jacket had gotten tangled in the exposed hook. She'd probably cried for my help, but I was all the way across the house, on the second floor, snoring and recovering from a bitch of a hangover.

The bottom line was this—our house wasn't insured for fire caused by an asshole teenager who couldn't keep his friends in check and fulfill a small promise he'd made to his sister. In other words—we were screwed. We had no house to live in, because soon after my mother dragged my father out of the house, the fire spread and the house pretty much collapsed in on itself.

We were suddenly broke, poor, and homeless.

We moved in with my aunt, Carrie, for the first few weeks, while my father and his coworkers "Band-Aided" the house as much as they could to make it livable again. My father, who owned a blueberry field and a small farm, had to neglect his business and throw himself into putting a roof over our heads. Every night, he pulled himself into bed and closed his eyes without even taking a shower.

I could swear he went weeks without taking a shower.

Months, maybe.

Neither my mother nor my father could bear looking at me. They didn't blame me explicitly, but they didn't have to. I'd killed Aubrey. At the very least, I was responsible for her death. And not in some vague ass way—the way people sometimes blamed themselves for someone else's death because they didn't insist hard enough on them going to get a mammogram or whatever. I'd straight up made this happen.

If only I'd dragged my sorry self out of bed and kept my promise, Aubrey would be here. With us. Happy, partly toothless, and alive.

I broke up with Whitley a week after the fire. She cried and told me I'd change my mind, but I knew I wouldn't. I didn't deserve happiness, and a girlfriend definitely equaled happiness.

Once we moved back to our house—or whatever was left of it—my parents threw themselves headfirst into the arms of depression and didn't leave the bed. They dwelled on their pain, neither of them working or trying to support whatever was left of the family. The blueberry fields were left unattended, the fruit unpicked. I quit football and took a job at Chipotle to help pay the bills. Coach Rudy begged me to reconsider, but once I explained my circumstances to him, he dropped it.

I was worried my parents and I would become homeless and neglected my social life indefinitely, but East stuck by me, even when I spent months not being able to look at his face without lashing out.

Then senior year happened.

Dad decided to get out of bed on my first day of school. I still remember the morning it happened. He put on his working clothes—The North Face jacket and Blundstone boots—and went down to the farm to see the damage. After months of neglect, nothing was left. He'd let the fruit in the fields die, and whatever animals he had, he'd given away for free.

Dad went downtown the same day and got himself a fisherman's job. Grandpa St. Claire was a fisherman, so he didn't have to learn the ropes, but by God, it must have been fucking humiliating to get a starter job so late in the game, especially for someone who'd been self-employed since he'd graduated from high school to support his small insta-family.

Mom emerged from her room a few weeks later. She was the first to actually talk to me, and by that time, it had been almost a year since any of them looked me in the eye, much less acknowledged my existence.

I'd been invisible.

They didn't ask me how I felt.

How I was coping.

Didn't feel me.

Clothe me.

Ask me how school was going.

Fuck, they didn't even know I quit football. I was an invisible ghost, hovering in their way to the kitchen occasionally, and nothing more.

She sat me down and told me it was not my fault. Said she appreciated how I'd stepped up and paid the bills, and that from now on, things were going to be different.

But I knew that it was my fault, and that the quicker I got out of my parents' hair, the better.

In the weeks leading to my eighteenth birthday, my parents made an effort to talk to me. Mom got on some meds after being diagnosed with major depression. Dad constantly smelled of fish. They were pretending to be okay. I didn't buy it. They spent almost a year virtually ignoring me. There was simply no way they were over what I'd done. Even if they were—I wasn't over it.

On my eighteenth birthday, they bought me a cake.

I returned from a shift at Chipotle. Walked straight past the cake with the lit candles, up to my room and locked the door.

I vowed not to celebrate birthdays ever again that day.

Shortly after my eighteenth birthday, I moved to Sheridan. East insisted on going wherever I was going. I didn't fight him on this, mostly because I knew I'd be all alone in the world if it wasn't for him.

Instead, I chose a D1 college where I knew he'd ride a full scholarship and enjoy his time.

The fights at the Sheridan Plaza were the start of my parents' financial recovery, but they weren't enough. My dream was to make it up to them the best I could. And that meant rebuilding their house from scratch and getting Dad's business back on its feet.

But in my quest to find an answer to all of their trouble, I forgot to ask myself where the hell I fit into this equation.

Forgot how to breathe without hurting.

Forgot that there was more to life than earning money and surviving.

Forgot that when you played with fire, eventually, you get burned.

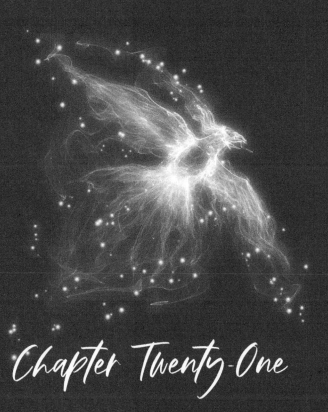

Chapter Twenty-One

West

IN THE END, IT ALL BOILED DOWN TO THIS: I COULDN'T HAVE KADE Appleton and his scouts know that Grace was my girlfriend. He had eyes everywhere, and confirming she and I were together was going to put her in the line of fire.

I couldn't do that.

So I did what I had to.

Dumped my ugly past at her feet.

Aubrey didn't die in a car accident.

She died because of me.

I'd be lying if I said I didn't think about Aub the first night I laid eyes on Grace Shaw. That it wasn't why I took the job at the food truck. Sure, the extra money was helpful, but mainly, I wanted to see what Aub would be like had she survived the fire. What kind of person she'd grow up to be.

I realized how majorly fucked up that was to look at this chick and see my sister. But that was the thing—I *didn't* see Aubrey in Grace. Not at all.

Grace was Grace. A madly unique person. Sweet-mannered and kind and funny, but also sarcastic and feisty and intelligent. She was gorgeous—scratch that, fucking breathtaking, apart from those scars that didn't even matter to me—and the more I spent time with her, the more it was impossible to think of her as a replacement to the sister I loved so desperately.

Texas thought I pitied her. That she was a pet project. And I'd confirmed her darkest suspicions to make sure Kade Appleton and his rats think the same thing.

But I never pitied her. Not even for one second.

If anything, I *envied* her strength. I couldn't have dealt with half the shit she's been through and still survive.

Hell, I still couldn't talk to my own parents without breaking into goddamn hives.

Now, the guilt of what I did to her at the cafeteria ate at me alive like the fire that consumed Aubrey.

"You're such an idiot." East shook his head. He was cruising around town, clutching the steering wheel like he was ready to yank and throw it out the window. We'd been doing that for an hour now. I sat next to him in his Toyota Camry, wallowing in the sheer volume of my stupidity.

"School's full of rats. Couldn't chance Appleton finding out about Grace and getting to her." I fixed my gaze on the view outside the window, reminding myself to fucking breathe.

"Appleton doesn't want to hurt your girlfriend, you moron. He wants to hurt *you*."

"He's hurt women before."

"That was his own girlfriend," East argued.

"Exactly what makes you think Grace, who is a stranger, is safe when his own goddamn baby momma isn't? Not to mention, one of his errand boys has warned me that he knows where Grace lives."

I referred to the incident at the intersection, where the guy on the Harley commented on Tex.

"Then why did you say yes to the fight?" East growled.

"That was before I hooked up with Grace."

"Why didn't you cancel?"

"He wouldn't fucking let me!" I boomed. "Were you not there when I gave you the rundown five thousand times?"

"Why didn't you tell her the truth?" Easton kept pushing, and that was when I officially lost it.

"Because she had enough on her fucking plate and didn't need my shit on top of it!"

My roar shook the entire car, reverberating between us. I didn't even tell him the whole truth. The truth I was able to admit only to myself. That I knew Grace would have broken up with me, and that she had the right to know. The right to get rid of my ass before things got ten times more complicated. It wasn't a noble thing to do, to lie to the person you love, but I'd long realized that love made you do twisted things.

Easton got back to being annoyingly quiet, and I drew a breath, gluing my gaze back to the monotonous view of yellow ranch-styled houses, the water tower, and cactuses.

Maybe if things had been different with Aubrey, I wouldn't be so paranoid about the people I loved. But Aubrey had died, and keeping Grace safe was my top priority, even if it gutted me inside out.

Even leaving here wouldn't have changed that. If anything, I'd be leaving her unprotected, in the same zip code with that asshole, Kade Appleton.

I'd already come to terms with the dreadful fact that I loved her.

It was the kind of love that made me roll my eyes to oblivion when I saw it in movies and TV. The intensity of it scared the shit out of me, because I never thought I could be this way with someone who wasn't blood-related to me.

I couldn't stop thinking about her.

Wanting to touch her.

Wondering what she was thinking, where she was, what she was doing.

It was different from the fairy tales, because I knew that I *could* go on without Grace Shaw. It wouldn't kill me. Not physically, anyway. I'd just go back to being the same miserable jackass I was prior to falling in love with her.

But I wouldn't be alive. Not really. I would be wasting oxygen, space, and resources, going back to not-so-secretly wishing I'd die.

The realization dawned on me like a cold shower.

I didn't want to die when I was with Grace.

I wanted to live. To laugh. To love.

To date her and nibble on her neck and listen to her talking about plays and nineties movies and defending fanny packs vehemently.

I'd been relishing life—actively enjoying it, even—for months, and I didn't even realize it.

I didn't want to die anymore.

Somewhere along the road, the idea of veering my bike off the road when I picked up speed stopped appealing to me. I no longer imagined what it would feel like to hurl myself off a cliff. I stopped walking into the ring wanting the asshole in front of me to throw a punch that would send me into cardiac arrest.

And it was all because of Grace 'Texas' Shaw.

"Still don't understand why you didn't just tell him the fight wasn't happening." East huffed. "How could Appleton force you to fight?"

"Easily, by playing dirty. As soon as I got it on with Texas, I went to Max and told him I was bailing. Max said he'd try, and from the moment I got the text that Appleton wanted to go ahead and make it happen, I'd been threatened, ambushed at the food truck, and slammed at an intersection on my way home. Kade has eyes on me everywhere. He wants to see me in that ring—and not in one piece."

"*Fuck.*" Easton scratched at his stubble.

"Yeah."

"Well, even if you're not going to be with Grace—which, by the way, I think is a fine decision, seeing as there's *no* chance she is going to take your sorry ass back after the public humiliation you put her through—I still think you should explain yourself. You made your point. Everyone on planet Earth knows you guys are not a couple. Now's the time to apologize."

"I will," I said with conviction. "I'm going to kiss her fucking feet and bow to her after this is all done. But I can't contact her right now. I haven't even visited her the entire week. I need to keep this shit on lock. Slipping now would just confirm everything she said is true. That we are a couple."

"You *aren't* a couple."

He didn't have to remind me.

The hole in my heart did the job.

The week leading to Friday was the worst of my life.

Well, maybe the second-worst week.

The week after I'd lost Aubrey, I knew, without a shadow of a doubt, that I would never see my baby sister again in the flesh. She could only taunt me in my dreams. But Grace—she was everywhere. She was on campus. In the cafeteria. In the provisional auditorium. She walked past me—always accompanied by Karlie and her new un-likely ally, Tess.

It was both comforting and taunting.

We both acted like the other person didn't exist.

I couldn't make it plainly obvious I was pining after her, even if it killed me.

Seeing her at work was no longer an option, as my ass got fired after the cafeteria scene. Not even an hour after I broke up with Texas publicly, I received a text message from Mrs. Contreras, advising me that my employment was terminated. She left a check and a formal letter in my mailbox the following day. She didn't even give me the good luck in the future bullshit. Straight up cut me loose and didn't look back.

To make my pathetic-o-meter ding even louder, I found myself driving around her neighborhood often. Each morning and every evening, skipping gym time. It wasn't like I was capable of thinking about anything beyond her. I even managed to forget sending my par-ents their weekly stipend.

I spotted Grace a couple times during my stalking.

One time, she was coming home from a shift at the food truck. Sensing being watched, she turned around and impaled me with a death glare.

I pretended not to notice her, and drove off.

Another time, she threw a goodbye party for Marla. I saw Mrs. Contreras, Karlie, and a few other people through the window. Grace made Marla cupcakes and delivered a pretty neat speech (yeah, I creeped around long enough to listen to most of it).

Eventually, Marla got out of the house and trudged over to me, spotting me from way across the street. The old lady clutched my arm in her bloated, oily hand and shook it as hard as she could.

"I heard what you did to Grace, and I'm here to tell ya just because I'm movin' to Florida don't mean I won't be watchin' her, makin' sure she's okay. You better turn around and go back to the hellhole you came from, because if I hear you're following her, I swear to God I'll tell Sheriff Jones, and make sure he kicks your butt outta town. And if that don't work, just remember: *shotgun.* I ain't afraid to use it."

As dearly as I wanted to see Grace, it was pretty obvious the feeling wasn't mutual.

The clock ticked more slowly as Friday approached. I couldn't wait to get it over with so I could finally talk to Tex, explain myself, and beg for forgiveness. I wasn't so stupid as to think I'd actually get another chance. All I wanted was for her not to think she was nothing but a fucking Band-Aid.

East and Reign told me I would be stupid to get in the ring. My mind wasn't in the game; it was with Grace.

Even Max said if I knew what was best for me, I'd skip town.

But I stayed, if only to lay eyes on Tex a few more times before school ended.

Wearing that little negligee, playing Blanche.

Thriving as I fell apart.

Chapter Twenty-Two

Grace

I GOT BACK TO WORKING AT THE FOOD TRUCK TWO DAYS AFTER THE cafeteria incident.

I couldn't afford the luxury of taking time off, even if that was exactly what I wanted to do. Luckily, Karlie had taken care of the West situation and had him fired faster than twice-struck lightning.

On Wednesday, I threw a farewell party for Marla. It was the least she deserved. It was the same day I finally asked her to tell West to get off my case and stay the heck away. I didn't know what kind of cruel game he was playing. Not only had he put a sword into my heart, breaking it in half for everyone to see, but he'd been driving around my block every day, making sure I was reminded of what I'd lost.

He did take a step back after Marla gave him the shotgun spiel, but that didn't stop him from shooting me looks whenever we crossed paths at Sheridan University.

I didn't know what he wanted from me. If he didn't like being my enemy—why did he make me one?

"The way he looks at you …" Karlie let loose a vindictive grin when we sat at the cafeteria on Thursday, a day before the fight. She tore a packet of hot sauce open and poured it over her basket of Doritos. "How does it feel to have the most unattainable man at Sheridan University at your feet?"

"Pretty crappy," I admitted.

What I didn't admit was that I had the nagging feeling West wasn't the only person to watch me.

That there was more. That I was being followed. I couldn't pinpoint what made me feel that way exactly, but the lingering feeling of danger hung in the air, bloated and hot. Like someone wished me harm.

Of course, telling this to Karlie without backing it up with facts was just overdramatic.

"Well, if you want a silver lining, here's something to think about—with the way he is staring at you, there's no doubt who *really* did the dumping."

But West's misery didn't comfort me one bit. It only made me hate him more for doing this to us for no reason.

As if things weren't reaching an alarming level of weirdness, Tess had begun to hang out with Karlie and me. I didn't stop it from happening. I was too emotionally exhausted to shoo her away. And she seemed genuine. Like she was back to being the girl I liked before West laid his eyes on me.

Maybe she was growing up.

Maybe we were all growing up.

I knew I certainly was, with the next decision I made.

"All right, Grams, it's showtime. You ready?"

I pushed the Chevy's door open on Saturday morning. I had to cancel Friday's rehearsal to spend the evening packing away all of Grams' belongings, with the help of Karlie and Marla.

Everything was last-minute, but when we got the call about the vacancy, we couldn't waste time.

Heartland Gardens Nursing Home was situated right outside of Austin. I actually found its brochure in one of the thick stacks West had left on my desk. It was full of glossy pictures of botanical gardens, open spaces, and fun activities, and offered dancing classes and bingo nights. It even had a small church. It was rated one of the best places in the state for people who were suffering from health issues, dementia, and other cognitive disorders.

In fact, the place specialized in taking care of people with Alzheimer's. And the real kicker was I never really bothered looking at the stack, but West had not only found me potential nursing homes, he'd also called each of them and gave them a rundown of the situation. There'd been a note attached to the brochure.

T,

I did some digging. Called the place, took your insurance card out of Mrs. S's purse, and ran a check. Your insurance covers most of the cost for this one. If Mrs. S goes through her tests and the results determine she needs assisted living, you're gold.

—W.

Sadly, I knew that the tests would turn back positive. So I gave Heartland Gardens a call. The director answered and we did a virtual tour, after which I drove up to see the place for myself. Grams had been mostly out of it that week, but in the hours she was lucid, she'd asked about West.

I didn't have the heart to tell her she was never going to see him again.

"So. Whaddaya think?" I tried to make myself sound playful, happy, now that Grams and I were in front of her new home. I still couldn't believe my luck in securing an immediate spot.

Grams slid out of the passenger seat as I grabbed her suitcases and bags from the bed of the truck, examining the regal, alabaster exterior of the place.

It looked like a small mansion. Manicured, lush front lawns, a tennis court, a pool, and impeccably tended flowers.

There were individual, luxurious cabins speckled around the main building, but since Grams required assisted living, she was going to reside in the main property, in a room that looked very much like a five-star hotel apartment.

"I think …" She looked around us, her mouth falling open. Lord, I prayed she was coherent enough to understand what was going on, and that she didn't despise me for making the executive decision. "I think we absolutely cannot afford this, Gracie-Mae."

I whipped my head toward her.

Gracie-Mae?

Miraculously, I found my voice.

"We can. All we need is to run some tests. And if it turns out that you—" I stopped, taking a deep breath—"that you qualify, which both the director of this place and I think you will, you'll be given a special grant from this foundation. I've already talked to them. Don't you worry about the details, Grams."

It would probably cost me half of what I'd been paying to Marla, who constantly worked overtime, and anyway, that was exactly why we had money put aside.

Grams glared at the place with childish awe, her wrinkly hand pressed over her heart. I wished she would say something, *anything*, to give me the faintest idea of what was going through her head. I knew I could no longer look after her at home. Not just for me. For her, too.

She needed to be cared for professionally.

And she needed company.

She needed to interact with people her age and to move far away from the town of Sheridan—a town haunted by memories that broke her heart and soul.

My mother.

My dead grandfather.

The fire.

And perhaps even me.

"Oh, Gracie-Mae …" She clutched the top of her dress, bowing her head down. To my surprise, tears formed on the edges of her eyes, threatening to spill over. "This is beautiful. I don't know if I deserve all this. This is too fancy. They'll probably think I'm a hick."

"Grams!" I chided, feeling like we were the old us, and for the first time, realizing that we weren't—never would be—and that it was okay, too.

"What?

"They'll be lucky to have you."

"Not sure they'll survive your grandmomma, sugar, but that ain't my problem."

A pretty, middle-aged nurse in a baby blue uniform rushed toward us from the automatic doors, picking up our suitcases.

"Hello! Mrs. Shaw?" She smiled at Grams brightly, her chestnut ponytail swinging in perfect harmony with her sunshine approach. "My name is Nurse Aimee, and I'm here to help you settle in. We are *so* excited to finally meet you. Your roommate, Ethel, is waiting for you. She is quite the firecracker, but your granddaughter is telling me so are you. I've a feeling you're going to get along just fine."

Something moved over Grams' face.

A mixture of excitement and shyness I hadn't seen before.

I ushered her in, holding her hand. She looked around timidly, like she was unwelcome. I realized, in our town, she wasn't. That's what she'd come to expect from people. The condemnation of being the mother of Courtney Shaw and the grandmother of the freak who'd set her own house on fire.

This was her own chance for rebirth. To become a phoenix. To start over, spread her wings and fly.

Why had I waited this long? What was I so scared of? Why couldn't I give her the gift of being treated the way she deserved?

Because I felt guilty. And guilt drives you to do mad things, as West proved to me.

Nurse Aimee led us to the reception area, where she entertained Grams while I went through all the paperwork with the director in the back office one more time.

Every time I glanced at Grams and Aimee through the glass window of the office, my heart was about to burst.

That was how I knew I'd done the right thing.

I spent six hours in Heartland Gardens, helping Grams settle into her new room. Her roommate, Ethel, was indeed there, for all of ten minutes, quickly greeting her hello, asking if she needed any help, and when Grams said her beautiful granddaughter had it covered, Ethel excused herself and dashed out, because she didn't want to miss the hot yoga class.

"I'm not ashamed to say I am completely enamored with a certain gentleman." She winked at my grandmother. Grams' eyebrows shot up to her silver curls.

"I didn't know people here are datin'."

"Oh, they are, sometimes. But I'm talkin' about the thirty-year-old fitness instructor! He's the one we're drooling over."

Nurse Aimee, Grams, and Ethel all burst out laughing. I grinned to myself, folding all her clothes in her closet and arranging her toiletries on her nightstand the way she liked them.

Saying goodbye was the hardest part. I knew it was time to leave, but I didn't want to go before I knew what her reaction would be when she was the *other* Grams. The one who still thought I was Courtney or the Devil's daughter.

"Just go. It's not going to get any easier if you stick around to see the meltdown. And the meltdown *will* come. They always do. Besides, right after we get those test results back, we can adjust her medicine accordingly, and her mood swings will subside," Aimee reassured me.

I wanted to tell her Grams was taking no medicine whatsoever for her condition but ended up just nodding. She was right. I couldn't keep Grams under wraps from the world forever.

Still, when I got back into the pickup, all I did for the first ten minutes was stare at the facility and let the guilt consume me. Grandma Savvy had raised me. She'd been the only mother I'd ever known. And now I was going to see her over the weekends, only for brief visits. I wouldn't live with her anymore. It was the end of an era.

I reached for my glove compartment and took out something Karlie had written to me. A letter she'd asked me to open only after I was done today. I guess she wanted to make sure I'd see it through.

I removed the letter from the envelope.

Shaw,

You did the right thing. I'm proud of you. Now take off that broken flame ring. You are better than holding on to the ashes of your mother.

#PhoenixForTheWin.

> *—Karlie.*

My eyes filled with tears. I did as she asked. Took off the ring and placed it in the envelope, resealing it. The paper between my fingertips was wet with my tears. I put it away on the passenger seat, sniffing and reaching for my phone for the first time in hours.

I swiped my finger across the screen, and my breath caught in my throat.

Twenty-five unanswered calls.

Easton Braun.

Maybe: Tess Davis.

Karlie Contreras.

Blocked Number.

There were text messages, too:

Easton Braun: It's Easton. Tried to call you.

Easton Braun: Pls call me back.

Easton Braun: It's an emergency. Please.

Tess Davis: Did you hear about West???

Tess Davis: Aren't you going to do something about it?

Karlie: You need to call me when you see this.

Easton Braun: PICK UP THE GODDAMN PHONE GRACE.

Tess Davis: Let me know if you need to talk. <3

Karlie: Seriously. The world is imploding and you're probably playing bingo with Agnes and Elmer over there, Shaw.

I deliberately hadn't checked my phone today, because I didn't want any interruptions, and I definitely didn't want to know the outcome of West's fight with Appleton.

Finally, I snapped out of my shock and decided to call Easton. I knew he was the person who was most likely to be next to West, so it made sense to call him first.

He picked up before the line even connected. So fast I was pretty sure we were calling each other at the same time.

"Hello? Easton? It's Grace."

"Grace!" he bellowed, sounding out of breath. I heard his footsteps squeaking on a linoleum floor. "Jesus Christ, the whole world has been looking for you."

"Is he okay?" Despite my best efforts, my voice shook.

I didn't want to care.

Then Easton asked the one question no recipient of bad news wants to hear.

"Are you sitting down?"

Chapter Twenty-Three

West

The night before.

"HOLY SHIT, DUDE. YOU'RE FORTY MINUTES LATE!" Max greeted me by throwing his arms around me, like we were a couple or some shit. I pushed him out of my vision, making him stumble back and fall flat on his ass. I zigzagged my way into Sheridan Plaza, the sound of my Ducati collapsing sideways behind me thudding in my ears.

I forgot to park it properly. My bad.

There goes my precious fucking paint. *Sorry, Christina.*

I stumbled over my own feet, soldiering forth. The faster I could get it over with, the better. Max regained his footing and managed to catch me—barely—groaning for help. East, Reign, and Tess appeared by his side.

"Oh, wow. Finally found a West nuttier than Kanye," Reign deadpanned. Tess cupped her mouth, shaking her head as she judged me hard.

"Ohmigod, Westie."

"Dude. He's trashed." East hoisted one of my arms over his shoulder. Reign took the other side. Tess scurried behind us, a curious little mouse I wanted to throw to the lions.

"You need to cancel the fight, Max," East pressed. "It can't happen. He can't even stand straight."

"*Yerrucan*," I slurred, pushing them away as I tried to make my point. East and Reign let go of me, and sure enough, I managed to stand upright.

See? No problem. Perfectly capable of …

Thwack!

It took me long seconds to realize the heat spreading across my cheek wasn't me pissing on myself.

"I fell on maface, didn't I?" My voice was muffled by the gravel sticking to my tongue. Since when did concrete feel so nice and cozy? It was outrageously nappable.

"Is nappable a word?" I inquired.

I heard East groan.

Max sighed. "I'm gonna go talk to Shaun. See if we can postpone it by a few hours. But we can't cancel. They made that pretty clear, and I want both my balls intact."

"The fight is happening," I heard myself say as I dusted myself off, rising up to my feet slowly. I felt seasick. A reasonable side effect to polishing off an entire bottle of the cheapest whiskey I could find at the grocery store. "I'm getting into that ring and finishing this thing."

"Are you crazy?" Tess thundered behind me.

I turned around to face her. I had a bone to pick with Miss Davis. Not only as she appeared in front of me, but I saw multiple images of her. They blurred into one another, like an accordion of cut out Tesses.

"What kind of heinous crimes have I committed in a previous life to deserve seeing six Tesses?" I pondered aloud. The need to barf in my mouth punched me in the stomach. "And to think all it took was one fucking Tess to screw things up between me and my girlfriend." I leaned forward, tapping her nose. I missed by a few inches and poked her eye. *My bad, take two.*

Reign stepped between us, swatting my hand away and furrowing his brows.

"*Ex*-girlfriend now, and don't dump this on Tess. It's not her fault you kept this from Grace. Did you really think no one was going to tell her?"

"I was hoping to tell her closer to the fight. You told Tess I was holding back on Grace, and she told her because she missed my dick too much."

My snarl came out with a burp. Extra classy.

"I'm sorry, okay?" Tess winced. "Really sorry. I never thought it would be this bad. I didn't want to ruin things for you. Just make them … difficult."

My phone rang in my pocket. Ignoring Tess' apology, I fumbled to take it out. Max was pacing back and forth, talking on his phone, explaining shit to Appleton and his crew, probably.

I checked my screen.

Mother.

How drunk was I to think it might actually be Grace?

I had my chance. A few of them, if I was being honest with myself. And I blew 'em all to hell. Good news was I was finally thinking clearly. I knew what I had to do to make sure Grace would be saved.

"He looks like he's planning something, which cannot be good, considering his current state." Easton's voice stabbed through Reign and Tess' simultaneous groveling. They said they were going to get me water and something to eat. It took me a few minutes to gather myself before someone propped me against the wall, like I was a piece of furniture. Upstairs, I could hear the crowd roaring and cheering.

Full venue. Sold out tickets. The whole enchilada.

And I was unfashionably late.

A few minutes later, Max killed the call. A senior lab nerd jogged toward us with a wrapped sandwich and a bottle of water.

"Here." He passed it on to Easton, who shoved the food and the drink in my face. "Chug it down. All of it."

"Want me to piss myself by round two?" I murmured around a stale bite. Who'd made this sandwich? It was next level bad. The bread was sour, the cheese too soft, and the ham was probably my age.

Fuck, I missed That Taco Truck's food.

"I'm not against you soiling yourself if it means it'd stop the fight," East gritted.

"Nothing will stop this fight," I said flatly. "And don't you fucking try."

"Why is it so important to you?" Reign crouched beside me. "I don't know how to break it to you, but you ain't gonna win this, not in your sorry ass state. Damn, I could put you against a cheerleader right now and you'd still lose."

"A dead cheerleader," Max pointed out helpfully.

"I don't lay a hand on chicks," I murmured. *Unlike that idiot Appleton.*

"It'd never come to that. You'd confuse her for a cardboard box before she throws the first punch." Reign clapped my shoulder reassuringly.

Sometime later—an hour, a week, a freaking minute, I wasn't sure—Max clapped his hands together and announced, "Okay, the moment of truth has arrived. I can't postpone this any longer. I'm an event organizer, not a magician."

"You're a class-A cunt, and you'll be paying for tricking him into a fight he can't back out of." Easton bared his teeth, offering me a hand. Max visibly winced. Reluctantly, I let Easton hoist me up to my feet. I glanced at the stairway leading up to the ring, as footfalls pounded on the concrete.

"Hey." Tess put her hand on my chest. I slapped it away. I wasn't in the mood to talk to the person who'd made this shit snowball into a fucking storm.

"Hands off, Tess."

"I'm sorry, okay? Look at me." She bracketed my cheeks.

Even through my state of drunkenness—which was a goddamn lot—I could still see the regret swimming in her eyes.

"I never thought it would go down this way. I was bitter and jealous and couldn't understand why Grace was getting every single thing I'd wished for myself. I wanted a little crisis, not a full-blown catastrophe."

I grabbed her wrists, shoving her hands away. "Sorry my tragedy is not tailor-made for your ass."

I turned around, about to go upstairs and get the fight over with, when my pecs collided with someone else's.

I looked down.

Appleton.

He was sweaty and bare-chested, his face smeared with enough Vaseline to lather the Statue of Liberty.

"St. Claire. Heard you have a girlfriend and that she is into … *toast.*"

He oinked out a rancid laugh, showing off his crooked teeth as he pushed me. Shaun and another clown from his team stood on either side of him, cackling evilly.

Not that I expected anything better from three people with the combined IQ of twelve, but I found myself unable to resist throwing a punch square to his nose, making him tumble backwards as blood shot out of his nostrils in two thick streams.

"Dafuq!" Appleton whined, pinching the bridge of his nose. He waved a hand in my face. "He is doing it again. Getting a few punches in before the bell rings."

"You sent people to my workplace, asshole."

"You can't prove that."

"I can prove that I can kill you." I bared my teeth.

"All because of a chick." He tsked, blood dribbling down his chin. "Talk about pussy-whipped."

I was about to correct him in saying that Grace wasn't my girl—not anymore, anyway—but held back. It was part of the reason why Grace had always had her doubts. I never owned up to our relationship. Never held her hand in public. Kissed her when everyone was watching. Showed the world how I felt about this girl.

I also knew that Kade Appleton wasn't going to leave Grace alone. That sooner or later, he was going to get to her, because she was linked to me, and I was a sore subject for him.

Unless …

Unless I lost. Monumentally. Unless I had my ass handed to me in the ring. Unless I threw the fight. It was all clear now.

Everyone had a phoenix moment.

This one was mine.

I started for the stairs, breezing past Appleton.

"C'mon. Let's get this shit show over with."

He chased me, leaving a trail of scarlet drops in his wake. I stormed into the makeshift ring, pushing through the dense, rabid crowd. Appleton followed closely. Behind us, Shaun, Max, East, Reign, and Tess were trying to keep up with our pace.

I turned around to face him. "Come at me."

I knew I wasn't going to win.

Wasn't going to *let* myself win.

I'd never thrown a fight in my life, but for Grace Shaw, I was willing to bite the bullet.

Max looked between us, uncertain. I was still far from the realm of sober, but dangerous nonetheless.

"Ready?" Max asked.

"Hell yeah."

I zeroed in on Appleton, pretending to give a shit about what was going to happen next.

It was showtime.

I only remembered fragments of the fight.

Appleton throwing a sucker punch to my jaw, sending me flying and crashing over a pile of wooden boxes.

Pretending to try to dodge him as he directed a roundhouse kick straight to my abs.

Appleton elbowing my side. The sudden gush of pain when I realized he'd managed to fracture a rib or two.

Me, twisting on the floor, gargling on my own blood like it was mouthwash.

I kept telling myself that if I lost, I wouldn't have to go to bed every night worrying about what Kade Appleton and his asshole friends may or may not do to Grace. She was my Achilles' heel. No matter how I turned it around, Kade needed his pride restored, and me? My ego wasn't worth half as much as Grace meant to me.

Everything had moved in slow motion. The excited chants around us had dissolved to panicky cries for Max to end the fight. But no matter how much I prayed to a god I wasn't sure was even up there for Kade to throw a knockout and put me out of my misery, the final blow never came.

At some point, I considered manufacturing a KO, but I didn't trust my own abilities to look passed out. Still, I didn't fight back. Didn't pretend to try. It wasn't a fight. It was me letting Appleton have his way, my punishment for defeating him.

Kade shoved me to the mat and wrestled me, trying some Jiu-Jitsu move that made it look like he wanted to eat my ass. There, when we were flush against each other, I finally grated through a bloody mouth.

"Just finish the job. You know I threw this shit before I walked in the ring, why are you dragging it?"

"I'm well aware of that, St. Claire." He threw me back a partly toothless grin. "But winning is not enough, see. First, I'm going to humiliate you."

I woke up in the ICU the following day.

I glanced around, gradually coming to, and found that I'd been hooked up to an IV drip, with my pulse monitored, and was wrapped in bandages with a casted hand ...

My eyes shifted downwards. I was wearing a hospital gown. I'd never worn one before. Let's just say I didn't think powder blue was my fucking color.

"Good mornin', sunshine!" Easton's voice sounded way too loud and cheerful for the occasion. The door flapped open, and he sauntered in. I closed my eyes, refusing to deal with his bullshit before I had a strong cup of Joe.

"Fancy seeing you awake. You gave us quite the scare last night."

"Why are you talking like you're eighty?" I croaked, trying to swallow some of my saliva. *Bad idea.* I had no saliva whatsoever. My throat was drier than Max's hookups. I grunted.

East sat beside me on a nearby stool, and I heard more shuffling around the room. He wasn't the only one here, but opening my eyes to see who entered the room wasn't on my agenda.

"You almost died last night," East pointed out.

"Thanks, Captain Obvious. Don't you have any other places to be? Maybe stand next to the Hudson and let tourists know that it's wet, or go to Alaska and point out the chilly weather?"

"Oh my God, he didn't only lose a tooth. His sense of humor got whacked, too." Reign exhaled dramatically from the other side of the room.

My heart sank at his voice. Who the hell was I expecting to be here?

Grace. I'd been expecting Grace.

"Your parents are on their way, and I don't want any goddamn lip about it," East warned. "They dropped a kebab when they heard what happened to you."

My first instinct was to bite his head off for telling them. Then again, he didn't have much choice. How else would he explain my taking a lengthy trip to the hospital?

Which brought me to my next question.

"What did you tell the hospital staff?"

"Bike stunt." Reign plopped on the bed beside me. "Which was easy to believe, seeing as poor Christina was trashed by Kade and his minions shortly after the fight." He tsked. "Hope you weren't counting on a joyride, because your bike ain't feeling very joyful right now."

I grumbled, my eyes still closed.

"According to Max, Appleton is a happy camper now, so at least we know he's not out and about trying to cause more shit," East offered me the glass-half-full. Of piss.

"Hunky-dory."

"Who is being eighty now, eh?" East cracked a can of Coke and brought it to my lips, not bothering with a straw. *Asshole.* I took a slow sip, letting the liquid burn a path down my throat. It felt good.

"What's the verdict?" I finally opened my eyes and motioned to my face.

"Broken nose, three broken fingers from before the fight, two cracked ribs, and an indefinite amount of bruises." East counted with his fingers.

"Isn't that against the HIPAA rules to give non-family members personal info?" I frowned.

"Oh, the medical staff didn't volunteer this information. I just have two working eyes," Easton deadpanned.

"Even that wasn't enough to make us drag your ass to the ER," Reign confessed from my other side. "But then you decided to take a long-ass nap on the ground after the fight, and we couldn't wake you up for ten minutes. Easton insisted it was a concussion. Finally, Tess, AKA my girlfriend, to whom you were a jerk, made the executive decision to call an ambulance. Good thing she did, because apparently some of your inner organs got hella swollen. Still hatin' on my girl?"

"Always," I managed to rasp. He laughed, flicking my ribs. I let out a curse.

"Where are your boundaries? I just broke the bastards."

"That's for sleeping with my girl."

"In that case." I swiveled toward him, grabbed his wrist and twisted it until it almost broke. Reign let out a cry. "That's for calling my girl names."

We were acting like twelve-year-olds, but if there was a time to act this way—it was now, when I could blame the painkillers.

"For the last time, St. Claire, she is not your girl anymore."

"We'll see about that."

My eyes drifted to Easton. I didn't have to spill it for him. He knew damn well what I was asking.

Where is she?

Was she coming for me?

Did she know what I'd done?

Why I'd done it?

East's throat bobbed. He looked away, busying himself by removing snacks he brought for me from a plastic bag and putting them on my nightstand.

"We're trying to reach her. I'm sure she'll pick up soon."

"Yeah," Reign added in a cheerful tone. "It's the weekend. People are not exactly sitting around staring at their phones."

"She's going to come." Easton patted my hand.

"On your face. Many times. You'll see. Chicks love it when you take a punch for them. You almost died for her," Reign pointed out. "That's worth at least a couple blowjobs, right?"

I closed my eyes, falling asleep, wishing I'd never wake up.

Chapter Twenty-Four

West

THE NEXT TIME I WOKE UP IT WAS LATE EVENING.

My parents were in the room, their silhouettes wrapped together, engulfed by the darkness. They stood by the window, embracing each other, exactly as I saw them on the snow the morning Aubrey had died.

The familiar lump in my throat thickened. For a moment, I was tempted to pretend I was still asleep. But if Grace Shaw taught me one thing about this world, it was that running away from your issues was a bad idea, and it always came back, biting you in the ass.

I righted myself on the hospital bed, making a show of clearing my throat.

They turned around simultaneously. Mom didn't gasp or cry. Her eyes traced my face like fingers, touching me softly. Dad—who looked a decade older than he had the last time I saw him almost five years ago—flinched, like he was the one who'd taken Appleton's blows.

"Son."

One word, and it sounded like it came from the bottom of the ocean, echoing everywhere in my body.

My parents looked worn-out—and had lost about twenty pounds between them. I barely recognized them, and yet I recognized that I was a huge part of why they were the way they were.

Dad was the first to rush toward me. He leaned over the hospital bed, his whole body brushing mine, giving me the gentlest, least touchy hug I'd ever received. We hadn't hugged in half a decade.

"You can go ham, Pops. It's your one and only chance at a hug I can't escape," I muttered. I felt his warm body quaking against mine as he tightened his grip. He was laughing and crying at the same time. When he stood up and stepped away, it was Mom's turn.

I ran my eyes over both of them, flashing them a crooked grin.

"Got all worried when I didn't send money this week, huh?"

It was so shitty and yet so classic me to say something like that. Neither of them winced or apologized. Mom's eyes were hard on mine. Something had changed since the last time she saw me. I saw in her expression more of the mom she was before Aubrey died. Determination lit her eyes, coupled with a promise to give me hell if I misbehaved.

"We're here to tell you we're not going to let you kill yourself over what happened to Aubrey. We get that you are upset. *We* are upset, too. We'll always be upset. We've lost our darling girl. But by God, West Camden St. Claire, we are not going to lose another child. Not to grief. Not to guilt. Not to *anything*. Ever again. You will outlive us, and you are going to goddamn enjoy it."

Her spine straightened, and she looked me in the eye with a ferocity that gave me fucking chills.

"I hate myself." The admission fell from my lips with a croak. "A whole fucking lot. And I don't see how you don't."

"It is not your fault." Dad took my hand. I looked away. The possibility of crying was getting too real to risk eye contact. "Even if it was—we'd still love you, still forgive you. Could you have done things differently? Yes. But you didn't. You did not commit a crime, West. The consequences of your bad decisions just happened to be exceptionally tragic."

"I broke my promise to Aub."

"We all break our promises sometimes." Mom took my other hand, and now I had nowhere to look, because my parents were everywhere. I could no longer avoid them. Ghost them. Dodge them. Pretend I could silence them with a check.

"It was never about the money." A warm tear fell from Dad's face onto my arm. "We never wanted you to pay our way out of this thing. At first, we thought maybe it was your own way to deal with the grief, to quiet the demons. By the time we knew better, it was too late. You were far away, and we didn't know how to find our way back to you."

"We were a mess," Mom interjected. I turned to look at her. She was crying, too. "The period we went through right after Aubrey's death—"

"You had every right," I interrupted, my voice thick with emotion. *Don't cry. Don't you dare fucking cry.*

It had been so long since I'd let myself feel, that I wasn't sure I could even if I wanted to.

"No. We had *no* right, Westie. We still had you to think about, to take care of. Instead of considering the consequences, we let ourselves slip into depression."

"You don't slip into depression. It grabs you by the foot like Pennywise and drags you down a deep, dark sewer full of shit. Depression is never your fault. So don't apologize for that."

I couldn't hold it any longer. My eyes and nose burned, and a hot tear slid down my cheek. I wiped it with my palm quickly.

"We love you, Westie." Mom dropped her head, burying it in my shoulder. "We love you so, so much. We never wanted the money. We just wanted to talk to you. We want our son back, and we refuse to get a dime from you from this point forward. When Easton told us what you've been doing to help us pay our loans, you know what I did?" she asked.

Quickly disowned your son for being so goddamn stupid?

"I slapped Easton in the face for never telling us. For never warning us. You've been risking your life every Friday to help us. Please forgive me for not knowing what you went through in the last five years." She grabbed my cheeks in her palms. It hurt like hell, but now wasn't the time to point it out. "I know it's a lot to ask, but I'm willing to work hard to show you what it means to me."

Another traitorous tear rolled down my cheek.

I opened my mouth and said the two most liberating words in the English language.

"You're forgiven."

Grace

The sun had dipped below the tall trees by the time I parked my pickup at the hospital parking lot, and it was almost completely dark. The traffic was insane, there had been two car accidents on the way, and most of the roads were blocked due to festivals. Each moment away from West sent me into the arms of despair, and I was so sick with worry, all anxiety about Grandma Savvy's first day at Heartland Gardens had magically disappeared.

West was awake when I got there.

Tess was the first to greet me, throwing her arms over my shoulders. "Grace! I'm so glad you're here. He just woke up." I patted her back awkwardly, shell-shocked. There was something weird about being on good terms with her again after everything that went down, but if I'd learned one thing from the moment I met West, it was that even though forgiveness is the underdog in the battle of feelings, it should always win.

Easton and Reign were plopped on a narrow seat outside West's room, napping in positions that couldn't be comfortable. Tess took a step back, scanning me. "Easton said he asked about you."

Exhilaration bubbled in my gut, but I made myself swallow it down. "Is he in a lot of pain?"

Tess nodded slowly. "I haven't gone in yet. Didn't think he'd appreciate seeing my face after everything that happened. But Reign and Easton say he's looked better. Go. He's waiting for you."

I pushed the door open just as his parents were leaving. I recognized his mother immediately. A petite woman with striking, dark features. She wrapped her arms around me in a recharging hug.

"Grace. Thank you for coming to see Westie."

"Of course." I rubbed her arm, smiling nervously. "I came as soon as I could."

"I prayed every night that you two would work things out. I'm glad you did," Caroline said. I grimaced, because West and I were as far as geographically possible from being worked out.

West let a low groan from the depths of his room. His parents blocked his figure, so I couldn't see him.

"That's enough, Mom."

Caroline did an exaggerated eye roll that made my heart surge, because if she could joke about it, maybe he didn't look as bad as he sounded.

"Take care of my son."

She kissed my cheek and left.

Closing the door behind me, I spun to face him. Heat crawled up my neck.

He looked horrible.

His nose was misplaced, his eyes swollen and purple, and it looked like he'd been stitched together five times over, bunched into a West I hardly recognized and was a far cry from the flawless Adonis I'd known.

An urgent need to look away took hold of every fiber in my body, but I soldiered through, training my eyes on him.

He loved you at your worst, knowing what you look like. Now it's time to prove you love him as he is. Scars and all.

"How do I look?" He gestured toward himself with his casted hand, giving me a humorless wink.

"Alive," my voice broke mid-word. "Which is more than I could ever wish for, everything considered. East told me on the phone you showed up trashed and didn't even put up a fight. What the hell were you thinkin'?"

With every step I took into the room, my muscles had loosened. His friends had already brought him Coke, snacks, flowers, and an iPad. I hadn't had time to buy anything to bring to him. I'd driven straight from the nursing home to the county hospital, which was even farther away from Austin than Sheridan. Heck, he didn't even know Grandma Savvy was *in* Heartland Gardens. So much had happened in the short time we'd been apart.

"I was thinking I needed to protect you at any cost." His jaw tightened. "Even if part of the price was getting my heart broken."

I took a seat in front of his bed, my eyes never wavering from his face.

"I knew after Kade sent people to raid the food truck, that if word got out I had a girlfriend, you'd be a target," West explained.

"Why didn't you tell me?" I choked, careful not to touch him. If I started, I'd never stop. I'd hold and kiss and drown myself in him, never coming up for air.

"Bringing the authorities into it was out of the question. My illegal fight scene would have come up, and everyone would have gotten screwed. They wouldn't have just thrown my ass in jail, but Max, East, and Reign, too." His eyes searched my face, looking for clues as to what I was thinking. "I decided I'd do whatever it took to keep you safe. At first, I tried to cancel the fight, like you'd asked. Told Max I was out at Reign's party. Max called Shaun, but he had none of it. See, for Kade, it was a pride thing. So I figured I'd throw the fight, let the asshole get his moment in the sun, and get this nightmare over with.

"But I underestimated just how crazy Kade Appleton is. He nearly killed me before the fight. Had me attacked at the food truck and thrown off my bike on my way home from yours. It wasn't about money anymore. I wanted to lose so he wouldn't hurt those around me. Still, I couldn't dump all this bullshit on you. You had Grams to take care of, a caregiver to find, and Professor McGraw's threat hanging over your head. I never planned not to tell you, Tex. I just wanted to do it on my own terms."

He took my hand in his. His skin felt wrong. Cold and dry, claylike. His mortality crashed into me like a wrecking ball.

He could have died.

He almost *had* died.

"Well, suffice it to say, things didn't work out the way you wanted them to." I sniffed, brushing my thumb over his knuckles. "You humiliated me beyond belief, West. You took the promise you made me and crushed it into dust in front of everyone we know."

He screwed his eyes shut, drawing a breath. The scars from that day were rawer for me than anything I'd worn on my face and arm. Because the person I loved the most made them.

"You said you were my girlfriend, and you *were*. Fuck, part of me is pathetic enough to hope you still are, and all I could see was Kade Appleton's little rats running back to him and telling him about the pretty blonde that had my balls in a grip. I knew you'd be a target. I needed to throw him off your scent. To make sure he stayed far away from you. And the only way I could have done that was to make you straight up hate me that week and ensure you stayed the hell away."

"Mission accomplished. But you still visited my house. Spied on me."

He shrugged, a sad ghost of a smile passing through his face.

"I never pretended to possess admirable self-control where you're involved, Texas Shaw. Hence why we're in this mess. If only I could stay away from you."

"You'd still be in this position. He wanted to ruin you because you were better. And you let him."

Silence blanketed the room. Eventually, he turned his face toward me. "Baby"—he smiled triumphantly—"You're not wearing any makeup."

My mouth dropped. I put a hand to my injured side, feeling my eyes narrowing. *Christ.* My face was completely bare. I'd spent the entire day at the nursing home without a drop of makeup and hadn't even noticed people's reactions. No funny looks. No disgusted frowns. No children pointing and laughing at me. No hushed whispers or judgmental sneers.

Huh.

"I'm proud of you, Texas."

"You'll be prouder when you hear this—know where I've been today?"

He closed his eyes, pretending to say a little prayer.

"Wherever it was, I hope there aren't any attractive men in this story."

I chuckled, rolling my eyes. "I helped Grams unpack her things. She moved to a nursing home just outside Austin. The one from the brochure you left me—Heartland Gardens. She's adaptin' well and has an equally eccentric roommate to keep her company."

"Holy crap," he boomed. His voice was so loud, Mrs. St. Claire rushed into the room to make sure everything was okay.

"Westie? You all right?"

"Yes, Mother. I'm injured, not six. Shut the door."

She laughed when she saw the grin on his face, shaking her head and closing the door again, giving us privacy.

"I'm so fucking proud of you, it's unreal. You taking part in the play. Doing the right thing by Grams. You're like my hero, Tex. Can I get an autograph?"

"Sure can." I laughed.

"Anywhere on my body?" He wiggled his brows. I took his casted palm in mine and kissed the tips of his fingers.

It was late evening, and I needed to go. Not because I wanted to, but because I *had* to. Staying with West was tempting, but facing the music was part of my healing process. I had to see tonight through. It was my first night alone in the house, without Grams. My first night alone, *period*. I had to get used to that.

"I'm glad you're okay, West. I'm sure you need your rest, so I'll be goin' now." I stood up, sliding my hand out of his. His grip tightened around mine. His throat worked around the word that slid out of his mouth.

"Don't."

I studied him silently.

"Don't leave me. I've been getting real good at recognizing good-byes, and once you go through that door, you are not going to come back."

He wasn't wrong. I couldn't do this anymore. Put my heart on the line and hope he'd keep it safe. Not when he'd handled it so carelessly before.

"You'll survive without me," I whispered, a tear sliding down my cheek. It slipped into my mouth, its saltiness spreading over my tongue.

"Surviving is not gonna cut it anymore. I survived for five years before I met you. It wasn't enough."

He took a deep breath, groaning. Every breath put him in pain, and I was the reason he'd gotten beaten up so badly.

"I can't unfeel, unlaugh, undo everything that went down between us." He shook his head. "I can't unlove you, Grace Shaw. You're inked in my fucking DNA, to a point I've completely lost my ability to think straight. One second I mauled you like a bobcat, the other I pushed you away, not wanting you to get tangled up in my shit. I pushed you and pulled you and chased you and hurt you and worshipped you every which way, because I couldn't say those fucking words the first time they sprang into my mind. I love you."

I couldn't breathe.

"You love me?"

"Shit, Tex. There's no word for what I feel for you. That first night we hung out? When Grams went missing? It was the first time I felt like my old self again, before Aubrey died. Something about it was light and fun and just … *real.*" He let out a sigh. "You were stressed, and worried, and suddenly, I needed to step up. It was the first time I saw crumbs of my former self. I think it was because you gave me so much shit." He laughed, covering his eyes with his forearm. "You just gave zero fucks about who I was. What my name meant in this town. I was drawn to that. And ever since that night, I couldn't get enough of you. I consumed you in every form possible—friend, lover, roommate, colleague, peer. I just needed you around. Constantly. I tried to fight it. I tried telling myself it was nothing. But every time I took a step back, you, or Easton, or Reign—*any-fucking-one in my life*—put me back in my place and made me see I was all about this Grace Shaw life."

I bowed my head, biting my lip to keep myself from bawling like a baby. I'd dreamed of this moment every night for weeks. Months, even. Yet now that he'd finally confessed his love to me, the words felt like beautiful, empty bullet cases.

He hurt me.

Not once.

Not twice.

I wasn't stupid enough to put myself through it a fourth time without some sort of commitment. A sign that he would at least try to protect me from himself next time things didn't work out.

"I love you, too, West. Which is why you have to let me go. What you are offerin' me is not enough. I want everything. The fairy tale. The romance. I want a man who will parade me around like I'm the most beautiful girl in the world—precisely because, fixed or not, I will *never* be pretty in my own eyes. I need someone who is good for me." I slipped my hand from his, watching him taking a ragged breath that nearly tore his chest apart. "And I'm dead scared that someone is not you."

His eyelids fluttered shut. He was giving up. I could practically see the fight evaporating out of his body.

I wanted to drop to my knees and beg him not to.

Convince him to give me everything I needed so we could be together.

But it wasn't on me.

It was West's commitment to make.

His fight to win.

I turned around and walked away.

This time, I didn't look back, as I left both the love of my life and my old, insecure Grace behind.

Slipping into bed that night was surreal.

The lack of sound Grams usually made around the house was jarring to me. Moving objects, snoring, talking, *breathing*—all those things were missing, and the loud quiet leaked into my bones like poison.

Karlie had texted me earlier, asking if I wanted her to drop in for a spontaneous slumber party. Nineties-themed movies, cheap wine, and *this or that* games. As tempting as it was, and as much as I wanted to get away from the chaos teeming in my own head, I knew my new self was better than running away like that.

I needed to see tonight through—and come out of it a better version of myself.

Still broken.

And wonky.

Asymmetrical.

But also whole.

And independent.

Stronger than I'd ever been.

As I tossed and turned in a bed that felt strange without West in it, after making sure the doors were locked, and the TV on, its static light dancing across my face so I wouldn't feel quite so alone, I had a feeling I was on the right path.

It was going to be a bumpy one, for sure, but wherever this road was taking me—I was ready.

Chapter Twenty-Five

Grace

I THREW MYSELF INTO BOTH WORK AND SCHOOL FOR THE NEXT week.

The premiere for *A Streetcar Named Desire* loomed large, casting its shadow across everything else in my life.

West was discharged from the hospital three days after I'd visited him. I sent food and get-well cards while he was at the hospital, but I hadn't summoned the courage to visit him again. The ball was in his court now.

A couple days after West got back to Sheridan, he showed up in the middle of rehearsal. He was still banged up, his face puffy, and a few pounds down, but that didn't stop my breath from catching when he appeared between the grand double doors of the auditorium, flashing his signature cocky grin, a candy stick peeking from the side of his mouth.

I was onstage when I saw him. Aiden stomped in with a dummy package of meat. The scene was our first encounter as Stanley and

Blanche. Even though I knew I needed to retune my mind to the play, I couldn't help but follow West's movements with my eyes as he took a seat directly under the stage, in the front row, watching me with his cool, attentive eyes.

"H'lo. Where's the little woman?" Aiden rumbled, puffing his chest.

I finally realized how West had felt when I came to see him fight all those weeks ago. We couldn't be in the same room and not be consumed by one another somehow.

Pretending to light a cigarette and puff on it, I tore my gaze from West, throwing myself into the role.

"In the bathroom."

Aiden shot his lines at me, and I quipped mine right back. We had good chemistry onstage. The more time had passed, the more I began to forget West was there and allowed myself to drown in the sweet magic of performing.

When the scene came to an end, with Tess walking in delivering her lines, Finlay clapped from his place in the first row, next to West, springing up to his feet.

"I can't believe I'm saying this, but that was utter perfection. Take five. Grace—don't go too far, please."

I nodded, hopping offstage. West sauntered over to me. My pulse jackrabbited, pounding against the side of my throat. We stood in front of each other. I waited for him to say something, anything, to relieve me of the gushing rip-your-veins pain that I experienced every time I thought about him.

He was already turning back to being his old, beautiful self.

"Tex."

"Maine."

He grinned. I rarely called him that, but when I did, it always had a dazzling impact and made me feel like a siren taking her clothes off for the very first time.

"Look at you," he whispered in awe.

I ducked my head down, blushing. "We've been workin' pretty hard. Thanks."

"We? I've only seen you. Were there other people?" he said matter-of-factly, a hint of possessiveness in his voice.

Ask me out.

Tell me you can't live without me.

That I'm not the only one feeling like I'm walking around with half a heart.

He shoved his fists into his front pockets, shifting from foot to foot.

"Wanna grab coffee later? As friends," he rushed to clarify. My heart sank. *Friends.* Of course. I'd told him I wouldn't settle for anything less than everything, and he figured I wasn't worth it. That was fair. I needed to come to terms with that. I couldn't ask him for something he was incapable of giving me.

"Sure." I mustered a weak smile. "Coffee sounds great."

"I'll pick you up in a couple hours."

He turned around and walked away. I spun back to the stage, catching Tess' gaze. She looked miserable. My cheeks heated when I realized she'd heard our exchange.

They say the bigger they are, the harder they fall.

I was anxiously waiting to hear the thud that West's love for me would make when it finally overpowered his stubbornness.

West

Payback and Karma had one thing in common—they were both bitches.

Today, I got to deliver them to Kade Appleton, wrapped in a toxic bow.

I'd tried to accommodate his small-dick syndrome. Truly, I had. I'd gone to extreme lengths to minimize the damage in this situation. I'd bitten my tongue and let him have his moment in the sun, but now all bets were off.

I wanted to ensure he was never coming after me and mine again.

Not only because I wasn't going to put up with his bullshit, but also because I wanted my girlfriend back.

This time, she was going to be safe.

From him.

From *me*.

From anyone who wished her harm.

I parked my trashed Ducati in front of Max's house. Christina was at the shop for days, and still looked like shit.

I'd never been to Max's place before. Come to think of it, I didn't even know who he lived with. By the nice, Craftsman-style digs and manicured front lawn, I bet he lived with his parents. Sad, because he didn't need any more obstacles standing in his way on his quest to lose his virginity.

Baked leaves crunched beneath my boots as I made my way to the door. Max opened up with a somber face, glancing behind my shoulder, to see if I brought reinforcements.

"Is he here?" I stepped into his house without technically being invited.

Max nodded quickly. "Told you I'd make it work."

"Alone?" I stressed.

He tugged his shirt down his round belly. "I ain't stupid. Don't want you to kill me."

"The former isn't true, and the latter is still fucking likely." I sauntered into a neat living room full of flowery furniture and family pictures that proved Max wasn't the only person in the family who was grossly unfuckable.

I found Kade slumped on the couch, smoking a blunt, watching a football rerun on a flat TV screen, a can of beer in his lap.

"Somethin' stinks." He sniffed the air, refusing to unglue his eyes from the screen.

I took a seat on a recliner to his right, studying him. He fidgeted, his fingers dancing around his beer. I noticed a tic in his right eye.

"Heard you were in the hospital." He made a show of flexing his muscles as he rearranged himself. "You sure look fine to me."

"Thanks for the medical assessment, Dr. Shit-for-brains."

He took a sip of his beer, trying to appear calm. But his knee was jerking, and his lower lip trembled. He knew as well as I did that I could thrash him right here, right now, and end things the way they were intended to happen if I wanted to. There was no dispute I was a better fighter. The fact of the matter was, I'd thrown the fight for him, and he'd greedily decided to almost kill me, punishment for my being better.

I stared at him wordlessly, watching him unravel.

"Why'd you call me in here, anyway?" He huffed. "An apology?"

Max slouched next to him, shoving his face between his own knees.

"Just want y'all to know my parents should be here in an hour, so dirtying up the carpet with blood ..."

"Better spit it out, then, St. Claire." Kade ripped his eyes from the screen, eyeballing me. "You wanted to do this without the buffer of our boys. That means whatever's gonna go down should stay between us. Tell me why I'm here."

Maybe he wasn't as dumb as a brick. Maybe he was just as stupid as a rock. Still an object, but half as deadly.

"I want half the money from the fight—and a promise you will never go after me, my friends, my parents, and *most* of all ..." I raised an octave, my tone cutting the air like a blade. "My girlfriend."

Grace and I weren't together, but a guy could dream.

Kade rolled his head on the couch, a metallic laugh slipping between his lips.

"You ain't getting a dime of my money. I won it fair and square, and while you have my word I won't hurt your girl, I can't promise I won't hit on her. A nice piece of ass, you got yourself there. And I hear she's newly single now. Well, whaddaya know? I happen to have lost my Vegas contract and moved here permanently. Can't think of better entertainment than pounding into your sexy ex."

"Now, Kade, let's not—" Max started, but Appleton hurled his half-full beer can across the room at the TV. The thick, white fluid rolled down on it, foam hissing on the floor.

"Shut your suck, Riviera, the men are speaking now."

"I ..." Max stuttered.

"Go clean it up," Kade barked. "Pretty sure Mr. and Mrs. Fugly don't want beer on their carpet just as much as they don't want blood."

I choked my armrests, feeling my jaw flexing. I needed to play this right, even if my natural response was to kill the bastard. Getting dragged into his hysterics would be amateur and unconstructive to the end goal.

"You might want to rethink that, Appleton," I said serenely.

"Oh, yeah? And why's that?" He shot me a stony glare.

I hunted my phone out of my front pocket, found what I was looking for, and held it out for him to see. He crouched forward reluctantly, watching.

It was a video of him and Shaun, launching two pit bulls at each other. The dogs ripped at each other savagely, with Kade and his manager cheering them on, laughing and making faces. There was a circle of people around the bloodied canines. You could see their faces clearly, and you could tell none of those assholes knew they were being taped.

One of the dogs plowed its teeth into the other's neck, producing so much blood, the injured dog whimpered and plopped sideways, fighting violent spasms as it bled out. It didn't stop the winning dog from tearing into it.

One of the pit bulls ate the other one alive, while it was crying for help.

It was so brutal, even my desensitized ass couldn't watch it. When Kade's ex-girlfriend agreed to send me those videos, I'd promised I would put an end to his dog-fighting days. That wasn't a promise I intended to break. In fact, I was going to make sure that from this point forward, every time I promised someone anything, I'd see it through.

"Where'd you get this?" He sat up straight, looking alert now. He tried to snatch the phone from my hand, but I swiftly tucked it back into my pocket.

"None of your goddamn business. Now, just so we're clear, you arranging dog fights with the human brick also known as Shaun, on top of the probation you're on for beating up your ex-girlfriend? Yeah, that's a big ol' pile of offenses. Me thinks your fighting skills may be handy in prison, unless you're fine with being everyone's little bitch."

"I'm not doing that anymo—"

"Spare me the bullshit. I have copies of these videos all over my cloud. These videos are recent. That's your new gig, now that you can't get into the ring anymore. I'll make sure this is all over YouTube and on the sheriff's desk by nighttime if you don't listen very carefully.

Now, I'll ask again—half the money from the fight, plus a promise you never get close to my people. Ever. That especially applies to Grace Shaw. If I hear you as much as farted in her direction, I will kill you twenty-six times, a death for each of your birthdays. Am I clear?"

His throat worked, his jaw moving back and forth. Whatever he was stoned on had worked its way out of his system completely. He was clearheaded now and aware of the massive pile of shit I'd just dumped at his feet.

"I mean it," I growled. "I threw one fight for you. I will not extend my good intentions beyond that. I *will* kill you if you harass her."

"If I do this, I'll want those videos back." He stabbed his finger against the table.

Didn't this schmuck know how the internet worked?

"I'm keeping the videos as a guarantee," I said, point-blank.

"How do I know you won't flip your shit on me?"

"A—because I'm a man of my word." At least, I was going to be. I'd been shitty about keeping up with my promises. But that was about to change. "And B—because no part of me wants your newborn daughter to grow up with a daddy who's in jail, even though that's exactly where you belong. So if I walk away from here after being assured you'll be getting a legal job, stop the dog fighting, provide for your ex, and leave me and mine alone, you've got yourself a deal."

I sounded like the morality police, but the truth was, uncovering everything that went down in the last few years at the Plaza was going to drag all of us into shit, and deep down, I believed in second chances.

I didn't trust Kade Appleton a hundred percent. But that was why I had Max. He was going to keep an eye on him. Make sure he was keeping up his end of this bargain.

Kade looked away. "Fine. *Fuck.*"

"I'll expect that money in my mailbox in the next twelve hours. Oh, and, Kade?"

I stood up. He turned his head to face me reluctantly. My mouth quirked.

"I mean it. If I hear there was a dog fight with your name on it, or that you got anywhere near my people, I'm killing you, and that's a promise I won't break."

Grace

West and I went for coffee every day that week. Always at the same place—the little diner on the outskirts of town, where Grams went the night he helped me.

They didn't even have my kind of coffee. I liked cappuccino, which wasn't on the menu. I noticed West wasn't touching his filter coffee either. We were just bracketing our cups with our hands, talking.

We talked about everything, other than us.

About how his parents made him swear he wouldn't fight again, and he'd agreed—and that this time, he intended not to break his word.

About my upcoming visit to Grams on Saturday. How she was adjusting well to the nursing home, even though she had her ups and downs. It had been a struggle to get her to the CT test, but Nurse Aimee called to tell me that by the end of the day, Grams was so exhausted that she went to bed at seven and woke up the next morning brand-new, singing along with Ethel in the breakfast room.

She was now being medicated, and even though it was going to take time to find the right medicine and doses that would work for her, it was a start.

I loved spending time with West. Just talking and laughing, rebuilding what had been broken that day in the cafeteria. And it wasn't just our daily coffee that pieced my heart back together. West had made it a point to pick me up from my house for school every day—even on days our schedules weren't aligned—and waited for me outside my lectures.

The new auditorium theater was finally ready, and we moved our final rehearsal into the massive newly built hall.

West carried my backpack and laughed at my jokes, even when they weren't funny. When I showed up at the cafeteria, taking a seat next to Karlie, he somehow materialized out of thin air to sit beside us. He didn't even seem to mind when all we talked about was nineties shows. He was content just spending time with me.

It was sweet.

And romantic.

It made me want to kill him.

"I want to strangle him," I confessed to Karlie the day before *A Streetcar Named Desire*'s premiere. I truly did. Wholeheartedly. Which was ironic, because I got so freaked out when it was Kade Appleton who'd almost ended his life.

"You'll need to be more specific. Even though I'm not his biggest fan, he hasn't done anything shitty recently. Definitely nothing to inspire murdering him." Karlie flipped through a thick textbook, highlighting the hell out of it.

I plopped down next to her on her bed, blowing a lock of hair out of my face. I was no longer wearing ball caps. Just a healthy amount of makeup. It felt extremely liberating, both for my body temperature and scalp.

"He's actin' like the perfect boyfriend." I groaned.

"Yuck!" Karlie pretended to gag. "How dare he? The bastard."

"But he is *not* my boyfriend. He hasn't asked me out. We haven't discussed our relationship ever since he got out of the hospital. We're just … platonic."

The word tasted like acid in my mouth. I didn't regret the fact we'd broken up. But I didn't understand why he insisted on spending time with me and didn't make any move to become anything more. The ball was in his court now. He was the one who needed to figure out if he was ready for this commitment, and I made it clear to him at the hospital.

"Maybe he is treading carefully. He screwed up pretty royally when you were together," Karlie suggested, capping her yellow marker and producing a green one. She had a highlighting system that made her textbooks look like a rainbow.

"Maybe he is just tryin' to make it up to me. Maybe this whole thing is just him being nice to me before he finally graduates and moves away."

It was West's last semester before graduation. Technically, he could be out of Sheridan as soon as next month. Nothing kept him here anymore.

The thought made me break out into a cold sweat.

Karlie noticed and slammed her textbook shut, scooting over next to me, wrapping an arm over my shoulder.

"Dang, you really love him, don't you, Shaw?"

I closed my eyes, nodding.

"I don't know what to do, Karl," I whispered. "I can't move away from the Austin area. Grams is here. But watchin' him go …" I tried to take a breath but couldn't suck in enough air. "Watchin' him go is going to be the end of me."

Karlie rubbed my arm, perching her chin over my shoulder.

"Sorry, Gracie-Mae. That's what you get for playing with fire."

Chapter Twenty-Six

Grace

THE MORNING OF THE BIG PREMIERE, I WOKE UP TO A TEXT message from West.

West: Check your front door. See you tonight (I got a front row seat).

Giddy, I padded barefoot to my door and opened it. There was a huge basket full of pastries, freshly brewed coffee, and flowers. I had no idea where he'd gotten something like this. You certainly couldn't buy it here, in Sheridan. He'd either had it delivered from a nearby town or made it himself from scratch. I brought it into the house and put it on the kitchen table, noticing there were numerous cards in it.

I plucked the first card out.

So proud of you, honey pie.
Then. Now. Forever.
Your number one fan.
—Marla.

I flipped the card around. It was written on the back of a picture of Marla smiling to the camera, both her grandchildren sitting in her lap, the palm trees and ocean her backdrop. I grinned. She was having so much fun in Florida.

I took out the second card.

You removed the flame ring and became your own fire.
Thank you for teaching me strength.
—Karlie.

I turned the card. It was a picture of both of us hugging and smiling for the camera. What I loved about it, more than anything else, was the fact that this picture was taken *after* the fire. In fact, it was the only picture I'd agreed to take with Karlie since I'd gotten my scars. I had my old, gray ball cap on. I knew why Karlie chose this photo. It was the new me, before I'd upgraded to my current version.

Yes, I was scarred, and looked a little different, but I was no less worthy.

I took another card.

Vivien Leigh got nothing on your ass.
#SlayTonight!
—Tess.

And another.

Good luck tonight, Grace.
Your boyfriend sure knows how to make a grand gesture.
Reality is overrated. Say yes to magic.
—Professor McGraw.

My tears and mirth blended together, and I wiped my face and nose, laughing uncontrollably.

Proud of you, Shaw.
(for the record, I knew you had acting chops the day you pretended to be interested in me to get back at Jackass St. Claire).
—Easton.

And also this surprising card:

Grace,
Sorry I was a tool.
Thanks for not being a tool back.
—Reign.

There was one card left. It was the one I'd been waiting for. I removed it from among the croissants, muffins, and cookies.

I'll walk through fire for you.
Love you.
—Your old flame.

I turned the card over. It was a picture of me I hadn't recognized. Maybe because I'd never noticed when he took it. We were in the food truck. I was wearing my pink ball cap, laughing, my eyes closed, holding a slushie, biting the tip of the straw.

I remembered that moment. He'd been lying on the floor, looking up at me like he was stargazing. I'd felt beautiful. Vibrant. Alive.

Why did you break up with him? What have you done?

Washing my face in the kitchen sink, I hurried about, slipping into something comfortable and jumping into my pickup. It was the final rehearsal before the big night. Tickets were sold out, and Professor McGraw and Finlay were on the verge of a nervous breakdown.

The rehearsal went flawlessly, and when we retired home to get showered and ready, there was another basket waiting for me at my door, this time full of dishes that looked and smelled awful, so my guess was West had tried to make them himself. This time, there was only one card.

Tried something new.
Wasn't very successful.
I did order you pizza, though.
Love, West.

"Don't peek. It's bad luck." Tess swatted my butt as she walked past me in the backstage area. I didn't listen. I shoved my face between the curtains, glancing around. The auditorium was jam-packed with people. Completely full. I didn't recognize ninety percent of the faces. Probably out-of-towners who wanted to enjoy the show. But the front row was full of Sheridan University staff, including Professor McGraw, and there were people I'd gone to high school and middle school with. They were all going to see my new face in a few minutes.

My real face.

My *scarred* face.

Oddly, I was prepared for that.

What I wasn't prepared for was West's conspicuous absence. He was nowhere to be seen.

Tess shoved her face next to mine behind the scarlet curtains, pouting. "Seriously, Grace, what are you looking at?"

"West is not here," I croaked. She tugged me backstage by my vintage dress.

"I'm sure he'll be here soon. Reign said he bought tickets."

"Tickets? Plural?"

She shrugged. "Yeah. Like, a good amount of 'em. He's probably bringing his eternal date, East Braun, and I know Reign's coming, too."

I laughed, before sobering up. "He wouldn't buy the tickets just to help the play, right?"

Tess stared at me like I was insane. "This play kicks ass. We don't need any help. He bought the tickets because he wants to show you off, silly."

By the time I was on the verge of going mad about West not being there, the show was starting, and I had to shove my anxiety aside to focus on being Blanche. It was surprisingly easy. I forgot just how much I loved having eyes on me. How addictive people's responses to what was going on onstage was.

Every laugh, gasp, and clap from the audience settled in my stomach, fueling me.

It was during my second scene when the doors to the auditorium opened and West walked in looking like a million bucks, wearing a tux, no less, his date hanging on his cast-clad arm.

It wasn't Easton Braun.

It was Grandma Savvy.

Following closely behind them was Nurse Aimee, who had her arm looped around Easton Braun's. He was her date.

Followed by Marla, who'd come all the way from Florida, and was accompanied by Reign.

My heart was in my throat as I recited all my lines, moved around, did all the things Blanche did. I watched from the corner of my eye as they settled in the first row. Grandma Savvy was wearing her beloved sequined gown. She waved at me with a bright smile.

She recognizes me.

West offered me a small wink with a hint of a smile, sprinkling his gesture with an approving once-over to let me know he liked the nightgown I was clad in—and was fully planning to destroy it by the end of the night. By the time I finished my scene, I was nearly bursting with happiness. I'd never felt so delighted in my life.

The rest of the show went without a hitch.

I was a phoenix, slicing the air, flying farther away from the ashes that had buried me for years.

I knew I would always remember how they'd felt against my wings.

But that I would never let them bring me down to the ground again.

And still, I rise.

West

The crowd cheered for ten minutes straight after the show ended.

Every time I thought the claps and whistles had subsided, a new wave started. On one hand, my chest was on the verge of exploding with pride, watching Grace slaying the play, leaving Aiden and Tess in a pile of dust behind her. On the other, I wanted to get the next part over with, because I'd been working toward it from the moment I left the hospital.

"That's my granddaughter over there, Gracie-Mae!" Grams took a break from clapping to point at Grace, yelling in Aimee's ear.

Aimee kept clapping. "I know. She was fabulous."

"Smart as a whip and beautiful as an angel. She's been touched by God, this one."

Finally, the cast began to retreat backstage.

Professor McGraw got onstage with a microphone, tapping Grace's shoulder and signaling her to stay behind.

Here goes fucking nothing, Tex. Accompanied by its friend, public humiliation!

They exchanged a few murmurs. Then McGraw addressed the crowd.

"Thank you so much for coming here and watching our production of *A Streetcar Named Desire,* the American classic by Tennessee Williams." She proceeded to gloss through the credits for the director, producer, and main actors, before cutting to the chase.

"While the show is over, I've been asked by one of our students to pass along a message I think is important for everyone in this day and age. I'm a huge believer that the amphitheater is a thought-provoking, emotionally stimulating space, and after listening to what this student had to say, I've a feeling he is going to stir those exact same feelings in you. A show of courage, bravery, and heart is just as much a show as the one you've just witnessed. And so, without further ado, I am thrilled to call West St. Claire to the stage."

My feet began moving as I tuned out the cheers around me. I glanced at Grace and saw the confusion in her eyes. Doubt reared its ugly head. Was I a complete moron for doing this?

She'd asked for a perfect boyfriend. For grand gestures. Things to make her feel beautiful. If this doesn't work, I might throw in the towel.

Ten seconds later, I was standing onstage. Professor McGraw handed me the microphone and gave my shoulder a squeeze.

"Knock 'em dead, honey."

I stood in front of Texas. She blinked back at me, waiting for an

330 | L.J. SHEN

explanation for this odd scene. I turned around from her and addressed the audience instead.

"I didn't know the play *A Streetcar Named Desire* before the start of this semester. Honestly? I don't think I know much about any piece of art that doesn't include explosions and Megan Fox in it."

I received some snickers and howls from men in the audience. Not exactly a blue-blooded crowd. That worked in my favor.

"But then Grace Shaw, this girl over here, was working as a stage assistant for the play, and I was interested in her, and she was interested in *it*, so I decided to read it. I wanted to know what enchanted her about *A Streetcar Named Desire*. And I get it. I truly do. What Tennessee Williams was trying to say here. The burning desire to call some place—*any* place—home. I'm no literary expert, but what I liked about this is the notion that we all at times ride on a road so dark, sometimes we don't even realize when our eyes are closed. Not until a fissure of light cracks through."

I took a deep breath, getting to the punch line.

"I've been spending the last few years running away from home in the dark. Not literally—my ass was right here, in Sheridan. But I didn't want to belong to a place I ruined because of one stupid mistake. Then I met Grace Shaw. She turned my life upside down. Whoever told you that's a nice thing never had anyone change *their* lives. That shit was brutal." I shook my head.

That made everyone laugh, Texas included. She clutched her side, giggling into her fist. That was good. Encouraging. Maybe this speech wasn't a complete bust.

"I think what made me fall in love with her, was that every time we were together, we smashed each other's walls with a hammer. It was ruthless. She put a mirror to my face. I put a mirror to hers. We saw each other at our best and worst. We made each other face our fears and insecurities and loneliness. At the end of it, I was so completely, ridiculously, pathetically in love with her, I couldn't even see straight. And I screwed it up. Big time."

This was the hard part. The own-up-to-it part. The part I loathed. I turned to look at her. Her face was searching, her stance lax.

"I'm sorry I was less than you deserve, Tex, but I'm afraid I can't let you walk away from this. You see, it's too good, too rare to give up.

I said in the cafeteria you weren't my girlfriend, and you weren't." I paused, watching her face twist with shock again. "You were my *everything*. Still are, baby. You wanted me to make you feel beautiful, but there's no one half as pretty as you are in this whole goddamn world. Please …" My voice broke, and I bent the knee, like I'd always planned to.

"Don't break my heart so soon after putting it back together."

The air was thick in the auditorium as everyone held their breath. I was pretty sure for every second that ticked without her reaction, I lost an entire year of my life. Silver lining: a full minute of that, and I'd drop dead and wouldn't have to witness my own, very open disgrace.

Finally, Grace found her voice. "On your feet, St. Claire," she whispered under her breath. "A king doesn't bow to others."

I got up and scooped her up, giving people something to look at and talk about for years in this godforsaken town, pressing a dirty kiss to her lips and almost breaking her jaw in the process.

"He does for his queen."

Acknowledgements

I wish I could take credit for *Playing with Fire,* but the truth of the matter is, I only wrote the book. West and Grace came to me in a dream, and the story belongs to them, not me.

Grace, especially, was born out of my need to write a woman who is less than perfect in a genre where….well, many heroines look kind-of perfect. I love her fiercely and wanted to protect her with everything I had, so this book was a difficult process, but an amazing adventure to take.

I would like to thank the people who stood by me and helped me with this book. To my editors: Angela Marshall Smith, Tamara Mataya, Max Dodson, and Paige Maroney Smith. Thank you so much for giving West and Grace the love and attention they deserved!

To my PA, Tijuana Turner, who has read this book too many times to count, and knows me and my process inside-out. You're my favorite (and only) Momager.

To my beta readers, Vanessa Villegas, Amy Halter and Lana Kart. A million Thank You's are in order!

To my BESTIES, Charleigh Rose, Ava Harrison and Parker S. Huntington, who cheered me from the sidelines, and to my awesome street team and reading group, L.J's Sassy Sparrows.

Huge thank you goes to my agent, Kimberly Brower, and also my cover designer, Letitia Hasser, and formatter, Stacey Ryan Blake. You are all so creative, talented and good at what you do!

Special shout out to the bloggers and readers who have supported me throughout this journey. I am forever indebted to you! And to my PR team, Social Butterfly. Jenn, Shan, Catherine. Thank you, thank you, thank you!

If you enjoyed Playing with Fire (or even if you didn't, but feel strongly about it), I would appreciate it greatly if you choose to leave an honest review.

Thank you so much, from the bottom of my heart.

L.J. Shen xoxo

Contact me

Join LJ's mailing list for exclusive material : eepurl.com/dgo6x5

Facebook: www.facebook.com/authorljshen

Reading group: www.facebook.com/groups/813953952051284

Website: www.authorljshen.com

Instagram: www.instagram.com/authorljshen

Or text SHEN to 313131 to get new releases alert (US only)

Other Books by L.J. Shen

Standalones

Tyed

Sparrow

Blood to Dust

Midnight Blue

The End Zone

Dirty Headlines

The Kiss Thief

In the Unlikely Event

The Devil Wears Black

Series

Sinners of Saint:

Defy (#0.1)

Vicious (#1)

Ruckus (#2)

Scandalous (#3)

Bane (#4)

All Saints High:

Pretty Reckless (#1)

Broken Knight (#2)

Angry God (#3)

Boston Belles:

The Hunter (#1)

The Villain (#2)

The Monster (#3)

The Rake (#4)

More to come…

Before you leave, make sure you try my signature series of standalones, SINNERS OF SAINT. *Vicious* is the first book in the series. Here is the first chapter. Hope you enjoy!

VICIOUS

SINNERS OF SAINT

Chapter One

Emilia

MY GRANDMAMA ONCE TOLD ME THAT LOVE AND HATE ARE the same feelings experienced under different circumstances. The passion is the same. The pain is the same. That weird thing that bubbles in your chest? Same. I didn't believe her until I met Baron Spencer and he became my nightmare.

Then my nightmare became my reality.

I thought I'd escaped him. I was even stupid enough to think he'd forgotten I ever existed.

But when he came back, he hit harder than I ever thought possible.

And just like a domino—I fell.

Ten Years Ago

I'd only been inside the mansion once before, when my family first came to Todos Santos. That was two months ago. That day, I stood rooted in place on the same ironwood flooring that never creaked.

That first time, Mama had elbowed my ribs. "You know this is the toughest floor in the world?"

She failed to mention it belonged to the man with the toughest heart in the world.

I couldn't for the life of me understand why people with so much money would spend it on such a depressing house. Ten bedrooms. Thirteen bathrooms. An indoor gym and a dramatic staircase. The best amenities money could buy…and except for the tennis court and sixty-five-foot pool, they were all in black.

Black choked out every pleasant feeling you might possibly have as soon as you walked through the big iron-studded doors. The interior designer must've been a medieval vampire, judging from the cold, lifeless colors and the giant iron chandeliers hanging from the ceilings. Even the floor was so dark that it looked like I was hovering over an abyss, a fraction of a second from falling into nothingness.

A ten-bedroom house, three people living in it—two of them barely ever there—and the Spencers had decided to house my family in the servants' apartment near the garage. It was bigger than our clapboard rental in Richmond, Virginia, but until that moment, it had still rubbed me the wrong way.

Not anymore.

Everything about the Spencer mansion was designed to intimidate. Rich and wealthy, yet poor in so many ways. *These are not happy people,* I thought.

I stared at my shoes—the tattered white Vans I doodled colorful flowers on to hide the fact that they were knock-offs—and swallowed, feeling insignificant even before *he* had belittled me. Before I even knew *him*.

"I wonder where he is?" Mama whispered.

As we stood in the hallway, I shivered at the echo that bounced off the bare walls. She wanted to ask if we could get paid two days early because we needed to buy medicine for my younger sister, Rosie.

"I hear something coming from that room." She pointed to a door on the opposite side of the vaulted foyer. "You go knock. I'll go back to the kitchen to wait."

"*Me?* Why me?"

"Because," she said, pinning me with a stare that stabbed at my conscience, "Rosie's sick, and his parents are out of town. You're his age. He'll listen to you."

I did as I was told—not for Mama, for Rosie—without understanding the consequences. The next few minutes cost me my whole senior year and were the reason why I was ripped from my family at the age of eighteen.

Vicious thought I knew his secret.

I didn't.

He thought I'd found out what he was arguing about in that room that day.

I had no clue.

All I remember was trudging toward the threshold of another dark door, my fist hovering inches from it before I heard the deep rasp of an old man.

"You know the drill, Baron."

A man. A smoker, probably.

"My sister told me you're giving her trouble again." The man slurred his words before raising his voice and slapping his palm against a hard surface. "I've had enough of you disrespecting her."

"Fuck you." I heard the composed voice of a younger man. He sounded...amused? "And fuck her too. Wait, is that why you're here, Daryl? You want a piece of your sister too? The good news is that she's open for business, if you have the buck to pay."

"Look at the mouth on you, you little cunt." *Slap.* "Your mother would've been proud."

Silence, and then, "Say another word about my mother, and I'll give you a real reason to get those dental implants you were talking about with my dad." The younger man's voice dripped venom, which made me think he might not be as young as Mama thought.

"Stay away," the younger voice warned. "I can beat the shit out of you, now. As a matter of fact, I'm pretty tempted to do so. All. The. fucking. Time. I'm done with your shit."

"And what the hell makes you think you have a choice?" The older man chuckled darkly.

I felt his voice in my bones, like poison eating at my skeleton.

"Haven't you heard?" the younger man gritted out. "I like to fight. I like the pain. Maybe because it makes it so much easier for me to come to terms with the fact that I'm going to kill you one day. And I will, Daryl. One day, I will kill you."

I gasped, too stunned to move. I heard a loud smack, then someone tumbling down, dragging some items with him as he fell to the floor.

I was about to run—this conversation obviously wasn't meant for me to hear—but he caught me off guard. Before I knew what was happening, the door swung open and I came face to face with a boy around my age. I say *a boy*, but there was nothing boyish about him.

The older man stood behind him, panting hard, hunched with

his hands flat against a desk. Books were scattered around his feet, and his lip was cut and bleeding.

The room was a library. Soaring floor-to-ceiling, walnut shelves full of hardbacks lined the walls. I felt a pang in my chest because I somehow knew there wasn't any way I'd ever be allowed in there again.

"What the fuck?" the teenage boy seethed. His eyes narrowed. They felt like the sight of a rifle aimed at me.

Seventeen? Eighteen? The fact that we were about the same age somehow made everything about the situation worse. I ducked my head, my cheeks flaming with enough heat to burn down the whole house.

"Have you been listening?" His jaw twitched.

I frantically shook my head *no*, but that was a lie. I'd always been a terrible liar.

"I didn't hear a thing, I swear." I choked on my words. "My mama works here. I was looking for her." Another lie.

I'd never been a scaredy-cat. I was always the brave one. But I didn't feel so brave at that moment. After all, I wasn't supposed to be there, in his house, and I definitely wasn't supposed to be listening to their argument.

The young man took a step closer, and I took a step back. His eyes were dead, but his lips were red, full, and very much alive. *This guy is going to break my heart if I let him.* The voice came from somewhere inside my head, and the thought stunned me because it made no sense at all. I'd never fallen in love before, and I was too anxious to even register his eye color or hairstyle, let alone the notion of ever having any feelings for the guy.

"What's your name?" he demanded. He smelled delicious—a masculine spice of boy-man, sweet sweat, sour hormones, and the faint trace of clean laundry, one of my mama's many chores.

"Emilia." I cleared my throat and extended my arm. "My friends call me Millie. Y'all can too."

His expression revealed zero emotion. "You're fucking done, *Emilia.*" He drawled my name, mocking my Southern accent and not even acknowledging my hand with a glance.

I withdrew it quickly, embarrassment flaming my cheeks again.

"Wrong fucking place and wrong fucking time. Next time I find you anywhere inside my house, bring a body bag because you won't be leaving alive." He thundered past me, his muscular arm brushing my shoulder.

I choked on my breath. My gaze bolted to the older man, and our eyes locked. He shook his head and grinned in a way that made me want to fold into myself and disappear. Blood dripped from his lip onto his leather boot—black like his worn MC jacket. What was he doing in a place like this, anyway? He just stared at me, making no move to clean up the blood.

I turned around and ran, feeling the bile burning in my throat, threatening to spill over.

Needless to say, Rosie had to make do without her medicine that week and my parents were paid not a minute earlier than when they were scheduled to.

That was two months ago.

Today, when I walked through the kitchen and climbed the stairs, I had no choice.

I knocked on Vicious's bedroom door. His room was on the second floor at the end of the wide curved hallway, the door facing the floating stone staircase of the cave-like mansion.

I'd never been near Vicious's room, and I wished I could keep it that way. Unfortunately, my calculus book had been stolen. Whoever broke into my locker had wiped it clean of my stuff and left garbage inside. Empty soda cans, cleaning supplies, and condom wrappers spilled out the minute I opened the locker door.

Just another not-so-clever, yet effective, way for the students at All Saints High to remind me that I was nothing but the cheap help around here. By that point, I was so used to it I barely reddened at all. When all eyes in the hallway darted to me, snickers and chuckles rising out of every throat, I tilted my chin up and marched straight to my next class.

All Saints High was a school full of spoiled, over-privileged sinners. A school where if you failed to dress or act a certain way, you didn't belong. Rosie blended in better than I did, thank the Lord. But with a Southern drawl, off-beat style, and one of the most popular guys at school—that being Vicious Spencer—hating my guts, I didn't fit in.

What made it worse was that I didn't *want* to fit in. These kids didn't impress me. They weren't kind or welcoming or even very smart. They didn't possess any of the qualities I looked for in friends.

But I needed my textbook badly if I ever wanted to escape this place.

I knocked three times on the mahogany door of Vicious's bedroom. Rolling my lower lip between my fingers, I tried to suck in as much oxygen as I could, but it did nothing to calm the throbbing pulse in my neck.

Please don't be there...

Please don't be an ass...

Please...

A soft noise seeped from the crack under the door, and my body tensed.

Giggling.

Vicious never giggled. Heck, he hardly ever chuckled. Even his smiles were few and far between. No. The sound was undoubtedly female.

I heard him whisper in his raspy tone something inaudible that made her moan. My ears seared, and I anxiously rubbed my hands on the yellow cut-off denim shorts covering my thighs. Out of all the scenarios I could have imagined, this was by far the worst.

Him.

With another girl.

Who I hated before I even knew her name.

It didn't make any sense, yet I felt ridiculously angry.

But he was clearly there, and I was a girl on a mission.

"Vicious?" I called out, trying to steady my voice. I straightened my spine, even though he couldn't see me. "It's Millie. Sorry to interrupt, y'all. I just wanted to borrow your calc book. Mine's lost, and I really need to get ready for that exam we have tomorrow." *God forbid you ever study for our exam yourself*, I breathed silently.

He didn't answer, but I heard a sharp intake of breath—*the girl*—and the rustle of fabric and the noise of a zipper rolling. Down, I had no doubt.

I squeezed my eyes shut and pressed my forehead against the cool wood of his door.

Bite the bullet. Swallow your pride. This wouldn't matter in a few years. Vicious and his stupid antics would be a distant memory, the snooty town of Todos Santos just a dust-covered part of my past.

My parents had jumped at the chance when Josephine Spencer offered them a job. They'd dragged us across the country to California because the health care was better and we didn't even need to pay rent. Mama was the Spencers' cook/housekeeper, and Daddy was part gardener and handyman. The previous live-in couple had quit, and it was no wonder. Pretty sure my parents weren't so keen on the job either. But opportunities like these were rare, and Josephine Spencer's mama was friends with my great-aunt, which is how they'd gotten the job.

I was planning on getting out of here soon. As soon as I got accepted to the first out-of-state college I'd applied to, to be exact. In order to do so, though, I needed a scholarship.

For a scholarship, I needed kick-ass grades.

And for kick-ass grades, I needed this textbook.

"Vicious," I ground out his stupid nickname. I knew he hated his real name, and for reasons beyond my grasp, I didn't want to upset him. "I'll grab the book and copy the formulas I need real quick. I won't borrow it long. Please." I gulped down the ball of frustration twisting in my throat. It was bad enough I'd had my stuff stolen— *again*—without having to ask Vicious for favors.

The giggling escalated. The high, screechy pitch sawed through my ears. My fingers tingled to push the door open and launch at him with my fists.

I heard his groan of pleasure and knew it had nothing to do with the girl he was with. He loved taunting me. Ever since our first encounter outside of his library two months ago, he'd been hell-bent on reminding me that I wasn't good enough.

Not good enough for his mansion.

Not good enough for his school.

Not good enough for *his town.*

Worst part? It wasn't a figure of speech. It really *was* his town. Baron Spencer Jr.—dubbed Vicious for his cold, ruthless behavior— was the heir to one of the biggest family-owned fortunes in California. The Spencers owned a pipeline company, half of downtown Todos Santos—including the mall—and three corporate office parks. Vicious had enough money to take care of the next ten generations of his family.

But I didn't.

My parents were servants. We had to work for every penny. I didn't expect him to understand. Trust-fund kids never did. But I presumed he'd at least pretend, like the rest of them.

Education mattered to me, and at that moment, I felt robbed of it.

Because rich people had stolen my books.

Because this particular rich kid wouldn't even open the door to his room so I could borrow his textbook real quick.

"Vicious!" My frustration got the better of me, and I slammed my palm flat against his door. Ignoring the throb it sent up my wrist, I continued, exasperated. "C'mon!"

I was close to turning around and walking away. Even if it meant I had to take my bike and ride all the way across town to borrow Sydney's books. Sydney was my only friend at All Saints High, and the one person I liked in class.

But then I heard Vicious chuckling, and I knew the joke was on me. "I love to see you crawl. Beg for it, baby, and I'll give it to you," he said.

Not to the girl in his room.

To me.

I lost it. Even though I knew it was wrong. That he was winning.

I thrust the door open and barged into his room, strangling the handle with my fist, my knuckles white and burning.

My eyes darted to his king-sized bed, barely stopping to take in the gorgeous mural above it—four white horses galloping into the darkness—or the elegant dark furniture. His bed looked like a throne, sitting in the middle of the room, big and high and draped in soft black satin. He was perched on the edge of his mattress, a girl who was in my PE class in his lap. Her name was Georgia and her grandparents owned half the vineyards upstate in Carmel Valley. Georgia's long blonde hair veiled one of his broad shoulders and her Caribbean tan looked perfect and smooth against Vicious's pale complexion.

His dark blue eyes—so dark they were almost black—locked on mine as he continued to kiss her ravenously—his tongue making several appearances—like she was made of cotton candy. I needed to look away, but couldn't. I was trapped in his gaze, completely immobilized from the eyes down, so I arched an eyebrow, showing him that I didn't care.

Only I did. I cared a lot.

I cared so much, in fact, that I continued to stare at them shamelessly. At his hollowed cheeks as he inserted his tongue deep into her mouth, his burning, taunting glare never leaving mine, gauging me for a reaction. I felt my body buzzing in an unfamiliar way, falling under his spell. A sweet, pungent fog. It was sexual, unwelcome, yet completely inescapable. I wanted to break free, but for the life of me, I couldn't.

My grip on the door handle tightened, and I swallowed, my eyes dropping to his hand as he grabbed her waist and squeezed playfully. I squeezed my own waist through the fabric of my yellow-and-white sunflower top.

What the hell was wrong with me? Watching him kiss another girl was unbearable, but also weirdly fascinating.

I wanted to see it.

I didn't want to see it.

Either way, I couldn't *unsee* it.

Admitting defeat, I blinked, shifting my gaze to a black Raiders cap hung over the headrest of his desk chair.

"Your textbook, Vicious. I need it," I repeated. "I'm not leaving your room without it."

"Get the fuck out, Help," he said into Georgia's giggling mouth.

A thorn twisted in my heart, jealousy filling my chest. I couldn't wrap my head around this physical reaction. The pain. The shame. The *lust*. I hated Vicious. He was hard, heartless, and hateful. I'd heard his mother had died when he was nine, but he was eighteen now and had a nice stepmother who let him do whatever he wanted. Josephine seemed sweet and caring.

He had no reason to be so cruel, yet he was to everyone. Especially to me.

"Nope." Inside, rage pounded through me, but outside, I remained unaffected. "*Calc. Textbook.*" I spoke slowly, treating him like the idiot he thought I was. "Just tell me where it is. I'll leave it at your door when I'm done. Easiest way to get rid of me and get back to your…activities."

Georgia, who was fiddling with his zipper, her white sheath dress already unzipped from behind, growled, pushing away from his chest momentarily and rolling her eyes.

She squeezed her lips into a disapproving pout. "Really? Mindy?"— My name was Millie and she knew it—"Can't you find anything better to do with your time? He's a little out of your league, don't you think?"

Vicious took a moment to examine me, a cocky smirk plastered on his face. He was so damn handsome. Unfortunately. Black hair, shiny and trimmed fashionably, buzzed at the sides and longer on top. Indigo eyes, bottomless in their depth, sparkling and hardened. By what, I didn't know. Skin so pale he looked like a stunning ghost.

As a painter, I often spent time admiring Vicious's form. The angles of his face and sharp bone structure. All smooth edges. Defined and clear-cut. He was made to be painted. A masterpiece of nature.

Georgia knew it too. I'd heard her not too long ago talking about him in the locker room after PE. Her friend had said, "Beautiful guy."

"Dude, but *ugly* personality," Georgia was quick to add. A moment of silence passed before they'd both snorted out a laugh.

"Who cares?" Georgia's friend had concluded. "I'd still do him."

The worst part was I couldn't blame them.

He was both a baller and filthy rich—a popular guy who dressed and talked the right way. A perfect All Saints hero. He drove the right kind of car—Mercedes—and possessed that mystifying aura of a true alpha. He always had the room. Even when he was completely silent.

Feigning boredom, I crossed my arms and leaned one hip on his doorframe. I stared out his window, knowing tears would appear in my eyes if I looked directly at him or Georgia.

"His *league*?" I mocked. "I'm not even playing the same game. I don't play dirty."

"You will, once I push you far enough," Vicious snapped, his tone flat and humorless. It felt like he clawed my guts out and threw them on his pristine ironwood floor.

I blinked slowly, trying to look blasé. "Textbook?" I asked for the two-hundredth time.

He must've concluded he'd tortured me enough for one day. He cocked his head sideways to a backpack sitting under his desk. The window above it overlooked the servants' apartment where I lived, allowing him a perfect view directly into my room. So far, I'd caught him staring at me twice through the window, and I always wondered why.

Why, why, why?

He hated me so much. The intensity of his glare burned my face every time he looked at me, which wasn't as often as I'd like him to. But being the sensible girl that I was, I never allowed myself to dwell on it.

I marched to the Givenchy rubber-coated backpack he took to school every day and blew out air as I flipped it open, rummaging noisily through his things. I was glad my back was to them, and I tried to block out the moans and sucking noises.

The second my hand touched the familiar white-and-blue calc book, I stilled. I stared at the cherry blossom I'd doodled on the spine. Rage tingled up my spine, coursing through my veins, making my fists clench and unclench. Blood whooshed in my ears, and my breathing quickened.

He broke into my friggin' locker.

With shaking fingers, I pulled the book out of Vicious's backpack. "You stole my textbook?" I turned to face him, every muscle in my face tense.

This was an escalation. Blunt aggression. Vicious always taunted me, but he'd never humiliated me like this before. He'd stolen my things and stuffed my locker full of condoms and used toilet paper, for Christ's sake.

Our eyes met and tangled. He pushed Georgia off his lap, like she was an eager puppy he was done playing with, and stood up. I took a step forward. We were nose to nose now.

"Why are you doing this to me?" I hissed out, searching his blank, stony face.

"Because I can," he offered with a smirk to hide all the pain in his eyes.

What's eating you, Baron Spencer?

"Because it's fun?" he added, chuckling while throwing Georgia's jacket at her. Without a glance her way, he motioned for her to leave.

She was clearly nothing more than a prop. A means to an end. He'd wanted to hurt me.

And he succeeded.

I shouldn't care about why he acted this way. It made no difference at all. The bottom line was I hated him. I hated him so much it made me sick to my stomach that I loved the way he looked, on and off the field. Hated my shallowness, my foolishness, at loving the way his square, hard jaw ticked when he fought a smile. I hated that I loved the smart, witty things that came out of his mouth when he spoke in class. Hated that he was a cynical realist while I was a hopeless idealist, and still, I loved every thought he uttered aloud. And I hated that once a week, every week, my heart did crazy things in my chest because I suspected he might be *him*.

I hated him, and it was clear that he hated me back.

I hated him, but I hated Georgia more because she was the one he'd kissed.

Knowing full well I couldn't fight him—my parents worked here—I bit my tongue and stormed toward the door. I only made it to the threshold before his callused hand wrapped around my elbow, spinning me in place and throwing my body into his steel chest. I swallowed back a whimper.

"Fight me, Help," he snarled into my face, his nostrils flaring like a wild beast. His lips were close, so close. Still swollen from kissing another girl, red against his fair skin. "For once in your life, stand your fucking ground."

I shook out of his touch, clutching my textbook to my chest like it was my shield. I rushed out of his room and didn't stop to take a breath until I reached the servants' apartment. Swinging the door open, I bolted to my room and locked the door, plopping down on the bed with a heavy sigh.

I didn't cry. He didn't deserve my tears. But I was angry, upset and yes, a little broken.

In the distance, I heard music blasting from his room, getting louder by the second as he turned the volume up to the max. It took me a few beats to recognize the song. "Stop Crying Your Heart Out" by Oasis.

A few minutes later, I heard Georgia's red automatic Camaro— the one Vicious constantly made fun of because, *Who the fuck buys an automatic Camaro?*—gun down the tree-lined driveway of the estate. She sounded angry too.

Vicious was vicious. It was too bad that my hate for him was dipped in a thin shell of something that felt like love. But I promised myself I'd crack it, break it, and unleash pure hatred in its place before he got to me. *He*, I promised myself, *will never break me.*